||| || | |||||||| || | ||| ||||||||||| ||| |||

W9-BHM-255

What people are saying about …

COMPOSING AMELIA

"What a phenomenal story! I can't think of a more accurate way to describe this novel. Strobel touches on so many aspects of real life. *Composing Amelia* gives readers a glimpse into varying emotional landscapes. It shows effective and ineffective communication, uncovers scars from dysfunctional families, exposes discord due to different marriage goals, shows how guilt and suppressed pain often lead to out-of-control depression, outlines couples searching for a balance between their needs and their dreams, exposes the agony of secrets, and explores the definition of genuine faith. Strobel is a master at exploring the inner workings of the heart. I love the way she writes her characters."

> **Michelle Sutton,** author of over a dozen
> novels, including *It's Not About Me* and
> the best-selling *Danger at the Door*

"Alison Strobel keeps getting better and better. *Composing Amelia* is a novel I consider to be a lasting work of fiction. Within its pages, Strobel plumbs the depths of emotion in a subject fraught with prejudice and misinformation within the church. With characters your heart will embrace, it is a story of pride and depression without being depressing. From the first page until the last, I was caught up in Marcus and Amelia's world, unwilling to stop reading. A beautiful love story, you'll see God's grace through unconditional love. Alison Strobel is quickly proving she has what it takes to be a best-selling author, book after book. Novel Journey and I give it our highest recommendation. It is a five-star must-read. Bravo, Alison!"

Ane Mulligan, editor of Novel Journey,

www.noveljourney.blogspot.com

Praise for …

REINVENTING RACHEL

"A fascinating story of one woman's search for God, of falling and rising and finding that we're never alone. In Rachel's struggles, many readers will recognize their own."

Lisa Wingate, best-selling author of

Beyond Summer and *Never Say Never*

"This honestly written book is a must-read for any survivors of 'churchianity.' Realistic and transparent, Rachel Westing will strike a familiar chord with anyone who's ever felt disenfranchised with contemporary 'Christian' culture. I lent this book to a friend—and she called it a life-altering story. Way to go, Alison!"

Melody Carlson, author of The Four Lindas

series and 86 Bloomberg Place series

"*Reinventing Rachel* is one of the most emotionally powerful and insightful books I've read in years. The author's intimate understanding of spiritual truth and the frailties of the human heart is evident in this well-written story. The conflict was so genuine and believable that it took my breath away and moved me to tears. God is really going to use this book to reach the hearts of people who are floundering in their faith."

Michelle Sutton, author of over a dozen
novels, including *It's Not About Me* and
the best-selling *Danger at the Door*

"*Reinventing Rachel* is the story of a young woman who finds herself questioning her faith and engaging in dangerous behaviors when her relationships are torn apart. Author Alison Strobel draws the reader into Rachel's world where, after spiraling into disbelief and brokenness, she begins the uphill, grace-filled journey back to God and a life punctuated by hope."

Tamara Leigh, American Christian Fiction
Writers' "Book of the Year" author of
Splitting Harriet and *Nowhere, Carolina*

"Alison Strobel delivers a tsunami of emotion in *Reinventing Rachel*. I haven't read another book that grew with as much intensity and depth. Deceptively innocent in its first chapters, *Reinventing Rachel* will grab your heart and hold it captive, leaving you breathless until the end. Novel Journey and I give it a high recommendation."

Ane Mulligan, editor of Novel Journey,
www.noveljourney.blogspot.com

"Alison Strobel's novel depicts the painful unraveling of a self-righteous soul—and her reascent up a daunting spiritual mountain. Strobel's passion for her character's journey and pursuit of truth comes through loud and clear on the page. For every reader who has doubted God through troubled times, this book is for you."

Rene Gutteridge, author of
Listen and *Never the Bride*

composing amelia

a novel

alison strobel

David C Cook
transforming lives together

COMPOSING AMELIA
Published by David C Cook
4050 Lee Vance View
Colorado Springs, CO 80918 U.S.A.

David C Cook Distribution Canada
55 Woodslee Avenue, Paris, Ontario, Canada N3L 3E5

David C Cook U.K., Kingsway Communications
Eastbourne, East Sussex BN23 6NT, England

David C Cook and the graphic circle C logo
are registered trademarks of Cook Communications Ministries.

All rights reserved. Except for brief excerpts for review purposes,
no part of this book may be reproduced or used in any form
without written permission from the publisher.

The website addresses recommended throughout this book are offered as a
resource to you. These websites are not intended in any way to be or imply an
endorsement on the part of David C Cook, nor do we vouch for their content.

This story is a work of fiction. All characters and events are the product of the author's
imagination. Any resemblance to any person, living or dead, is coincidental.

Unless otherwise noted, all Scripture quotations are taken from the Holy Bible, New
International Version®, NIV®. Copyright © 1973, 1978, 1984 by Biblica, Inc™. Used
by permission of Zondervan. All rights reserved worldwide. www.zondervan.com.

LCCN 2011928812
ISBN 978-1-4347-6773-8
eISBN 978-1-4347-0419-1

© 2011 Alison Strobel
The author is represented by MacGregor Literary.

The Team: Don Pape, Nicci Jordan Hubert, Nick Lee,
Renada Arens, and Karen Athen
Cover Design: Amy Konyndyk
Cover Photo: iStock 13255924; 8841420

Printed in the United States of America
First Edition 2011

1 2 3 4 5 6 7 8 9 10

062911

ACKNOWLEDGMENTS

Nicci Jordan Hubert: I feel like I owe you both an apology (didn't I promise not to do this to you again?!) and a coauthorship credit. Once again, you kicked both my butt and my story's, and made us both better. Thank you for your encouragement and support, and for still wanting to work with me after two very messy books.

Rachel Hauck: Thank you for playing therapist to both me *and* my characters. Without your help I wouldn't have figured either of them out, and I probably would have gone loonier than Amelia's mom. You saved the story and my sanity!

The women who shared their stories: Johanna Verburg, Kimberly C. Simpkins, Amy G., Catherine Boyd, Jodie LaRiviere, Erin, and Margaret W. Roney. Thank you for your honesty and openness. Because of you, Amelia's story rings true.

Lisa Klein, Kari Holt, and Veronica Huffines: Thank you for sharing your NICU and preemie-care experiences.

Dr. Kate Hrach: Thank you for making sure I didn't do anything medically impossible.

Dan, aka Husband of the Year: Thank you, babe, for everything. I love you more than I can say.

My parents, Lee and Leslie: Thank you for everything you do for my family. None of this would happen without you.

My Creator, Guide, and Savior: Thank You for the ability and opportunity to write. I am humbled to be a part of Your plan.

For Jen

CHAPTER 1

The bus ride to LA Café was a soul-sucking experience.

Amelia Sheffield's head bounced with each pothole as she attempted to doze. She'd never been a morning person, but her boss didn't seem to care. The shop opened at six, and if she wanted a paycheck, she needed to be there in time to get the bread baking and the sandwich fixings organized for the crowd that picked up lunches on the way to work. Never a big meat eater, she found chicken and shredded turkey and sliced roast beef even more difficult to handle at five thirty in the morning.

She stepped off the bus at Sunset and Echo Park, then walked the last three blocks to the shop. LA wasn't a pretty city at any time of day, but at least at o-dark-thirty it was a bit more calm. She'd walked this route long enough now to have figured out the regulars and locals, and they exchanged sleepy nods as they passed on the sidewalk. Familiar faces, friendly conversation—it was all that kept her at this job. Well, that and the need to eat and pay rent.

When the manager switched on the Open sign and unlocked the front door, Amelia gathered her resolve and wiped the mope off her face. She began to greet the customers as though they were close personal friends.

"You way too chipper, *chica*," Maria told her. "Ain't gonna find a producer in here, you know. They all eat downtown."

"Touché," Amelia admitted. "But either way, I can't stand the thought of grunting my way through the day and never actually talking with anyone." Then, in a lowered voice, "This job is bad enough without my attitude making it worse."

"You saying my attitude is bad?"

Amelia grinned and popped Maria on the shoulder. "Your attitude? Naw, *chica,* you're the picture of optimism." That started Maria laughing.

But despite her best efforts, Amelia could feel the creativity draining from her blood every day that she punched in and then out again eight hours later. Every day, she would drag herself to the bus stop and slouch against the shelter, feeling isolated despite the people around her, and she would pray that today would be the day she got an offer for the job she really wanted.

To her surprise, her husband, Marcus, was home when she let herself in to their fourth-floor studio, his hair still wet from what was likely a post-jog shower. She hardly ever saw him during the day; he worked so much. Between his tutoring jobs, his surf instructing, and his part-time shifts behind the register at Target, he was rarely home and awake for more than an hour or two at the most. Going for a run was one of the ways Marcus blew off steam.

"Hey, you're home," she said, leaning against the door and breathing hard. "Can you believe the elevator is broken—again?" She shuffled in, flopped onto the couch, and groaned. "I am so tired."

"You've got to stop going to bed so late."

"I know, I know."

He leaned down and kissed her cheek. "Mmm, the heavenly scent of fresh bread and mustard."

She smiled. "Eau de hoagie?"

"Bottle it, babe, you'll make a mint."

"Don't I wish." She leaned over, stretching her back. "Remind me again that we're not just killing time."

"We're not just killing time."

Amelia sat up and cocked her head to the side. "Yeah, I don't buy it."

Marcus gave her a small frown. "His ways are not our ways, love. And neither is His timing. We can't see what He's orchestrating behind the scenes."

"But if God exists outside of time, then He doesn't have any timing at all, right?" She couldn't help playing devil's advocate, especially when he got all pastorly on her. It triggered a need to prove she was just as smart as he was, even if her theology wasn't as polished. "In which case, maybe He just doesn't realize how long we've waited."

Marcus laughed. "Not as long as some."

She sighed. "Yeah, you're right. Sorry I'm so impatient."

"Don't apologize to me."

She looked to the ceiling. "Sorry I'm so impatient. It's just that I'd much rather be, you know, playing piano like I've been training to do for the last ten years, rather than building sub sandwiches. But please don't take this as a prayer for patience. It's just an apology."

Marcus snickered. "Nice."

"Hey, it's honest. He likes honest, right?" She stood. "I'm gonna take a shower."

"And wash away all that delicious cold-cut goodness?"

She laughed. "Sorry, babe. I know how much you love your wife smelling like the deli case."

He wagged his eyebrows, then looked at the clock and sighed. "Guess I'll see you later, then; I'm leaving in ten."

She said farewell with a lingering kiss that made her shiver. "Just a little preview of later tonight," she said with a wink.

"Looking forward to it." He kissed the small diamond ring and wedding band on her finger, and she turned with a smile for the bathroom, humming Mozart and thinking happy thoughts of her husband. Despite the uncertainty of their futures, Marcus's confidence that God would take care of them comforted her. She loved the stability his faith gave their lives.

But alone in the steam, she prayed more seriously. *I wish I knew what You were waiting for*, she thought toward heaven. *It would make it easier. And I wish I had Marcus's faith. And patience. I probably should be praying for patience, huh? Even if I could just get some studio work or something, I'd feel so much better. This sandwich gig makes my existence feel positively meaningless.*

As she showered, her thoughts bounced from one thing to another—from Marcus and what their night held, to the motif she'd found herself humming on the bus and had meant to chart at home, then to the call she owed her best friend, Jill—which sent her thoughts to the two years they spent together at Juilliard and the double wedding they'd shared six months ago. Eventually her mind made its way to the audition she'd had two days ago. She'd done well, and had been sure she'd get a callback, but so far she hadn't heard anything. Hadn't they said they'd contact everyone in a day or two? Maybe the whole gig had fallen apart. There were already scores of theater troupes in LA—was there really a need for one that only did musicals? For her sake, she hoped so. She prayed she'd land the position—it would keep her playing and performing and practicing for when something bigger came along.

She left the shower with a plan in place for the short time she had before leaving for job number two: tutoring piano students at the community center. Tugging a comb through her long hair, she hummed the motif again as she walked to the bedroom to get new clothes. With her mind on other things, she returned to the bathroom and checked her reflection in the mirror—and stood there in surprise. For the second time that week she couldn't avoid noticing the striking resemblance: her mother looking back at her.

She pulled her damp hair into a ponytail to dispel the similarities. *Maybe I should get a haircut or something,* she thought. *Maybe dye it.* Her fingers fumbled the elastic ponytail band twice before she managed to pull it around her thick red locks. To further mark the distinction, she applied only mascara and a quick sweep of blush. She couldn't remember ever seeing her mom without full makeup.

Amelia went to the keyboard to chart the motif but found she couldn't concentrate. She cursed her mother silently and put the pencil down so she could play instead. She needed to refocus her head, distract it from the memories recalled by seeing her mother's visage in the mirror. She mentally flipped through her repertoire and selected a simple, calming Brahms piece, one she'd learned after her mother's disappearance three years ago. Playing anything her mother had heard would only make things worse. She played from memory, eyes often closed as she pictured the music and called upon the memory of the dozens of other times she'd played the song. Soon the familiar piece had her centered again, and her thoughts returned once more to her earlier prayers.

This was what she was meant to do. Not refill mayo containers, not walk an eight-year-old through finger exercises and "Twinkle,

Twinkle Little Star." She was meant to sit behind a sleek grand piano on a stage somewhere playing the compositions of masters. When she played piano and imagined herself on stage, her soul seemed to open up. In her more honest moments, she admitted to herself that it was the only time she ever felt that God really did exist.

Thoughts of her mother pushed aside, Amelia glanced at the clock on the DVD player and sighed. Time to leave. At least this job let her put her talents to use, even if it was with a bunch of uninterested kids.

She arrived home four hours later, damp from a surprise winter shower that struck on her walk back from the community center. The apartment was dark and empty; Marcus was working until ten at his third job. She hated how much they both worked—Marcus especially. *Enough already with these dead-end jobs,* she prayed as she hung up her dripping coat and kicked her shoes to the corner beside the front door.

It wasn't until she'd changed into dry clothes and toweled her hair that she noticed the blinking light on her cell. The ringer was still off from her lessons. She flipped it open and hit the voice mail button, then opened the fridge to pull some dinner together.

"Amelia, hi, this is Ross Gunther. I wanted to see if you could come back for a second audition on Friday at eleven. Give me a call." He rattled off a number, but Amelia wasn't listening. She was too busy jumping around the kitchen.

She dialed Marcus's number, knowing she'd get his voice mail since he was tutoring but too excited to wait. "Guess what, guess what, guess what?" she sang into the phone. "I got the callback!" She shut the cell and let out a squeal, then closed the fridge and sat down at her keyboard. The piece she'd used for her audition came to her first, and she played it at double time until she switched mid-measure to Mozart's "Alla Turca" to accommodate her excitement. Maybe this was the break she'd been waiting for. It was hardly a prestigious position—heck, the troupe was still forming; it technically wasn't even in existence yet—but all you needed in LA was to be seen. Or heard, in her case. And if she got this job, who knew what contacts she might make?

This could be it, she thought as she ended the piece and danced to the kitchen to forage for dinner. *This could be the beginning of it all.*

Marcus smiled as Amelia's message played on his phone. "Good for you, babe," he murmured to himself in the quiet of the library. He wasn't surprised that she'd made it through the first round of auditions. She was so gifted. He wasn't very knowledgeable when it came to music, but the first time he'd heard her play he'd known she had a future. She just had that "it" factor. And although he knew that musical theater wasn't her dream job, it was better than nothing. If only it paid a little better so she could ditch the dreaded sandwich shop.

His excitement for Amelia morphed to guilt when he returned the phone to his pocket and his hand felt the letter he'd stuffed there. He'd had plenty of chances to tell Amelia about it since its arrival yesterday, but each time he'd chickened out. Granted, he'd written off the job opening at first. But the longer he had it, the more he found himself considering it. He just didn't know what to do next.

The rain that had begun falling a couple hours ago showed no signs of letting up. He hoped Amelia had reached home before it started. He sat in the library's reading room, eyes trained on the street light outside that illuminated the falling rain, waiting for it to lighten up so he could walk home without getting drenched. His thoughts began to wander, first to the letter, then to the positions he'd applied for but had lost to other candidates, then to the ministry dreams he'd held for the last four years: a city like LA or Chicago or New York; a multicultural church making a difference in its community; Amelia playing in the worship band or working with disadvantaged youth like she'd done alongside him during college. He would be a pastor, one of a handful who shared the responsibilities of teaching and shepherding the congregation, and would help lead the church even deeper into the plights of the city, showing its members how to shine their light in the darkest corners.

The job described in the letter was nothing like this. Not in a big city—not in a city at all. Not multicultural. Not team led. Which meant he should have stopped thinking about the invitation it contained ten seconds after reading it, not cart it around in his pocket all day. And if that didn't do it, the description of a congregation left wounded and confused from a decade under a legalistic and downright heretical leader, from what he could tell, should have made up his mind. He was a theologian, not a therapist. But somehow he couldn't stop thinking about it.

The rain finally turned to mist. Marcus shouldered his messenger bag and headed for the sidewalk.

He wasn't naive. He knew God's plans could be different from what he'd expected. God had proven Himself far better at providing what Marcus needed than Marcus had ever been. Amelia was evidence of that. He'd courted education and youth-ministry majors during his undergrad years, thinking such a person would be the obvious match for a pastor in training. But then he'd found Amelia one October night as she'd played on the darkened campus chapel's Steinway, and somehow, he'd known immediately she was the one. She was nothing like the girls he'd dated before, nothing like he'd ever imagined himself wanting. But he'd definitely wanted her. And God had been faithful to them, guiding their relationship, speaking to them through their mentors and friends, and assuring them that the unlikely match was just what He had intended.

The only person not convinced had been Marcus's father. He insisted they were too young, too immature, and too blinded by emotion to enter into marriage wisely. His mother had done her best to make up for his lack of enthusiasm, and Marcus and Amelia had refused to let one lone voice of dissent ruin their plans—but even so, the indictment had hurt.

Marcus fiddled with the letter. Memories of God's faithfulness with Amelia made him willing to concede that the career path God had in store for him may not be the path he'd planned. He was confident God wanted him to be a pastor—and he knew that how it played out might end up looking very different from the vision he had. But he knew that Amelia held more tightly to her dreams. There was no room in her mind for a life that didn't include a career for her as a professional musician—hence the reason she still knew nothing about this interview request. Marcus worried about how her young faith would respond if the job discussed in the letter came to fruition. Though he had to admit she had a penchant for being wildly encouraging of him and his career; it was one of the things he most appreciated about her. Maybe she'd surprise him and be enthusiastic instead of mortified. He prayed she'd at least have an open mind.

He walked quickly toward their apartment complex, head down against the December wind, and debated when to tell Amelia about the letter. Perhaps he should wait until he'd figured out whether to pursue it. He still had a hard time believing the church had contacted him in the first place—since when were inexperienced wannabes fresh out of seminary invited to interview for senior pastorships? Maybe it would all turn out to be a mistake.

But that thought made him nervous. The hope of finally having a full-time ministry job, the hope that had prompted him to pocket the letter rather than recycle it, was growing in influence with every hour that passed. And the more he thought about it, the more enticing the position was. How many of his fellow seminary graduates were interviewing for top positions, rather than taking slots at the bottom of the totem pole? This wasn't a ground-level job. This was a pulpit of his own, a flock to manage and care for, a chance to help a congregation recover from a toxic past and reinvent itself. And he knew he could do it. It was an unconventional offer, yes, but all the more reason why God had certainly ordained it.

I hope.

The next afternoon found Amelia longing for nighttime. She had gone to bed too late again last night, her thoughts jumbled with excitement over the audition, and now as she trudged to the community center to teach, she admonished herself to be in bed by ten. Not every night. But tonight at least. And maybe tomorrow. The audition was in three days and she didn't want to botch it because she was too tired to think straight.

She'd begged and pleaded with her boss to have Friday off, but it wasn't until Maria had offered to trade shifts with Amelia that he'd relented. She was nervous; between lessons and the deli she didn't have much time to brush up on her second audition pieces. In the past, pressure often brought out the best of her abilities. She hoped that was still true.

Part of her felt a little silly for being as excited as she was. This wasn't the philharmonic—heck, it was just barely a paying job. She had so much further to go if she wanted the kind of career she'd always dreamed of, and wondered if her time would be better spent seeking out more prestigious opportunities. But then she remembered how long it had been since she'd played for an audience—besides church, which didn't count—and reminded herself that the right people were a lot more likely to hear her at this troupe's shows than in some hotel bar somewhere. There was nothing wrong with starting at the bottom. She zipped her coat to the top and stuffed her hands into her pockets. Everyone had to start someplace.

The same was true for Marcus, and she wondered when all his résumés and interviews would finally lead to a position. He'd interviewed four times so far without success, and had sent résumés to scores of ministries. There were thousands of churches in the country; certainly one of them wanted a charismatic young pastor on its staff. His talents and education were going utterly to waste right now, and while he didn't complain about it as Amelia had a tendency to do, he had to be frustrated with the wait. She was certainly frustrated for him. But whenever she'd lament that her years of training and sacrifice would amount to nothing more than after-school piano lessons for children whose parents forced them to play, he would remind her that her talent was God given, and that whatever career He led her to would bring her joy because she'd be doing what God had created her to do.

"I won't go so far as to promise you'll get record deals and sold-out concerts," he'd say, referencing the future she'd always envisioned for herself. "But whatever you end up doing will be as wonderful as you think that life would be. You just wait."

So wait she did, although not sure if she really believed it.

Amelia entered the community center an hour before her first scheduled lesson. The shouts of teens on the basketball courts outside penetrated the thin window beside the piano in the main hall where she taught. The community center's Yamaha upright was a quality instrument, a gift from a local philanthropist who wanted to provide musical instruction to children whose families would never otherwise be able to afford it. A grant from the NEA kept it tuned and paid for Amelia's time. Three days a week she taught three different students for an hour, the majority of whom didn't really want to be there. She tried to make it fun, tried to cater her instruction to each child's personality and share her own joy for performing with them in the hopes that it would rub off. Three months into the job, and the fruits of her labor were still hard to see. But she kept the smile on her face and a hint of mirth in her voice as she cheered on her pupils, figuring that, if nothing else, it kept her own spirits up.

Amelia waved to one of the directors and the gaggle of children in paint smocks who followed him to a craft room, then sat down and pulled off her jacket and gloves. She planned on spending as much time here as she could until her audition. Music didn't just *sound* different on a real piano, it *felt* different. She was grateful for the high-end digital piano that sat in her living room—without it her skills would have atrophied long ago—but there was no substitute for playing on the real thing.

She pulled the sheet music for Gershwin's "Prelude no. 2 in C-sharp Minor" from her bag and laid it out on the stand. Then she started scales to limber up her fingers and followed them with Beethoven's "Für Elise" to warm up. Once she felt her hands were ready, she started in on the prelude, one of her audition pieces, paying specific attention to the fingering and stopping now and then to drill a few troublesome measures. Every once in a while she'd notice from the corner of her eye that someone was watching her, but she kept her focus on the music. It was good practice doing this in such a public place. She'd be less likely to become distracted at her audition.

After she felt confident with the improved fingering, she let her mind wander a bit as she played the first page over and over. In her imagination she was on stage in Carnegie Hall, then the Sydney Opera House, decked out in the pale yellow satin dress she'd spotted in a downtown shop last week, with her hair cascading in curls down her back. Her heart ached with the daydream, and after a while she pulled herself back to reality just to save herself from getting depressed. *It's never going to happen,* she thought. Then Marcus's words came back to her, and she tried to make herself believe them.

When she finished, a smattering of applause made her smile. "How do you do that?" asked one girl doing homework at a nearby table.

Amelia smiled. "A lot of practice."

"I never seen somebody's fingers move that fast before."

She began playing the piece again at half the speed. "The first time I played this piece I had to play it very slowly so I could figure out how my fingers were supposed to move. I couldn't play it that quickly until I'd done it quite a few times."

"I don't think I've ever heard you play anything—well, *real* before," said a director who was doing paperwork at the front desk. "Just the scales and the stuff you do with your students. You really are talented."

Amelia could feel her cheeks warming with the praise. "Thank you."

"You ought to play professionally."

She sighed and forced herself to smile. "Well, that's the plan. But I guess we'll just have to wait and see."

❈

Marcus let himself into their studio apartment quietly, knowing Amelia was attempting to get to bed early this week. But as soon as he locked the door, she said with chagrin, "Don't worry about being quiet. I'm still awake."

"I'm sorry, babe." He dropped his bag on the table and went to the bed at the far end of the room to give her a kiss. "Can you not sleep?"

"Too nervous."

"Understandable." He kissed her again before pulling his sweats from the dresser.

Amelia sat up and leaned back against the wall. "I keep getting myself all worked up, and then I remember this is such a small gig it might not actually lead to anything, and then I get depressed that I'm never going to be a professional pianist, and then I remember what you always say about God having a plan, and then I get excited again because I think maybe this is that plan finally coming together. Over and over and over for the last hour and a half. How am I going to last two more days?" She gave him a sheepish look. "I must sound like a total mental patient."

"No, babe, of course not." He chuckled, but inside he was debating whether to change his game plan. He'd decided to tell her about the letter if she was awake when he got home, but he hadn't expected her to be so emotional over the audition. Now he wasn't sure it was such a good idea. She was usually so relaxed about playing—even for her senior performance she hadn't been this nervous. "Don't analyze it, babe. Just go in there and do your best, and whatever is supposed to happen will happen. God's got it all under control."

She pulled her hair through her fist, eyes trained on the end of the bed. "I know. You're right. But I can't help it." Amelia continued talking, something over-the-top about chucking it all and just teaching for the rest of her life, but Marcus wasn't tuned in as he pulled off his T-shirt and climbed into bed. He didn't want to keep the letter from Amelia any longer, but this obviously wasn't the right time. But how much longer could he put it off?

On his walk home from the library, he'd tried to temper his growing enthusiasm with reality checks about how the odds were stacked against him, but it didn't help. Besides being an ego boost, it was encouraging to know that someone out there believed in him enough to pursue him. It made all the previous rejections sting just a little bit less. He couldn't help imagining his father's face when Marcus finally got to tell him he had a job—and telling him he had a senior pastorship would be even better—

"Yoo-hoo, earth to Marcus."

He blinked, looked at Amelia. "Sorry, what did you say?"

"I didn't say anything. I was trying to give you my 'come hither' eyes, but you were all spaced out. What's on your mind?"

"Nothing." He slid closer to her beneath the sheets and kissed her neck. This would probably be a better use of their evening anyway—they both needed a diversion.

She giggled. "Liar. What were you thinking about?"

He kissed her again. "I was thinking about how much I like those pajamas on you."

She brought her hands up to his chest, pushing him back enough to look him in the eyes. "You are so lying to me right now. What are you hiding, Marcus Sheffield?"

Her smirk told him he wasn't being let off the hook. He should have known better than to think he could distract her. "I'm not sure this is the best time to bring it up. I don't want you to be preoccupied during your audition."

She nudged him farther back and sat up again. "Well, now you *have* to tell me. Spill it."

A brief staring contest sealed his fate, and he sat beside her on the bed and took her hand. "I got an interview."

She squealed and grabbed his arm. "Marcus, that's fantastic! Oh my gosh, I'm so proud of you. Which church—was it that one in New York? Because I had such a good feeling about that one."

"No, not the New York one. I got a 'thanks, but no thanks' letter from them the other day. Remember how I decided to send out a couple résumés to some smaller churches that we thought had potential?"

"Sure, the suburban ones."

"Right. Well, this church isn't one of the ones I applied to. Apparently one of those suburban pastors gave my résumé to the pastor of this church."

She gave his knee a shake. "So? Details? Where is it, what's their story?"

He took a deep breath. "Well ... It's in Nebraska."

Her features froze. "Nebraska?"

"Yes."

"Omaha or Lincoln?"

"Neither." He forced himself to keep eye contact. "A little town called Wheatridge."

He saw the look he'd been dreading start to form on her face. "How little?"

"Well, there's a college campus there, so during the school year there are a lot more people. Like twenty thousand."

Her eyes narrowed. "At the school?"

"In the town."

She slumped back against the wall. "How many are at the church?"

"I don't know, the letter just said 'small.'"

She groaned. "Are you really considering it?"

He could practically see the wall going up between them. He started in on all the positive angles he'd come up with. "Well, here's the thing. They're offering me a head pastorship. I'm only twenty-six and I could be a senior pastor. That's a tremendous opportunity."

She gave him a sidelong glance. "You don't think it's a little sketchy that they'd offer a position like that to a guy fresh out of school with only an MDiv to his name?"

He tried not to look as hurt as he felt. He was well aware how rare an offer like this was for a new graduate, but did she really not think he was worthy of the responsibility? Did she really not think him capable? He always pointed out how talented she was—why couldn't she return the favor?

"They want someone young who can lead the church in a new direction. They want to focus on community outreach, on addressing the town's social issues. It's the kind of thing we want to do, but just in a smaller venue than we'd expected. And it's totally possible that nothing will come of it. They didn't offer me the job. I still have to interview. But I've been trying to let go of this and I just can't. I think God wants me to at least give it a shot. I keep thinking of the verse in Luke that says 'nothing is impossible with God.' Sure it's unusual and the chances are slim. But God does the unexpected all the time. Why can't He do it with me?"

She stared at him, lips thin and eyes narrowed. He didn't like the vibe he was getting from her.

"Amelia, look—"

"We need to pray about it." Her tone issued a challenge, as though he hadn't been doing that already.

"Yes. Absolutely." He pretended she'd been gentler in the suggestion, hoping she'd come around if he acted as if she wasn't as upset as he knew she was. "Let's pray right now. Do you want to or should I?"

"You."

He cleared his throat and took her hands. He prayed aloud for wisdom and guidance. He tried not to think too much about the fact that Amelia's hands were limp in his own.

When he said "Amen," she pulled away, turned off her lamp, and rolled to her side beneath the covers. "I need to sleep."

He squeezed her shoulder and kissed the back of her head, receiving a prim pat on the hand in return. It hadn't gone as badly as it could have—she could have said a flat-out "no"—but she wasn't exactly supportive. He turned off his light and stared into the black, letting the words of the letter come back to him. He knew Amelia was nowhere near being onboard, but he couldn't help being excited. And if this job was meant to be, then God would bring her around eventually.

CHAPTER 2

Amelia slipped into the booth across from Jill and let out a sigh. "So sorry I'm late. Stupid city buses between here and the community center are never anywhere on time."

Jill nodded. "Tell me about it. What's Marcus up to tonight?"

Amelia made a face. "I don't know. Working, as usual. He took on another tutoring student, although he must have petitioned God for another hour in the day because I don't know where in his schedule he could possibly stick another one."

Jill arched a brow as she handed Amelia one of the menus from beneath the napkin dispenser. "Bitter, party of one?"

Amelia flipped over the menu to make sure her favorite salad was still there, then slouched back in the seat. "Yeah, but not about that, really. He got an interview."

"But that's fanta—"

"In Nebraska."

"Oh." Jill sobered. The waitress appeared and took their order, leaving them with their drinks. Jill stirred her water with her straw as she resumed the conversation. "So, why did he apply out there in the first place?"

"He didn't. Apparently someone passed his résumé on to this church. The town is so small it only hits twenty thousand when the local college is in session."

Jill winced. "Yikes. Well, so what? There's no law that says he has to interview there, right?"

"Right. But he wants to anyway."

"Why?"

Amelia leaned in. "It's for a senior pastorship."

"But he's only—"

"I know."

"Wow." Jill's head tipped side to side. "Now I understand why he wants to interview though."

"Yeah, but *I* don't want to go out there." Jill smiled gently and Amelia's heart sank, knowing what was coming. She held up a hand to stop Jill from continuing. "Look, I know, God's will, blah blah blah. But if this is His will, wouldn't He make me more excited about it?"

"I'm not saying it *is* God's will, Ames. I was just going to say that you have no idea where this might lead, or what role this might play in the grand scheme of things, and that you shouldn't jump to conclusions. Maybe you could let it play out, see what happens?"

"But what do we do if he gets the job and I still don't want to go?"

"Cross that bridge when you get to it. Until then, don't borrow trouble."

Amelia smirked. "Any more where those came from, Queen Cliché?"

"Girl, you have no idea." She winked. "So, any word on that audition?"

Amelia smacked her forehead. "I can't believe I forgot to tell you. I got the callback!"

Jill gave a little squeal. "That's awesome! When do you audition?"

"Friday."

"Break a leg. What are you going to play?"

"They asked for two pieces in differing styles, so I'm doing 'Hot Honey Rag' from *Chicago* and a Gershwin prelude."

"Nice."

"But that's the other thing that has me so frustrated. What if I get this and Marcus gets his job too? Who has to quit?"

"Seriously, Ames, don't dwell on this."

The waitress reappeared and set their salads before them. Jill prayed briefly for their meal, then poured dressing on her salad and continued. "You're freaking out about something totally far-fetched and miles away from certain. You have far more interesting things to dwell on, like your audition and my delicate condition."

Amelia froze, her forkful of salad halfway to her mouth. "Your what?"

A conspiratorial grin spread over Jill's face. "I'm pregnant."

Amelia let out a shriek that turned heads around the diner. "Oh my gosh! That's awesome, Jill! Right? Is that awesome? I mean, it happened awfully fast, huh?"

"Yes, six months was indeed a little quicker than we'd planned. But even so, *I* think it's awesome. Dane, not so much."

Amelia frowned, recapturing the salad that had dropped back to the bowl with a stab of her fork. "Oh no. I'm sorry."

"He's worried—no, actually, he's panicking that our marriage is doomed because of it, as though every couple that has a baby this soon divorces. And the money, of course." She sipped her water. "I feel bad. I feel like it's my fault. I know Dane is trying not to be mad, but I can tell he is."

"That's stupid. It's not like you did it on purpose."

"I know, but still … We dated such a short time, and now we have less than a year to get settled as a couple before we become a family. Kids were supposed to come five years down the road. What if this *does* damage our marriage?"

Amelia squeezed Jill's hand. "You guys are going to be fine. You love each other like crazy. That's really all you need, right? Listen to the Beatles, they know what they're talking about."

Jill nodded, eyes on her salad, then gave Amelia a wicked smirk. "Maybe you should take your own advice."

Amelia gave her a pointed look. "Ahem. Moving on. I'm very happy for you. And, no offense, but I'm so glad it's you and not me."

Jill chuckled. "Still not big on kids, huh?"

Amelia snorted. "Um, no. Not with how my … No, there's just no way." She didn't want to delve too far into why and risk ruining the night with that toxicity; Jill knew enough to draw the right conclusions. "Besides, with my wonky body I doubt I could get pregnant if I wanted to. I haven't had a real cycle since August."

"Still dealing with that anovulatory stuff, hm?"

"Yes, still. But at least it means we don't have to budget for birth control. That stuff's expensive."

Jill let out an unladylike snort. "Don't I know it. If we'd had a little extra cash one night about, oh, three months ago, I might not be in this situation."

Jill raised a single eyebrow to punctuate her statement as Amelia giggled. "But in this situation you are. Let's think of baby names."

By the time they finished dinner Amelia was in better spirits. She decided on the way home not to even acknowledge this ridiculous

job interview. Marcus would eventually come to his senses and realize
that it was not only a long shot, it was a terrible idea. Taking a job so
far ahead of his experience level could only be setting up himself—
and the church—for disaster. He'd realize that soon enough. Until
then she'd concentrate on winning this audition. Her fingers itched
to play, and she ran them through the audition piece on her knees as
the bus bounced over potholes on its way back toward her neighborhood. *Just focus on the audition,* she told herself. *Marcus will come
around eventually.*

✳

Relishing the fact that she didn't have to be at the sandwich shop
at the crack of dawn, Amelia slept in Friday morning and woke
feeling better than she had in weeks. Marcus had already left for
his morning surf-instructing job, so she cranked up the stereo with
a Tori Amos mix to psyche herself up for her audition and treated
herself to a serious breakfast. She remembered while she ate that
she'd dreamed about the audition. She'd won it, and the director
for *Les Misérables* happened to come to the first show. He hired her
right out of the orchestra pit for the next tour. *If only.*

   She finished breakfast and then showered, remembering to avoid
the mirror until her hair was pulled back, and ran through her audition pieces a few more times before deciding she couldn't play the
arrangements anymore without jinxing them. But she had an hour
left before she even had to leave. How to kill the time?

   Inspiration hit like lightning. She grabbed her jacket and
nearly ran down the street to the strip mall that housed a cheap

hair salon. "I just want a cut, but I'm short on time. Can I be out of here in less than an hour?" she asked the woman behind the counter.

"Oh sure, honey." The woman popped her gum as she entered Amelia's information into the computer and then ushered her back to the sinks. "So what are we doing for you today?"

Amelia freed her hair from its ponytail and shook it loose. It fell halfway down her back. She studied herself in the mirror, doing mental battle with the resemblance she saw to her mother, then held up her hand at her shoulder. "Cut it to here."

The woman's heavily lined eyes went wide. "That's a lot of length you're losing. Sure you wanna do that?"

Amelia smiled as the woman draped a plastic cape over her chest. "As long as I can still pull it back to a ponytail, I'll be happy. And … maybe some bangs."

"Alrighty, honey. You've got it." The stylist began to spray down her hair and engaged Amelia in chitchat, but Amelia was only half listening. The rest of her concentration was focused on the transformation taking place in the mirror. With every snip of the scissors she felt a little more relief, hoping she wouldn't have any more run-ins with her mother's likeness.

When they were done, Amelia felt as though she'd had a full makeover. She walked to the bus stop with her head high, checking her appearance in every reflective surface she passed. She arrived twenty minutes early at the theater where they were holding auditions, but her bubble of happiness burst when she saw three other people waiting in the green room. "Auditioning?" she asked in general. All three heads nodded. "On piano?"

"Guitar," answered one, but the other two nodded to Amelia, and she sensed assessments being made. "Break a leg," she said with a smile. Might as well be friendly; who knew whom she might end up working with someday.

The guitarist was the next in, and the three pianists sat in silence as they awaited their turns. Amelia sat on the floor, closed her eyes, and went through the songs in her mind. *C'mon, God. Please give me this.*

When the first pianist emerged from her audition, Amelia stood and began to stretch. She had just barely heard the music through the heavy wood door—it sounded good. The pressure was on.

The second pianist appeared ten minutes later, looking smug. "Good luck," she said to Amelia as she held the door open for her. Amelia gave her a smile that was at odds with her competitive thoughts. "Thanks. You, too." She entered the hallway and followed it to the stage, where the piano sat waiting for her, flanked by the directors.

Ross and his cofounder, Gabe Reynolds, both shook her hand. "Thanks for coming back, Amelia," said Ross. His smile was warm and put Amelia at ease.

"Of course. Thanks for the invitation."

"We really enjoyed your audition last week," Gabe said. "I'm looking forward to what you play today. We'll take a seat"—he motioned to the front row—"and you can start when you're ready."

He gave her a smile, and Ross squeezed her shoulder before following Gabe to the steps that led to the seats. She rolled her shoulders and sat down, then ran her fingers over the keys and played a few bars of Brahms to calm herself. "I'll start with 'Hot Honey Rag' and then play 'Prelude Number Two in C-sharp Minor' from Gershwin's *Three Preludes*," she said, then took a deep breath, said a prayer, and began to play.

She pictured herself accompanying a cast as she played the *Chicago* tune, imagined a full house drawn in by her music. Her execution on "Hot Honey Rag" was perfect, better than she'd played it during any practice, and even before she started her second piece, she honestly believed it was one of the best performances she'd ever given. *Too bad there are only two people here to hear it.*

And then it happened. She missed a note. Then another. She continued on as if nothing had happened, but she knew even an untrained ear would have picked up the mistakes. The rest of the prelude went well, and she kept her head high as she stood and shook their hands, but she knew it didn't matter. She'd gotten cocky and lost her concentration. She only had herself to blame.

Big surprise, she thought. *Like mother, like daughter. Not only do you share your musical talent, you share your inability to pass up any opportunity to foil any chance of success.*

Amelia brushed a finger beneath her eye as she lifted her chin against the voice in her head. She would not fall for those comparisons. She would not let herself be dragged down into those lies. *They are lies, right?*

"Thanks again," she called over her shoulder as she headed for the door, trying to sound unfazed, as though the tears weren't already falling to her cheeks. She pushed the door open at the end of the hall and was relieved to see that the room was empty. She let herself crumble then, head down as she made her way to the street doors and out into the overcast December afternoon.

She shoved her hands into her jacket pockets and blinked against the tears. Despite her resolve not to listen to the condemnation in her mind, she couldn't help berating herself for her stupidity. She'd blown her audition on a song half as complicated as the one she'd led with and nowhere near as complicated as some of the pieces she'd played before without a problem. She'd played Chopin and Mozart flawlessly in front of hundreds of people—how could she flub an arrangement that was, to someone of her caliber, just a few steps up from beginner level? The memory of her face in the mirror before the stylist had made the first cut almost stopped her short. No matter how she changed her look, she couldn't escape the curse of her genes.

Amelia reached the bus stop at the corner and sat on the bench, wiping tears from her face and wishing she had a tissue for her nose. She'd never been so embarrassed. If God was merciful, she'd never see Ross or Gabe again. Opening her purse, she pulled out her cell phone and was about to call Marcus when she heard someone shouting her name.

"Amelia!"

She sat up straight and looked around. It was Ross, jogging up the sidewalk toward her. She wanted to die.

"I'm so glad I caught you," he said, breathing hard but smiling. The smile faded, though, once he got a good look at her face. "Are you all right?"

"Hey, Ross. Yes, I'm fine. I just—" Did he really not know why she was upset? "I just got some bad news," she lied. She flashed her cell phone as if the news had come by text. Then she pulled her shoulders back. "Forgive the tears. Anyway—what's up? Or do you always run on your way to the bus stop?"

Ross shook his head and gave a breathless laugh. "No, not usually. It's just that you ran out of there so fast, I didn't get the chance to tell you—you were brilliant. That was an amazing arrangement of 'Hot Honey Rag.' And 'Prelude Number Two' was beautiful."

She stared at him, confused. "But …"

"I know what you're going to say. So you're not perfect. Big surprise, no one is." His smile returned. "Overall, it was beautiful. You're hired if you want the job."

Amelia slowly shook her head as the words sank in. "What? Are you serious?"

"None of the other pianists came close to your talent. I was going to call you, but I thought it would be more fun to tell you in person. That was, if I could find you in time." His boyish grin returned. "Hope this makes up for the bad news you got. Congratulations."

Amelia let out a laugh. "Um, yes, it—it does. Thank you. I can't believe it. Thank you so much." She shook his hand and tried to tone down the smile that stretched her face, but couldn't. He filled her in on some of the details of the troupe until her bus pulled up, then promised to email her with the rest that evening. With the smile still on her face, she swung into a seat and caught her reflection in the window. *I may look like Mom sometimes,* she thought, *but maybe the similarities end there after all. Be it by dumb luck or divine providence, I've got my first break and I am* not *going to waste it like she would have.*

Marcus clapped a hand on Dane's shoulder when they met in the sports bar. "I hear congratulations are in order, Big Daddy."

Dane rolled his eyes and took a seat in a booth that gave them a clear view of the Anaheim Ducks game on the TV in the corner. "Yeah, apparently."

"You're not happy?"

Dane gave him a look. "Are you kidding me? I wait for how many years to get married, and then bang, she's pregnant practically right out of the gate? It's cruel, man."

Marcus got the drift and couldn't help laughing. "Get a grip, Dane. I don't think sex is off-limits during pregnancy."

"Not officially, no. But when your wife spends her whole morning puking and her whole afternoon working, she's not exactly in the mood at the end of the day. And once the baby comes, there goes ... everything. Or so I'm told anyway."

A waitress came to their table and took their order. When she left, Marcus tapped and spun the cardboard coaster she'd left as he talked, trying not to let his own feelings on the subject taint his words with bitterness. "You're a lucky man, Dane. I'd love to have a family sooner rather than later. I'm happy for you guys. Make sure you give us lots of opportunities to babysit, okay? Maybe it'll change Amelia's mind."

Dane eyed Marcus. "Seriously? I didn't know you were into all that."

Marcus smirked. "Into what? Procreating?"

Dane laughed. "No, I just didn't peg you as the paternal type. At least not yet."

Marcus shrugged. "Well, I'm not saying I want a whole football team. But the idea of being entrusted with that life—I mean, just the science of it, the fact that God makes a whole new human being that's got parts of you and your wife—I think it's cool. And I think Amelia would make a great mom." He paused to watch the fight that had broken out on the ice. "But she's made it clear she doesn't want children yet. Possibly ever. And if that's really how it turns out, then I'll be okay with it." That's what he kept telling himself, anyway. He grinned at Dane. "I'll just borrow yours every once in a while to make up for it."

Dane pointed a finger at him. "I'll send him to your house when he starts asking all those God questions. Your training has you a lot more equipped for it than mine does." He smacked a hand to his forehead. "Oh man, it better be a boy. What the heck am I gonna do with a girl?"

"Same things you'd do with a boy. But with pink gear."

"Ha, yeah," Dane said, then pegged Marcus with a stare. "So, hey, I hear you have some news, too. I can't believe you haven't told me about this job yet. What gives?"

Marcus gave him a skeptical look. "Dare I ask how Amelia described it?"

"Jill didn't give a lot of details, other than it's in … Nebraska, was it? There was apparently little discussion about the job itself and more discussion about how Amelia wasn't particularly thrilled about the location and timing."

Marcus couldn't help the sheepish smile that came to his face. "Yeah, she's not real excited at the idea. But I sure am. It's a senior pastorship at a small independent Bible church, and yes, it's in Nebraska. They got my résumé from the pastor of one of the churches I sent it to in Illinois; their head elder is old friends with the guy. They just dismissed their old pastor; the letter didn't say why, but it did say that they're coming out of a long season of legalism and heresy so I'm assuming the last guy was the reason. And now they're

looking for someone to help them redefine themselves." He spread
his hands. "I know it sounds off the wall, given the plans we had, but
the challenge has me seriously stoked."

Dane nodded. "Challenge sounds like an understatement. But
wow—senior pastor. That's a lot of responsibility. Think you're up for
it? I mean, I don't want to knock your abilities; I'm not saying you
couldn't pull it off. It just sounds like you'd be jumping into the deep
end."

Marcus's jaw clenched. *Don't get defensive,* he told himself.
*Dane's just looking out for you and trying to be a good friend. Respect
that.* "I hear you. And I understand the concern. I'm a little surprised myself at the invitation, but I've been praying, and they've
obviously been praying, and I figure it wouldn't hurt to explore
it and give it a chance, see what happens." Marcus wished that
everyone in his world would just be supportive for once.

Dane took his drink from the waitress who had returned. "And
Amelia's not happy."

Marcus winced. "No."

"I'll bet."

"And I can understand her reluctance, especially now. I assume
Jill also told you that Amelia won a position yesterday with a new
theater group that's starting in the city. All musicals, all the time, and
she's the resident pianist. Which is great, and I'm excited for her. She's
so talented; she deserves an audience. But I can't help thinking: What
about me? She didn't even bother to feign concern over the fact that if
she takes this job, I can't take the Nebraska position." He stabbed the
ice in his drink with his straw. "Anyway it's not like I've been hired or
anything, so who knows, maybe it won't matter in the end."

"But she knows you applied all over the country. Heck, she helped you look for listings, didn't she? And now she doesn't want to move?"

"Well, I applied in big cities. We both wanted—still want, honestly—to be in a metropolitan area. And that's the problem in her eyes: This church is in a small town in the middle of nowhere. Not a lot of opportunities for someone looking to launch a music career, unlike New York or Chicago or LA or Dallas. But if the churches in New York and the like aren't calling me for interviews or offering me jobs, then what else am I supposed to do? How can I turn down a possibility of a job when it's the first real possibility I've had? I can*not* work at Target forever."

"I hear you. Well, congrats on the interview, bro." He sat back and crossed his arms. "Marcus Sheffield, Senior Pastor. Pretty impressive."

The patrons around them cheered, and Marcus and Dane both turned their attention to the television to catch the replay. But Marcus was only half interested in the game. His thoughts were stuck on the job in Nebraska, the job that kept him up at night and felt more right every time he talked about it. Of course it would be a difficult position to handle without prior experience. But what was so wrong with him that made everyone think he was incapable of succeeding? *That's an exaggeration,* he told himself. Obviously the elders of New Hope Church in Wheatridge, Nebraska, didn't think that. They wouldn't have written if they hadn't considered him up to the challenge. *See? Not everyone thinks you're incapable.*

Just the people who should have been cheering him on.

Amelia looked at the clock again. The game had to have ended by now—what was taking Marcus so long to get home? He and Dane were good friends, but didn't have the tendency to forget time when they hung out the way she and Jill did. Marcus's dependability gave her a sense of security, something she'd always craved and was so happy to find, and when he deviated from his usual, predictable nature, it stressed her out. She'd already been mildly irritated that he'd spent one of his rare job-free nights at a bar with Dane, though she knew he needed time with his friends too.

She turned back to her keyboard and continued to play a piece she'd learned as a warmup at Juilliard. Muscle memory allowed her to play it without thinking; it gave her body something to do while her mind fidgeted.

She and Marcus hadn't had the chance to talk much since she'd won the position with the theater troupe, and the suspense was killing her. She really thought Marcus would capitulate and give up the notion of the Nebraska interview since she now had an actual job anchoring her in LA, but while he'd been enthusiastic for her, he hadn't said anything about his own plans. He couldn't still be thinking about going, could he? What was the point?

By the time he got home, Amelia had gone over her arguments for staying in California so many times that she had to swallow back the urge to dive right in when he walked through the door. Maybe Dane had talked some sense into him; she should give him the chance to admit he'd changed his mind before inundating him with her reasoning. She rose from the keyboard bench and met him at the door with a kiss. "What took you so long? I was getting worried."

"I'm sorry, babe. Game went into a shoot-out and we wanted to see how it ended."

She was relieved the reason was so mundane. "Oh, okay. That's cool. Exciting game, then, huh?

"Yeah, great game—Ducks won and Selanne scored the winning shot with a wicked move." He hung up his jacket and stretched. "Dane's cousin owes him some cash, so when he gets it he's buying tickets for the four of us for the Ducks-Avalanche game in January."

Amelia felt itchy waiting for the conversation to turn. "That will be fun."

"Yeah, should be." He planted another kiss on her cheek and took her hand to lead her to the couch.

"So … how's Dane?"

"He's good. Still not convinced this pregnancy isn't the end of the world, but I think he'll come around eventually." He smiled, though he looked unsure. "I told him we'd help out, babysit and stuff so they could go out. We'd do that, right?"

"Oh—definitely, of course." *We can't do that if we're in Nebraska,* she thought with relief. "So you're turning down that interview, then?"

Marcus visibly tensed. "No, I'm still going to interview. I actually booked my flight this afternoon."

She gaped at him, shocked. "Are you serious? We didn't agree that you would go. We only agreed that we would pray about it. Why didn't you ask me? I have a job now—I can't just up and leave."

A flash of defiance shone in Marcus's eyes. Had he intentionally avoided the conversation? "Look," he said with his palms out, as if protecting himself from her, "it's not like I've accepted a position.

But just like you, I want to move forward with my career. I'm just as tired as you are of dead-end jobs. I just need to see where this goes."

She took a deep breath. She did understand his position. But still … "So what happens if you *do* get an offer?"

He shrugged. "I'd have to consider it."

Her understanding turned to anger. She rose from the couch. "Marcus, this is my point. Don't put yourself in the position of even being offered the job if it's going to tempt you to take it seriously. We can't move to Nebraska. It makes no sense."

Marcus's expression remained infuriatingly set. "Amelia, I can't just write this off. I told you, I feel like God is prompting me to consider this. I can't say no."

Amelia rolled her eyes. "Oh, sure, play the God card. I can't argue with that, can I? No, wait—I can. How is it that *you* getting offered an interview is God working, but me actually getting a job isn't? Does it only count because your job is ministry? Does that make your career more important than mine?"

"No, of course not." He ran his hand through his hair, and Amelia could see she'd rattled him. "I can't speak to what, if anything, God was doing when you got that job. All I know is that I really feel God is leading me to pursue this." He stopped, his eyes closing briefly, then continued with a quieter tone. "Look, why don't you come with me? Maybe if you saw what Wheatridge is really like, instead of just assuming it's a cultural black hole, you'd deci—"

"No." The word was out before she could craft a more diplomatic response. At this point it was as much about principle as it was about the actual job. "You obviously don't value my career. If you did, you wouldn't be going out there in the first place. I don't support this, Marcus, I'm sorry. The whole thing is …" She threw up her hands, her words cut off by her exasperation. She sat down hard on the keyboard bench and pulled on her headphones, then began to play Tori Amos's "Precious Things." She needed to pound the keys and blast the sound without bothering the neighbors. Plus, playing with the headphones on was the closest she could get to having some privacy in their tiny apartment. From the corner of her eye she saw Marcus throw up his hands and sit down on the couch to watch television. It was getting late; both of them should have been getting ready for bed, but Amelia wasn't about to open herself up to more conversation by disengaging from her music.

It took over an hour, but eventually Marcus made the first move toward bed. Anger and energy spent, Amelia's playing had dwindled to lullabies and scales, and she turned off the sound in her headphones so she could tell without looking when Marcus had finally gone to bed. The sound of the bed creaking beneath his weight was the signal she'd been waiting for; she sat five more minutes before turning off the keyboard and going to the bathroom to brush her teeth.

Be asleep, she thought as she emerged from the bathroom to pull on her pajamas. She didn't want to go to bed with this unresolved issue clouding the atmosphere, but neither did she want to hash it out anymore. She slipped between the sheets, careful to keep to her side of the bed, and was startled when Marcus's voice broke the silence.

"I won't take it if you really don't want to go."

She froze. "What?" Surely she must have misunderstood.

He took a deep breath, as though saying the words required more strength than he had. "If they offer the job, and you really don't want to go, I won't take it."

There had to be a catch. "For real? How can you say that? I thought it was God's decision." Her tone was more sarcastic than she'd intended, and the moment of quiet before he spoke made her think he might recant. Instead he said, "It *is* God's decision. But if He wants us to go, He'll give you the desire too. That's how we'll know it's the right thing to do."

Wow. *This* was the man she'd married. And she could accept his logic—even if admittedly it was because she was positive she would never desire to move to Nebraska. Still, she slid closer to Marcus and wrapped him in a hug. "Thank you."

Marcus stared at the lights that shifted on the ceiling from the traffic on the street outside. He should never have said it. But he just hadn't been able stand the thought of Amelia being so angry with him. Irrational as his head knew it was, his heart worried she wouldn't love him if he didn't provide some kind of compromise. He couldn't risk that. And the more he thought about it, the more it made sense that God really would make Amelia excited about moving if it was the right thing to do. Or, if not totally excited, at least willing. *Inaction until unity* was the phrase their pastor often used when discussing decision making in marriage. It had always made sense. But ... could couples always be united? Sometimes a decision had to be made. What then?

Change her mind, he begged God. *Please, give me this job and change her mind.* He was out of options, and he was out of patience. If he wasn't offered this job, what then? Not to mention that the job description—aside from the location—sounded even more exciting after having heard back from Ed Donovan, the head elder at New Hope.

While Amelia had been playing—or rather, what seemed to be assaulting—her piano, Marcus had watched the news, then checked his email to kill time before bed. He'd emailed Ed earlier in the day to let him know when he'd be coming to town for the interview, and Ed had written back to confirm the date and answer some of Marcus's questions about the position. He now knew that the old pastor had descended into heresy so gradually no one really noticed until they were in the thick of it. When the elders had finally come to their senses, they'd ousted the man and nearly caused a church split in the process. They were limping along now, in need of a pastor who could unify them again and retrain them in biblical Christianity. The elders were taking turns preaching, but none of them was a gifted speaker, and none of them had any formal training in theology or doctrine. The church was multigenerational, but with far fewer young families and couples.

"We'd love to see that change," Ed had written. "Wheatridge has a growing population of people under thirty-five. To have someone in that demographic at the helm would help in attracting them to the church."

I want this, God. Please make it happen.

Marcus knew his prayers were selfish, but he figured he might as well admit his feelings; God knew them anyway. And he was as sure as he had ever been about anything that this job was for him, so he was confident he was praying in agreement with God's plan.

But he couldn't help worrying that he and Amelia would come to an impasse.

Deep breath, he told himself. *One thing at a time. Do the interview, get all the details, and then start pleading with God.*

Marcus flipped to his stomach and pulled the pillow over his head to shut out the light from the window. He had to sleep—he had an early start with his surf class tomorrow. But his head throbbed with stress.

He never should have said it.

CHAPTER 3

The Santa Ana winds had finally blown away the cold weather and brought back the winter warmth LA was famous for. Amelia checked the weather for Nebraska before heading to sushi with Jill and couldn't help smiling. The forecast predicted freezing rain and possible snow that night. Marcus had never lived anywhere with snow. *We'll see what you think of Nebraska after this.*

He'd left that morning for his interview, and while Amelia felt much better about everything given the promise he'd made her, she was still nervous about his trip. She didn't think it was right to interview for a job he obviously wasn't going to take. It felt like tempting fate.

Amelia swept powder over her nose and examined herself in the mirror. Her new hairstyle still took her by surprise now and then, but she was glad she'd done it. Her copper hair now rested on her shoulders, and the loss of the extra weight made the natural curl more pronounced. Marcus had been shocked at the unplanned change but loved it. Amelia had no memory of her mother's hair being any shorter than her triceps, and she'd always worn it down. She'd never had bangs, either. Amelia hadn't realized how stressful those sightings in the mirror had been until she knew she wouldn't have them anymore. She'd almost completely stopped flinching when she looked in the mirror.

She arrived at the sushi bar just as Jill was emerging from the ladies' room. "I swear I go to the bathroom every ten minutes," she said as they slipped onto stools at the bar. "And I drink, like, five gallons of water a day. Am I pregnant with a baby or a fish?"

Amelia eyed Jill's middle. "Don't ask me."

"Dane said Marcus did an admirable job of trying to cheer him up about the baby. I had no idea he was so into having kids."

Amelia tilted her head. "Who—Marcus?"

"Yeah." She looked concerned. "You didn't know that?"

Amelia shifted uneasily on her seat. "No, I did. We talked about it before we got married. Once or twice, anyway. I told him I didn't want any kids, at least not for a long time, and he was cool with it." But what if he wasn't anymore? Amelia didn't know if she could handle any more life-changing surprises from Marcus. *He'd better not come back from Nebraska with some dream to start having babies.*

"So, speaking of which, Marcus is in Nebraska now, right?" Amelia had texted Jill about her conversation with Marcus the morning after their fight, to which Jill had replied with the famous quote from *My Big Fat Greek Wedding:* "The man is the head, but the woman is the neck …"

Amelia looked at the time on her cell phone. "Yep, he should be there. The weather's miserable there right now; you should see the weekend forecast."

"Aw, poor guy."

"No—this is good. He's such a California boy. The man still surfs, for Pete's sake. Can you imagine Marcus shoveling snow and scraping ice off the windshield? I know it's a little evil of me to think this, but I'm hoping he realizes he doesn't want to live through those winters. It'd be nice if he comes to realize that he doesn't want this job, versus me having to cash in on his promise."

Jill gave her an admonishing look. Amelia's chin raised a bit. "What?"

"I don't know," Jill said, focusing her gaze on the dragon roll on her plate. "Never mind, it's none of my business anyway."

"No, seriously. What?"

Jill shifted on her stool, her eyes only briefly meeting Amelia's. "I guess it just seems a little … cold … that you're not even considering the possibility. Isn't there any room to be at least a little open-minded?"

Amelia sat up straighter. "Why? The odds are against him, and I got the job I wanted here. Would God have set me up with that if His plan also included us moving? That doesn't make sense."

Jill's gaze flickered back and forth between her plate and Amelia. "Yeah, but it seems you and Marcus have conflicting ideas of what God wants right now. I just wonder if it's good to believe that when something happens the way you want it to, God won't mess with it. What if God really does want this job for Marcus?"

"What are you saying—that God is going to rip my success away from me just to teach me a lesson?"

Jill gave Amelia an imploring look. "Come on, that's not what I mean. It's just … God does what's best for us, and if we carve in stone our idea of how things should be, then it's really painful when God's will trumps ours. Isn't it better to recognize that we can't see how or why God orchestrates things the way He does? That His plans have a greater purpose?"

Amelia clenched her jaw and focused on her sushi in silence. Why couldn't Jill just support her, or at least play along?

The noise of the restaurant filled the space between them as they ate their dinners in silence. When it started to get awkward, Jill was the first to speak. "I'm sorry, Amelia, I know that's probably not what you wanted to hear."

Amelia chased a grain of rice with her chopsticks. "Not really, no."

"Don't take this the wrong way, Ames, but I guess … I just worry sometimes that your faith is still so … young. I mean it wasn't that long ago that we were at Juilliard and you were committing your life to the Lord, and campus ministry isn't exactly the 'real world.' Living as a Christian is complicated."

Amelia felt the weight of those words. "I know … But I feel like it's harder for me than it should be. It certainly seems harder for me than it does for you, or Dane, or Marcus. Especially Marcus. I never hear God like you guys do, or feel Him. And when Marcus gets all preacher on me and launches into some theology lesson out of nowhere, it just annoys me. I mean, if I wanted to be a theologian, I'd have gone to seminary, right? But then I feel guilty, because if I'm a Christian, shouldn't I want to know that stuff?"

"Well …" Jill ducked her head, trying to look Amelia in the eyes. "I can't tell you if you are or aren't a Christian, Ames. That's between you and God. What does your gut tell you?"

This turn in the conversation was making Amelia uncomfortable. "What do you mean?"

"I mean, do you think you are a Christian?"

Amelia answered quickly. "Of course I am."

"I'm not trying to say you're not," Jill said. "I just—"

"But if you didn't question it, you wouldn't be asking. Right?" When Jill's words seemed to get stuck in her throat, Amelia felt her face flush as the heat rose in her cheeks. She could feel herself overreacting, but she couldn't help it. "You never struck me as the judgmental type, Jill."

"I'm not—"

"Never mind." Amelia pulled her wallet from her purse and opened it. "Dinner's on me. Enjoy." She threw down a twenty and shoved the wallet back into her purse, then slid off the stool and headed for the street.

How dare Jill accuse her of not being a Christian. Didn't Jesus tell people not to judge? Jill had been the first Christian Amelia had ever known when they met as roommates their first year at Juilliard, and Amelia had been surprised at how cool she was in spite of it. Apparently Jill had been a lot more accepting of people's differing views on spirituality back then.

Her bus was just pulling up to the corner. She hopped on and slouched into a seat just in time to see Jill power walking up the sidewalk. Amelia almost got off the bus, but then turned her back to the window and pulled her iPod from her pocket. She scrolled to Joni Mitchell's *Court and Spark* and lost herself in the music as the bus bounced over potholes and tears burned in her eyes.

The last thing she'd expected tonight was to have her friendship with Jill upended. But how could she be vulnerable with Jill anymore, knowing her friend's assessment of her? Maybe she'd make some new friends in the theater group. Maybe they would accept her, flaws and all.

The 757 hit a pocket of turbulence, jarring Marcus from his thoughts and sending him fumbling to keep his plastic cup of Coke upright. His neighbor in the center seat flashed him a nervous smile and gripped his bag of pretzels tighter. "Reason 243 why I hate flying."

Marcus laughed politely. "That's a shame. I don't mind it, though I don't fly often."

"You're lucky. I have to do it all the time."

"For work?"

"Yeah. Salesman. How 'bout you?"

"What, my job?" Marcus chuckled. "Right now it's anything that pays the bills. But I just did an interview about an hour outside Omaha for a job, and I think it went well."

Really well, actually, even considering the bad weather. Before the plane had dipped, he'd been lost in daydreams about preaching his first sermon from the church's intricately carved oak podium, Amelia and his parents beaming with pride in the front pew.

"That's great. What's the job?"

"Senior pastor."

The man's face registered surprise. "Impressive."

"Thanks." He couldn't help smiling. "I'm pretty excited."

The man glanced down at Marcus's hand. "Married? What's your wife do?"

"She's a pianist." His good mood faltered. "And she's not quite as excited as I am about Nebraska."

"Ah."

"Yeah."

The man's head bobbed in a slow nod. "My wife's not crazy about my job, either. Takes me away from home too much. But in this economy you do what you can, right?"

Marcus agreed and shifted his gaze to the window, where the Rocky Mountains stretched below them in snowcapped splendor. The man was right. In this economy, you took what you could get. Even better when what you could get was your dream job. Another reason why Amelia really should just accept that this was a good thing—no, a God thing.

And it certainly wasn't the only reason. There was the way he'd clicked with the elders, despite the disparity between his age and theirs, which averaged around sixty. The way he'd taken to quaint Wheatridge, which made him think of *It's a Wonderful Life's* Bedford Falls. The way his heart had raced when they'd laid out the challenge the job would set before him—being not only a pastor but a spiritual doctor, helping the congregation heal from a decade under a toxic pastor. When Ed Donovan had given Marcus a tour of the church, they'd stopped for a moment in the pastor's office, and Marcus had easily imagined himself sitting at the mahogany desk in conference with a parishioner. The whole feel of the place suited him perfectly. He never would have expected it, given the pull he'd felt to the trendier young churches that met in movie theaters and industrial parks and nightclubs in downtown LA. But his attraction to the small, traditional church had been surprising, and undeniable.

And when Ed had offered him the job as they drove to the airport that afternoon, Marcus had almost accepted it then and there. In fact, had Ed not followed the offer with "We know you need to talk it over with Amelia first," he probably would have.

And now he really knew: He should never have made that promise to Amelia.

The plane touched down at LAX, and Marcus and his neighbor wished each other well as they parted ways in the terminal. Having only his carry-on, Marcus skipped baggage claim and headed straight for the exit, where his eyes scanned the shifting crowd for Amelia's face. It was the kind of thing she'd typically do: show up to welcome him home, even though they'd already made plans to meet up at their small group's Sunday night community dinner at Jill and Dane's. But after a few minutes spent swiveling in place as he searched in vain, he headed for the ground transportation exit to take the light rail, alone.

It was a calculated move, and he knew it. Were he returning from any other trip she'd have been there; that's just how she was. It hurt to know that she was still closed off to this whole thing. He took a seat in the nearest Metro car and thought over the things he'd brought back for her. He'd meant for them to be fun and enticing, to help her see that moving to Nebraska wouldn't be the end of the world. But the locally grown popcorn, the mug from the Omaha Performing Arts Theater, a schedule of its upcoming season, and the "I'm kind of a big deal in Nebraska" T-shirt he'd seen at the airport no longer struck him as amusing souvenirs.

He stared out the window as the city came into view. *It's clear to me what You're doing, God,* he prayed as his eyes took in the smoggy sky and shining buildings—such a contrast from the cold, snowy, and overcast weekend he'd spent in the very flat town of Wheatridge. *But if You're making it clear to me, why aren't You making it clear to Amelia? I'm supposed to take this job, aren't I? I don't want to go back on my word. I know I shouldn't have promised not to go if she didn't want to, but I really thought You'd change her mind.*

Though maybe He still would. He shouldn't despair yet. God was known for His eleventh-hour saves.

The Metro pulled into his station, and Marcus filed off with a few others and headed for the street. He had to remember this wasn't over yet. Who knew what Amelia's response might be when he told her he'd been officially offered the job? God could make anything happen.

He just hoped God would work His miracle soon.

Amelia's eyes kept drifting to the clock on Jill's kitchen wall. She'd been so close to going to LAX and meeting Marcus in baggage claim, but when the time had come to leave she hadn't been able to do it. It was the thought of the ride back into the city that had stopped her. All that time to talk—for *him* to talk, to gush about Wheatridge (as she was sure he would, given how excited he'd been about the place when they'd talked on the phone the last two nights), to try to convince her to move. She couldn't handle it, not in public. Instead, she'd made up the dip she'd signed up to bring to dinner and had gone to Jill's fifteen minutes late to make sure she wasn't the first one there. They hadn't spoken since their conversation that had gone south at the sushi bar, and Amelia had enough on her mind without adding to it by being alone with Jill.

But she'd kept track of where Marcus likely was, knowing he'd eventually show up, and she had to be prepared. Right now he was probably ten minutes out, maybe less. She couldn't wait to see him and yet feared it at the same time. She wondered if she'd be able to read his face and know before he even spoke if he'd been offered the job. And what if she did see it written there? What would she do?

Amelia was helping someone rearrange the potluck spread on the table when a voice behind her said, "Hey, Marcus!" She caught Jill's eye briefly, and her friend gave her a supportive half smile before Amelia turned to see Marcus. And when she saw his face she knew. It was the eyes that gave it away. The rest of his face looked tired, even uncertain. But his eyes were shining.

He spotted her immediately and dropped his duffel by the front door and crossed the room to wrap her in a hug and whisper "Hey, babe" in her ear. She'd have melted if she hadn't seen that look in his eyes.

She let him give her a quick kiss, not wanting to make a scene in front of everyone else. "I missed you," he said when he pulled away.

"I missed you, too." It was true, 100 percent. She had missed him terribly, even if she'd been irritated that he'd gone away in the first place. "How was the flight?"

"Oh—fine."

"Great." She nodded to the dining room table, where the others had already begun to serve themselves. "Come get some dinner. "

That's what she'd do: Keep the conversation on the periphery, and avoid a discussion about the trip until they went home. At least that way no one would see them fight. And, sadly, she was pretty sure there would be a fight.

Her plan to keep things on the surface worked perfectly until someone asked Marcus why he had the duffel. "Just got back from Nebraska," he said.

"Nebraska? What the heck is out there?" someone else asked.

"Job interview."

Amelia eyed Marcus carefully. She could tell he was trying to keep his excitement at bay, probably for the same reason she'd tried to steer clear of the topic. He didn't want a public argument any more than she did.

A smattering of "Congrats" and "What for?" rained down on him, and as the discussion progressed, Amelia found her spirits buoying. Marcus didn't mention anything about a job offer. *Thank You,* she prayed as she twirled spaghetti on a plastic fork. God had come through. Who said she wasn't a Christian?

The dinner came to an end and guests began to leave. Amelia packed up the leftovers of her dip before everyone else had gone and they were the only couple left; she didn't want Jill or Dane to have the chance to ask Marcus how the interview had been. After their usual "See you later," they walked out together and headed for home. "That was fun," Amelia said as she hooked an arm through Marcus's, trying to keep the conversation light until they were safe in the apartment. "Did you have a good time?"

"Yeah."

She elbowed him. "That wasn't particularly enthusiastic."

He gave her a smile. "Sorry, just … thinking."

"About …?" She caught him staring at her after a silent moment. "What?"

"You haven't asked me at all about the trip."

Why was she suddenly nervous? "We talked both nights you were gone, it's not like I didn't get to hear about it."

"I know, but … Come on, Amelia, I know you're avoiding the whole thing. That's not going to make it go away, you know."

She smirked, though her heart was starting to pound. "No, you're right, I can't make an entire state disappear with the power of my mind. At least not one so big. I'll work on Rhode Island first."

He wasn't laughing. "It really hurts that you don't care at all about something that I care so much about."

"I just don't want to get into it here, in public."

"Get into what? You make it sound like we're going to have a knock-down drag-out."

"Fine." She dropped her hand from his arm. "It hurts me, too, that you don't care at all about the thing *I* care about so much," she said, eyes focused on the sidewalk ahead of them.

"What do you mean by that?"

"Maybe you don't care about my career like I once thought you did."

"How could you possibly say that?"

"If you did, you wouldn't have even taken that interview."

He muttered something under his breath. "Amelia, we've gone over this already."

"I know, I know—*God* told you to go."

"You say that as if you're mocking me."

"I'm not mocking you. I'm trying to explain that you've played the ultimate trump card. But it's not fair. What about the fact that I believe God gave me the theater troupe gig? You're being selfish, and you're using God to support it."

Marcus went quiet. Amelia gripped the Tupperware tighter as her heart sank. She had hurt him. She hadn't meant to do that. But it was as if he wasn't hearing her at all. She didn't want to wound him, but she didn't want to get walked all over, either. She didn't know where the balance was between sticking up for herself and not being harsh when her words didn't seem to get through.

"I'm sorry," she said as their apartment building came into sight. Marcus said nothing, and she felt her palms begin to sweat. Great, now she was getting the silent treatment. "Really," she said. "I'm sorry, I'm not being very nice. But … from what I gathered at dinner, it doesn't matter … right? Maybe this week we can start looking for new job postings and—"

"Amelia." He reached out to take hold of her arm, stopping her on the sidewalk. "I got the job."

She was dumbfounded. She shut her mouth when she realized it was open, then shook her head, disbelieving. "They—they actually offered it to you?"

His jaw slid back and forth just slightly. "Yes," he said, irritation tinting his tone. "They *actually* offered it to me."

"And of course you told them no."

"No, I didn't. I told them I'd talk to you, and we'd pray about it and get back to them by mid-January."

A terse laugh escaped her throat. "But we're not going. You promised."

"I didn't promise we weren't going. I promised we wouldn't go if you didn't want to."

"And I don't, so case closed."

"No—we haven't prayed about it. *You* haven't prayed about it."

Her eyes narrowed as the arrow hit her heart. "I'm getting really tired of people making assumptions about my spiritual life."

"Well, I'm sorry. Maybe if you didn't act so cocky people wouldn't make assumptions."

"Cocky?!"

She turned and headed for the apartment at double speed, knowing she couldn't hold her tongue much longer in the face of such an insult. She heard Marcus's steps behind her but did nothing to acknowledge him, making a beeline instead for the staircase that led to their floor as her mind turned over and over the words Marcus had spoken. *"I got the job."*

She nearly slammed the door behind her, but Marcus caught it and closed it quietly. His even-keeled emotions drove her nuts. She needed a yelling match, not some calm, logical voice of reason. She pulled off her jacket and threw it on the back of the couch. "You promised, Marcus. Don't split hairs. If my mind was going to be changed, God would have done it by now, don't you think?"

"I don't know what to think," he said. "Which is why I think we should pray about it together."

She let out a snort. "I love that you think your job is worth praying over, but when I told you I was auditioning you acted like it was no big deal."

"I prayed about that."

That surprised her. "You did?"

"Of course."

She crossed her arms. "Prayed I wouldn't get it, I'll bet."

His face fell, and she winced inside at the look in his eyes. "How could you say that? Of course I didn't pray that. I prayed God would guide your career, just like I've been praying since the day we started dating. I prayed you'd get it if that was His will, and that He'd comfort you if you didn't. You know I always try to support you and encourage you. How could you ever think I'd be so mean as to pray against you like that?"

Amelia had let her anger carry her too far, and she knew it. Guilt began to gnaw at her stomach. What had she prayed for Marcus? "I'm sorry," she said again. "I—I didn't know you did all that."

"Of course I did," Marcus said, sounding weary. "I love you."

Wounded by the realization that she had never even thought to pray like that, as well as by the fear that Jill might have been on to something, Amelia struggled with what to say next. She didn't want to hurt him anymore. But she wasn't about to give in on Nebraska, either. She sank to the couch beside Marcus and held out her hands. "All right then," she said, unable to soften the challenge in her voice and unwilling to meet his eyes, "let's pray about it."

He paused a moment, then grasped her hands tightly and began to pray aloud. Amelia listened for a moment, then tuned out his voice, knowing his words didn't matter. Nothing was going to make her move.

Christmas Day dawned with a chill in the air that matched the mood in the Sheffield apartment. The last three days had been navigated carefully by both parties, with no mention of the decision before them outside of the twice daily prayers they said together—or rather, that Marcus said in Amelia's presence. Amelia was counting down the days until January 18, when the theater group began rehearsals for their first show, *Pippin*. Despite it not paying enough for her to quit either of her other positions, the mere knowledge that she would soon be performing again made the less-enjoyable parts of her day far easier to bear. However, it did nothing to soothe things between her and Marcus, and that was the part of her life that most concerned her.

Amelia loved Marcus, but she wondered if he'd begun to doubt it. The way they interacted had changed so much since he'd returned from Wheatridge. She didn't feel comfortable being herself anymore. She worried she'd inadvertently say something to hurt his feelings again. He, too, seemed guarded, more measured with his conversation, more careful with his touches.

She glanced at the clock as she woke and calculated their morning schedule. They had nearly two hours before they had to be at church, which gave them plenty of time to exchange gifts, eat breakfast, and get ready for the day—as well as time to reconnect in a more intimate way.

Amelia slipped closer to Marcus beneath the covers and twined her limbs around her husband, whispering "Merry Christmas, baby" in his ear as he stirred from sleep.

He gave her a slow smile that lit his face in the way it had before this mess had begun. "Hey. Merry Christmas to you, too."

She laid her head on his shoulder. "I'd like to propose a truce."

"A truce?"

"A Christmas truce. Let's pretend we haven't been fighting, and that we don't have this giant decision looming over us. Let's just … go back to how we were and let today be magical the way Christmas should be. Agreed?"

His arms came around her, and he kissed her in the way she'd missed so much. "Agreed."

During breakfast, Marcus pulled a small box from beneath the table-top Christmas tree that adorned a TV tray beside the couch. "For you," he said, handing her the box with a flourish.

She smiled and ripped the sparkly red paper, then opened the package to find a black velvet jewelry box. "Oh my," she said. "Fancy." He wagged his eyebrows, making her giggle as she pulled up the lid. Inside sat a silver rectangular frame-like pendant with a snippet of sheet music inside.

"From Mozart's 'Alla Turca,'" he said, looking almost shy at the explanation. "Not the real thing—I mean, it's a reproduction." He shrugged. "I know you like that piece."

"Oh, Marcus. It's beautiful." She pulled it off the velvet pillow and clasped it behind her neck, then leaned across the table to hug him. "Thank you so much." She never would have thought he could name a single classical piece she liked. She always assumed she bored him to death when she talked to him about her favorite composer. That he not only listened, but remembered, chastised her. Could she name any of his favorite ... favorite what? Theologians? Missionaries? What kinds of profession-specific favorites did pastors have, anyway?

Unwilling to break the good mood with thoughts of her own shortcomings, she stood and retrieved the gift she'd placed beneath the tree the night before. "For you. And, I am ashamed to say, not nearly as unique."

He chuckled as he unwrapped the gift. "My cologne. Thanks, I'm almost out."

"I noticed. And you can't run out of that. It's too delicious."

He kissed her. "Thank you."

"You're welcome. I wish I could have gotten you more."

"I wish I could have gotten more for you, too. But that's all right. It's the nature of low-paying jobs in a high-cost-of-living city. Someday we'll be able to shower each other with gifts." He kissed her again, then brought their empty breakfast dishes to the sink. "But until then I'll be perfectly content knowing I've got an amazing wife who loves me and keeps me well stocked in cologne."

He left to shower and dress, leaving Amelia feeling wretched. How lucky was she, to be married to someone who was so kind and sweet and caring? What kind of fool was she to cause such a fuss over this move? *Surely we can find a way to compromise.*

The thought triggered a long-forgotten memory. The same words, spoken by her father, which were met with a heated diatribe by her mother. Amelia had been young, maybe five or six, and the events her mother had been ranting about had happened long before she'd been born. Amelia didn't quite know what her parents were arguing about. But later, when she'd asked her older sister why they'd been fighting, Evie told her about how the family had come to live in Pennsylvania. Their father hadn't liked his job anymore, so he got a new one. But it was in Philadelphia, and their parents had been living in New York. Mom was on Broadway then—this was before even Evie was born—and she had to quit for the move. Since then, Dad had considered changing jobs again, but their mother didn't want him to drag her away from their home like he had done the last time.

It was the first time Amelia had heard about her mother's life before children. How Evie knew the details, Amelia never learned, but from then on Amelia's ears were fine tuned to catch more tidbits about the kind of life her parents had once led. The older she'd grown, the more she'd discovered, and the angrier she'd become at both her parents—at her father for pulling her mother away from such a successful life that, even decades later, she longed to recapture; and at her mother, for allowing herself to be dragged away. For not bouncing back and finding another outlet for her creativity. For compromising. It was that compromise that had set off the chain of events that led to her disappearance.

Amelia shivered, suddenly cold. She loved Marcus; of course she did. But she wasn't about give up her dreams for him. She'd seen what that kind of regret could do to a soul.

❋

After the service, Marcus and Amelia drove north to Ventura to have dinner with Marcus's family. Despite being less than an hour's drive from them, Amelia had only seen them a handful of times since meeting Marcus in college and had never spent Christmas with them. Marcus's father was a second-in-command associate pastor at a large church, and was often swamped with work. His mother, who had lived as a full-time homemaker until her children had all left the nest, now volunteered full-time at the church in a handful of positions. Amelia sometimes wondered why they had a house at all—they practically lived at Ventura Bible Fellowship.

His family was nice on the surface, but there was some prickliness there that kept Amelia on the defensive. Marcus's two older brothers were outgoing, albeit a bit too full of themselves in Amelia's estimation. His mother was kind, always well dressed and making sure everyone was comfortable and had what they needed, but quiet, almost never talking about herself. She, at least, made obvious attempts to fold Amelia into the family. His father reminded her a bit of her own: He had a strong presence that kept her always aware of him, and he was short on chitchat. He asked straightforward questions, and although she hadn't been raised to do so, Amelia always felt like she should address him as "sir."

On the drive home from the first holiday she'd spent with Marcus's family, Amelia had confessed that she didn't understand how Marcus had turned out so normal. "Not that your family is abnormal," she'd assured him. "It's just … Well, I definitely like you the most out of all of them."

Marcus had found that amusing. "I'm glad to hear that."

"Although your mom is pretty cool."

"Yes, she is. She and I have always been close."

"Your brothers …"

"Are conceited."

She'd gasped. "That's not what I was going to say!"

"No, but only because you're too kind to talk about people that way," he'd said with a smile before kissing her. "But it's true, they are. Very popular, very successful … It went to their heads."

"It didn't go to yours."

He laughed. "That's because I've never been popular or successful." He'd distracted her then, drawing her attention to the way the sun was setting over the Pacific, and Amelia had sensed he was done with the discussion. When she'd tried bringing it up again, to ask why his father always seemed so critical of him, he'd shrugged it off and insisted he was like that with everyone. She knew better than to bring it up again.

When they arrived at the spacious home where Marcus had grown up, Amelia was disappointed to notice no other cars were in the driveway or on the street. When Marcus's brothers were there with their families, the house felt less stifling, and the other wives kept the conversation going. Amelia and Mary Sheffield never seemed to have anything to say to each other.

Amelia helped Marcus carry in the gifts, which they placed beneath the tree that looked as though it had been decorated by a Macy's window dresser. "Merry Christmas, Mom!" Marcus called into the silent house.

"Merry Christmas," she called back from the kitchen. Amelia followed Marcus there, where they found Mary assembling a broccoli casserole. "Hello, sweetheart," she said, kissing Marcus on the cheek. "Hello, Amelia," she said, hugging her lightly. "Help yourselves to egg nog. Any sign of the others?"

"Nope, not yet," Marcus said, pouring drinks for himself and Amelia. "Where's Dad?"

"Still at church. He should be back in time for dinner, though."

Amelia glanced at the clock. Dinner was to be at four. It was now just past noon. Their church's services were surely finished by now. What would keep him at work so long on a holiday?

She noticed that neither Marcus nor Mary seemed fazed. Obviously there was a lot more for a pastor to do than Amelia realized. "Can I help, Mary?"

"Oh, you're sweet, Amelia. Thank you, but I'm fine." She smiled at her, then nodded in the direction of the living room. "Make yourselves comfortable. The others ought to be here soon. I stacked the Christmas movies on the coffee table, Marcus—how about putting something in?"

Sensing they were being banished, Amelia followed Marcus to the living room and sat on the leather couch while he chose a DVD from the pile. Amelia caught a glimpse of the case. *It's a Wonderful Life.*

The movie was half over before Eddie and his family arrived, followed closely by John, the middle son, and his wife and six-month-old twin sons. Amelia was relieved by the presence of more people, even if two of them seemed to do nothing but cry and three of them were less than four feet tall and ran around the house as though possessed. Amelia followed the women into the kitchen, not wanting to get stuck in sports-laden conversation as was sure to happen if she remained in the living room with the brothers. Kendra and Renee, her sisters-in-law, dived right in to helping prepare dinner, leaving Amelia feeling inadequate and useless until Renee smiled at her and tilted her head toward the car seat on the floor where one of the twins was wailing. "Would you mind taking Jackson out of there, Amelia? He hates the car but I thought he'd calm down once we were inside. Guess I was wrong."

"Oh—sure." Amelia knelt and studied the buckle a moment before attempting to open it. Some fumbling eventually did the trick, and she lifted the squirming little boy from the velour and held him awkwardly against her as she gently bounced. She could count on one hand the number of babies she'd held in her life. She never knew what to do with them.

Renee gave her another smile, but then started talking to Mary about the preschool their church was starting. Amelia was soon shut out of the conversation by virtue of being unable to contribute to the debate over sending or not sending children to preschool. The same type of thing had happened the last time the family had been together, at Thanksgiving. Amelia and Marcus had arrived late that night, and she'd assumed it was simply a matter of people already being in a groove with their discussions, but to find it happening again when she and Marcus had been earlier than everyone else made her feel snubbed.

Jackson was still crying, but Renee showed no interest in rescuing Amelia, and in fact volunteered to begin preparing the hors d'oeuvres. *Maybe one of the men would do a better job taking care of the baby,* Amelia thought. Still bouncing her fist-waving nephew, she went into the living room where Marcus and his brothers were watching a basketball game and Jackson's twin was lying asleep in his car seat.

"... tried out for the seventh-grade team, remember?" Eddie was saying as John laughed. Marcus rolled his eyes at his brothers and turned back to the television. "You couldn't even make a layup, you were so short."

"Like that was my fault?" Marcus said, then glanced at Amelia. "Aw, Jackson's not happy, huh?"

"Watching you do those drills in the driveway—man, I thought I'd die laughing."

"Shut up, Ed." Marcus reached his hands out Amelia. "Here, give him to me."

"Lighten up, Marc," John said. "You're always so defensive."

Amelia noticed how Marcus completely ignored his brothers once he had Jackson in his arms. "Hey, kiddo," he said as he gently bounced him on his knees. "You're just not a happy guy, are you? Your brother is conked out, you know. You should try that. Naps are good stuff."

Jackson's eyes locked onto Marcus's face and his crying abruptly ceased. Marcus smiled at him. "There you go. You don't need to cry. Life is good for you right now. Believe me." He lifted the baby into the air above his head, and Jackson let out a belly laugh. Amelia thought back to Jill's comments about Marcus as a father and frowned. This was pressure she definitely did not need.

Eddie and John continued to rib Marcus, but he focused all his attention on his nephew. Amelia was disturbed by his brothers' degrading teasing, though Marcus seemed almost unfazed. Except for the set of his jaw.

Amelia returned to the kitchen in the hopes of at least being helpful in the dinner preparation. Actually getting in on the discussion would be icing on the cake.

But it appeared the other women had everything under control. Mary and Kendra had already finished what they were doing, and were sitting on barstools at the island drinking sparkling apple cider while Renee finished prepping the tray of finger foods. "Can I get you a glass?" Mary asked when Amelia came in, raising her own with the question.

"Oh, thanks, I'll get it myself."

"So, any luck with the music thing?" Kendra asked. It always bothered her the way Marcus's family talked about her chosen career, as though it were a teenager's current obsession that was likely to be forgotten in a month. She was glad she had an answer for once besides "Not yet, still looking."

"Yes, actually—I just got hired as the in-house pianist for a new theater troupe. They're going to do all Broadway musicals, but with new arrangements and scripts reworked to fit the current social climate."

The three Sheffield women looked at her like she'd just spoken in tongues.

"That's … interesting," Mary said.

"And this is a full-time job?" Renee asked.

"Not really, no. They're working off of a pretty meager budget right now, but hopefully once the shows start, the ticket sales will bump everyone's salary up a bit. Since rehearsals and shows are in the evenings, I can keep working my other jobs until I find something else."

"It's a bit risky, that whole industry, isn't it?" Kendra swirled her cider as one patent leather–shod foot tapped on the rung of the barstool. "I mean, if no one buys any tickets, you're doomed."

Amelia wanted to wring Kendra's neck, but she tried to keep her tone positive. "True, but I'm not in it for the money. With this job in particular, I'm really just hoping to make some new connections. For example, one of the directors has worked on the music videos of some big names in hip-hop. So if he—"

"But that's not the kind of music you want to do, right?" Mary asked, looking concerned. "You don't want to taint your image with those kinds of associations. Plus, it would be a waste of your talent." She gave Amelia a motherly smile. "What you need to do is connect with someone in the Christian music industry. And that's all in Nashville, I think."

Renee picked up the thread and launched into a review of the most recent digital issue of *CCM Magazine,* once again leaving Amelia out in the cold.

She turned to leave but was called back by Mary. "Would you mind bringing the hors d'oeuvres tray with you if you're going to the living room? I'm sure the boys are getting hungry."

Amelia took the tray as her own stomach growled and walked as far as the hall before stopping to eat a couple of the cheese cubes and club crackers. Eddie was just hanging up his cell. "Dad's going to be another couple hours," he said to the room in general.

"What's keeping him?" Amelia asked. The look Marcus gave her over Jackson's shoulder made her think her conversation wasn't welcome here, either.

"His job, obviously." John scooped a handful of crackers from the tray before Amelia could set it on the coffee table.

"But—on Christmas? Everyone else must have already gone home—"

"That's just Dad's way," Marcus said. His mouth was smiling, but his eyes were not.

"His work ethic is important, both to him and to the church," Eddie said in a tone that hinted at condescension. "A little family get-together doesn't take precedence over the needs of the flock. God comes first."

Amelia didn't appreciate the insinuation that she didn't agree, but at the same time it didn't ring true to her. "Ooo-kay," she muttered under her breath, then spotted her salvation down the hall. "Marcus, do you think it would be okay if I played the piano in the family room?"

He smiled as he played "so big" with Jackson. "Sure, go ahead."

Relieved, she turned and fled the living room with as much speed as she thought allowable without appearing as if she was running away. The upright Boston was high-end for its type, but after so much time spent on her digital model she wouldn't have cared if it was an Everette. She sat on the bench and folded back the keyboard cover, then placed her fingers on the keys and contemplated what to play. Christmas carols were the obvious choice, but she didn't want to waste this opportunity on songs that were so elementary to play. Eventually she chose Mozart's "Alla Turca," hoping Marcus would recognize it as a nod to his gift to her.

Once she began to play, the time passed more quickly, and much more pleasantly. But when the low tenor of Marcus's father's voice reached her ears, she stopped midphrase and shut the cover as though caught committing a crime. She glanced at her watch and realized it was well past their originally scheduled dinner time. What on earth would keep a man at church five hours past the end of the last service?

"Ah, Amelia. I thought I heard you playing back there," he said when she reached the kitchen where everyone had congregated. He reached out a hand to shake, answering for Amelia the question of whether or not she should try to hug him. "Shall we eat, then?"

She noticed that no one mentioned how hungry they were as they went to take their seats, and given how little food had been on the hors d'oeurves tray, Amelia figured everyone had to be starving. *Unless they load up before coming over,* she thought as she took her seat beside Marcus. She'd have to remember that when they came on Easter. The table was crowded with food. They passed around dishes and plates piled with roast beef and mashed potatoes and a variety of casseroles, but no one ate until everyone had been served and Pastor Sheffield said, "Let us pray." The sentiments that followed were long-winded and, in Amelia's opinion, far more showy than God could possibly care for, but everyone's faces were straight and solemn when he was done. They soon became more animated, however, as they began eating and conversation started again. Pastor Sheffield said little, but when he did it seemed as though everyone stopped talking, even if they weren't a part of his conversation.

"I hear you got a new job," he said to Amelia halfway through dinner. The voices around them went silent. "Congratulations."

"Thank you. I'm excited about it."

"You using that talent of yours at your church?"

"On occasion, yes. There are a few of us who play, so we rotate."

"It's a shame you're so far away. We could use a new organist."

Amelia chuckled. "I'm afraid I wouldn't have any idea how to play an organ." The faces around the table registered skepticism. "I mean, yes, I could play the keyboard—but all those stops and pedals are what make an organ so unique, and I have no clue what to do with any of them. The technique is actually really different—the way you use your body, the expression of … the …" Their blank stares told her no one was that interested in hearing her explanation.

"It can't be that hard; I'm sure you'd figure it out," Pastor Sheffield said definitively. "Not that it matters—you're too far away to come play for us anyway."

Amelia cast her eyes back to her plate, feeling chastised but not sure why. Under the table, Marcus squeezed her knee. Then he cleared his throat, a tic she recognized as meaning he was nervous about what he was about to say. She glanced up at him, curious, as he said, "I had an interview last weekend."

"That's wonderful," his mother said. "For what?"

"For a senior pastorship, actually. At a church in Nebraska."

"Wow," Renee said, eyebrows raised like everyone else's. "Where?"

"Nebraska." John snorted.

Marcus frowned. "That makes its ministry less important?"

"No, it just makes it crappy. Who wants to live out there?"

"I'm not saying we'd be out there for the rest of our lives. But it would be a pretty prestigious first position, and hopefully a stepping stone to something back here in California someday."

"You have no experience," Marcus's father said. "They knew this and still let you interview?"

Marcus straightened in his seat. "Actually, they invited me to interview. I hadn't applied."

"Hm. Makes me wonder what kind of church they are that they'd be willing to put someone fresh out of seminary at the helm. Seems like a poor decision."

Amelia kept waiting for Marcus to tell them the rest of the story and defend himself, but instead the conversation shifted and Marcus did nothing to bring it back into focus. She gave him a questioning look, but his face warned her to leave it be.

After dinner they all moved into the living room to open gifts and have dessert. By the time Mary asked if anyone else wanted more coffee, Amelia thought she'd wither and die if she had to stay there a single minute more. She begged Marcus with her eyes to start their good-byes, and to her relief he nodded and stood. "We really should get going," he said. "Long drive back, and Amelia has the early shift in the morning."

Brief half embraces with the women and waves from the men wrapped up their Christmas visit, and when they were safely ensconced in their car Amelia let out a groan. "I'm sorry, love, but your family drains me. They're nice and all, but … man." Marcus grunted a response as he backed out of the driveway. She turned in her seat to face him. "And why didn't you say anything about actually getting the job?"

He gave her a sidelong glance. "You don't even want me to take it. Why should I brag about it?"

"I'm not saying you should have bragged. But you didn't even tell them you got it. Why not?"

Marcus focused with more concentration than necessary on the road before them. "It wasn't the right time."

"The right time? You make it sound like you'd be breaking bad news to them or something."

"It's just …" His voice trailed off and he shook his head. "Just trust me. I'll tell them eventually."

Amelia frowned and turned straight in her seat, straining in vain to decipher the words Marcus muttered under his breath. She just didn't get the Sheffields. And she knew better than to push Marcus to explain himself. She took his hand, which he kissed gently, and settled in for the silent drive home.

CHAPTER 4

In the days after Christmas, Marcus prayed even more fervently that God would change Amelia's heart about Nebraska. He was dying to tell his dad about the job offer, but until he knew it was really happening he wasn't going to mention it again. And if Amelia didn't come around, there would be no point in bringing it up at all, and he'd have lost what might have been the first achievement that made his father proud of him.

He couldn't let that happen. He hated feeling as if he and Amelia were on opposite sides, working against each other, but the longer this went on and Amelia continued to be stubborn, the truer it became. She was definitely not being a team player. Should he have to suffer because of it?

He'd read an email from Ed Donovan that morning, wishing him and Amelia a safe and happy New Year's Eve. "Hope to see you again this year" was the only hint Ed had dropped about whether or not the church was growing impatient for his answer. He hated making them wait like this—not that it was his fault—but their deadline for an answer was looming and Marcus didn't want to wait until the last minute to respond. He feared it would look bad, like he'd been on the fence the entire time. He didn't want to badmouth Amelia by telling Ed she was the one holding things up, but he wished he could at least convey his own eagerness to accept the job so as to save his reputation.

He was halfway through the day when he decided to do just that. Surely he could come up with a diplomatic way to word things. His fear was that the church would start looking into other people just in case he said no, and would then find someone else they preferred and recant on the offer. He wasn't willing to risk it any longer.

Before his last tutoring client of the afternoon—his evening appointments had all canceled to take advantage of the holiday—he logged in to one of the public computer terminals at the library and pulled up his email. *Hello, Ed! Thank you for your note. I appreciate the well-wishes and pray the same for you and the whole New Hope Church family.* He paused, thinking a moment before trying out a few sentences and then deleting them. It didn't matter how he worded it, they all read like indictments again Amelia—though his frustration, which he'd kept bottled up for the last two weeks, was quickly building. Why was she putting him in this position? He still agreed that inaction until unity was a sound approach *most* of the time, but did it continue to apply when one party was holding out due to sheer bullheadedness?

A new approach dawned on him that he had not yet considered. What would his father do in this situation? He almost chuckled aloud—he couldn't imagine his father *in* this situation, because his mother would acquiesce to his desires without a second thought. But that right there was telling. Their marriage was great, their life as close to perfect as it could get in this world, and what was their approach? That someone had to step up and take control. Someone had to be the point person, the decision maker who made sure things happened. His parents would never stagnate, waiting around for one of them to change their mind. And it's not like his mother had no say. He could recall plenty of times when she'd played devil's advocate or expressed concern over a choice that needed to be made. But in the end his father had the final word. And while Marcus liked the idea of him and Amelia always reaching an agreement on things, he was realizing now that such a goal might not always be attainable.

The bottom line was that, of the two of them, Marcus was certainly the most spiritually mature. Amelia had come to the faith only three years ago, and while he didn't doubt her sincerity, he did sometimes wonder about her growth. Was her faith sound enough for her to be able to discern what God was telling her? Wasn't it his job, as the more knowledgeable, the more seasoned Christian in the relationship to make the final call?

A smile of relief spread over his face. He wouldn't have been at all surprised to learn that God had kept Amelia from conceding simply to help him reach this new understanding. An intoxicating warmth pulsed through him as he set about completing his email. With every word Marcus felt more sure, more settled with his verdict, and a weight lifted from his shoulders as his fingers tapped the keys to tell the elder that he would be thrilled to accept the position.

Amelia woke from her nap when Marcus returned from his afternoon tutoring appointments. With the community center classes canceled for the holidays, she'd been taking advantage of the extra time to catch up on her sleep and leisure activities—mainly more sleep—and she'd been doubly sure to get a nap in that afternoon in preparation for the church's New Year's Eve party at Venice Beach.

She rolled herself upright and ran her fingers through her hair to tame it. "Hey, babe. How was tutoring?"

"Oh—fine." Marcus nodded to the couch. "Come sit with me?"

She smiled in anticipation. "Why, sure." He kissed her when she sat down, then gave her a look she couldn't decipher. "I need to tell you something."

This wasn't what she'd been expecting. "Oh. Okay. Is everything all right?"

He smiled, but she could see hesitation in his eyes. "Yes. Everything is—great." He paused, taking hold of her hands. "I've been really thinking about this job."

"Mm-hm." She tried not to smile prematurely. Surely he was finally giving this thing up.

"And I started thinking about how my parents handle these kinds of impasses, in light of the whole 'inaction until unity' concept."

Suddenly she wasn't so confident, especially since his voice was taking on that lecturing tone he used when he was about to slip into preacher mode. "Okay."

"And I think that, in situations like this, that are this important, it falls to the husband to make an executive decision, especially when the husband is the more spiritually mature of the two."

Now she knew she didn't like where this was going. She pulled her hands from his. "This isn't a dictatorship. You don't get to order me around just because you've been a Christian longer."

"I'm not," he said quickly, eyes wide. "I'm just saying that we have to reach a decision eventually, and I'm just not confident that you're willing to listen to God over this because you're so against it."

Her muscles went rigid. She was embarrassed by his assessment, because in her heart of hearts she knew he was right. But
she wasn't about to admit it and risk losing her job. "How dare
you."

He blinked. "I didn't mean to—"

"How dare you judge me like that." She stood and crossed to
the other side of the coffee table. "You've always said marriage was
a partnership, that we each had an equal say in everything. And you
think you can just change that to suit your own situation?"

"I think we need to be open to growing in how we interpret
and understand biblical—"

She laughed. "Spare me. How convenient you'd grow just now,
huh?"

"Amelia—"

She held up her hand. "Don't even talk to me." She stared at
him, every muscle twitching. "If you think for a second you can
just waltz in here and tell me how it's going to be, you're wrong."

Marcus opened his mouth, then closed it again. She could see
his jaw sliding sideways and back. *How dare he be angry.*

She crossed the room and grabbed her jacket from the hook
near the front door. "For your sake, I'm going for a walk. I suggest
we pretend this never happened when I get home."

"It's too late for that," he said quietly. "I've already accepted
the job."

Her chest constricted and she lost her breath. The betrayal was
physically painful. What happened to the support? To the dependability? When she found her voice she said the first thing on her
mind, knowing she meant every word. "Then you're going alone.

I'll research divorce tomorrow." And with that, she shut the door behind her and headed for the street.

Amelia didn't head back to the apartment until after nightfall. Marcus had phoned and texted a dozen times, and she'd erased every message without listening or reading. After walking aimlessly for half an hour she'd headed for a piano dealer she passed on her way to the deli every morning. After perusing the shop long enough to warm her hands, she asked if she could play the glossy black Bösendorfer that sat in the front window. She'd started with the "Lento" from "Marche funèbre," part of Chopin's *Sonata no. 2 in B-flat Minor,* then revisited Tori Amos's "Precious Things," mourning that she'd been driven to play the angry song twice in such a short period of time. She never would have thought Marcus would wound her that deeply. It wasn't until the manager told her the shop was closing that she'd realized it was nearly seven o'clock. She'd returned to the street, where shops were all closing early for the holiday, and slowly made her way back to the apartment, deleting Marcus's attempts at communication every time she heard her cell beep.

When she walked into the apartment Marcus jumped from the couch like he'd been bit. "There you are." He ran a hand over his face. "Why didn't you answer me? I've been worried about you."

"So sorry," she said with plenty of sarcasm. She passed him without so much as a glance and opened the closet to find an outfit for the party.

Marcus came up behind her. She tensed in anticipation of his touch, but it never came. She was glad. "Amelia, look, I'm sorry if

you were hurt by what I said. You have to know that wasn't my intention. But if God is telling me to take this job, then what choice do I
have but to assume you're shutting Him out rather than letting Him
change your mind?"

She pulled a butter-yellow poor-boy sweater and brown tweed
jacket from the closet and tossed them on the bed, careful to avoid
Marcus's eyes as she turned. Ignoring him, she changed clothes and
then reapplied her makeup and brushed her hair. He stood watching
her the entire time, saying nothing, and the ball of tension in her
stomach grew tighter with every second that she thought over what
he had just said. Now she knew firsthand why so many people hated
Christians. Thanks to Marcus and Jill she was beginning to rethink
her decision to call herself one.

"Are you going to ignore me all night?"

Amelia could hear the strain in his voice and wanted to hit him
for being mad. He had no reason, none whatsoever, to be anything
but a groveling mess of guilt and remorse. She said nothing, moving
to the kitchen to fix a snack before leaving for the party. Though the
more she thought about it, the less sure she was she wanted to spend
the evening with people from church. They were probably all just as
two-faced as Jill and Marcus.

"Amelia, come on."

She bit her sandwich, poured a glass of milk.

"This is ridiculous. You can yell at me all you want, I'm okay
with that, just … do *something*."

She took her plate and glass to the table and sat down, staring
out the window and clinging to her spite to stop herself from giving
him what he wanted. He sat down across from her and stared at her

as though he could subdue her by the sheer force of his thoughts. "Look." His voice was calm, though she heard the irritation behind it and was pleased to know she'd finally shaken Mr. Even Keel. "I know this is painful. I know it means giving up the theater job. I know you see it as a step backward for your career. But do you not trust God to take care of you in Nebraska? Do you think He's incapable of bringing you opportunities? It's not a third-world country we're moving to, you know. There are musicians there too. We'll start looking for jobs tomorrow, since we both have the day off. We'll get you a whole list of them to work off of."

This was his best offer? *Please*. She ate her last bite, swallowed the last of her milk, and checked her watch. Only then, as she stood to leave for the party, did she respond. "There's no need. I'm not going." She pulled gloves and earmuffs from a basket on the floor by the door and pocketed her phone and keys. "Don't wait up." Without waiting to see if he planned on joining her, Amelia left for the bus stop, wishing she was going to a party with spiked punch and hoping the new year would start better than this one was ending.

"Amelia!"

Amelia groaned inside as Jill's voice rose above the din of the crowd around the bonfire. It had been easier to avoid a serious conversation with Jill at the community supper because there had been so many people crammed in their apartment, but out here with everyone spread out on the beach, Amelia knew she wouldn't be so lucky. And she'd had so much on her mind she hadn't given any thought to how to respond when, and if, Jill finally apologized.

Jill reached Amelia's side, and the look on her face told Amelia she was contrite. "I'm so glad you came. I was worried you wouldn't."

Amelia shrugged. "Not a lot of other options."

"Yeah, but still. I'm glad you came. I've been trying to get ahold of you; didn't you get my messages?"

Amelia nodded. They'd all met the same fate Marcus's messages had that afternoon. "I did, yeah. Just … didn't feel like responding."

Jill nodded. "I know. I understand. And I'm really sorry. I really wasn't trying to say you weren't a Christian. I can't see your heart; only God can do that, and it's all between Him and you anyway. It's none of my business. Do you forgive me?"

Amelia swirled her Styrofoam cup of lukewarm hot chocolate. "Yeah. I forgive you."

Jill smiled. "Thanks. I really mean it."

"I know you do."

Jill glanced around. "I still haven't seen Marcus. Did he come? Dane saw you first and was all psyched you guys were here."

"No, he's not here. And I don't know if he's coming." Normally she'd have called Jill to vent and cry the second she left the apartment, but obviously she hadn't wanted to do that. But even now that Jill had apologized, Amelia felt weird telling her what had happened. "We … We had a fight."

Jill frowned. "Oh no. What happened?"

"He took the job in Nebraska, even though he promised not to if I didn't want to go."

Jill's face registered the appropriate shock and Amelia felt a little safer. "Are you serious? That doesn't sound like Marcus."

"It gets better. He tried to use the 'I'm the man, it's my call' card."

"Wow. I don't know what to say. What did *you* say?"

"I told him I wasn't going." She left out the part about divorce, knowing Jill would overreact. "I have a job, he made a promise, it's that simple."

"What did he say?"

Amelia drained the rest of her hot chocolate and wandered toward the trash can as Jill fell in beside her. Marcus's actual words had left her, but the gist of them had left their mark. "That his job was more important than mine. That he knew God better than I did. That I didn't have any faith."

Jill's mouth hung open. "He said all that? Marcus?"

"Not those exact words, no, but that's what he meant. If he keeps this up I'll be glad to see him leave."

"But … he wouldn't really leave without you, would he? And you wouldn't really let him go—right?"

Amelia took a slow breath, sensing Jill's support was not going to extend as far as Amelia had hoped. "I'm not the boss of him. If he wants to leave, he can leave, that's his choice. But I'm not going to chase him and beg him to say, and I'm sure as heck not going to follow along behind him like a will-less Stepford wife. If he breaks his promise and decides to go, then I'll be glad I saw this side of him six months into our marriage instead of six years."

"Amelia, what are you saying?"

"Hey, guys." They turned in tandem to see Dane and Marcus approaching. Amelia was stunned that he'd even decided to come, and could tell by the look on Dane's face that Marcus had already shared his side of the story. Marcus's face told her nothing had changed for him, and she bristled, crossing her arms and squaring her stance in the sand, preparing herself for a face off.

"Marcus told me what happened," Dane said. Jill nodded, her face telling him she knew as well. "I don't want to see you two split up over this."

Marcus shoved his hands in the pockets of his cargo pants. "What am I supposed to do?" His mouth worked as though preparing to speak again, but then clamped tight as he cast his eyes to the sand.

"There's got to be a compromise," Jill said. "There's got to be some way to fix this."

"I don't think this is necessarily the place to try to work this out," Amelia said, not liking the feeling of such a serious discussion in the middle of so many other people. "I kind of wanted to forget about it all for the evening and just enjoy the holiday with my friends." She would have preferred to spend it with her husband, too, but not when he was acting like this.

"You know …" They all looked to Dane, though Amelia wasn't as interested in what he had to say as the others appeared to be. Unless he flat out told Marcus to stay in LA, she doubted she'd appreciate his idea. Dane looked at Jill. "We have that second bedroom. It'll be the nursery next year, but we won't need to do that for a long time …" He scratched his chin, thinking while the rest of them wondered where he was going with this. "Okay, so, this might sound crazy, but what if you guys both took a trial run with your jobs? Amelia could stay with us, Marcus could move to Nebraska, and when Amelia's first show is over she can reevaluate to see if it's where she really wants to be."

Amelia gave him a dark look. "Why am I the one who has to reevaluate? Shouldn't Marcus have to do the same thing?"

Dane thought a moment. "Well … when does your first show end?"

Amelia thought back to the conversation she'd had last week with Ross. "Just before Easter, I think?"

"Okay, perfect. At Easter you can both talk it over and see where you stand. It *should* be a mutual thing, both of you agreeing to be open to the possibility that you're not in the right place. No gloating from the other party allowed."

As little as she wanted to admit it, Dane's suggestion had merit. She'd have to move anyway if Marcus left; it took both their incomes to pay the bills. And Amelia was certain it wouldn't be her packing bags and booking a flight come April. What did she have to lose? She swallowed hard. *Here goes nothing.* "Okay."

The other three looked at her with varying expressions of surprise. "Really?" Marcus said. "You're willing to stay behind?"

She cocked a brow. "You could always just stay, you know."

"No," Marcus said, head shaking. "I appreciate the idea, Dane, but no."

"You know, Marcus," Amelia said as a new angle dawned to her. "When we were dating you always said you'd be okay if one of my gigs toured around a little. This isn't really any different. This is what it would be like, you know? Well, except you're the one moving, and not me. But the result is the same. If you were okay with that, then why is what you're doing any different? I mean, sure it's longer than we were thinking I'd be gone, but three months is still less than a typical tour."

"Yeah, but ... I just ..." Marcus rolled his eyes heavenward. "It's just different."

"It's really not."

"There has to be another solution."

Amelia shrugged. "If there is, none of us are thinking of it."

Marcus blew out a breath that fogged in front of him. "All right. Fine. Three-month trial run."

Amelia found herself smiling. She never would have expected a somewhat happy ending to this. She even had it in her to peck Marcus on the cheek. "Thanks, babe."

He gave her a sidelong glance and sighed. "You're welcome, I guess."

She hooked an arm through his and tugged him toward the table of food. "Come on, let's get a snack. Fighting always makes me hungry."

✳

Marcus stared as his phone, willing his finger to dial but not able to make it happen. He didn't often feel such conflict, but Randall Sheffield had an uncanny ability to make Marcus feel all sorts of things he didn't like. *And yet I keep after him. I'm such a glutton for punishment.*

He'd almost called his parents a dozen times to tell them the news, but he knew trying to explain the arrangement with Amelia was going to ruin the moment. Part of him was tempted to conveniently forget to mention that part. But, besides the fact that he didn't want to lie to his parents, he knew somehow it would come out eventually, and the last thing he wanted was to give his father another reason to be disappointed with him. That was the catch, though—there was no way to spin this so that he wouldn't be disappointed. He prayed that, for once, his father's pride in his son's achievements would overshadow what he knew his father would perceive as Marcus's weakness as a husband.

Finally his finger jabbed at the buttons, and before he could change his mind his mother had answered. "Hey, Mom," he said, mentally cursing the nervous break in his voice. "I've got some good news."

"Oh, wonderful—what is it?"

"That job I told you about at Christmas? I got it. I'm the senior pastor of New Hope Church in Wheatridge, Nebraska."

At least he could always count on his mother for enthusiasm. "Oh, Marcus, that's fantastic, congratulations! I'm so proud of you."

Marcus smiled. "Thanks, Mom."

He heard his father's voice in the background. His stomach tensed. "Your father heard me cheering and wants to know what the fuss is about. Here he is." A brief crackle on the line ensued, then his father's voice was in his ear. "What's going on, Marcus?"

"That job, in Nebraska—I got it."

"Didn't Amelia just get a job?"

"Yes, she did." Leave it to his dad to hone in on that and not Marcus's accomplishment.

"So she's giving it up for you, eh?"

Marcus couldn't believe his ears. Either he was mistaken, or a note of pride had infiltrated his father's voice. The temptation to say yes was almost too strong to withstand, but knowing he'd have to get Amelia to lie along with him made him tell the truth. "No, actually—she's going to stay in LA with some friends of ours. At least until her first show is over. After that she'll probably come out." He winced at the half truth, but just couldn't help himself.

"Wait—she's staying here? You're going to lose her to her career, you know. If you weren't able to convince her to come now, she never will. You'll be divorced by this time next year, mark my words. And what kind of a church is this that they're putting you in charge at twenty-six and no experience? Either you'll drive it into the ground or they'll chew you up and spit you out. You've taken on more than you can handle, Marcus. Amelia has the right idea. Stay in LA."

The crackle hit his ear once more, and he heard his father's voice receding in the background before his mother spoke up. "I'm sure you'll do fine," she said, her tone as smooth and soothing as it always was when she was salving the wounds of her husband's bite. "God will work it all out, don't you worry."

"Yeah. Thanks, Mom." With all the joy sucked out of him he no longer had the energy to keep up the conversation. "I'll keep you updated."

Marcus hung up the phone and dropped it to the cushion beside him on the couch. Once again history had repeated itself. His father always knocked him down, and Marcus kept getting up and asking for more.

One day, though, he'll be supportive, Marcus told himself. *He has to be eventually, right?* And Marcus was determined to give him something to be supportive about. He'd been working at it for this long—he wasn't going to stop now.

Ten days later Marcus was sealing up the last of his boxes in preparation for their shipment to Nebraska, eager to get on the road. He'd experienced a brief moment of paralyzing doubt after speaking to his father, and had very nearly called Ed Donovan to rescind his acceptance. But it had been Amelia, of all people, who had encouraged him to stick it out.

"Is this or is this not what you've always wanted? And you're going to let your pessimistic, hypercritical father ruin that for you? You give him an awful lot of power, don't you?"

She'd said the words with venom, and it took Marcus by surprise. He'd had no idea she felt that negatively about his father. He'd never met anyone who spoke of him with anything other than respect and admiration. But even though the words stung, the more he thought about them, the more he had to agree. Besides, what was the worst that could happen? He'd get fired for not knowing what he was doing and prove his father right. Again. It was definitely a worst-case scenario Marcus didn't like to contemplate, but eating humble pie was more savory than tasting regret for the rest of his life.

And for a brief moment, Marcus had basked in what was the closest thing to a supportive comment Amelia had made about this whole situation. Her attitude toward his new job hurt far more than he'd ever let on to her. He understood why she was angry, and didn't want her to feign support out of guilt, so he'd never admitted it to her. But he sorely missed the encouragement he craved and that, until now, she'd always provided.

The planning of the move went faster than he'd expected, and when Ed floated January 20 as Marcus's start date, he'd found he had no reason not to accept it. He'd given notice at his jobs as soon as he'd taken the position with the church, and the days passed quickly as he packed and prepared for the move. The busyness had been a welcome distraction from the one hitch in this whole plan that still made his heart hurt: leaving Amelia.

At first he'd thought she was completely cool with the arrangement. He watched carefully for signs of sadness or anxiety, but she seemed her typical, chipper self—until he recognized her upbeat demeanor as the same smoke screen busyness was for him. And when he caught her crying in the bathroom the night before he left he'd felt both awful and relieved at the same time. She *was* going to miss him. She did love him. They connected at that moment more intimately and passionately than they had in months, and set aside packing for a while to just talk.

"I was crazy when I said I didn't mind if you toured," Marcus said, nuzzling the base of her neck and inhaling the coconut scent that lingered in her hair from that morning's shower. "I was a stupid, ignorant boy in my youth."

She chuckled. "The youth of that whole year and a half ago?"

He smiled. "I've grown a lot since then."

"Oh, yes, you're a sage."

"You're sure you can trust these theater guys, now? The theater kids always made me nervous in high school."

She looked at him, confused. "What do you mean, trust?"

"Oh, you know—they're not going to try to make any moves on you or take you out and get you drunk?"

She laughed. "Seriously not the kind of thing you need to worry about. I think Ross and Gabe are okay people, and theater guys are pretty harmless. It was the guys in the automotive classes you had to be careful about. Never knew when they might jump on the hood of the wreck they were fixing and bust out with 'Greased Lightning.' You know what that kind of choreography does to a girl's senses."

They both lost their breath laughing, and Marcus held Amelia tighter as they both recovered. This was the Amelia he loved. He'd missed her the last few weeks. How was he going to handle the physical distance for three months when he'd barely handled the emotional distance of the last twenty-four days?

Amelia looked around the living room. "You're way ahead of me. I'm going to be up all night getting my stuff packed up."

"I think I'm done; I'll help you."

She was quiet for a moment, then sighed and pressed herself closer to him. "I miss you already."

"I know." He squeezed her hand. "I'll call every night."

"We'll need to get a better cell phone plan."

"That's all right. I've got a real salary now, remember?"

"Yeah, but …" She pulled her hand from his and wiped her cheek. "Do you hate me?"

The question came from nowhere, taking Marcus by surprise. "What—hate you? Are you nuts?"

"I'm making this all so difficult. I know it's all my fault."

"Hey, babe, ease up." He gave her a squeeze and rubbed her back. "Listen, you were absolutely right about what you said at the beach. This is no different than you going on tour. Yeah, it's longer than we ever expected to be apart, but think of it this way: If we can handle this, then we'll be able to handle any little trip you—or I— might have to take for our jobs. And yeah, I wish you were coming with, but … I'm okay with this. Really."

The next day went so quickly that Marcus had no time to get emotional. He and Dane moved Amelia's boxes over to Dane and Jill's apartment, then they'd taken the boxes that didn't fit in Marcus's hatchback to the shipping store and sent them on their way. Back at their apartment, Amelia showed up with sandwiches for everyone at lunch and, despite Marcus's protests, insisted he leave as soon as he was done eating.

"I told you I'd help you clean the apartment," he said.

"It's a Friday afternoon—you really want to wait until two or three to get on the road? The I-15 is going to be locked up with the Vegas-bound before then. You know you don't want to start the trip at a snail's pace through the desert."

She was right, but he still felt rotten leaving her with all the work. When he said as much, she gave him a pointed look that told him she wouldn't be able to maintain dry eyes for much longer. "I'd sort of like the time alone. "

Dane had wisely taken his leave with his lunch after giving Amelia a copy of the apartment keys. With a final look at the clock Amelia had nodded to the door. "You need to go."

"Right. Okay." Marcus pulled out his keys and took off the front door and mailbox keys from the ring and placed them on the counter. "I'll call you from the road, let you know how things are going."

"Okay."

"I told the management company we'd be out by tomorrow night, so you've got some extra time if you need it."

Amelia nodded but said nothing.

"I love you, Amelia."

That broke the dam and brought her into his arms. She cried into his shoulder and he hugged her close, telling himself again that this was the right thing to do, even though it no longer felt that way. When they pulled apart she gave him a gentle push for the door. "Get out of here. Drive safe."

"I will." He kissed her again and then left for the parking garage, not wanting to linger and make leaving any more difficult than it already was. When he reached the car, packed with suitcases and boxes, he prayed nothing would go wrong—with the car, the drive, or their plans. He sensed a long stretch of quiet on the horizon and quickly climbed inside and pulled out, eager to get on the freeway with his music blaring and his thoughts focused fully on the road before the silence got the best of him.

❀

Amelia closed the door behind Marcus and allowed herself a good cry on the couch that would soon be hauled away by Goodwill. Did she really want this job this badly? This barely paying, super-off-Broadway gig that might or might not bring the connections she was hoping for? She'd been telling herself for days that "no pain, no gain" was a cliché for a reason. But now, with the apartment nearly empty and Marcus gone, her heart hurt so much she had to wonder if she'd reached the point at which the gain wasn't worth the pain it caused.

No—you're not there yet, she told herself while she mopped her tears. *Give it another couple years and then we'll see. If you give up that*

easily you'll never know what you can do. You'd regret quitting now. And
worse, you'd be just like her.

Crumpling her tissue, she went to the kitchen to get the cleaning
supplies and start working on the apartment. She set her iPod to
Little Earthquakes and sang along as she pulled on rubber gloves and
started on the kitchen. If she worked nonstop she'd be out of here
in just a couple hours and could get back to Jill's to put her room
together.

She'd been cleaning for an hour when her phone's ringing came
through between songs. She yanked out the earbuds and raced to
grab it, thinking it might be Marcus, but the number on the screen
was unfamiliar. "Hello?"

"Hey, Amelia, it's Ross."

"Oh—hey, hi."

"I know this is last minute, but I wanted to see if you were
free tonight. Gabe and I selected the last troupe member yesterday and thought it would be fun to get everyone together for a
celebratory drink or two at the Melody Lounge near Chinatown.
We'll get there around five to take advantage of happy hour. Can
you make it?"

Her first impulse was to say no, but then she thought it might
help put her in a better frame of mind. Plus, it would be nice to meet
everyone before the first rehearsal. Jill's apartment was only about ten
minutes from there by bus; she'd just stay for an hour or so and then
go. "Sure. Why not."

"Great! I'm glad you can make it. I'm looking forward to it."

She hung up and went back to work, feeling a little less morose. It
would be fun to finally meet the others she'd be working with—and

to get her mind off missing Marcus. Maybe she'd even make some new friends.

The bar was packed, but Amelia spotted Ross and Gabe in a back corner booth with a handful of others. She unzipped her jacket and straightened her blouse, hoping the freshening up she'd done at the apartment had lasted the bus ride over. She'd forgotten she didn't have any clothes or even her makeup at the apartment, and hadn't finished cleaning in time to stop at Jill's. Threading her way through the crowd, she noticed with dismay she was the only woman in their party. *It was last minute. Who knows who else might show up later, or just couldn't come tonight. Maybe you'll click with someone at rehearsal on Monday.*

"Amelia! So glad you made it." Ross and Gabe both stood to give her a brief embrace, then Ross pulled out the empty chair beside him for her and started the introductions. "Gentlemen, this is Amelia Sheffield, our wicked-talented pianist." He pointed to each of the others as he named them and their position within the troupe. Only two of the five were musicians; the others were actors. "Blythe, Dana, and Carson can't make it tonight, but you'll meet them Monday. Carson's our drummer, Dana and Blythe are actors." He nodded to two appetizers in the middle of the table. "Help yourself. Can I get you a drink?"

"Cherry Coke, thanks."

He saluted and stood. "Coming right up."

Amelia helped herself to a plate and a handful of chips for the guacamole as the conversation continued where it had left off when she'd arrived. She eyed each of the other musicians, wondering what their stories were. For the first time she worried they'd be better than her, that her performance would lack something special they each possessed. She decided to start practicing more, just to be safe.

"… UCLA for two years. What about you, Amelia? Where did you get your degree?"

"Oh—started at Juilliard but transferred to LA Bible College to complete my bachelor's."

The brief silence that followed told her this was likely not a crowd that often rubbed shoulders with Bible-college grads. She hoped her embarrassment didn't show on her face. *Quick, change the subject!* "So what else do you all do to pay the bills?"

The conversation took off from there as everyone compared stories of how they stayed afloat financially while they pursued the careers they really wanted. As they talked over each other in friendly one-upmanship, Ross returned with her drink and set it before her with a flourish. "*Senorita,*" he said as he smiled and sat down. She saw him glance at her wedding ring. "Ah. *Senora,* I mean." His face changed slightly. "How long have you been married? You're so young."

"Last June, straight out of college."

"A nice Christian boy?" the guitarist asked.

Ross looked from the musician to her. "Huh?"

"Oh—my alma mater. LA Bible College. And yes, he is a nice Christian boy." She sipped her drink, tipping her head downward to hide the surprising onset of tears.

Ross was perceptive, however. "Are you all right?" he asked, leaning in and speaking quietly while the others returned to their conversation.

"Yeah, I'm fine, thanks," she said with a brief smile. "My husband just got a job in Nebraska and left today."

Ross frowned. "Like—contract work or something?"

"No, it's a head pastorship at a church out there."

"So ... he left you here?"

"It was a mutual decision. I already had this gig—"

"He got the job after you signed on with us? And he still took it?"

"Well, yeah. I mean, that's his dream. And I could have quit and gone with him, but this is *my* dream, so I'm staying. It's like touring. Not that big a deal."

Ross shook his head. "He left behind a woman like you?" He whistled. "He must really trust you."

Amelia didn't know what to say. She settled on a meek "He does" and turned her attention to the food on her plate in the hopes he'd engage someone else. It worked. Amelia tried not to read too much into Ross's statements, figuring her discomfort was more keen because Marcus had just left. On another day she'd have likely appreciated the compliment.

She stayed longer than she meant to, completely forgetting the time until the violinist stood and nodded for the door. "Early shift in the morning; I need to run."

"What time is it?" Ross asked, fishing for his cell phone.

"Eight."

Amelia nearly choked. "I have the early shift in the morning too. And a new room to unpack." She stood and pulled on her jacket. "It was really nice meeting you all. Thanks so much for inviting me, Ross."

"Of course, Amelia. Looking forward to Monday."

She returned his smile, shook hands with the others, and followed the violinist to the door where they parted ways. The streets were crowded with Friday night fun seekers, making her feel safer as she made her way to the bus stop and looked up the bus she'd need to take to Jill's. She took a seat on the bench and took out her phone to check the time, and saw a text from Marcus. *In UT hotel. Easy drive. Luv u.* She texted him back with *On my way 2 J&Ds. Will call when I get home. LUV U.* She was mad she'd missed him; if she'd seen it when he'd first written she'd have called him right back. She kept checking her phone, waiting for a response, but none came.

By the time she got home, the emotional and physical strain of the day had started to take their toll. She was relieved to see the note on the door telling her Jill and Dane had gone to a movie—but, even though she'd been to their place scores of times, she felt awkward being there alone. She tried to unpack but was completely unmotivated. Instead, she pulled her pajamas and toiletries from the suitcase, readied herself for bed, and called Marcus once she was under the covers. It rang four times before going to voice mail, and then she remembered Utah was an hour ahead and Marcus had likely gone to bed early after such a long day of driving. She shut the phone, set it on the nightstand, and stared at it, willing it to ring, until she fell asleep.

CHAPTER 5

The furnished apartment Marcus now lived in was easily more than twice the size of the studio back in LA, and the extra space was driving him crazy. He kept the door to the second bedroom closed and had rearranged the furniture twice since arriving yesterday, trying to get things to take up more room, but still he felt uncomfortable.

It was his own fault. When he'd talked to Ed about the move, Ed had offered to get a short-term apartment lined up for them so they didn't have to commit long-term to something sight unseen. At the time Marcus had still been sure Amelia would eventually come around, so he'd asked Ed to find a two-bedroom unit, knowing how much Amelia hated the cramped quarters of their studio. When they'd decided on their three-month compromise, he'd already forgotten about the apartment, since he'd only been planning on staying in it for a month or two at the most while they looked for something else.

He was contemplating the layout of the living room once again when his cell rang. "Welcome to Nebraska," boomed Ed's friendly voice. "Would have called yesterday but wanted to give you two a chance to settle in. How was the drive out?"

It took Marcus a moment to answer. He was stuck on the fact that he'd somehow managed to neglect telling Ed that Amelia wasn't coming. "Um—fine, yes, the drive was fine."

"And the apartment, is it all right?"

"It's great, Ed, thank you."

"Glad to hear it. So, Lucy and I would love to take you two out for dinner tonight. Would that be all right or do you already have plans?"

Marcus rubbed a hand over his eyes. "No plans, no. Where should we meet?"

Marcus recorded the address and directions in his notebook and hung up with a lump in his stomach. How could he have forgotten to bring this up? *Please don't let this be a big deal,* he prayed as he lugged a love seat to a new spot. The last thing he wanted to do was get off on the wrong foot with the church.

Pete's Bar and Grill was a pub-like restaurant that bustled with a middle-aged crowd taking advantage of the happy hour. Ed and Lucy already had a table, and when he reached it both their faces registered concern. "Is Amelia feeling poorly?" Lucy asked after giving him a warm embrace in welcome.

"No, she's fine—she's just not in Nebraska yet." He took a seat and dived in, wanting to get the explanation out of the way. "She's 'on tour' in a sense—she got a job with a local theater group right before I interviewed with New Hope, and she's going to stay there through the end of their first production."

"Oh my," said Lucy. "I imagine that must be difficult for you both, being separated for such a long time."

"When will she be coming out?" Ed asked.

"Well, the show ends right before Easter." It wasn't the whole answer, but it was a truthful statement, and Marcus wasn't about to get into the nuances of his and Amelia's agreement.

"Three months! And you two are newlyweds." Lucy tsk'd. "What an unfortunate situation."

"We knew going into our marriage that this might eventually happen. Amelia is a very talented musician; with a little more experience under her belt she'll likely get offers to tour with all sorts of productions." He felt like a shyster advocating for the opposite team. He'd only been gone two days and he was already certain he never wanted Amelia to tour anywhere. "So this is good practice, really. She's rooming with close friends of ours, and once I've got a rhythm down here I'll go back to LA to visit her. She works two other jobs besides the theater group, so it's hard for her to get time off."

Ed pushed his spectacles up on his nose. "And I'm sure you'll find that rhythm quickly. Are you still prepared to start tomorrow?"

"Absolutely." He couldn't help smiling at the thought. "I've been looking forward to it."

"Excellent. Why don't you come by around nine, and I'll introduce you to Lillian, our secretary, and we'll sort out when you'll start preaching."

The thought of finally standing behind that pulpit in the center of the church's sanctuary platform made his blood pump harder. "Sounds good," he said, toasting them with his ice water.

They began to discuss the menu, but in the back of his mind Marcus was imagining himself preaching, his leather-bound ESV Bible in hand, and his father in the audience. Smiling.

The next morning Marcus emerged from the apartment unprepared for the weather. The previous two days had been far warmer than when he'd visited in December, and he'd assumed the worst was over and the spring thaw was coming. Instead, the night had brought three inches of snow and encased his car in a thin layer of ice and a thick layer of snow.

He went back to the apartment, pulled on a second sweater and his earmuffs and gloves, and went back out to chip his way into his hatchback.

He'd succeeded in brushing the snow off when he heard a voice behind him say, "Need a hand?" A young woman in a black wool trench coat held up a small can. "De-icer. Let me get your locks for you." She sprayed the can's contents over the lock as Marcus fought embarrassment over having a car so old there were no power locks. "There you go," she said. "Open it quick before it ices back up. It's got to be twenty degrees out here."

He turned the key and pulled hard on the handle, shattering the ice that had filled in the space around the door as it swung open with a creak. He slid in with a prayer that was rewarded when the car started on the first try, then got out to thank the Good Samaritan. "Marcus Sheffield," he said, then nodded to the back license plate of his car. "New to Wheatridge, as you can see."

She smiled, revealing chattering teeth, and shook his hand. "Karis Bloom. Welcome to Wheatridge. Make sure you let your car run for a good five minutes before you go. Older models like that don't take well to the cold in the morning. Ask me how I know." She nodded to her own car, a boxy Volvo from the eighties. "I'm going back in to wait, and I've got coffee—want to join me?"

"Sure, thanks." He followed her back into the building and down the hall to her first-floor unit. The smell of coffee when she opened the door was heavenly. "Let me call my boss and let him know I'll be late," he said and stepped back out into the hall.

Ed had a good laugh over Marcus's predicament. "Should have warned you about that last night. My apologies. Get here when you can, and be careful in the parking lot; the gentleman from the congregation that plows it for us hasn't come through yet."

Karis met him at the door with a steaming mug. "Milk or sugar?"

"Normally both, but I think I need it straight this morning." He smiled. "Thanks again for your help. Guess I need to pay closer attention to the weather forecast, hm?"

She nodded, looking mirthful. "That would be wise. Probably not a lot of use for that in California."

"That's the truth." He took a long sip, relishing the heat in his throat. "Guess the alarm clock will have to get set back ten minutes."

"Even more when there's more snow. The management here is awful about plowing. It's usually done by the time I get home, but that doesn't help when I have ten minutes to get to work in the morning."

"And where do you work?"

"The library—I'm the children's librarian. You?"

"I'm the new pastor at New Hope Church."

Her eyes gave a glimmer of recognition. "That's the one on First and Cherry, right?"

"That's right."

"Hmm."

She sipped her coffee but said nothing more. Marcus gave her a cautious smile. "Do you know anything about them?"

"A little, yes." She studied her coffee, then gave him a frank look. "Let's just say I'm glad to know they're under new management."

"Really … so you've been there?"

"Tried to go when I first moved here, about a year and a half ago. They didn't like that I was a single mother." She glanced to the corner of the living room where a basket of toys sat along with a stack of picture books. "I have a four-year-old. Harriet Miles up in 3B watches her for me. I got the impression it might have been okay if I'd admitted that my husband had left me or something, but the fact that I'd never even married didn't go over very well."

Marcus shook his head. "That's really unfortunate. I'm so sorry that happened."

She smiled tightly and shrugged. "Not your fault."

"No, but still. I can assure you it won't be like that now. The pastor they had was … Well, let's just say there's a good reason he's not there anymore. They know they were off course, and they want to change."

"And that's why you're here?"

He grinned. "That's why I'm here."

She tilted her head, studying him. "Well, then I'm even more glad to welcome you to Wheatridge."

There was a subtle change in her tone that told Marcus it might not be appropriate to stay any longer. He took a long sip from the coffee, then handed her the mug with a smile. "This is supposed to be my first day on the job. I should probably attempt to actually get there."

She laughed and set both their mugs on the dining room table. "I'll follow you out."

When they reached their cars, Karis gave him a plastic scraper. "For the windshield. It's my extra; you can keep it."

"Thanks," he said, attacking the glass in front of the driver's seat. "I'll pick one up today and bring this back down."

The heat that had started to kick in inside the cabin warmed the windshield and made scraping easier. He finished his car and helped Karis finish hers after a brief pause to consider whether or not he should. Unless he was mistaken, she'd started flirting with him, and he didn't want to encourage her. But neither did he want to pull out while she was still hard at work. When they finished he handed back the scraper, insisting he'd be better prepared that evening, and said good-bye.

"Feel free to stop on over if you're looking for company at dinner," she said. "Audry and I always have plenty to share."

Friendly offer or flirting? He couldn't tell. "Thanks, I'll remember that." He hoped that was noncommittal enough, and as he pulled slowly out of the snowy parking lot he marveled at her gall—until he realized he'd never removed his gloves. He groaned. She had no way of knowing he was married. He'd have to explain that the next time he saw her. *But definitely not over dinner.*

❄

Day fifteen. Amelia had figured by this point she'd be used to Marcus's absence, that she wouldn't get weepy whenever she thought of how long he'd been gone or still fall into bouts of self-doubt for putting them both through this. But unfortunately that morning brought instances of both, and she found it particularly difficult to drag herself out of bed and down to the bus station in time.

Even when she wasn't feeling morose, she wasn't feeling great. It was as though the gloomy January clouds that had rolled in off the Pacific had taken up residence directly above her head. The only time she didn't notice it was at rehearsal, which she had three nights a week, but even then the emotional high she experienced only lasted as long as it took to get home. By the time she was in bed, the gloom returned.

Tonight wasn't a rehearsal night, but it was a social night. The troupe had gelled well at their first couple rehearsals, and after the first week they decided to institute a bonding night for whoever was free to attend. The first had been at a karaoke bar; tonight's was at the guitarist's flat, twenty minutes by bus from her new home. Amelia was grateful for the activity; she felt like she might just sit in bed and cry all night otherwise.

Even though she was looking forward to the evening, it took her a while to get out the door. By the time she arrived, with a shopping bag of chips and salsa as her contribution, everyone else was already there. Ross answered the door when she rang the bell, and before she was halfway in the room he'd thrust a glass of wine in her hand. "Lousy weather again, isn't it?" he said. "This will warm you up."

"Thanks." She was about to give it back, since she abstained from alcohol as a general rule, but a recently developed bout of apathy toward her personal protocols made her hold on to it instead. The taste made her pucker, but Ross was right: It was warm going down. She held up the shopping bag. "Where should I put this?"

"There's a table over there." He pointed toward the living room, where she could see everyone gathered around a Rock Band drum kit. "Here, let me take it for you. You can put your coat in the bedroom; door's over there."

She dropped her coat on the pile on the bed and returned to the living room where their drummer, violinist, and guitarist were all playing plastic versions of instruments that they normally wouldn't touch as the actors sang together into the microphone. Ross came to stand beside her and nodded to the ensemble. "Ever played?"

"No. I don't suppose there's a keyboard that goes with that setup?"

He chuckled. "Nope, sorry. But I bet you'd do great on the drums."

She smiled and wrinkled her nose. "Not sure I'm in the mood for that kind of thing tonight."

Ross frowned. "Everything all right?"

"Eh, you know." She took a sip of her wine and focused her gaze on the television where the prompts for "Ballroom Blitz" scrolled for the players. "It's been a long two weeks."

He nodded slowly, then said, "Ah. Marcus, you mean."

"Yeah."

"I see. Are you regretting things?"

She settled on the arm of the sofa and gave him a small smile. "Good question. I don't know. Sometimes I do; sometimes I'm mad at him for making me choose, or for leaving. I shouldn't be—I mean, I could have gone with, right? But still—"

"I think you have every right to be angry. He was selfish."

"So was I."

"But you had a job here first."

She sighed. "I know." She'd run these circles in her mind a million times since Marcus had left; it was never going to get any less complicated. "I need to just get over it. This is life, it's not the end of the world—we'll see each other soon, I'm sure. And in a few months, who knows where things will be."

"What do you mean?"

"We agreed to reevaluate at Easter. We'll be done with *Pippin*, he'll be three months into his job and have a clearer idea of what it's like. We're going to have an official debriefing of sorts at that point and decide who's staying and who's moving."

"So we may lose you after *Pippin?*"

She shrugged. "I don't know. I guess it's a possibility. I really didn't see myself leaving, and honestly I still don't. But ..." She shrugged again, but had to admit that the idea of staying separated from Marcus beyond that point seemed incomprehensible to her now. "We'll see."

Ross wrapped an arm around her shoulders. "I'd hate to see you leave." He grinned down at her. "I'll have to talk to Gabe and see if we can't figure out a way to sweeten the deal to get you to stay."

Amelia batted her eyes playfully. "I'm flattered."

"Hey, you're a brilliant musician and a perfect fit for the troupe. I can't imagine having to replace you."

A moment later, "Ballroom Blitz" ended and everyone swapped positions again. "Want to jump in, Amelia?" someone asked.

"No thanks," she said with a wave. "I'd be the weak link, seriously. Besides, I need to eat something."

"Ross?"

"No thanks, guys." He followed Amelia to the table and they both filled paper plates with appetizers.

"You know," Ross said after they'd settled on the sofa with their food. "I was just thinking about something. Have you ever considered session work?"

"Sure—just haven't figured out how to get my foot in the door."

"Well, I know one of the sound engineers down at Atlantic, and while I can't say for sure that he'd have the connections that might get you in, chances are he'd know someone who knows someone, et cetera, et cetera—"

"Wait." Amelia shut her eyes a moment, making sure her brain was properly engaged and she didn't misunderstand what Ross was saying. "You know a sound engineer at Atlantic Records?"

"Yes."

"And you'd be willing to talk to him about me?"

He shrugged with a smile. "Sure."

"Atlantic Records—like, the huge label that produces major musicians."

"That's the one."

"Um ... wow."

He smiled. "I'll take that as a yes, then? It's been a while since I talked to him, I'll admit; I'll have to see if I still have his phone number somewhere ..."

Amelia put a hand to her forehead. Her thoughts were chasing each other through her head, and she couldn't focus. What confused her most was the realization that, inside, she wasn't jumping up and down at this development. She wasn't even sure she wanted to pursue it. *What on earth is wrong with me?*

She put a hand on Ross's arm. "Could I maybe think about it?"

Ross was silent a moment. "Think about it? What's there to think about?"

"Honestly, I don't know, I just—I just don't feel as sure about it as I thought I would. And I don't want to waste anyone's time."

Ross cocked an eyebrow and fixed her with eyes that bore a little too deeply. "You do know that's practically the only way you'll ever get what you want in this industry—people who know people talking you up to them. You're star quality for sure, but unless the right people hear you no one will ever know. You can't overthink these opportunities. You have to grab them when they come and ride them as far as you can."

"I know, I know." She broke their staring contest and concentrated on her plate, suddenly uncomfortable. "I know you're right, but—I don't know, I feel like I need to talk to Marcus first about it."

Ross shook his head. "That kind of hesitation is going to kill you, Amelia. I won't talk to Atlantic if you don't want me to, but seriously, you never know what connection will be the one to get you the kind of career you want. This could be it, but you won't know if you don't pursue it."

Why couldn't she feel excited? Why didn't this feel right? Everything Ross said was completely true. "Okay," she said, forcing out the word before she could think about it anymore.

Ross's smile returned. "Awesome. I'll dig up his info tonight and call him first thing in the morning."

"Thanks." She returned the smile, though she didn't feel happy. Instead, a sinking feeling took up residence in her chest that made her worry she was going crazy. Or worse: that God was killing her desire to play. Was this the beginning of Him changing her mind so she'd move to Nebraska? *It better not be,* she thought as she ate and half listened to Ross talk about the previous night's rehearsal. *Changing my mind is one thing—but taking away my music isn't playing fair.* She hadn't given Him permission to mess with her like that. If He thought He could fool around with her heart that way, then she'd fight Him for it. She'd take Ross up on every connection he offered to exploit for her. *It's my life,* she reminded God in her angry head. *And if You're going to work that way, then You can just back off.*

※

A week and a half into his job, Marcus was wondering when he'd get to do the kinds of things he'd always envisioned a senior pastor doing: reading commentaries as he studied for a sermon, meeting with the elders to discuss the budget and the church's future, weddings, baby dedications. He'd pictured spending his days drinking coffee at the desk in the office as he wrestled with Scripture to discern the message his congregation needed to hear, but that had yet to happen. Instead, he'd spent the last week and three days listening and … listening. That was pretty much it.

When he'd finally made it to the church that first day, he'd discovered a small stack of phone messages already awaiting him on his desk. Each had been from a member of the church who claimed he or she wanted to meet him and hear about his vision for the church. He'd appreciated this show of involvement and interest and had asked Lillian to schedule the meetings as soon as possible. Once word got out that he was willing to meet with people, however, nearly every member called to claim his or her thirty minutes of face time. And not a single one of those meetings had been about getting to know him or hearing his plans for the church. They'd all been gripe sessions aiming to either badmouth or defend the old pastor, gossip about other congregants who either still supported the old pastor or had been instrumental in driving him away, or express concern over the installation of Marcus as the replacement. And it didn't seem to matter where anyone stood on the issue of the previous pastor, they all were dubious about Marcus.

He couldn't blame them. He was well aware, thanks to the doubts raised by his own friends and family, of how he might be viewed. He'd been ready for the questions and concerns. He just hadn't expected them to be laid out so frankly to his face, one meeting after the other, for over a week.

On his drive out to Nebraska, Marcus had brainstormed sermon-series ideas based on the recent struggles the church had endured. He'd talked them through with Ed on his first day in the office, and Ed had been impressed with the list he'd created. They'd decided Marcus would preach the first weekend in February, figuring that would given him enough time to get into the swing of things. But here he was, a week from his first sermon, and he hadn't so much as outlined the talk, much less started researching.

The fact that he had so much to do should have kept him busy straight through the day. Instead, he'd lapsed into daydreams at the slightest break in concentration, thinking about Amelia and what she was up to that day. He missed her. Badly. They talked every night, but it wasn't enough. He had plenty to keep him busy, but putting nose to grindstone wasn't keeping thoughts of her at bay as he'd hoped it would—and not for lack of trying. He kept his work spread out on the dining room table so he could get to it at any time, but he couldn't track with the books he read or keep his thoughts focused long enough to write any notes.

Part of the problem was that he was alone. Amelia still had all her old friends, plus her new ones in the theater group. Who did he have besides the elders, who held that title not only for their role at the church but also for their stage in life? The closest he'd come to making a friend was meeting Karis, and he hadn't even seen her since the morning they'd met. Where did a pastor go to make friends, anyway?

"This is ridiculous," he spoke aloud in the depressing quiet of the apartment, then forced himself up from the couch where he'd settled after dinner to watch a movie and carried his dinner dishes to the kitchen. "Get a grip," he muttered as he stuck his plate in the dishwasher. Not even two weeks in and he was already slacking off. He was on track to proving all the naysayers right, and he couldn't afford to let that happen. *I can't keep wasting my time like this.* He looked at the clock. An hour left until he could call Amelia. *All right then. Get in a solid hour's worth of work, and then you can call her.* He poured a cup of coffee and took it to the dining room table, then surveyed the notes he'd made earlier. They were scant, but a start. *I can do this,* he told himself as he ripped out the page and turned to a fresh one in the notebook. He stared at the notes, the blank page, and back again, waiting for inspiration.

Both God and Marcus's creativity, however, were silent. Or, if not silent, then drowned out by the doubt that slowly began to coalesce in his mind. *He* was supposed to get up in front of this church in six days and speak with authority? *He* was supposed to assume the role of shepherd and teacher and act as though seminary had provided the necessary wisdom to walk the members through the process of detoxing from the spiritual abuse they'd been under? Just how was he going to do any of this?

In all the time he'd spent imagining himself in this job, he'd never considered the possibility that he would have no idea what he was doing once he arrived. In the back of his mind, he'd assumed God would zap the ability into him once the right position came along. But now, faced with the task of actually doing his job, he realized how inadequate he not only felt, but truly was. Apparently God's plan was more along the lines of saying, "Jump," and then sitting back to watch just how high Marcus could go on his own. He was determined to prove his worthiness to both God and the church—and to everyone else—but he would have appreciated a little help.

Profound disappointment joined the doubt. This wasn't anything like he'd expected. The griping congregants, the writer's block, the fear—the absence of Amelia. He tossed his pen atop the notebook and sat back from the table, arms crossed. If he weren't spending so much time missing her, worrying about her, being jealous of her friends, his brain wouldn't be so tangled and cluttered. He'd be able to think straight, to reason and write clearly about the things the church—*his* church—needed to hear. This was all her fault.

A knock at the door made him jump. He glanced through the peephole and saw Karis holding a plate wrapped in tinfoil and a little blonde girl leaning against her leg.

He put on a smile and opened the door. "Karis, hey."

She smiled. "Hi, Marcus. Are we interrupting anything?"

"No, not at all." He wasn't sure whether to invite her in or not. He didn't want to be unfriendly, but he also didn't want to encourage anything more than an acquaintanceship. Although this would give him a chance to make sure she knew he was married. "Come on in, if you'd like."

"Sure, thanks." Taking the little girl's hand, she stepped in and handed him the plate. "These are for you. Audry and I made them for you this afternoon. Say 'hi,' Audry."

The girl smiled but said nothing. Marcus smiled down at her and couldn't help feeling a twinge of jealousy. "Hi, Audry. Thanks for the cookies; I'll bet they're really good."

"They're chocolate chip."

"My favorite." He gave her a grin. "Would you like to share one with me?"

Audry looked to her mom, who nodded. "Just one. And we can't stay too long; it's nearly bedtime."

Marcus pulled back the foil and held out the plate. "This was very kind of you, Karis. Thanks."

"You're welcome. I would have done it earlier, but it's been a crazy week. I'm trying to get a second job, and I've been working on my portfolio."

"What kind of portfolio?" He motioned for her to sit on the sofa and took for himself the armchair at its corner.

"Graphic design. I took night classes a few years back but never pursued anything after finishing the program. But the library job just isn't cutting it financially, and the graphic design I could do independently on my own time."

"So you're looking to work with a firm somewhere?"

"Actually, I'm hoping to just find random clients. That way I have the freedom of my own hours and can set my own rates. Oh— Audry, honey, feet off the sofa."

Marcus waved a hand. "It's all right, I don't mind." He was struck by how different the apartment felt with more people in it. Even just sitting five feet from another person made it feel less empty and cavernous than it usually did. *This is how it's supposed to be. Me and Amelia and another little person … maybe even two. There should be a family here.*

He caught Karis staring at him and realized he'd gone silent. "Sorry," he said with a shake of his head. "It's been a weird day. I'm spacing out on you. I apologize."

"That's all right. We'll get out of your hair."

"No, it's all right," he said, holding up his hand.

He saw her finally notice his ring. "Oh," she said, looking bewildered. "You're married?"

"Yes, I am. My wife is back in LA. I'm sorry I didn't mention it before—it didn't even cross my mind, and I didn't realize until later that there was no way you could have known."

Her cheeks bloomed with color. "Oh. I see. Is she going to join you soon?"

"I'm hoping so, yeah."

She looked surprised. "You're not sure?"

"It's a long story."

"Ah."

Not wanting to leave anything to Karis's imagination, Marcus told her the basics, after which she told him a little about Audry's father. Marcus enjoyed the conversation. Other than at dinner with Ed and Lucy almost two weeks ago, he hadn't interacted on a purely social level with anyone since leaving California. It was nice to just sit and talk with someone.

When Marcus's phone rang, it took him by surprise. He glanced at his watch and groaned as he jumped to his feet to answer his cell. "It's almost eleven thirty." He was supposed to call Amelia at nine o'clock Pacific. He was half an hour late.

Karis's eyes went wide. "Are you kidding me? How did that happen?" She shifted on the couch and a sleeping Audry whined as she awakened.

He answered the phone with a wince, fearing Amelia would be angry, and turned his back to Karis as he spoke. "Hey, babe. Sorry I didn't call."

"That's all right. Did you fall asleep?"

"No, I just got caught up. Are you home?"

"No, I'm still out with the group."

"All right. Can I call you back in a couple minutes?"

"Oh—yeah, sure."

"Okay, great. Seriously, just two minutes."

"All right. Bye."

He hung up and turned just as Karis was about to close the front door. "I'm sorry," he said, catching the door, though he wasn't sure what he was apologizing for. He just knew he felt bad that the evening was ending like this when it had turned out to be so enjoyable.

"That's okay. I shouldn't have stayed."

"I'm glad you did, though." The second he said the words he knew they sounded different from what he'd meant. "I mean, I've been here two weeks and don't really know anyone outside of work, and … It was nice to get to just hang out with someone."

"It's all right. Trust me, I know what you mean." She gave him a smile as she shifted Audry in her arms. "Have a good night."

"You, too. Thanks again for the cookies."

They said good-bye and he shut the door, feeling frustrated that what had turned into a great conversation had so abruptly ended, and feeling guilty for having such a good time talking with a woman who wasn't his wife.

His wife. He needed to call Amelia back.

He pulled the phone from his pocket and sat on the sofa. He caught the scent of perfume that he'd noticed in Karis's apartment the morning she'd invited him for coffee. He liked the scent, which for some reason made him feel even more guilty. He stood and moved back to the dining room as he dialed.

"What's got you so busy?" Amelia asked when she answered.

"I was working on my message for the weekend, and then a neighbor stopped in to welcome me."

"Aw, that's nice. Anyone interesting?"

"A mom and her daughter. They brought chocolate-chip cookies."

"Lucky you."

"Yeah. They were … friendly. So, where are you?"

"Mike's apartment. He's the guitarist."

"A lot of people there?"

"Yeah, most of the troupe. I had an, um, interesting talk with Ross."

"Really? About what?"

"Well …" Amelia's hesitance made him nervous. Had she been talking with Ross the way he'd been talking with Karis? The fact that the possibility stirred his jealousy made him uncomfortable. "He knows someone at Atlantic Records, here in LA. A sound engineer.

He's going to talk to him and see if he can get me in as a session player."

Marcus frowned. "What's that?"

"Someone that plays on recordings. Like, if you have a band with a guitarist and a drummer and a bassist, but you have songs that are arranged with violin and piano as well, then they hire session players to play those instruments."

"Oh—so a musician for hire."

"Yes."

"Wow. That would be cool."

"That would be *huge*. Not because session work is so fantastic, but because there's a chance you'll get asked to tour with them later—if they tour, that is."

No, no touring! "Oh. That's ... wow."

"I know, right?"

Amelia's voice didn't reach the level of exuberance he expected from her about such news. "You don't sound that excited."

"Well ... It's all, you know, hypothetical at this point."

"Ah."

They both went silent. Marcus realized that, for the first time since leaving home, he really didn't want to talk. "I have to be up early for church," he said. "I really need to go."

"Oh. Okay."

"And I don't want to keep you from the party. Have fun with everyone."

"Thanks. Have a good night."

"You, too."

"I miss you."

His heart hurt. "I miss you, too."

They traded I-love-yous and good-byes and then Marcus hung up, feeling lousy for so many reasons he couldn't even sort them all out. He dropped the phone to the table and hauled himself off to bed.

Valentine's Day spent apart from Marcus was worse than all the dateless Valentine's Days she'd endured though high school and college. And what really compounded things was seeing Jill and Dane so lovey-dovey with each other. Even though Dane's excitement about the baby was still tempered, he had turned into the doting husband who fretted and worried about his pregnant wife, and Amelia watched him pamper her with more than a little jealousy. Jill certainly deserved it; the pregnancy had been hard on her, and Amelia had been doing her fair share of doting and pampering too. But seeing how the pregnancy had drawn them closer made Amelia's longing for Marcus even more painful, and today the pain was a thousand times worse.

It was Sunday night, and she was cleaning the kitchen for Dane so he and Jill could spend the evening in front of a romantic comedy. She'd called Marcus earlier than usual because she just couldn't wait any longer, but once they were on the phone she kept falling into the trap that seemed to suck her in every time they talked these days: Somehow, she'd lost her ability to be completely honest with him. She couldn't bring herself to admit that she was more miserable every day, that she hated her deli job so much she'd almost quit twice, that as much as she loved Jill and Dane she couldn't stand living with them because seeing them together just made her miss Marcus more. Admitting she wasn't brimming over with happiness felt like admitting defeat. How could she complain when she'd fought so hard to stay? She was living her dream—she was supposed to be excited about it, even if it meant sacrifice. But she wasn't. *Suck it up,* she'd tell herself. *It could be worse.* She could be in Nebraska and living within arm's reach of the toilet with perpetual morning sickness like Jill. *Just don't let on—don't give Marcus any ammo.*

So she lied. "Yeah, the deli job is great. Maria is gone, but the new girl is nice. We get along really well." *When I'm not cleaning up after her mistakes.*

"Rehearsals are going great! I really enjoy the music, and the actors are doing a great job. I can't wait for opening night." *As long as I don't let myself remember you won't be there to see it.*

"The apartment is great. Jill and Dane are fun to live with; we're having a great time." *When Jill's not too sick to carry on a conversation and I don't catch them being all snuggly and cute.*

Great became her go-to word. The weather? Great. The community center job? Great. Everything was great. It had to be. If it wasn't, it might mean she didn't really want to be there. And that meant she had no reason not to go to Nebraska.

Marcus walked his usual circuit through the apartment as he listened to Amelia gush about how great things were in LA. Dining room to kitchen, through to the living room, around the couch, past the front door, and all over again. Each room had its own distinct, Amelia-shaped emptiness that tugged at his chest whenever he passed through it. The dining room was doubly painful, not only because Amelia was not there, but because no number of commentaries spread on the table seemed to make the work he did there any easier.

To hear her talk about it, LA was heaven on earth. Everything was fantastic. He was happy for her—he didn't want her miserable, obviously—but it would have been nice to hear that, while things were going well, they'd be better if he was there. But when it was his turn to report on life in Nebraska, he ended up doing the same thing. He didn't want to sound needy, as if all he did was sit around pining after her—not if she wasn't pining on her end. He was already struggling with worry that their marriage didn't mean as much to her as it did to him, given how easily she'd thrown around the idea of divorce. He didn't want to scare her away. So the job was "challenging, but in a good way" and it was "great to be able to finally do what I love." The apartment was "spacious and bright—makes the studio look like a cave." The weather was "a welcome change from the predictability of Southern California—can you even say they *have* real weather there?"

Hearing the updates on Jill and Dane compounded his misery, especially the way Amelia described them. It was clear from her report that living with a pregnant woman had done nothing to jump-start her own maternal longings. Quite the opposite, in fact. "You should see how sick she is. And it's *all the time*. I'd rather be celibate the rest of my life than go through that for nine months! And, oh my gosh—the stuff. The insane amount of *stuff* you apparently have to have to take care of a baby. The hall closet is completely packed with all this random gear. She hasn't even had her shower yet and they've already run out of room to store it all." He could practically hear her shuddering in disgust.

As he listened to her rant, Marcus's eyes caught sight of the flyer he'd left on the dining room table as he passed it on his route around the apartment. Part of him wanted to mention it to her, but the practical side of him knew that Amelia might think he was trying to manipulate her, and the harder he pushed her about coming to Wheatridge the less likely it was that she ever would. He picked up the flyer and just stared at it as he continued his meandering pace. He'd pulled it from the plastic box mounted to the "For Sale" sign he'd seen while taking a new route home from work. The house was small, but sat on a quarter acre and was within walking distance to downtown. The pictures on the flyer showed hardwood floors that gleamed in the sun and quaint rooms with big windows and fancy crown molding. Details like wainscoting on the lower half of the dining room walls, a fully finished basement, and an updated kitchen with stainless steel appliances gave the house both charm and bonus points for livability. But what he knew would really reel Amelia in was the petite grand piano that sat in the front window and came with the house.

If only he could tell her about it.

When they'd hung up, Marcus stuck the flyer to the refrigerator door. Despite the unlikelihood that it would still be on the market when they were looking to buy, he couldn't bring himself to throw it away. It gave him warm thoughts of his and Amelia's future—of fires in the fireplace while a winter storm raged, of evenings spent reading in the living room while Amelia practiced for her next gig. And even though Amelia's thoughts on the matter were clear, he couldn't help picturing a redheaded girl sliding down the hall in her socks into her daddy's arms.

She's going to change her mind eventually, right, God? You'll bring her out by the summer, surely. Until then he'd ask Ed for a recommendation for a Realtor. It wouldn't hurt to start getting all their ducks in a row. Maybe God would save that house for them if Marcus showed Him just how hard he was willing to work for it.

Amelia came home from her deli job feeling oddly anxious. It was an emotion she'd been struggling with all day, and while she figured it would get better after she left work, she could barely concentrate with the flurry of jittery activity in her stomach.

It had to be opening night that was causing all the commotion. She pulled off her jacket and headed straight for her keyboard. The music for *Pippin* was spread across the music stand, and she launched into "Corner of the Sky" without warming up, hoping the playing would calm her down. It was her favorite song in the show—she could relate to Pippin's longing for purpose and fulfillment, and Jeff's voice soared when he sang it, making it even more enjoyable to play in rehearsals. But tonight would be the last night they rehearsed. Tomorrow was opening night.

When she reached the end of the song, Jill's voice startled her from her thoughts of the performance. "Sorry I scared you," she said when Amelia spun in surprise. "That sounded great, by the way."

"Thanks. I didn't wake you up or anything, did I?"

Jill smiled and rubbed a hand over her belly, which was just beginning to swell. "No, no worries. I love listening to you play."

"You should get your violin out one of these days; we could duet."

Jill let out a snort. "Yeah right. Do you know how long it's been since I played?"

"Too long."

"Hm. Maybe."

Jill had been one of Juilliard's finest when they'd attended together. They'd played together all the time—Jill had been the only person Amelia could stand to play with. But she'd broken under the pressure at the school, and after graduating she'd put away her instrument "for good." Amelia hoped she'd be able to coax her to take it out again someday.

She thought of her mother. Just like Jill, she had given up on her talents. Amelia didn't want that for herself. She found so much peace in her music, so much fulfillment. She prayed in that moment that her passion would never fade the way theirs had.

Amelia returned her gaze to Jill. "So what's up then?"

Jill shifted against the doorjamb. "Tomorrow they're launching the new Saturday service at church. I wanted to see if you'd go with us."

"I can't—opening night, remember?"

Jill smacked her forehead. "I *knew* there was something going on. I told Dane I had a feeling you'd be busy. I can't believe I forgot that, I'm sorry."

Amelia chuckled. "Hey, when you spend most of every day puking in the bathroom, you get a free pass on remembering what day it is."

Jill gave a wan smile. "Thanks."

"I won't even be offended if you don't make it to a performance. And I mean that. I know how sick you are."

"Thanks. I really want to try to make it, though. I'll take the seat closest to the door."

Amelia smiled. "There you go."

Jill's warm expression faded. "We miss you at church."

She smirked. "You see plenty of me here, don't you?"

"C'mon, Ames, I'm being serious. The folks in the small group, the music-team people—whenever I make it there I get asked a thousand times where you are."

Amelia shrugged. "Sundays are the only days I get to sleep in, and the only day that I don't have rehearsal or work. I have to take a day to just veg."

"I know, but still. You need Christian community."

I do? were the first words in Amelia's head, but she kept them inside for fear of confirming Jill's suspicions about her lame spirituality. Honestly, she didn't see why Christian community was any better than any other community. It wasn't like they sat around talking about the Bible all the time. The only difference between the people at church and the people in the theater troupe was that the church people didn't swear as much. Oh, and the theater people didn't pray aloud before meals. Big deal.

"I have Christian community—I live with you guys."

Jill rolled her eyes. "That's not the same."

"Why not? It's better than nothing, anyway. Seriously, Jill, I do get what you're saying, but I think you're concerned over nothing. I know we both have plenty of memories of the artsy people we hung out with back in college. I know as a whole that group wasn't the most wholesome. But this is a job; it's adult and professional. We're working, we're busting our rears trying to make it in this business—no one has time to waste like we did in school. So really, you don't have to worry about me being pulled over to the dark side or something."

Jill studied her for a moment with tired eyes, then nodded. "I hear you. I hope you don't think I'm hounding you or anything."

Amelia smiled. "Of course not. You're my friend, you care, I get it."

Jill nodded. "Cool. I'm going to talk to Dane about coming to the show."

"Great! I'll save you the worst seat in the house. It's the closest to the bathroom."

Jill chuckled and wandered away, leaving Amelia to wonder why it was so all-important to Christians to surround themselves with even more Christians. To Amelia, people were people; she didn't care what they believed in. And sometimes it felt easier being around non-Christians—she didn't have to worry about saying or doing something that would make them question her beliefs. Her own doubts where more than enough to contend with.

By Saturday night, Amelia's nerves were barely holding it together. She'd never felt this anxious before a performance, not even her Juilliard audition. She went to the theater early to rehearse, hoping it would calm her, but instead it drove her to full-on dread. Her fingers tripped over themselves, missed keys, fumbled during quick fingering changes. By the time Ross and Gabe arrived, Amelia was nearly in tears.

"Hey, it's going to be fine," Ross said, massaging the knots from her shoulders. "You need to get away from the piano, not spend more time at it. Go take a walk or something; you have plenty of time."

She turned and gave Ross a nervous smile, then heaved a deep sigh, hoping to smother the butterflies, but it didn't work.

She let him rub her shoulders a bit more, appreciating the gesture and praying it made a difference while trying to ignore the way his touch warmed her blood. When he left to help Gabe hunt down a missing prop, she stood, shaking the feeling of intoxication from her head, and took a walk around the block, wishing the LA air was cleaner so that every deep breath didn't taste like exhaust. *I'll bet the air in Wheatridge is purer than Mother Mary,* she thought, remembering how Marcus continually waxed eloquent about the small town. But then the thought of Marcus brought tears to her eyes. He'd been at every performance she'd had since they'd met. It broke her heart that he wouldn't be there tonight.

She hadn't let herself think about it much, but his presence had always been such a clear communication of how much he loved her and appreciated her talent that *not* having him there, even though she knew the reason, felt like a deliberate rejection. She'd have to get used to it if she wanted to tour—he couldn't follow her around the country like a groupie. But she'd never realized how many ways she'd miss him when she let him go alone to Nebraska.

I can't think about this now. She wiped tears from her eyes and rolled her head and shoulders, trying to work out the tension. A glance at her phone told her she had less than fifteen minutes before the curtain went up. She stuffed her hands into her pockets along with her phone and walked back to the theater to take her place. As she'd told Jill, this was professional. No angst allowed.

Ross spotted her as she entered the backstage area. "Feeling better?"

She nodded and lied, "Yeah, much. Thanks."

He smiled and gave her a hug. "Break a leg."

"You, too."

She left her jacket in the dressing room and went to the orchestra pit to warm up with the others. The house lights were halfway up, and she could see pockets of people scattered around the red velvet seats. It wasn't a sold-out show by any means, but they'd had better sales than they'd expected for their first show, so everyone was hopeful that the launch might receive more attention than they'd planned. Amelia tried to be encouraged by the people she saw coming in through the doors and down the aisles to their seats, but instead they fueled her nerves' dance of fear. She shook out her hands and rolled her shoulders. *C'mon, relax already.*

When the lights dimmed, Ross stepped up to the conductor's stand and a shot of adrenaline jolted Amelia's butterflies to a standstill. Baton raised, he gave each member of the band a quick look, ending with Amelia, to whom he also gave a wink, then cued them into "Magic to Do," the show's opening number. Once the production was actually under way, Amelia felt her body settle in to the familiar rhythm of performing: Play a song, take a break, play a song, take a break. In between numbers in the first act, Ross leaned over her keyboard and whispered, "Feeling better?"

"I am, thanks."

"Good." He gave her another wink, and Amelia couldn't help smiling at his encouragement. She was lucky to work with someone so understanding.

Things went well until the second act. Ross cued them in for "Love Song," and Amelia heard the romantic lyrics in a way she hadn't before. Her thoughts instantly went to Marcus, to missing him and to the fact that he wasn't there for opening night. Her fingers fumbled.

She caught her place quickly, but the damage was done. The arrangement Ross had created was dominated by the piano, so there was no chance that her mistake went unnoticed. Her face couldn't let go of the wince she'd pulled when her fingers had hit the sour notes; her shoulders came up around her ears as her muscles tensed against the glares she expected from the other musicians. She kept her eyes on her music, barely watching Ross for fear of catching the disappointment on his face. When the song ended, she covered her face with her hands, mortified.

An arm came around her shoulder. She thought it was the guitarist who sat beside her, but then Ross's voice was in her ear. "Don't beat yourself up. It's not the end of the world."

Amelia peeked over her shoulder and gave a small smile. "You sure about that?"

"You have nothing to worry about, believe me." He squeezed her shoulder, then went back to the conductor's stand. Amelia pulled up her posture and tried to regain her confidence, but she wavered. A sense of fear began to grip her. What if she'd been deluded about her abilities all along? What if she couldn't cut it professionally? The scope of this show was nothing compared to the gigs she'd envisioned herself playing once her career was in full-swing, but if she couldn't handle this, how would she ever handle concert halls and orchestras?

Her mother's face surfaced in her mind. Amelia worried that the image of her mother had become some kind of prophetic specter. *Maybe there's no use fighting it. It really is in the genes.*

She shook off the unnerving thought and fought her way through the rest of the show. When the house lights came up, embarrassment kept her eyes down on her instrument as she packed it away while the other musicians congratulated each other and debated where to go celebrate.

"Hey, Amelia." Ross's voice snapped her from her thoughts. "You coming out with us? We're trying to figure out where to go."

"I don't think I'm up for going out tonight. Thanks, though."

Ross frowned, his arms crossing over his chest. "Amelia, I know what this is really about. Why are you taking it so hard? You need to ease up on yourself."

Ross was overly forgiving, a touchy-feely "we're all okay" kind of guy. There was no sense in trying to explain to him how wrong he was about her. She waved away his words and shoved her binder in her bag.

"I'm not giving you a choice," Ross persisted. "Consider it part of the job. You don't attend the opening-night party, you don't get paid."

"Oh, come on—"

"No, I'm serious. Zip that bag and come with us." The twinkle in his eyes told her he was joking, but he was probably right that she should go. The thought of wallowing in her misery alone in her bedroom made her want to cry right there.

"Okay …" She offered her best playful smile. "I'm in."

"Good girl." He held out a hand. "Let me take your bag. You've got enough weight on your shoulders." She let him take it, then let him lead her by the hand out of the orchestra pit to the dressing room where everyone had stashed coats and bags. Hugs and accolades were traded with the actors, then the musicians left for a bar down the street.

"I'm buying you a drink when we get there," Ross said as they walked behind the others.

"I don't normally drink."

"Well, I'm not going to try to push you into it, but it might help you unwind a bit and sleep well tonight. You sure could use it."

The night air was cold, but the only place the band could find a table big enough for all the members was in the beer garden out back. They dragged a second heater over to their table and Ross bought the first round for everyone, which included a spiked coffee for Amelia. "It's decaf," he said with a grin as he handed her the drink and took the seat next to her. "I knew you'd be cold, though, so I figured the coffee would be a good bet."

Amelia took an exaggerated sniff of the brew. "Mmm. It's perfect, thanks."

He moved his chair closer and leaned in when he spoke. "Look. I know you're putting on your best face, but I can tell you're still freaked out by the performance tonight. Why? You're so talented. There's no need to be so tortured over such a little thing."

Amelia took a long sip of her coffee, which was cooling quickly in the chilly February air. She could taste the alcohol, which made her throat tingle as it went down. "I'm not—I'm not *tortured*. I'm just … a perfectionist."

"Hmm. I think it's more than that."

Amelia raised a brow. "Do you now? What are you, an armchair psychologist?"

"No. Just perceptive. You're staking a lot on this job. You have big plans, big dreams—and you're right to have them, because you have the talent to achieve them, if I may sound for a second like an after-school special." They shared a laugh, then he continued. "You feel like you're on the clock to make this happen because of this ridiculous three-month deadline you have, as though three months would be enough to determine whether or not a career was going to take off. And you're terrified that if you screw it up, even just one little mistake, it'll be all over."

Amelia wrapped her hands around her mug. "Perceptive is an understatement, Ross." He smiled, but was clearly waiting for her to respond. She swallowed some of her coffee in a few slow, small sips, then began to explain. "But it's not just that. It's—see, my mom was a Broadway singer, and she screwed it all up. She threw away every-thing she had, and her life was miserable because of it." Thoughts she'd never articulated were tumbling from her mouth faster than she could censor them. "I don't want to be like her. I don't want my life to be a giant ball of regret. The thought of wasting my life playing nothing but hymns every Sunday, or teaching piano lessons, or barefoot and pregnant—"

Amelia shut her mouth, shocked at the things she was saying to someone she barely knew. "I—it's not that—I mean I don't—" She didn't want to give Ross the impression that Marcus was trying to subjugate her, but couldn't figure out how to say what she really meant. "Never mind." She downed the rest of her coffee. "This was good for me, Ross; thanks for 'forcing' me to come out. But I really should go." She felt bad for not reciprocating the conversation with Ross, but she was just so tired.

Without looking to see his reaction, she grabbed her keyboard case and hefted it over her shoulder as she clumsily threaded her way between tables to get to the bar. She was halfway to the front door when she felt the case lifted from her arm by a silent Ross. She let him take it, unwilling to argue in public, and muttered "Thank you" when they reached the sidewalk.

"Don't go."

Amelia shook her head. "You're sweet to show concern, but I don't have my head on straight tonight. The longer I stay the more likely it is I'm going to say something even more stupid. I *know* nothing is as bad as I'm making it out to be—I just can't get my emotions to understand that."

"I understand. Honestly." Ross pulled her into a hug, and Amelia, hungry for a caring touch, melted into him. Over a month without physical affection had taken a toll she hadn't fully realized until now. And when Ross slowly pulled back and kissed her, she kissed him back without thinking—until her head cleared and she realized what she was doing.

She broke the kiss, heart pounding in her ears, eyes wide with shock. Ross held up his hands in defense. "I'm sorry, Amelia, I got carried away. Forgive me—"

She didn't give him time to finish. She grabbed the case from where it leaned against the bar's facade and took off down the sidewalk, not caring it was the wrong direction. Tears threatened as she dodged people to jump onto a bus that stood at the corner. She pulled her bus pass from her purse with shaking hands, then found a seat and fell into it, her keyboard across her lap. The bus pulled away from the curb and passed the bar; Ross still stood on the sidewalk, and his eyes caught hers. She saw the regret on his face, but it was nothing compared to the shame she felt inside.

Her own mother's affair had basically destroyed her marriage. Less than a month later her father had filed for divorce, and days later her mother had left, leaving her car at a beach two hours from home and disappearing without a trace. Her life ended the same way she'd lived it: leaving destruction in her wake and her family limping along behind her. And now Amelia was following in her footsteps.

It was almost one in the morning by the time she got home. The hour she'd spent on the buses had given her plenty of time to think, and every thought had served to remind her that she was doomed. Forget being stronger. Forget being smarter. All her work, all her focus had been for naught. Underneath it all she was a loser, a tramp, a stupid girl who couldn't grab success with both hands if it stood still in front of her.

Wait. Calm down. She was overreacting, she knew it. She and Marcus were both so lonely, and at an impasse in their relationship. It hadn't been a premeditated action. And she had put a stop to it. *So maybe I'm not a lost cause.*

But what would she do now? She couldn't face Ross. And she certainly didn't deserve to take up space in the troupe when she was just going to drag them down—but then again, she couldn't quit and leave them in the lurch. And if she did quit, she'd have to go to Nebraska. She wouldn't be able to justify staying in LA, not without a gig. But how could she ever look Marcus in the eyes again, knowing she'd kissed someone else?

Her thoughts felt out of control, like someone else was thinking them. She could sense herself blowing things out of proportion, but had no idea how to rein it all back in. Ashamed as she was to even talk to him, she dialed Marcus, hoping he'd be able to calm her down.

But when he answered she realized she'd made a huge mistake. His groggy "Hello?" told her she'd woken him. She suddenly remembered the time difference—and the fact that he was supposed to preach in the morning.

"I'm so sorry," she said, voice quavering. "I forgot the time. Go back to sleep."

"Wait, Amelia—are you okay? Is everything all right?"

She took a deep breath, fighting the lump in her throat. "Yes, everything's fine. Just—got in late from the show and wasn't thinking. I'm sorry."

"No, don't apologize, it's all right. How did it go?"

"Fine. It was fine. Went great. We can talk tomorrow, though, okay? Go to sleep, break a leg in the morning."

"Yeah, okay. You're sure you're all right?"

"Yes, fine, totally fine."

"All right, babe. I love you."

"I love you, too."

The line disconnected and Amelia clenched her jaw and fists. Angry, nauseated, and shaky, Amelia crawled into bed and burrowed beneath the covers and prayed for the mercy of sleep.

CHAPTER 6

Marcus shut his phone and set it on the nightstand, but he couldn't fall back asleep. Adrenaline had shot through his chest when the ring had awoken him, and even though Amelia had insisted she was fine, he could tell she wasn't. Between the chemical alertness and the concern for his wife, there was no point in even staying in bed. Trying not to dwell on the time, Marcus got up and headed for the kitchen.

It felt weird to be up and about in the middle of the night. Sleep didn't usually evade him, and back in LA their apartment had been so small that he'd never wanted to risk waking Amelia by getting up on the rare nights he experienced insomnia. Here someone could be up and watching TV and you'd never hear it in the bedroom. *We'd be so comfortable here together,* he thought as he ate the bowl of cereal he'd poured himself. *And if she were here, I'd know why she was on the verge of crying.*

It had only been five weeks. It felt like five months. Already he felt the wall between them, the unfamiliarity that set in after so much life lived apart. And if it was this bad already, how much worse would it be in April? And how long would it take before things went back to normal?

Will they go back to normal? His father's comments about Amelia came back to haunt him.

Marcus couldn't let himself think about that. He finished his cereal and dumped the bowl in the sink. He noticed the flyer for the house on the fridge as he passed and thought of the conversation he'd had with a Realtor from the congregation. She'd laid out various mortgage plans based on how much he could offer for a down payment, and unless he took a second job, they wouldn't have enough for at least another year. Was it worth it to him to look for more work?

If it was the right job ... the right pay ... and Amelia liked the house, then yes. And—who was he kidding?—it would keep him too busy to allow for moments like this when his thoughts started to betray him and his devotion to his vision began to waver.

That was settled, then—he'd spend his Monday off searching for another stream of income, and with any luck, that house on the fridge, or something like it, would be theirs sooner rather than later. He returned to bed, telling himself that of course Amelia would be happy when he told her.

"Didn't sleep well last night?"

Marcus gave Ed a rueful smile. "It's that obvious?"

"Sorry, but yes. Is everything all right?"

Marcus folded the church bulletin in his hands, giving his eyes somewhere else to focus. "Yes, for the most part. Amelia called, upset about something, but when she realized what time it was she told me never mind and hung up. 'Course, then I was wound up and worried about her—I don't think I fell back asleep until nearly five."

"That's too bad. I'm sorry."

"Ah, well—nature of the beast. Something else for both of us to get used to: not being able to comfort each other when we need it." Ed's concerned gaze made Marcus uncomfortable. "It's all good, though, no worries. I'm ready for this morning."

"I wish I could invite you to lunch. You seem like you could use some company. Lucy and I are headed out to Denver this afternoon, though, for a last-minute vacation. One of the perks of being retired; you can take advantage of great airfare when it pops up."

Marcus forced a brighter smile. "Oh, it's no big deal, Ed. Have fun on your trip."

A parishioner came up to greet them, and their attention turned to the people trickling in through the vestibule. Marcus had the warm smile and handshake down to a science, and greeted the congregants with a cheery "Good morning" that reflected the opposite of what was going on inside. But that was part of the role, wasn't it? No one would put their faith in a pastor who was an emotional mess.

His third sermon was more polished than the first two, and when the service was over, Marcus felt that he'd finally found his preaching groove. At least one aspect of the job was coming together—unlike the ministries and events he'd tried to launch over the last month. He thought they would appease the parishioners who subtly and not-so-subtly expressed their expectation that he improve the climate of the congregation, but participation had so far been meager, and he was on the verge of canceling them all. He didn't know what else the church expected from him.

When the service ended, Marcus planted himself at the front door to shake hands with people as they left. He was the last one out of the building, which he locked up before heading to his car. The gravel parking lot was already empty, and the gray February afternoon mirrored his mood. He got into his car, shut the door, and sat there, feeling morose. He didn't want to go home, but didn't know what else to do.

A jog, perhaps, just to kill some time. And maybe Karis would be around and in the mood to hang out. At least she would be able to relate to his loneliness.

※

Ross's kiss sent Amelia into a downward spiral that only grew worse with time.

She blamed it on all sorts of things. On missing Marcus. On how Jill and Dane's deepening relationship made the slow breakdown of her own even more obvious. On the strain she felt now whenever she and Ross were within ten feet of each other. On how much she hated her deli job. On how she was her mother's daughter. This one in particular became the backdrop of her tumultuous emotions, and as a result she found it harder and harder to get out of bed in the morning.

Her emotions were out of control. She'd always had a small melodramatic streak, but it was worse now than it had ever been. She cried at the stupidest things—greeting card commercials; the sight of a camo-clad soldier waiting for the bus to LAX with his duffel slung over his shoulder; a mild correction from her boss at the deli. And dark thoughts about her doomed marriage were always close to the surface, along with the depressing resignation that this was as far as her career would ever go.

When she awoke one Saturday morning with flu symptoms, she felt as if God was punishing her. It wasn't bad enough that her mind was sick; now she had to struggle with a sick body, too. She fought the nausea and went in to work anyway, knowing she couldn't afford to miss a day if she was going to keep saving money for the divorce she was sure would eventually come.

She was feeling a little better by that night, but dragging herself to another performance of *Pippin* made her feel worse. She couldn't take the awkwardness between her and Ross anymore. His affection for her was so obvious to her now. He hadn't hit on her or even flirted with her since opening night, and they'd never spoken of what had transpired on the sidewalk, but the tension was still there. What made it worse was her growing affection for him, which only added to her self-loathing.

Amelia descended the bus steps with heavy feet, which plodded ever slower along her route to the theater. She'd never *not* wanted to perform before, but there was a first time for everything. She was dreading the night, even though it was their first sold-out show. She didn't feel like she could trust her fingers not to betray the chaos in her head.

Tears began to fall for the second time that day. She just wanted to crawl back into bed and sleep until Monday. No—she just wanted everything to stop. Expectations, stress, the shows, the ache for Marcus. Life. All of it, just to stop.

She froze on the sidewalk as the gravity of her thoughts became clear. She, Amelia Sheffield, who until now had embraced life with passion and verve, wanted it all to end? Even when her mother had disappeared Amelia hadn't felt this low. Pressure had always made her perform better, made her rise to the challenge it posed—it had never beat her down. Until now. Now she felt like she was drowning.

The curse uttered by another pedestrian as he narrowly missed walking into Amelia jolted her from her thoughts. She continued to the theater, hands clammy, tears still running. Once she arrived, she scrubbed at her cheeks with her sleeves and willed herself to pull it together. *I can't fall apart now. I can't. The whole troupe is depending on me.* She freed her hair from its ponytail and kept her head low as she made her way to the orchestra pit. She was later than usual and had only a few minutes before curtain. She knew Ross would leave her alone, and tried her hand at ESP to keep the rest of the band away from her. Luckily everyone else was busy tuning up, and other than a couple high fives for making it in the nick of time—which Amelia played along with—conversation was minimal. The knot in her stomach tightened as the lights went down, and she channeled all her energy into focusing on the performance.

The night was more draining than usual. By the finale, she was struggling to keep her concentration—even to stay awake. It would figure that the sleepless nights she'd experienced recently would choose that evening to catch up with her, and when the curtain came down, she folded her arms on the dash of the digital piano and laid down her head, utterly exhausted. The thought of having to pack up and take the bus home nearly brought her to tears.

"Amelia?"

Her whole body flinched at Ross's voice. She sat up, not caring if her misery was plain on her face. "Hey."

"Are you okay?"

Honesty or not? She didn't want to give Ross any more information than necessary.

"I'm fine. I think I'm … coming down with the flu or something." It wasn't a total lie—she'd been sick all morning, hadn't she?—and in fact that might have been the real reason she was so bone-achingly tired. *Though it doesn't explain why I've thought about*— She mentally batted away the thought and pushed herself to her feet.

"If there's anything I can do—" Ross's eyes would only meet hers for a few seconds at a time before darting away.

"No thanks, I'll be fine." She set to work on packing up her things, hoping he'd get the message and leave her alone.

"I know you take the bus here. Can I please give you a ride home? I promise I won't … you know …" His unfinished thought hung in the air, filling the space between them with awkwardness.

She wanted to turn him down, but getting home twenty minutes early sounded like heaven. "All right, thanks," she said, working to not sound too eager about it.

"Okay. I'll meet you at the back door to the parking lot. I just have to talk to Gabe for a minute. Take your time."

She broke down her setup and managed to shoulder the bag without falling over, which felt like a small triumph, then shuffled to the back door to wait.

The ride with Ross was blessedly silent, save for Amelia's occasional directions. "Thanks again. See you tomorrow night." She climbed out in front of her building.

"Yeah, see you." He cleared his throat. "Um, Amelia, look, if I'm the reason—"

"Good night, Ross." Amelia gave him a pointed look, hoping he caught her drift, and lugged her bag to the security door and let herself in. She couldn't stomach a heartfelt apology right now. She couldn't stomach anything but the feel of her cool sheets and feather pillow.

Leaving her keyboard in the living room, Amelia dragged herself to bed and crawled, fully clothed, beneath the covers.

She wanted nothing more than to sleep—for days, preferably, though she'd settle for a solid eight hours—but once again sleep fought her for most of the night. This time, however, it wasn't thoughts of missing Marcus or that stupid kiss that kept her awake. It was the thought she'd had on the way to the show that night, the one that ran so counter to her usual outlook, the one that made her wonder if she was starting to lose her mind.

※

Marcus stood once again at the vestibule door and shook hands with the parishioners as they filed out for home. He kept a smile on his face, though inside he wanted to hide, and searched his congregants' faces for signs of disappointment as they said good-bye. His sermon that morning had been weak, and he knew going in that it would be. He just hadn't had the time to prepare that he'd thought he would. It wasn't the tutoring he was now doing in the evenings at the private college that stole so much time—it was all the peripherals of his job that kept him from researching and writing. Meeting with the elders; meeting with other ministers in the area looking to network with New Hope's new pastor; meeting with the choir director, who wanted to coordinate his music selections to the sermon; visiting those who were technically still members but could no longer attend services due to age or illness—and, of course, more meetings with congregants who wanted to process their experience at the church under the old pastor, or who wanted to critique his sermon from the week before. He spent more time in meetings than he did actually preparing for the weekend.

So many people wanted him to fix them, fix their circumstances, fix their doubt, their frustrations. And he felt powerless to do so. All he could do was encourage and try to comfort. He had a feeling his father would be a lot more successful in this position than he had been so far.

It was this recurring thought that haunted him most—or rather, what it implied: that he wasn't the right man for this job. Maybe Amelia had been right all along. Maybe he hadn't heard God, and maybe this move had taken him out of God's will, rather than into the middle of it. Or maybe he was in God's will but just not up to the task of fulfilling it.

Marcus locked up the church and headed through the empty lot to his car. He caught a glimpse of himself in the car's window. By all appearances, he looked like a regular man in a suit. He looked smart, even accomplished—but there was a lack of sparkle in his eyes that made Marcus realize he *looked* as if he was just acting the part.

Nonsense. This was what he was meant to do. He was just still adapting. He'd never imagined himself at such a small church, where he was virtually the only staff member. He'd anticipated being on a team of pastors, with hundreds, if not thousands, of people to minister to—people who weren't bent on picking apart his sermon or whining about the previous leadership. Fresh out of seminary, he'd expected a more specialized position, a more focused job description. It would take time to adjust to his new reality, that's all. He just had to try harder.

Amelia was a big part of the problem. Every time they spoke on the phone these days, he sensed something was off with her, and his worry for her compounded how much he missed her. Maybe a visit would help. In person, he could see for himself that she was as fine as she insisted she was, reconnect with her, and hopefully clear his mind so he'd be more focused when he returned.

The thought of seeing her again brightened his spirit considerably. Forsaking the rumble in his stomach, he got on the Internet the minute he reached home and looked up flights for the next two weeks. He wouldn't be able to visit long, just a couple days, but he could leave right after church and get into LA in time to watch one of her productions, then spend another full day and come home the next morning. He found a flight two weeks from that Sunday that wasn't exorbitantly expensive and booked it before emailing Dane to tell him he'd be coming into town. *Don't tell Amelia,* he wrote. *I'm going to surprise her at that night's* Pippin.

He couldn't help smiling as he sent the email, then changed clothes to go for a run with the new energy his plans had given him. He wasn't sure how he'd make it two more weeks, but just knowing he'd see her before the month was out made him feel better.

Amelia burst through the door of the theater five minutes before curtain. The look of relief on everyone's faces made her palms even more damp than they already were. "I'm sorry, I'm sorry," she muttered as she set up her keyboard in the pit. "I overslept."

"Musta partied hard last night," said their violinist. The sarcasm wasn't hard to hear—she'd been showing up late more frequently—and Amelia's embarrassment grew. She hadn't joined the troupe for a post-performance get-together since opening night, and she could tell everyone else's friendships were deepening and slowly shutting her out. Just another thing to pile onto the heap along with the temperamental flu that wouldn't go away and the persistent thoughts of giving up on life.

Amelia set up her things in what felt like record time, but when Ross gave them all his final eye-to-eye check, Amelia's hands were shaking so hard she could barely line her fingers up on the right keys. She gave him an "Okay" nod anyway, knowing she'd already stressed everyone out enough—to make them all wait for her to calm down would only irritate them more. She didn't want to give them any more reasons to be mad at her.

Her head was a jumble of chaos and fear—par for the course these days, but exacerbated by the last forty minutes she'd spent scrambling to get to the theater on time. She kept her eyes on her music as she played, something she hadn't had to do since the third week of rehearsal, and in between songs she dug her fingernails into her forearm to give her mind something else to think about other than her restlessness. She needed to stay focused. Even Ross's forgiveness would expire eventually.

She prayed harder than she'd prayed in a long time—and for the first time in weeks. *Don't let me screw up. Don't let me mess up the show. Please just get me through tonight.* She blinked several times, then began to play. Her playing sounded emotionless—ironic, given how emotional she actually was—and she kept expecting Ross to throw her dirty looks. When the show was over she almost collapsed on the keyboard, so spent was she from wrangling her concentration and trying to herd her emotions away from what felt like a drop-off into insanity. She couldn't do this again. She had to get better. She had to stop feeling sick all the time, and thinking about a sleep from which she never awoke, and struggling to follow through on the simplest of tasks. She couldn't live like this much longer. She'd go crazy. If she wasn't already.

"Coming out?" asked the guitarist while everyone packed up. She could hear the note of challenge in his voice. She hated how they must all think of her now, but the thought of socializing made her almost physically ill. She just wanted to get home and call Marcus, even though he'd already be asleep. She needed to hear his voice.

"Amelia?" A voice—a familiar one—called out to her.

She sat straight up.

"Amelia, over here."

She spun, hope almost suffocating her, and saw him standing at the door to the orchestra pit holding a bouquet of roses.

"Marcus!" Her voice broke as she called. She dodged equipment to get to him, and she literally fell into his arms and began to cry.

"Hey, babe—whoa, it's all right, calm down." His arms tightened around her and she felt safe. Strong, stable, levelheaded Marcus. He'd help her get her head back on straight.

"Are you okay?" he said into her ear.

She nodded, holding him tighter. "I'm just—so glad to see you."

He chuckled and squeezed. "Me, too. I hope you don't mind that I surprised you."

"No, not at all—but I can't believe I played so badly, the one night you actually get to see the show."

He leaned back a bit, frowning at her. "You played great. What are you talking about?"

"It was awful."

"You're too hard on yourself. You were fantastic." He glanced around. "So what do you need to do? Post-show meeting? Or can you just go home?"

"I can go home," she said, wiping her eyes on her sleeves. "I have to pack up my keyboard though."

"I'll help you."

She led him to her setup, and as he helped her pack she had to fight the urge to cry again. She wasn't happy—she couldn't even remember what it felt like to be happy—but she was so relieved she thought she might actually be able to sleep tonight. She thanked God over and over as she led Marcus from the pit to the exit and out to the sidewalk. He carried her bag on his shoulder and wrapped his free arm around her waist. "I'm so happy to see you."

"I can't believe you're here. This feels like a dream."

"I made the reservations two weeks ago and have been going crazy ever since. I couldn't wait to get out here." He stopped, tugged her beneath a storefront's canopy, and set her keyboard on the ground. Then, his arms sliding around her, he pulled her close and kissed her.

She felt uncoordinated, as though she'd never done this before, and she almost pulled away. She had wanted to experience this very moment for two months, but now, when Marcus's hands slipped beneath her sweater and pressed against her bare back, she fought the feeling of violation it evoked. But she couldn't deny him, not after two months apart. At least they were in public; she had until they got home to figure out how to gently turn him down when he tried to go further. As much as she wanted to be near him, sex sounded like too much work—physically *and* emotionally.

She kept him talking as they rode the bus home, not wanting to give him a chance to ask her how she was. She needed his help and knew that would require telling him the truth about how she truly was doing, but even so, she wasn't about to admit the depths of her brokenness, not when he was in town for less than forty-eight hours. He wouldn't be able to fix her entirely, and she didn't want him going back to Nebraska with worry. She would have to tone it down, ask for some general advice, that sort of thing. And then be vague if he pushed for more details.

Dane and Jill were asleep when they got back to the apartment. Amelia led Marcus silently through the living room to her bedroom, and once they were there Marcus wrapped her in a bear hug and whispered, "I've missed you so much."

"I know, love. I've missed you, too. But … I'm still fighting the flu, and I'm so incredibly tired. Maybe, can we. … tomorrow …?"

He nodded, lips pressed tight, but understanding in his eyes. "No worries. Get ready for bed. It'll be nice just having you next to me."

She agreed with that completely. Just his presence in the same room as her made her feel a little better. They changed into their pajamas and snuggled together in the dark, and for the first time in weeks, Amelia slept through the night.

Marcus, still on Central time, awoke before Amelia did the next morning. He was glad she had Monday mornings off from the deli; he would have accompanied her to work, but it wouldn't have been the same. Instead he moved closer to her and draped an arm over her hip, relishing the feeling of her beside him again. How was he going to leave tomorrow?

She stirred but didn't wake. He knew she'd been sick; better to let her sleep in on her day off. He slowly rolled off the bed to go shower and dress. They'd have the whole day ahead of them once she was up.

Jill was in the kitchen when Marcus went to get breakfast. "Hey, Jill!" He gave her a hug, then smiled down at her growing stomach. "Wow, look at you. How are you feeling?"

Jill gave her belly the signature mother-to-be rub. "Better than I was. But man, pregnancy is *hard*."

Marcus smiled. "Yeah, but think of what you get for your trouble."

Jill smiled. "That's what Dane keeps saying, which, as you know, is an improvement." Her face changed when her eyes met Marcus's. She crossed her arms and leaned against the counter. "So, forgive me if I skip all the catching-up conversation, but I have a question for you. Has Amelia ... shared anything with you? About how she's doing?"

Marcus didn't like how that was worded. "Um ... I know she's been fighting the flu."

"She hasn't mentioned anything else?"

He thought back to the night before. "No. Why are you asking? Do you think something else is going on?"

"I don't know, to tell you the truth. She just … doesn't seem herself these days. When you emailed to say you'd be coming out I was so relieved—I had been debating whether or not I should say something to you, because I figured if she was giving me the whole 'I'm fine' thing, then she was probably saying that to you, too."

"Well … yeah, she has been."

"I was afraid of that."

He crossed his arms. "So what do you think is going on?"

She shrugged. "I don't know. And for all I know it's just a matter of us not connecting much these days because of our schedules. I wonder if the pregnancy is weird for her—I mean, I'm sure I'm changing, and will keep changing once the baby's here, so maybe she's just anticipating that our friendship might change too, and she's bothered by it. But …" She stopped, then shook her head. "I don't know, Marcus. Something's up."

He nodded slowly, processing. "Thanks." To have his fears confirmed didn't make him feel any better.

Just then Dane joined them, and after the three of them had finished breakfast and Jill and Dane had left for work, Marcus went back to the bedroom to wake Amelia.

"Hey, babe," he said, kissing her forehead and trying to keep his energy light. "Wake up and play with me."

Amelia stirred and faced him with a lazy half smile. Slowly the smile morphed into a grimace and she rolled out of bed. "Be right back." She disappeared from the room and reappeared a couple minutes later. "Sorry," she said as she slipped beneath the covers again. "This stupid stomach thing just comes and goes."

"Poor baby." He joined her beneath the sheets and held her close. "So what do you want to do today?"

"Um … could we just stay home?"

He gave her a squeeze. "Sounds good to me."

Twice her breathing seemed to catch and he expected her to speak, but nothing happened. When it happened a third time, he sat up and looked down at her. "Say it already."

"What? There's nothing."

"Come on. What's on your mind?"

"Really, it's nothing."

"I don't believe you." He sat up and folded his arms, deciding to get to the bottom of this before they did anything else. Better than waiting to have such a downer of a discussion ten minutes before he left for the airport. "I know something's going on, Amelia. Please just tell me."

Her back was to him, but he could tell from the set of her shoulders and the vibe of tension she gave off that she was on the verge of tears. He gently rested a hand on her shoulder, just to let her know he was there, and it was as though the extra weight finally broke her. She cried harder than he'd ever seen her cry. He lay back down and held her while she sobbed, saying nothing and praying that whatever was wrong wasn't nearly as bad as she seemed to think it was.

After a few minutes she reined in her tears and, still sniffling, sat up and let Marcus wrap his arm around her shoulder. She leaned her head against him and eventually said in a voice so quiet he had to close his eyes to hear it, "I think I'm losing my mind."

"Okay …" He waited for elaboration, but none came. "What makes you think that?"

"I can't focus … I can't sleep at night, but during the day it's all I want to do … And I'm so, so sad all the time. Like, to my core. I can't remember the last time I felt honest-to-goodness happy. Even when I saw you last night, I didn't feel happy. I just felt this immense relief, because I thought maybe you'd be able to figure out what's wrong with me." Her voice began to quaver. "I don't even want to play music anymore. I've never *not* wanted to play. Music has always been the one thing that made everything steady. Now whenever I play it sounds horrible to me and I'm sure everyone is laughing at me for thinking I could ever do this as a professional."

With every problem Amelia listed, Marcus felt the weight in his chest grow heavier. He recalled his psych classes from seminary and didn't want to tell her what he suspected the problem was because he knew it wouldn't go over well. *And I'm no doctor. Maybe I shouldn't say anything. Why make things worse?*

But as Amelia began to cry again, soundlessly this time as her body shook, Marcus knew he had no choice but to say something, because unless he helped her get on the right track for treatment, chances were she wouldn't do it herself. Not when the diagnosis might dredge up memories and comparisons that he knew she'd rather avoid.

"Babe, I think I know what's wrong."

She sat up and wiped her eyes with the edge of the sheet. "What?"

Please don't let her freak out, God. "I think you're depressed. Not just sad—I mean, clinically depressed. I think you should see a doctor."

She frowned, shook her head slowly. "No, I don't think … It's just—the separation. Right? We just need to come up with a new arrangement."

"It might be. But I think we should set an appointment with a doctor to make sure."

She went silent, but he could practically hear the wheels turning. Suddenly she sat up and slid from the bed without looking at him. "You're wrong." She yanked a blouse from a hanger in the closet, snatched a pair of jeans from the floor, and disappeared into the bathroom with a slam of the door.

The hot spray did nothing to ease the knots that had become chronic in her neck and shoulders. She'd been in the shower for ten minutes but still hadn't so much as picked up the soap. Marcus's diagnosis had to be wrong. Taking Psych 101 and pastoral counseling didn't make him a psychiatrist. What did he know?

At the word *depressed*, Amelia had heard her mother's voice. "Depressed? I'm not depressed. Artists are never depressed—they're creatively jammed." She saw her father roll his eyes and heard him curse as he left the bedroom where his wife had been hiding out for three days straight. Amelia had seen it all from her parents' closet where she'd run when her father had come home. He didn't like Amelia to visit her mother when she got that way. He never told her why. But she hated the thought of her mother all alone, even if she was choosing the solitude.

Amelia had been eight when she'd witnessed the exchange. She didn't know what *depressed* meant, so she'd looked it up in the dictionary that night. *Sad and gloomy; dejected; downcast.* The words had summed up her mother pretty well. But the description didn't carry the weight the word had when her father had used it. And the vehemence with which her mother denied it told Amelia there was more that the definition didn't mention.

By the time Amelia understood the full meaning of the word, she'd been living with the reality of it for so long that it didn't really faze her. Her mother didn't just "have" depression. She was depression embodied. Well, depression with a twist—nonsensical rambling and frenzied cleaning jags and days without sleep would creep up out of nowhere and throw the dynamic of the household into chaos. But after a week or two, her mother would settle back into the fog; her father would go back to his workaholic tendencies, and her sister Evie would go back to being the quasimother who made the meals and did the family's laundry.

And Amelia—Amelia would go back to her piano. Actually, she never left it. When her mother was depressed, she asked Amelia to play. When she was going on hour forty without sleep and insisted on having company while she rearranged the living room again, she asked Amelia to play. And when she was passed out drunk or finally asleep, Amelia played for herself. The girl and her piano, till death do they part.

Except now the piano did nothing for her, and the label that she associated with her broken, haunted mother hung over her head like a judgment. Her worst nightmare—the thing she had shoved far enough into her subconscious that she'd assumed she'd never recall it—was coming true.

Did that mean her fate would be the same as her mother's?

She barely had the energy to stand, but that thought was enough to get her moving. She bathed and dressed and joined Marcus in the living room where he was reading a Bible commentary.

"Feeling better?" he asked.

"Much," she lied with a bright smile.

"Good. Let's figure out what we can do."

"About what?"

"About the depression, babe. We can't ignore it."

She held her head higher. "I'm not depressed."

"Ames. Please."

"You're no doctor, Marcus."

"And you're no actress, Amelia. I know what you're trying to do, and I'm not buying it. Look, it's not the end of the world. Far from it. There are a million drugs out there you can take to treat it, a million therapists you can try—"

"Forget it. Drugs will kill my creativity and therapists will just tell me it's all my fault."

Marcus frowned. "What on earth makes you think that?"

"That's—um—I mean, everyone knows that." *Right?* She'd heard her mother throw back that excuse every time her father accused her of being depressed. Her mother wouldn't have said it if it wasn't true.

"Amelia." Marcus closed the book and stood. "You've got a choice to make. You can either get help, or you can get worse. And … I've been thinking about this, and I swear I'm not trying to use this situation to manipulate you … but if you were to come to Nebraska, it would be a lot easier. And cheaper. My insurance through the church isn't too bad, but I doubt there are many doctors in-network with them here in LA. And you wouldn't have to work at the deli anymore, or stay holed up in a single room. The cost of living is just so much lower. It would be … man, Amelia, it would be so much better if we were together. I miss you so much. And I can't take care of you if you're all the way out here, and that's what I'm supposed to do. I'm your husband, for Pete's sake. Please. Let me take care of you."

Amelia had no ammunition to fight with, but she tried anyway. "But the theater—it's my only opportunity to play right now."

"But you hate it. You don't even want to play. "

"My career—"

"Isn't going to go anywhere if you don't even want to touch the piano. Look, when you're better you can come back. Leaving doesn't mean staying away forever. It just means taking a break so you can get healthy."

Amelia swayed on her feet. She was so tired, even after a decent night of sleep. Her stomach was still making threats. The dark cloud that lived in her chest was there like always, solid and painful as ever. But the thought of quitting the deli, of having Marcus with her again, of no longer living with the daily fear of messing up a performance based on exhaustion sounded like pure heaven.

"Okay."

Marcus's face glowed as though lit with a spotlight. "Seriously? You'll come?"

"Yeah." She sat hard on the armchair, defeated. But also, ever so slightly relieved. "Yeah, I'll come."

Marcus knelt before her and took her hands in his. "I'll take care of everything, okay? You just give notice to your jobs and pack your things. Don't worry about the details. Okay?"

"Okay."

He kissed her hands, then her cheek. "Can I get you some breakfast?"

She felt her face go green at the mention of food. "No. No thanks. In fact," she said, forcing herself to her feet. "I think I'm just going to go back to bed."

"Okay, you do that. I'll start in on your move. Let me know if I can get you anything—"

She shut the bedroom door on his offer and slid between the sheets.

CHAPTER 7

When performances started, the troupe went down to just one rehearsal a week. The day after Marcus returned to Nebraska, where he promised he would continue to work out all the details of Amelia's move, Amelia went to rehearsal with mixed emotions over her announcement. Most of her was overcome with relief. Once they found a new pianist—or once the second week of April arrived—she'd be off the hook, no longer burdened with the fear of public humiliation. But there was still a sliver of her that was convinced her life as a professional musician was over. There would be no opportunities in Nebraska, and coming back to LA seemed unrealistic. Once Jill had the baby Amelia would have nowhere to stay. And while she had once sworn she'd do anything to advance her career, she knew now that it wasn't true. She'd be staying in LA if it were.

Amelia walked into rehearsal and saw she was one of the last to arrive; only Gabe and Ross were missing. She set up in silence while the others bantered and conversed around her. Her stomach knotted as she thought about how the directors, Ross especially, would react. She was well aware of the mess she was creating for them—hopefully they'd recognize that it was far less messy than her continuing to play would be.

Gabe came in two minutes before rehearsal was to start. "Sorry, gang," he said. "Awful traffic. Ross is about ten minutes out. I told him we'd get started without him. Everyone ready?"

As the others called out their answers, Amelia walked up to Gabe and forced herself to look him in the eye. "Can I talk to you a minute? In private?"

"Oh. Sure." He led her to the back of the theater, where he leaned against the wall and Amelia sat on the backs of the last row of seats. "Is everything all right?"

She took a deep breath and launched into the statement she'd practiced. "For personal reasons I'd rather not discuss, I'm going to have to quit."

Gabe's face remained neutral. "All right. When would your last show be?"

"I can play all the shows up until April ninth. But as soon as you find a replacement they can take over—I won't make them or you wait until I leave."

He nodded slowly. "Okay. I'm very sorry to see you go."

"Thanks, Gabe."

His eyes narrowed slightly. "This isn't because of Ross, is it?"

Amelia blinked, surprised. "No—not at all."

"I know that he, um—"

"No, really, it's not about him." *Please don't make me have this conversation.*

"Okay, I'll take your word for it. But if there's anything we can do to convince you to stay, just tell me what it is."

Amelia couldn't believe he wasn't jumping at the chance to let her go. "There isn't. But thanks."

He nodded. "Now, would you like me to tell the troupe, or would you prefer to do it?"

"You can." She was grateful to not have to bear that responsibility. Maybe he'd wait until after rehearsal and she'd be able to sneak out before he said anything.

Together they walked back to the front and Gabe motioned

to the stage. "Places, actors. I want to run 'Morning Glow' and focus on really nailing that ending. It was getting a little mushy this weekend."

He cued in Amelia, who launched the song, and she found she was better able to concentrate now that she knew her time with the troupe was limited. She was fine until Ross came in during the song and sat in the front row. Then her nerves kicked up again. What would he say when Gabe told him Amelia's plans?

The song ended, and Ross took his place on the podium to conduct the band. They ran three more songs before Ross declared himself satisfied and left the rest of rehearsal up to Gabe.

"I think we're good too," Gabe said, "but before I dismiss you we have some business to discuss." He glanced at Amelia, and she trained her gaze on her music notebook, unable to withstand the weight of everyone's stares as they followed Gabe's. "Amelia won't be with us after April ninth, so we're going to need to find a new pianist." A murmur arose from the group, but Gabe continued to talk. "Ross and I weren't thrilled with any of the other pianists we auditioned, so if you know of anyone you think might be interested, give them mine or Ross's number, and tell them we'll audition them immediately."

"Touring, Amelia?" asked the drummer.

"No. It's … It's a long story."

Amelia began to pack up, her face burning from the curious looks. She knew that several people in the group had never warmed to her—she could hardly blame them—and although she could swear she heard someone say "prima donna," she hoped that it was only paranoia.

"I can't believe you're leaving," Ross said when he came up beside Amelia as she tucked padding around her keyboard. "Is this because of me?"

"No, it's not. There are a lot of reasons."

"You're going to Nebraska, aren't you?" Ross ran a hand through his hair. "You know you're throwing your talent away, right? I mean, I get that your husband is there and all, but you're totally compromising here. What did he do to get you to leave? Threaten you with divorce? You'd be better off without him if that's the kind of guy he is."

Enough is enough. "That's *not* the kind of guy he is." Who did Ross think he was? Amelia shoved her binder in its pocket and stood tall. "Thanks for making this even harder than it already is, Ross. Thanks for bringing up every fear I've got and then trying to smear my husband's character. You're right, I should totally dump him and come to you. You're the most upstanding guy on the planet." Sarcasm wasn't a tool Amelia typically employed, but this time the words rolled off her tongue.

She was slightly mollified by Ross's obvious regret. "I'm sorry, Amelia, I didn't mean—I mean, I just can't believe—"

"Yeah, I know. Me neither." She shouldered her bag and turned for the door. "Don't follow me out, all right? I really don't need your 'help.'"

From seat 21F, Amelia watched the snowcapped Rockies slowly glide beneath her and shuddered at the sight of the snow. Marcus had warned her that a late winter storm was to move in over the next day, yet in some kind of subconscious defiance, she'd boxed her cold-weather clothes to be ground shipped and packed in her suitcase the outfits she'd been wearing for LA's unseasonably warm spring. She hadn't noticed until she'd boarded the plane in a tank top and skirt. Now she was freezing.

The drone of the plane and its subtle vibration lulled her toward sleep, but the cold air coupled with her thoughts kept her from nodding off. Nebraska. If she'd ever wanted proof that God didn't care about her—not that she was looking for it—this had to be it. Why would God bless her with talent and then ship her off to a place where it would atrophy?

The plane hit a patch of turbulence and her stomach lurched. She pressed a hand to her abdomen and closed her eyes, willing the nausea to abate. She'd finally gotten over her weird flu during the last week, and the thought of being dogged by that sick feeling again made her … well … sick. At least the flight was almost halfway over. They'd be in Denver soon, where she'd connect on a smaller plane to Omaha. Knowing those small planes, though, her nausea was only just beginning.

When they landed, Amelia dragged her carry-on on its rickety wheels to the new gate where she waited an hour for her next flight. She used to love flying, and especially loved layovers. More time to read, to listen to music uninterrupted, to people-watch while indulging in snacks she normally avoided. This time she sat at the window and stared at the runway, hardly noticing the aircraft that arrived and departed right in front of her. She felt numb. This couldn't possibly be her life. She was living someone else's existence.

There was only a single ray of hope that she felt in all of this. The depression, as Marcus had called it, seemed to be abating. Not that she was happy-go-lucky or anything, but the depth and opacity of her sadness seemed to have lessened over the last couple days. It didn't make sense, given she was abandoning her career and moving to a place she had no desire to be in. She figured it was just from the relief of not being separated from Marcus any longer and not having to waste her days in two jobs she hated. Regardless of the reason, she was glad. She just wished she knew whether or not to expect it to last.

She boarded the plane with the other passengers and her prayer for an introverted seat neighbor was granted. She closed her eyes and pretended to sleep, hoping to fool the rest of her body. But no, she was conscious for the entire bumpy flight, and after she debarked she sat in the gate for several long minutes while she waited for her stomach to settle.

Marcus was waiting for her at the end of the escalator. He'd already taken her suitcase from the baggage claim. "I was beginning to worry," he said after they broke their embrace. "I thought maybe you'd missed your connection."

She should have called him. "There was a lot of turbulence. I felt awful when I got off the plane, so I sat in the gate until I was sure I wasn't going to throw up."

"Poor baby." He kissed her forehead, then added her carry-on to the luggage cart. "Let's get going, before we hit the commuter traffic." She followed him to a set of double doors, where he paused and removed his coat. "You're going to need this."

"Oh. Thanks." His warmth enveloped her as she pulled it on, and the scent of his cologne brought a rush of equally warm memories—of their first date, their wedding, nights spent snuggling on the couch. She wondered if she'd ever be that happy again.

The next morning Amelia woke to see snow drifting from the sky. She groaned as she pulled the duvet over her head and burrowed deeper beneath the sheets. She'd be spending another day in Marcus's clothes. What kind of idiot packed shorts instead of sweats when heading to a place that hadn't gotten the memo that it was supposed to be spring?

But there was no going back to sleep once she was up. Within seconds of waking, her mind was going full throttle. Marcus was taking the day off to help her acclimate—drive her around town; help her find a doctor to give her a referral to a therapist (even though Amelia insisted she no longer needed help with her depression, Marcus wanted her to at least talk to someone to ensure it didn't come back); and buy her some winter clothes. Even though she had warmer things coming in her shipped boxes, they were meant for LA's version of winter, not Wheatridge's. She didn't want to do any of it, but she wasn't about to tell Marcus that. He'd made it clear yesterday through numerous hints that he couldn't afford to take a lot of time off right now. It was either today or waiting until Saturday, and she knew he wanted to get her an appointment with a doctor as soon as possible. She wasn't looking forward to that, but she didn't have a choice. She'd abdicated responsibility for herself the minute she'd agreed to move. Marcus was in charge now. And she had to admit it was sort of nice not to have to figure things out on her own anymore.

She pulled on the sweatpants and sweatshirt she'd worn yesterday, knowing she wouldn't go back to sleep now. Once again Marcus's
scent lit a tiny spark inside her, and even though it was brief, she was
glad she could still experience happiness, even if it was so small and
fleeting.

"There you are." Marcus's smile lit his face when Amelia came
out of the bedroom. He was sitting at the dining room table with
three thick books and his laptop open before him. "Breakfast or
lunch? It's almost eleven."

The clouds hiding the sun had made her think it was earlier than
that. She hadn't slept so well since Marcus had visited her in LA.
"Thanks, but I'm not hungry. I'm dying for coffee, though."

"You really should eat something, babe. You barely had any dinner last night."

"I will, I promise. Just a little later, okay?"

Marcus's face told her he didn't like her answer, but he said nothing as he entered the kitchen. "So I have a list of family doctors here
in Wheatridge for you to look over. I figure you can pick your top
three and we'll make an appointment with whoever can get you in
soonest."

She shrugged, though she knew he couldn't see the gesture.
"Okay."

"When you're ready to go out, we'll hit the mall and see what we
can find for you, clothing-wise. There won't be a lot to choose from,
but all you really need are a couple items for now, right? Your stuff
should be here by Monday at the latest, and they're predicting the
weather will turn by the weekend."

"Okay."

He set the coffee in front of her, then sat back down and reached out a hand across the table. She offered hers in return, and he grasped it, smiling. "I'm so glad you're here. The apartment feels totally different with you in it—in a good way. A really good way. I couldn't wait for you to come."

She smiled with genuine warmth. In spite of her ever-present exhaustion and her reluctance to move—okay, flat-out rejection of moving—she was happy to be with her husband. "I'm glad I'm with you." She pointed her chin toward the books. "Working on your sermon for Easter?"

"Yeah. I'll stop, though."

"No, go ahead. I don't really feel like talking, anyway. What sounds really great is a bath." She grabbed her coffee and smiled. "I'll be taking this with me."

"You rebel." He grinned as he stood and gave her a kiss whose chasteness she appreciated. "Let me know when you're ready to go."

The bath and coffee worked together to chase the chill that had lingered since yesterday, and when she finally emerged she felt better about the day's pending events. But when she followed Marcus to the car that he'd already began warming up, the brief time spent in the snow and cold irritated her. She hadn't been in true winter weather since her days at Juilliard. She hadn't minded it much back then, but now the gray expanse of the sky seemed to hang just inches from her head and made her feel claustrophobic, and the bitter wind that gusted just before she got into the car made her gasp. As Marcus backed the car out, Amelia doubted this place would ever feel like home.

"Isn't the snow beautiful?" Marcus said, contradicting her very thoughts. "That ice storm we had back in February was brutal but made everything look absolutely amazing. I'm not going to say the weather doesn't suck sometimes, but at least the aftermath is nice to look at."

She tried to fake agreement, but this time it didn't work. "I can't believe I'm here."

Thankfully, Marcus missed her real meaning. He squeezed her hand. "I know, me neither. Hey, let me know if you get hungry, because there's a great little bar and grill downtown I'd love to take you to, okay?"

"Sure."

She let Marcus play tour guide as they drove through Wheatridge toward the mall. The affection with which he described the town made it seem as though he'd been born and raised there. She never would have pegged him for a small-town kind of guy, but he really seemed to feel at home. And she could tell he was trying to engage her with the place—he kept pointing out places of musical interest, of which there were very few, but he hyped each one as though it was on Nebraska's list of most treasured spots. "Blue Note—that's the store I was telling you about. See that baby grand in the window? I went by there the other day and someone was playing it, though not nearly as well as you could. We should stop over there some time so you can try it out. I know how much you love the real thing. Oh, and the guys who work there are great—I think they even have a band, maybe you could jam with them some time. Do pianists do that? Jam with other musicians? Oh, and there's that coffee shop that has the live music on Friday nights. I've heard some of the other acts, and they're all right, but you'd blow them out of the water. When you're feeling better we'll stop by there and maybe you can sign up for a night. Maybe we could even find a recording studio somewhere; I bet there's one in Omaha. You could record a few tracks so you have a CD to sell. The gal I saw sing had some, and I know she sold at least a handful ..." He filled the silence, and for that Amelia was grateful, even if his words piled more expectations on her shoulders than she felt strong enough to bear.

She tried her best that day. And it seemed that Marcus was clueless about how much his plans for their future made her feel more hopeless, rather than hopeful. She knew he was just trying to show her that she could make a living as a musician in Wheatridge one way or another, but he'd say things like, "I looked into what substitute teachers make in this school district. You could sub for band, or orchestra, or general music classes and make a pretty decent amount of money," or "The Blue Note offers lessons, too. We should see if they need a piano teacher" and all Amelia heard was "You're never leaving here, so you might as well put down roots." By the time they got home from the mall, she was lower than she'd felt since arriving in Nebraska, and the turn her thoughts had taken scared her more than they had that day she'd first felt vaguely suicidal on the way to *Pippin*. She was in a perfect Catch-22: Drown in LA or drown in Nebraska. Either way she was doomed.

The final nail in the coffin came when they arrived at the apartment. Amelia had planned on begging off for a nap the minute they walked in the door, but before she could open her mouth, Marcus said, "Hey, there's something I want to show you."

Amelia sat on the couch and rubbed a hand over her eyes as he disappeared into the kitchen. When he returned, he held a piece of paper in his hand. "Now, I know it would take some saving, and we might not get enough in time. But I saw this place when I first moved here, and every time I look at the pictures I can practically see us in them."

He handed her the flyer. Pictures of a bare dining room space, of a modern kitchen flanked by 1930s woodwork, of a front room lit with large windows and graced by a shining petite baby grand slowly sank in. A house. He'd found them a house. He wanted to buy a house.

"The piano comes with the place. Isn't that incredible? Hardwood floors, tons of upgrades but all this gorgeous structural stuff— wouldn't it be amazing? Can't you just picture us there, in front of that beautiful fireplace, maybe a kid sliding around in socks—"

"A kid?" Her tone was sharper than she'd meant for it to be, but the rising panic in her chest shut down the filter between her head and her mouth.

"I—yeah, well, eventually, I mean. Like I said, this place might sell before—"

"I'm not moving here for good, Marcus. We discussed this. I'm just here until I've got this—this 'depression,' or whatever it is, figured out, and then I'm going back."

"I know, but—"

"No buts, Marcus. You act like it's ... like it's decided that I'm staying but I'm not, I ..." Her hand clutched her chest as it squeezed the air from her lungs. "I don't want to ... Oh God, I can't breathe."

Her body began to shake. She gasped for breath. Her hands clawed at her chest, as though she could dig a hole to her airway. The room began to go fuzzy. Marcus dropped to her side and gripped her knees with his hands. "Amelia, what's wrong?"

"I don't—I don't—"

Marcus tried gently to take her hands, but she yanked them away, not able to stand the feeling of being restrained. "I think you're having a panic attack," he said, a note of authority in his voice but his face belying his concern. "You need to try to calm down. Here—try to breathe as slowly as you can."

She gulped for breath, and suddenly Marcus stood and ran into the bedroom, then came back out holding her iPod and fumbling with her earbuds. "Wear these and we'll put on some relaxing music. Maybe that will help." He handed her the earbuds and she pressed them to her ears, unable to steady her hands enough to insert them properly. Marcus scrolled through her playlists and selected Bedtime, the list she'd made last month. Pachabel's *Canon* began to play, and Amelia shut her eyes and tried to let the music soothe her. Marcus sat beside her as she continued to breathe as slowly as she could.

Things were not improving, but suddenly Amelia didn't care. If she gave herself over to it, maybe it would overtake her. Could a person die from a panic attack? *That'd be nice.*

She stopped the slow breathing and dropped the earbuds. Marcus picked them up, but she pushed his hands away as he tried to give them back. She began to pant, and her chest spasmed tighter. Despite her terror, the thought that this might provide a way out was enough motivation to keep her going.

"Amelia, what are you doing?" Marcus grabbed her shoulders but she jerked herself away. "Amelia—"

"Leave me alone." She gasped out the words as she tried to stand and get away from him, but her legs were too shaky to support her.

She turned her back to him and closed her eyes. *Just take me. Please, let this be the end.*

It didn't work. Within ten minutes the crushing weight on her chest had subsided and her breathing had evened out. Marcus helped her to the bed and she lay unmoving, utterly spent, as tears gathered in her eyes.

Marcus pulled the duvet to her shoulders. "Get some rest. I'll start calling doctors." He kissed her cheek and closed the door behind him.

The doctor's waiting room needed serious redecorating. Amelia didn't have the best eye for design, but she knew outdated when she saw it. It didn't surprise her, though—somehow it made sense for the small-town setting.

She held a four-month-old copy of *People* magazine on her lap but didn't care enough to actually open it. Instead she stared at the framed Norman Rockwell print, faded from years spent across from the window, and tried to let her mind go blank. Since yesterday's panic attack she'd been nervous about a repeat, and her scattered, racing thoughts surely weren't helping matters. She meditated on the tranquil scene in the picture to no avail. She shifted her gaze to the white wall beside it, hoping it would fill her mind, but that didn't work either.

Her phone buzzed in the seat beside her. She glanced at the screen and saw Jill's name. Amelia hit a button to send the call to voice mail. Jill had called twice and emailed a handful of times, but Amelia hadn't felt like talking. She didn't have the energy right now to maintain that relationship. She was too busy trying to figure out how she was going to live in Wheatridge without losing her mind.

"Amelia?" A middle-aged woman in turquoise scrubs called for her from a door that led to the back of the office. "Please follow me."

Amelia obeyed and sat on the paper-covered exam bed, and the nurse took her vitals as she chatted amiably. "Dr. Robinson will be in to see you soon," she said after filling out the chart. "It's cold out there—can I get you some tea?"

That was an unexpectedly nice touch. "Thanks," Amelia said. "That would be nice." The nurse returned with the tea, and moments later the petite Dr. Robinson appeared. "I'm Dr. Robinson. Nice to meet you, Amelia," she said in a quick clip as she shook her hand. "Welcome to the practice. I see on your forms you had a panic attack yesterday—is that why you came in?"

Amelia scratched a thumbnail against the Styrofoam cup. "Partly, yes. My husband thinks I'm depressed, too."

Dr. Robinson's mouth quirked a small smile. "Do *you?*"

Amelia shrugged. "I don't know. Maybe. I was a lot worse, and then I started getting better. But then … Well, something's not right, I know that much."

Dr. Robinson scanned Amelia's chart again. "You checked off recent weight loss. Was that intentional?"

"No. It just … happened. Well, maybe not 'just.'" Amelia gave the doctor an apologetic look. "I lost my appetite so I just stopped eating."

"Ah, I see. That is a sign of depression." She scribbled something on the chart. "Let's see … insomnia, inability to enjoy life, weight loss, panic attack … It does sound like depression to me. There are plenty of ways for us to treat it, luckily. Let's go through this depression inventory real quick and see what we find." She ran through a list of questions, almost all of which drew a yes from Amelia.

"Depression indeed," the doctor said as she flipped to the second page of the chart and made notes. Then she went back to the first page of the chart and frowned. "Is this right? Your last period was in November?"

Amelia nodded. "I have ridiculously long and irregular cycles."

"Are they always this long?"

Amelia felt a flutter in her chest. "Um … no. I guess not. Not usually."

"And you're sure you're not pregnant?"

Amelia shook her head. "Uhh, nope. Not possible. When I was twenty I was diagnosed as being chronically anovulatory."

Dr. Robinson tapped her pen to her lips. "Okay. And you noted on your intake form that your most recent illness had been the flu?"

"Seemed like it, yeah. Tons of nausea, threw up a few times a week. Lasted for … I don't know, almost six weeks?"

Dr. Robinson gave Amelia a curious look. "All right then. We're going to do some routine blood work, just to make sure your thyroid is functioning properly—when it's off it can cause the symptoms you're dealing with, and even cause depression—but I'm also going to have you humor me and take a pregnancy test."

Amelia's mouth went dry. "Why?"

"Because not all antidepressants are safe in pregnancy, and we don't want to take any chances."

"But I can't be."

Dr. Robinson studied her with eyebrows raised. "Have you had sex since November?"

"Well—yes."

"Then there's always a chance; I don't care what diagnosis you've been given. Stranger things have happened." She closed the chart and pocketed her pen. "I'll have Linda come in and do your blood work in a minute, and she'll also bring in a pregnancy test. Bathroom's down the hall to the left."

Dr. Robinson shut the door, leaving Amelia to absorb information that felt like a mental hand grenade.

Linda came in with a wheeled cart carrying the blood work vials and tools. Amelia saw the pregnancy test beside them. "Can I do that first?" she said, pointing to it. She had to settle the issue, before she let herself get worked up.

Linda handed it to her. "Take off the cap; pee on the end. It'll take about three minutes to register. You can leave the test for me if you'd rather not sit there and stare at it."

"Are you kidding?" Amelia slid off the exam bed and picked up the test. "I'm not leaving the bathroom until I've seen the results."

Linda smiled. "Good luck—whatever you're hoping for."

Amelia ripped off the paper wrapper as she walked down the hall. She shut the bathroom door and examined the test, which showed two symbols beside the result window. A minus sign indicated she wasn't pregnant. A plus sign meant she was.

She took the test, set it on the counter, then righted her clothes. *Don't look,* she told herself. *At least count to a hundred first. Slowly.* Linda had said three minutes.

She couldn't help it. She looked.

Plus sign.

Chapter 8

Easter morning brought a veritable heat wave that Marcus hoped would brighten Amelia's spirits. Clouds had hidden the sun since she'd arrived, and he could see the toll it was taking. She'd gotten worse since her panic attack that past Tuesday. The doctor had prescribed an antidepressant, but had said it might take a few weeks to see any benefits. Marcus hoped it kicked in sooner than that, for both their sakes.

Maybe getting out in the sunshine would help, he thought as he showered and shaved. Maybe they could go for a walk that afternoon. Ed and Lucy had invited them to dinner, but Marcus knew Amelia wouldn't be up for getting together with strangers, and they had no big plans for a holiday meal. Maybe they could grill burgers in the courtyard.

He checked his watch as he dressed. They had to leave in less than an hour, and Amelia was still sleeping. He hated to wake her, but he also didn't want to be late on one of the two Sundays of the year that were sure to draw holiday-only attenders. He straightened his tie and went back to the bedroom to wake her.

"Hey, babe," he said, gently shaking her shoulder. "We need to leave at—hey, what's wrong?"

She wasn't sleeping. She was curled into her pillow and crying without a sound. He sat on the bed beside her and handed her a tissue from the box on the bedside table. "Is it just, you know, the new usual, or is something else wrong?"

She shook her head as she sat up and dragged the tissue against her cheeks. After some deep breaths that curbed most of the tears, she said, "It's ... It's nothing. Never mind. I'll get up now. How much time do I have?"

"About forty-five minutes. But ... You don't have to go if you don't want to, Amelia."

"No, it's fine," she said between sniffs. "Just let me shower." She stood, still not making eye contact with him, and pulled an outfit from the closet before leaving for the bathroom. He frowned, watching her. *What's really going on?* he wondered. It was the second time this week he'd found her like that, obviously deeply upset, but unwilling to tell him why. He didn't like to think she was keeping secrets from him.

Marcus went to the kitchen to pour her some coffee, figuring she'd need it this morning. The one improvement he had noticed lately was that she was eating again. Not much, but more than she had when he'd visited her in LA. He pulled a loaf of bread from the fridge, deciding to make her some toast. Peanut butter or butter and cinnamon? He went to the bathroom to ask her.

He knocked, and heard her call to come in. He opened the door and poked his head in, unable to help the smile that crossed his face when he saw her through the glass shower door. It had been a long time since he'd seen her unclothed, and he'd deeply missed the view. "I'm making you toast. What would you like on it?"

"Peanut butter."

"Okay." He went to shut the door, then looked in once more, paying closer attention. Her body looked ... different. He shut the door again and went back to the kitchen, thinking. It was probably the weight loss. The parts of her that looked skinnier must just be making the more ... curvy ... parts of her look larger. Things just seemed a little out of proportion.

Unfortunately the encounter sent his thoughts on to tangents that he couldn't afford to follow, not when he'd be greeting parishioners in an hour. He took a deep breath and blew it out pursed lips. *I can't deal with this right now, God. Focus me on You and this sermon.*

But all he could think about was how seeing her nude heightened his sexual frustration. It had been far too long since they'd been intimate—she just didn't seem interested any longer. He prayed it was because of the depression, and not because of him.

A knock on the front door brought his thoughts out of the bedroom. Through the peephole he saw Karis and Audry standing in the hall. Audry looked adorable holding an Easter basket.

"Happy Easter," he said as he opened the door, grateful for the distraction. He smiled down at Audry, who held up her basket. "Well, lucky you. Look at all that chocolate."

"She asked if we could come share some with you," Karis said with an apologetic grin.

"Aw, that's really sweet, Audry. Thank you. Come on in."

"We won't make you late, will we?" Karis asked as she eyed his suit. "I know this must be a big day for you."

"Yes, Christmas and Easter. They're the Super Bowls of the church world." Karis chuckled and Marcus waved them inside. "But there's still some time before we have to leave."

Karis's eyebrows nudged higher. "'We'?"

He acted casual, hoping to dispel the awkwardness. "Yes— Amelia is here now."

A clouded look flickered over Karis's face before she smiled. "I'd forgotten when she was coming. You must be so happy to see her.

Well anyway, we'd better get going, Audry. Why don't you give Mr. Marcus your gift and we'll leave."

"No, there's no rush, really," Marcus said as Audry began rummaging in her basket's plastic grass. "Besides, I'd love for you to meet Amelia."

Karis silently perched on the edge of the armchair while Audry placed foil-wrapped chocolate eggs in Marcus's hand. Marcus couldn't figure out why Karis was being so quiet. "So … any plans for today?" he asked, trying to draw her out.

"No, not really," she said. "Just—oh." She stood, one hand clasping the other against her middle as she stared over Marcus's shoulder.

Marcus turned and smiled at Amelia, whose dress and done-up hair were a nice change from the slumming look she'd been sporting lately. "Hey, babe. This is Karis and Audry, who I told you so much about. Karis, this is my wife, Amelia."

Karis offered a hand. "Nice to meet you," she said. "Marcus talks about you all the time."

Amelia's face was neutral as she stepped forward slowly and shook her hand. "Yes—he's told me about you, too."

"Well, it was lovely to meet you." Karis placed a hand on Audry's shoulder. "Sweetheart, we really need to go."

"'Bye, Mr. Marcus," Audry said as she hooked her arm through her basket's handle.

"Good-bye, Audry. 'Bye, Karis. Service starts at ten if you'd like to stop by."

Karis smiled but didn't look him in the eyes. "Thanks. Nice meeting you, Amelia."

"Yes, you, too."

Marcus shut the door. "I'm glad you two got the chance to meet," he said. "I really think you guys will get along."

Amelia said nothing as she walked into the kitchen. He followed her. "Amelia, are you all right?"

"Fine."

"No, you're not."

She set her plate of toast on the table with more force than necessary and sat down. "So that's Karis."

"Yes. So?"

Amelia rolled her eyes. "You didn't tell me she looked like Nicole Kidman's prettier younger sister."

Marcus frowned, thinking. "Well, she looks a little like her, I guess. I never noticed." Understanding dawned and he straightened from where he'd been leaning against the counter. "Ames, tell me you're not jealous of her."

"I'm not jealous of her." Her voice was flat and unconvincing.

"Oh, for Pete's sake." Marcus sat down across from her. "Seriously, babe, you have nothing to worry about."

"Why—not your type?"

His eyes narrowed. "Not my wife."

She licked peanut butter from her finger. "And it's just that easy for you, huh?"

"It is, in fact." Wait. What was that supposed to mean? "Why—isn't it for you?"

Their eyes locked and Marcus's blood chilled when her expression told him loud and clear that it wasn't. She stood abruptly, dumped the rest of her toast in the trash, and headed for the front door. "Come on. Let's go."

The ride to the church was almost completely silent. Amelia stared out her window as Marcus drove, her profile looking preoccupied and occasionally tortured. He tried not to jump to conclusions, but his imagination was having a field day concocting scenarios in which her fidelity had been tested. Was that what was bothering her? Was that why he kept catching her crying, and why she wouldn't tell him what was wrong?

He bit back his questions. This wasn't the right time. *After church, we'll take that walk. If I can get her to go, that is.*

The parking lot already had a handful of cars in it when they arrived. Normally only Marcus and Ed were there this early. "I'll show you where my office is, if you want to hide out," he said as he gathered his things from the backseat. "I need to do a meet and greet at the front door starting …" Another three cars pulled into the parking lot. "Starting now, I guess. I sit in the front right pew, right on the aisle, so when you're ready to come into the sanctuary, just come there. I'll put my Bible and notes there before I post myself at the door, so you'll see where to go."

They walked up to the front door and Ed greeted them with an enthusiastic handshake. "Good morning, Marcus. And Amelia! Such a pleasure to meet you."

She smiled brightly, but he could tell the smile wasn't reflecting in her eyes. He hoped Ed wouldn't notice. "Nice to meet you, Ed. Marcus has told me a lot about you."

"I've heard a lot about you, too. I'm so glad you're here. I hope we get a chance to hear you on the piano soon; I doubt our little Steinway has seen anyone as talented as you."

She chuckled. "Thanks, Ed."

"I'm going to take her to my office and then I'll come join you,"
Marcus told him. He took her hand and led her on the short walk
through the building to his office. "Here's the office key," he said,
pointing it out on his key ring before placing the keys on his desk.
"Lock up when you come down."

"All right."

He gave her a hug and felt her tense in his arms. It broke his
heart. "Amelia," he said quietly, "I know something is wrong. I know
this isn't the right time to talk about it, when I can't give you as much
time as you might need. But this afternoon, I promise, you'll have
my full attention for as long as you want it. I hope you'll be able to
share what's got you in so much anguish."

She finally looked him in the eyes. "It's that obvious?"

"I'm afraid so."

"I'll think about it."

He kissed her. "I have a stash of food in the lower drawer of the
desk. Help yourself if you get hungry."

She smiled slightly. "Thanks."

He kissed her again, hating to leave. "All right then. Showtime.
See you in a bit." He shut the door behind him, straightened his tie in
a window's reflection, and joined Ed at the front door just in time to
shake hands with a steady stream of attendees. As he traded "Happy
Easters" with familiar faces, he kept a mental list of women he might
introduce Amelia to after the service. Maybe if she connected with
someone it would help smooth the transition to Wheatridge and
make her more willing to stay once her depression had cleared. He
couldn't stand to think of her going back to California, especially if
he had competition there.

When he and Ed entered the sanctuary, Marcus saw Amelia sitting where he'd told her he'd be, surrounded by three of the women Marcus had hoped she'd meet. He gave a subtle fist pump as he made his way up the aisle. "Thanks for welcoming Amelia, ladies," he said when they greeted him. "I was hoping she'd get to meet some of you."

"We were just talking about trying to get together for coffee sometime," one of them said. "I know how rough it was when I first moved here, until I found some friends." She pulled a pen from her purse and began to write on her bulletin. "Here's my phone number and email address. Give me a call anytime; I stay home with our sons, so I'm always around."

The other women added their information, and when Ed came by to tell Marcus they were ready to start the service, they all gave Amelia a hug. Marcus was psyched for the new connections she'd already made, but as soon as the women left for their seats he saw the animation in her face die out completely.

"What?" he said quietly as the choir filed onto the risers and Ed welcomed the congregation in his jovial way.

Amelia tucked the bulletin into the back of her Bible. "I just doubt I'll have anything in common with any of them."

"You never know." He stood with the rest of the church as the congregation began to sing along with the choir.

Amelia remained seated for a moment, but then stood slowly with her eyes fixed on the choir. "It doesn't matter, anyway," she muttered just loud enough for him to hear. "I'm not going to be around for long."

Marcus continued to sing, but his heart and thoughts were conceding defeat. She wasn't even going to give the place a chance. She really preferred being in LA even though it meant being separated from him. Was it the depression? Or was there another man?

These were not the kind of thoughts he needed right now. He wished she had just stayed home.

The rest of the morning was one frustration after the other. Marcus had looked forward to Amelia finally seeing the church. He'd hoped Amelia would see the things he loved about it—the preference for hymns over contemporary choruses, the beautiful sanctuary with its stained glass and polished oak pews—and would find herself starting to like them too. But as the service unfolded around them, he could tell she wasn't engaged at all. She didn't even bother pulling out a hymnal so she could sing "Nothing but the Blood" and "Christ the Lord Is Risen Today" along with the choir. She stared glumly ahead when Ed stood at the front to receive and pray over the offering, not even joining in on the "amen" at the end. And the one time he allowed himself to look at her while he preached, she wasn't even watching him. She was slouched in the pew looking totally zoned out.

By the time the service was over, Marcus's sympathy was wearing thin. "I know it's not what you're used to, but this service was just as powerful to these people as our church in LA is for you."

"I don't doubt that. I'm sure it's great for them. It's just not my thing. I'm sorry."

"I know it's not the kind of service you're drawn to, but you could at least show some respect for the holiday and God while you're here."

He saw her lip quiver and didn't know what to do. "Ames, I'm sorry—"

"No, you're right. I was totally rude. I'm sorry." She blinked rapidly and busied herself with rearranging her Bible and purse in her arms. "I'll go back to your office while you do … whatever it is you have to do."

His anger was dampened some by her contriteness. "It'll be another ten minutes or so."

"Okay." She gave him a peck on the cheek and headed up the aisle without him. He followed, trying to shake the irritation and frustration from his spirit. He didn't like how angry he was, but he couldn't help it. He knew she was depressed, but that didn't mean she had to close herself off to Wheatridge and the church. Didn't she care at all about how that made him feel?

He smiled and shook hands and blessed and embraced as strangers and steady attenders filed out together to finish their Easter Sundays. When he'd realized Amelia would be there for the holiday, he'd envisioned introducing her to the congregation, standing with her at these doors and greeting people together. He'd imagined spontaneous invitations to dinners of honey-baked ham and green bean casseroles with members who were charmed by his wife's engaging personality and eager to welcome her to town. He hated that she was hiding in his office like some scared little girl.

A few families remained in the sanctuary, chatting in the aisles and the pews, but everyone else had gone. Ed shook Marcus's hand and said good-bye, and Marcus went to his office to collect Amelia. "We can go now," he said when he entered and found her playing solitaire on his desktop computer.

Amelia followed him to the doors, where they stopped short to let an elderly woman through ahead of them. "Happy Easter,

Pastor Sheffield," the woman said as she reached out to pat his arm.

"Happy Easter to you, too, Mrs. Sawyer."

"And who is this?" she said, reaching out a wrinkled hand to Amelia.

Amelia shook the offered hand with a small smile. "I'm Amelia, Marcus's wife."

"Oh!" Mrs. Sawyer's face lit up. "It's lovely to meet you, dear. Just lovely. I don't know how I've missed you all these last weeks since you all moved here." Marcus was about to explain just how that had happened when Mrs. Sawyer gave a little cluck of her tongue and said, "And congratulations on the baby, dear. How exciting that must be."

Marcus let out a surprised laugh, but it died in his throat when he saw how the color had drained from Amelia's face. "Oh, Mrs. Sawyer, I'm sorry ... but ... she's not pregnant." He expected Amelia to add an emphatic response of her own, but she looked stricken.

He also expected Mrs. Sawyer to apologize for her mistake, but instead she shook a finger at them and chuckled. "I was a midwife for forty years. I know a pregnant woman when I see one." She patted Amelia's arm, then cocked her head and said with a measure of authority, "It's a good thing, dear. Trust me."

With that, she walked out the door, leaving Marcus and Amelia alone in the foyer. "Amelia?" He didn't know what else to say.

She swallowed hard. "It's true." Her lip quivered as she turned to look at him with eyes bright with tears. "Marcus, I'm pregnant."

Amelia could tell Marcus was reining in his excitement because of her own obvious grief.

"You're positive?"

"Yes."

"When—"

"At the doctor's office on Wednesday."

His face fell. "You've known this long and haven't told me?"

This was the part she'd been struggling with, and this moment was what she'd been dreading. "I … I couldn't."

"Why not?"

"Because." She lowered her eyes, unwilling to see his expression. She dropped her voice to a whisper. "Because I wasn't sure I was going to keep it."

The silence was agonizing. Her gaze was glued to the worn carpet as she waited for Marcus to unleash his anger. When his arms came around her the grace was too much to bear. She began to cry.

"No wonder," Marcus said.

Amelia sniffed. "What?"

"Just … the last few days. The crying, the distractedness … I knew something was going on." He took a deep breath and let it out slowly. "I never would have guessed it was this, though."

He took her hand and helped her up and out to the car. She was grateful he didn't grill her for more information while they were still at the church. They drove home the same way they'd driven to church that morning—in silence—but this time it was more open, more companionable. He was right, as always. She should have told him sooner.

When they got home, Marcus brought her a glass of water and joined her on the couch. "So," he said, sounding uncertain. "When are you due?"

"Early Octoberish."

"So you're ..."

"About three and a half months."

"Wow."

"Tell me about it."

"I always figured it was going to take a lot of medical intervention for us to get pregnant."

"Me, too."

"Guess God had different plans." A giant smile spread across Marcus's face as he ran his hands through his hair and linked them at the back of his head. "Holy cow. We're gonna have a baby."

The words were arrows in her heart. "I'm still not sure."

The smile dissolved into a puzzled look. "Sure of what?"

Why was he making her say it again? It had been hard enough to admit the first time. "Whether or not I ... I want to."

He looked blank. "Want to what?"

"Want to keep it."

His arms dropped. "What? You can't be serious." His eyes narrowed. "Wait a minute. Is it ... someone else's?"

She clutched a hand to her chest. "No! No, Marcus, it's definitely yours."

He visibly relaxed, though a guarded look still clouded his face. "I thought ... given what you said this morning ..."

She groaned. "No. I ... no." She shook her head emphatically.

"All right," he said, "but then what reason would you have to not want the baby?"

She set the glass of water on the table so hard its contents sloshed over the sides. "Do you really not know me well enough to know how I must feel about this? About how devastating this is for me?"

"I know you didn't want kids this soon, but I always figured once you were actually pregnant you'd feel differently about it."

"Well, I don't." She stood and paced as agitation ramped up her anxiety. "This depression has set me back enough already. I've lost my job. I've lost the small amount of time I had to build up enough money to move once Jill and Dane had the baby. I've flaked out on what few connections I made in LA that could have gotten me better work. And now a baby? There goes my chance of a career. " She threw her arms out in an all-encompassing surrender. "So there it goes. No more career. All that money, all that time spent over the years—totally pointless. Instead I get to sit around at home in Nebraska with a baby I have no idea what to do with and have play-dates with women who probably went straight to the altar after high school graduation and never had aspirations beyond the borders of this crummy little town."

"Hey!" Marcus's tone was sharp. She hadn't heard that from him before. "If you're talking about the women who were kind enough to reach out to you at church today, then you really need to just stop. I don't know where this condescending attitude is coming from, but the people here are just as intelligent and accomplished as people are in LA. Choosing to live in Wheatridge doesn't mean they're stupid, or incapable of doing better. Just because it's not what you would choose doesn't mean it's a lesser choice. But that's all completely beside the point."

Marcus stood, but his arms were crossed and his stance told her to prepare to be schooled. "The bottom line is that it's not your decision what to do with this baby. It's ours. Because regardless of whether or not you want there to be, there is still an us. You still have a husband, and as your husband I am going to defend the life of the child that is just as much mine as it is yours. And come to think of it, even *that* isn't the bottom line. The bottom line is that you've stopped trusting God. You don't trust Him to lead you. You don't trust Him to have a plan for your life that you'd actually love. You seem to think your future success rests solely on your own efforts. What happened to you? What happened to your faith?"

It wasn't a rhetorical question, and she knew it. The force of his words had driven the fight out of her. She leaned against the wall that her pacing had brought her to and shrugged. "I don't know. Honestly, I don't think I ever had any."

"I don't believe that."

"I don't know what else to say."

Marcus ran a hand over his face. "So now what?"

"I don't know."

"Please tell me that you won't get an abortion."

She knew that everything he had said was right. This was as much his baby as hers. Especially now that he knew about it, there was no way she could ever live with herself if she had terminated his child's life. "I won't," she finally said.

"Well, thank God for that." He collapsed on the couch and pinched the bridge of his nose. "Okay. One thing at a time." He looked at her, and the sadness in his eyes wrenched her insides. "Do you still want me?"

It wasn't the question she'd expected. "Wh-what?"

"Do you still want me? To be married to me?"

"Of course—"

"No, not 'of course.' You've made it clear you want to go back to LA as soon as you possibly can. I was miserable without you. I couldn't wait for us to be together again. And if you felt like I felt, then you wouldn't be so eager to leave again. So what seems obvious to me is that you … you don't love me."

She began to panic. "No, Marcus—I do, I swear I do."

"Then how can you even think about leaving again?"

Her mother's words came back to her, along with her mother's pain, her mother's lost years, her mother's compromises. Hadn't Amelia always vowed not to make the same mistakes? Hadn't she promised herself she'd never let anything get in the way of achieving her dreams?

Then why did she get married?

Because she loved Marcus, pure and simple. She loved his stability and his intelligence and his balanced demeanor. He gave her things she'd gone without when growing up, and her life was better with him in it. And because she'd loved him, she'd made a promise to him—and to God, though right now that promise didn't mean as much, since she wasn't entirely sure what she thought about Him anymore. But her promise to Marcus, her love for him and his for her—those mattered. Still, she knew that they also put her at a fork in the road. Would she forever hate herself for giving up her career for her man, like her mother had done? Or would she forever hate herself for giving up a man who loved her this much, even when she acted so selfishly?

In the light of the child they'd created together, even though they hadn't meant to, she knew with a clarity she hadn't felt in months what her answer needed to be.

"I won't leave."

Marcus blinked, as though seeing her more clearly would help her words to sink in. "You won't?"

"No." A cavernous ache opened in her soul as she felt herself give up the last vestige of hope for success that she'd clung to. "I won't."

Marcus was up off the couch and wrapping his arms around her faster than seemed possible. And even though she felt numb, she couldn't help hoping he was right when he whispered, "It will all be better than you think."

CHAPTER 9

Marcus had a fine line to walk, now that he knew about the baby. He had to balance his euphoria with his consideration for how much Amelia was struggling with this new turn their lives had taken. He tried not to bring up the pregnancy or birth too often, and when he did it was with as much tact and care as he could. But when he was alone, or on the phone with Dane or talking with Ed, he let his true emotions out. He was going to be a dad, and he was thrilled.

A few days later, Amelia gave Marcus permission to tell his family. His mother's reaction was exactly what he'd been expecting: She gushed over the idea of another grandbaby, and offered to come when the baby was born since Amelia's own mother was gone. "What a year it's been since you graduated," she said with a laugh. "New wife, new job, new home, new baby. What amazing blessings God's giving you. How is Amelia doing?"

"She had some morning sickness, but it's gone now. She's doing great." He wasn't about to tell her about the antidepressants, or about how much she didn't want to be pregnant in the first place. That wasn't the kind of thing his parents needed to know.

He appreciated his mother's enthusiasm, and hoped his father would have some as well. He wasn't home when Marcus called, of course, and the childhood rule about not calling him at work unless there was an emergency was still burned into his brain, so he emailed him with the news instead.

Great news, Dad: Amelia's pregnant! She's due sometime in October. It's a total miracle—we really never thought this would happen naturally. Obviously God is to thank, eh? I know how much you love Eddie's and John's kids—it'll be fun having more of them to be proud of, won't it? Isn't it fantastic?

He'd achieved the trifecta: accomplished wife, esteemed job, and a child. This had to be it, what his father had been hoping for his youngest son. Marcus sent the email and waited eagerly for the response.

He was working on his sermon before lunch when his computer chimed the arrival of an email. He clicked over immediately, and smiled. His father had written back.

Marcus,

Congratulations. I hope Amelia is well. Have you discussed how many children you'll have? You need to do that sooner, rather than later. When a couple is not in agreement on that, or have not discussed it thoroughly, there can be unfortunate results. Children are expensive and require a great deal of time and attention. It has always been my belief that two is plenty for any family; anything more than that is a burden, especially on a ministry income. God's work is of the utmost importance, and anything that detracts from that should not be tolerated. I'm sure you're discovering this in your own life, given your new job. Tell Amelia we are happy for the both of you and look forward to meeting our new grandchild.

—Randall

Marcus had to read the email twice—he was sure he'd missed something that explained where this diatribe was coming from. Instead, the words finally sank in and dissolved the film of neediness through which he'd viewed his father all these years. For the first time he saw with crystal clarity how his father truly viewed him, and finally their relationship made sense.

His father hadn't wanted him.

He picked up the phone and called his mother. "Mom, was I an accident?" He didn't care how abrupt it sounded. At this point, he had a pretty good idea that his mother would know exactly what he meant.

The pause before she spoke confirmed his fears. "Accident is a terrible word for it, Marcus," she said in a weary voice.

"That's how Dad sees it, though, right?"

"Oh, sweetheart. What did he say to you?"

Marcus read the email to her, wishing he could hold out just a sliver of hope that he'd misinterpreted the entire thing. But the meaning was clear, he knew. Now he just wanted to find out what had happened.

"Money was always tight," she finally said, "and I had a hard time balancing my volunteer time at church with taking care of your brothers. Your father said we were done, but … I wasn't, not in my heart, even with all that was going on. And I prayed God would make me content with just John and Eddie, but He didn't. Your father wanted me to get my tubes tied, so I told God I was willing to have another baby, even if your father wasn't, but that I didn't want to argue with him over the procedure, and that God should just get me pregnant before I had it done if He really wanted us to have another baby." She sighed, but it sounded like a happy one. "Lo and behold, a month later I was pregnant with you."

Knowing the backstory didn't make it any easier to handle. "So he just … what, decided to write me off entirely?"

"Your father is a complicated man, Marcus. Sometimes it's difficult to understand his motives." It was the closest thing to criticism he'd ever heard his mother utter against his father. "It's always hurt me to see how he treats you, and to see how hard you've tried to win his affection without success. I wish I could have fixed it for you somehow, but a boy's relationship with his father—it's so different than with his mother. I know my praise has never meant as much as the same words would mean from him. But please know that I did my best to make up for the lack of them."

He appreciated her words, but just like she said, they did nothing to soothe his wounds. "Thanks, Mom," he managed. They said good-bye, and Marcus hung up the phone and stared again at the email on his screen. No wonder the harder he strove for his father's attention the harder his father pushed back. Who wants someone they don't love hounding them all the time?

He felt foolish. Angry. Embarrassed. Why couldn't he have figured this out on his own? How could he have been so blind? The signs were right there.

He wondered if his brothers knew. He hoped not. The thought made him ill.

Marcus shut down his computer and locked the door behind him as he left his office without his work. "I need to, um, leave early," he told the secretary.

"You have a four o'clock with Pastor Cort from Wheatridge Baptist. Shall I reschedule?"

"Yes. Thanks. Tomorrow's appointments, too; I'm not sure if I'll be in."

He walked halfway to his car, intending to pull out his spare outfit for jogging so he could hit the streets like he always did when he was stressed, but then stopped. He didn't want to jog. Not just right now—he wanted to give up the hobby entirely. He'd only started because his father valued his brothers' athleticism, and it was the only thing he could do remotely well in the sports arena. He didn't know what else to do, though, so he stood for a moment in the parking lot as though he'd lost the car that sat less than twenty feet away. How else could he preoccupy himself while he processed? Nothing came to mind. At a loss for other options, he set out for the sidewalk at a comfortable pace.

The pleasant spring day was at total odds with the tumult in his mind and soul. Everything he'd done since he was five years old had been for naught. It had never mattered what he did, how hard he tried; his father would never give Marcus the affirmation he needed. But now that he knew that, he found himself in a life that was driven, if he was going to be truly honest, by pointless ambition. Why else had he gone to seminary? Or taken the job that pulled him from his wife? Nearly everything he had done was in question. Nothing mattered now as it once had.

Which parts of his life had he actually wanted, and which parts had he chosen just to please his father?

One realization after another burst through his thoughts. He'd never questioned Christianity, but had accepted it as truth because his father said it was so. What if it wasn't? He'd never prayed that God would show him what to do with his life—he'd simply assumed that God would want him in ministry. Why wouldn't He? Wasn't ministry the highest calling, the most important thing a person could do with his life? But—what if it wasn't? What if there was something else he could—should—have done, something he could have done better, would have enjoyed more? What if he'd been meant to marry someone else, live somewhere else …?

Marcus walked, head down, through the oak-lined residential streets of Wheatridge for two hours. When his stomach rumbled for the lunch he'd missed, he turned back toward the church and forced himself to shelve the emotions that were churning. Regardless of whether he was meant to be or not, he was a pastor now, and he had a job to do. A breakdown would have to wait for later.

❁

Amelia picked at the spaghetti she'd made for dinner and tried to watch Marcus without him feeling her stare. Something was wrong. The last three days he'd been quiet, and Marcus was never quiet, not like that. No joking, no animation in his gestures … He looked the way Amelia had felt when her depression had first started. The fact that he'd quit tutoring the college students didn't bode well, either. Marcus wasn't the kind of guy who liked a lot of downtime.

Her own depression had been getting better over the last couple weeks, despite learning about the baby. Contrary to what she'd told

Marcus, she hadn't started taking the antidepressant yet, because she'd wanted to see if the slow but steady improvement she'd noticed right before she'd moved would continue on its own. Sure, she still had angry thoughts, and still felt sad, but nothing like she felt in LA. But she wasn't ready for Marcus to have the same problems. She was still trying to figure out how to take care of herself and keep her mood on an upward swing. She couldn't handle Marcus being depressed too.

What isn't he telling me? Marcus was a talker, a sharer. The fact that he wasn't sharing now must mean she was the source of his stress. Why else wouldn't he do what he always did: process aloud, bounce things off her, ask for her insight?

But what had she done?

Unfortunately, once she asked herself that question the possible answers came in hordes. He was turned off by her because she was pregnant. He no longer wanted the baby either. He was angry at her for not being more excited about the baby. He was mad at himself for insisting she move out to Nebraska. He was angry at her for being depressed. There really was something going on with Karis.

Honestly, she hoped it had something to do with her, rather than the baby or Karis. It was only his enthusiasm for the pregnancy that kept her from truly resenting it. Without his support and excitement, she'd never make it to October.

She shook her head as her thoughts became more jumbled and twisted, trying to dislodge them so they didn't start taking deeper root. She couldn't afford to add that negativity to the stockpile she already had.

And that meant she was back to square one. She had to be here in Wheatridge. And she had to figure out how to make Marcus glad that she was.

She analyzed the past two weeks since she'd arrived. What had she done, other than sleep, eat, and sit around? Nothing. *No wonder he's angry.*

She had to make some changes. She had to show Marcus she really did want to be with him, that she did love him, that she wasn't going to be a total drain on him. She had to keep the depression from worsening again—and sitting around moping was not the way to do it. She needed to start living a real life here in Wheatridge.

"I was thinking about looking for a job," she blurted over a forkful of pasta. She hadn't, really, but now that she said it, she knew she should.

He looked up at her, confusion on his face. "Huh?"

"I'm going to look for a job."

"Oh—that's great."

"Yeah. I thought, um ... maybe I can look into teaching lessons at Blue Note, like you suggested, and maybe subbing in the schools. I could stop subbing when the baby comes and just take a little break from lessons."

"Sure. Sounds good."

"And ... I think I still have that bulletin from Easter, with those women's info on it. Maybe I'll give them a call."

"Great."

Why were his responses so apathetic? Maybe because he had no reason to believe her. She cut the conversation off, already feeling overwhelmed by what she'd claimed to be planning, and decided to apply herself to those initial steps and see how they went. Maybe once he saw she was following through he'd be more enthusiastic.

The next morning, Amelia showered and dressed with more care than usual, then set out for Blue Note at a slow pace that accommodated a body that had grown unused to exercise. By the time she reached the shop, her legs and back ached, but mentally she felt better than she had in a long time. The manager gave her an application to teach piano, which she filled out on the spot. He assured her they were in fact looking for piano teachers and promised she'd at least get an interview. The news made her feel better than she'd expected. In fact, if she felt like being liberal with the definition, she might even say it made her feel happy.

She was on her way out when the sight of the baby grand that sat in the front window arrested her. She hadn't touched her keyboard since moving, and how long had it been since she'd played on the real deal? She went back to the manager, feeling uncharacteristically shy. "I was wondering ... would you mind if I played on the baby grand for a minute?"

"Sure, help yourself," he said. "I'd like to hear you play."

"It's been a while," she said quickly. "I just moved and haven't had the chance to practice in a while."

"Don't worry," he said with a smile. "I won't count it as an audition."

She sat down on the quilted bench and ran her hands over the keys. She wasn't really dying to play; it was more a feeling of not wanting to miss what was usually a rare opportunity. She played a couple chords, reacquainting herself with the feel of real keys, then began to play Mozart's *Piano Sonata no. 15 in C.* Her fingers fumbled a bit here and there, and she played more slowly than the proper tempo, but just as with riding a bicycle, muscle memory carried her through the song with relative ease despite not having played it in over a year. Satisfied with the impromptu performance, she started in on Kirby's "Dance of the Antilles," a piece she hadn't played nearly as much as Mozart's but which she had greatly enjoyed during the short time she'd worked on it. It felt good to be playing again, even though her fingers were awkward and her speed was gone. At least she knew what she had to work on before she auditioned for teaching lessons.

She stopped at the coffee shop next, just to relax before she walked back to the apartment. She felt bad spending money on herself—she didn't deserve it after being so lazy and dependent on Marcus—but she had forgotten her water bottle at home and knew she had to stay hydrated for the baby's sake, if not her own. She purchased a bottled water and sat by the window, taking in the shops along the street that she hadn't yet paid much attention to.

After a few minutes, she was vaguely aware that someone was watching her. She glanced to the side and saw one of the women she'd met at church—what was her name?

The woman snapped her fingers and smiled. "I thought that was you. Amelia, right?"

Amelia smiled, embarrassed. "Um, yes, hi—but I'm afraid I don't remember your name."

"Holly," she said, standing and shifting her chair over to Amelia's table. "The others were Lauren and Connie. In fact, they should be here—we do this every week—but Lauren's daughter has chicken pox and Connie is volunteering at some activity day at her sons' school. But since I'm a creature of habit I thought I'd come anyway. I'm glad I did." Her smile was genuine, and even though her look was stuck in the '90s, Amelia had to admit she was friendly. She remembered Marcus's indictment against her for being judgmental toward the people of Wheatridge, and she vowed not to let her California sensibilities stand in the way of getting to know people who might make life in this little town more bearable.

It had been a while since Amelia had tried to make new friends, but Holly made it easy. She was chatty enough to keep the conversation going but didn't dominate it. And she blew away Amelia's presuppositions about small-town people. Not only had she grown up in a city (well—in Lincoln), but she'd traveled abroad in college and graduated with a double major. She'd met her husband in college and they decided together to move to Wheatridge when they wanted to start having children. "We were living in Omaha before this, and sometimes I miss city stuff—the restaurants, the entertainment— but I love the pace of life here and how friendly people are." She'd motioned to Amelia with her iced mocha. "What about you? What do you think of Wheatridge so far?"

Amelia aimed for diplomacy and hoped she'd hit the target. "It's not where I expected to end up," she said, choosing her words carefully. "I have to be honest and say I miss LA. But ... I can't complain about the cost of living. And you're right, people are friendly." Friendlier than she'd allowed herself to believe.

They talked for an hour before Holly had to leave to pick up her daughter from preschool. "I'm so glad we met up," she said as she shouldered a clunky faux-leather purse. "Now you know when and where we meet; please just come join us whenever you want."

"I will," Amelia said. She was drained from the interaction, but pleased that she'd been able to handle it at all. "Thanks for the invitation. You all seem really nice."

Holly chuckled. "Thanks. I think we are. And you're sweet too. I think you'll fit right in." She waved and left, and Amelia headed for home.

As the week progressed, Amelia found herself feeling better and better. Her energy returned, her thoughts cleared, and for the first time she finally felt excited about the baby. She met Holly and the others at the coffee shop the next week, applied to substitute teach at the schools, and auditioned for—and was offered—the position at the Blue Note. She finally called Jill and caught her up on everything that had happened since she'd moved. And when she went to church with Marcus, she socialized, remembered people's names, and did what she could to make Marcus proud to have her there.

Unfortunately, none of it seemed to have any effect on Marcus at all.

She was agitated at his lack of reaction. Didn't he see how hard she was trying? Heck, not just trying—didn't he see how she was succeeding? Getting jobs, finding friends—what else did he want from her? She wanted to lay it all out for him, outline exactly how much she had improved and demand that he give her some recognition, but her pride stopped her from being so bold. Besides, it wouldn't mean as much as him actually noticing. Usually he was a lot better about that sort of thing.

Usually he was a lot better about sharing what was on his mind, too. So the fact that he was obviously troubled but unwilling to share why when she had asked him—he had given the passive "nothing" and changed the subject—fueled her imagination and sent it in all sorts of frightening directions.

Her thoughts grew more and more irritated and angry as the days passed without Marcus showing any recognition of her effort or revealing why he was upset. Her mind began to race as it had when she'd been depressed, except now her thoughts birthed an electric-like current that kept her body humming day and night. She stopped sleeping again, this time because she couldn't settle down enough. She stopped eating again too, mostly because she was so busy with other things she just didn't think to. When she did eat, it was in huge quantities that made up for lost time and left her feeling sick.

She started trying to pick fights with Marcus, just to get him to engage. He shrugged her off most of the time, but twice he fought back, and the sparks flew like fireworks. Amelia slammed doors and Marcus yelled; the next day they received a letter of reprimand from the management saying complaints had been filed for the noise, and Marcus went back to being sullen.

Amelia started staying out of the house when he was home. First she spent her time at Blue Note, where she played the baby grand for hours on end. Then she started taking the car to the mall once Marcus had come home from work, both because it was too far to walk and because she knew it stranded him at the apartment, and after how petulant he'd been acting, she spitefully enjoyed the thought of him wallowing alone. Whether or not he was willing to open up to her, which she had requested of him more than once, she was going to make progress.

On one such trip to the mall, she had been drawn to the baby store, and in the end spent hundreds of dollars on gear and clothes, despite not knowing the baby's gender. Two employees hauled the purchases to her car and packed them into the trunk and backseat, and the look on Marcus's face was priceless when he saw her dragging two giant bags behind her as she entered the apartment.

Unfortunately, as her energy spurt continued on into its second week, Amelia's irritation began to spread from Marcus to other areas of her life. She had a craving for sushi and nowhere to go, and it renewed her distaste for Wheatridge with a passion. Holly and the others annoyed her with their lack of culture and small-town mind-sets. Their clothes were lame, their lives were boring, and their conversation dull. They couldn't keep up with Amelia's intelligence. She couldn't help rolling her eyes at them, and started skipping out of their meetings after just half an hour.

And the church. That stupid, backward church. The only thing they had going for them was Marcus. She hated to admit it, since she was always so annoyed when he turned on the preacher mode when talking to her, but the man really could teach. Seeing the congregation in rapt attention when he paced the platform and exposited a passage always awoke a burst of pride in her. And even though it meant having to wait even longer to get home, she was pleased to see how many people stopped on their way out to compliment him on his sermons.

But for Pete's sake, when were they ever going to step into the twenty-first century and get some new music? Their love of the arcane made Amelia writhe in boredom as the uninspired choir sang all four verses of "More Love to Thee, O Christ." Amelia longed to push the pianist off his bench and introduce them to the Hillsong catalog. Their ministry offerings were equally lacking. There was a monthly tea for the ladies, a monthly coffee morning for the men, and a weekly youth ministry meeting that, as best as she could tell, consisted of playing ridiculous games and then memorizing Scripture. Marcus kept trying to start other ministries, but no one seemed to care. No wonder the little congregation was dying out.

As the days passed, Amelia's emotions began to take a turn south. Her frustration with the women made her lament that she would never find any real friends in Wheatridge. Her impulse purchases from the baby store sat unsorted on the floor of the living room; neither she nor Marcus were motivated to do anything with them, and their presence reminded Amelia every day of the impending birth she wasn't ready for. She had more flashbacks of her childhood relationship with her mother and began to truly fear the idea of raising a child. She was in no way prepared for it, in no way equipped. People like her shouldn't be allowed to have babies in the first place.

She could sense where things were going. The reprieve had been short-lived, and despite her best efforts to keep it at bay, the depression was returning.

Amelia vacillated between resigned and terrified. She couldn't do it again. It would kill her this time, she was sure. But who cared? And what about her baby? Wasn't she just dooming another generation to the fate her mother had passed on to her?

The prescription for her antidepressant still sat in her purse. She knew she should go get it filled, but now that she actually knew people here, she was paranoid someone would see her and ask what was wrong, or that the pharmacist would end up being a member of

New Hope. But she couldn't ask Marcus to do it—he'd be mad she'd never started them as she was supposed to. She was paralyzed, unable to see past her fear.

Back and forth, back and forth, until Amelia crept once again beneath the bedsheets, praying for sleep that wouldn't come and for peace that eluded her grasp.

※

Marcus had a sermon to deliver in less than seventy-two hours, and he still hadn't started the research. He hadn't been this bad the week before, though he'd been up until two o'clock on Sunday morning finishing his talk. This time he couldn't even decide on a topic.

Doubt consumed his mind, and he didn't know how to pull himself out of his quagmire. He'd been analyzing the last fifteen years of his life, trying to figure out which decisions, if any, had been driven by his own desires and interests. Extracurricular activities? No—he chose those based on what he thought his father would appreciate, or on his father's recommendation. The college he attended? His father's alma mater. His major—the same as his dad's. And now he questioned everything he did: Was that decision truly a reflection of his actual desires, or was it based on his attempts to be who he thought his father wanted him to be? Did he really care about the things he spent his time on, or did he pursue them in the hopes that doing so would finally win his father's love?

And what if he wasn't supposed to be a pastor? What if he'd missed his real calling because he hadn't bothered to listen for God's voice at all? It would explain why he still felt so out of sorts in his job and still didn't enjoy it. But what was he supposed to do—say, "Oops, sorry, my mistake," and leave? He'd prayed passionately for answers, for God to either assure him he was in the right place or tell him no, he wasn't. But God was silent, which fed into a whole host of other insecurities and worries.

There was only one decision he could think of that had been made purely out of his own will: marrying Amelia. Had he followed his father's lead on choosing a wife, he'd have ended up with one of the education majors he'd pursued during his undergrad days. But Amelia had cast all those other women in black and white. They were sweet, earnest, and predictable. Amelia was Technicolor and ... exciting. But more than that, she had been so encouraging, so supportive of him and his endeavors. Not that the other women hadn't been, but theirs had been delivered in a fawning sort of way. He always felt as if they were trying to puff him up so he'd return the favor. Amelia had never sought that kind of recognition; she'd encouraged him enthusiastically and sought to join him in what he was doing. But none of those things ever mattered to her as much as he did. She loved him, pure and simple, not because of what he might someday be, or because of what he did, but because of who he was. He was starting to think marrying her was the only right decision he'd ever made—but then he remembered how things had changed and how at odds they seemed to be lately, and went right back to wondering if their marriage was a mistake too.

He was still too embarrassed and unclear to talk to her about his father. Plus, he worried that his waffling about his choices would not only fuel her desire to return to LA, but would also make her think he hadn't been listening to God after all.

Marcus shut his book and stood. "I'm, um … going for a run," he told Amelia, who was curled on the couch with a book.

She nodded. "See you later then."

He changed clothes, gave her a kiss, and left, feeling guilty. He knew she was worried about him. He still hadn't told her—he couldn't bear to. If moving to Nebraska turned out to be a mistake, he wasn't sure he'd be able to admit it to her, not after the toll it had taken on her and their marriage. And he could tell there was something going on with her, too—he just didn't have the emotional reserves to confront it, which made him feel even more guilty.

Some husband he was turning out to be.

He stretched for a few minutes on the sidewalk outside the complex, then started out at a light jog. He still wasn't sure what he thought about running, but he couldn't deny how it helped clear his head, and that was more important to him right now than determining whether or not it was something he would have done without his father's influence. He focused on his route and his body as he waited to fall into his usual rhythm, and once he was there he released his mind to ponder his predicament.

If being a pastor wasn't the route he was supposed to take, he'd concentrated on it for so long he didn't even know how to begin figuring out what he really *did* want to do with his life. His choices had become a carbon copy of his father's, and without that template he didn't know who he was. He didn't like feeling like a stranger to himself—but as his feet hit the pavement in their steady stride, he realized he was afraid to find out who he really was. What if Amelia didn't love the real Marcus? What if the real Marcus was as rudderless and aimless as he felt these days? What if he had no ambitions, no desires that amounted to anything significant? What if he was only successful when he was following his father's footsteps and not laying down his own?

Marcus rounded the corner a block earlier than he usually did. Any farther and he'd have come across the church, and he didn't want to go anywhere near the place right now. Just the thought of it made him feel like a failure. In three days he'd be in front of the congregation as a fraud. He knew what the Bible had to say about the responsibility teachers had, and how much more strict their judgment would be, especially if they led people astray. How could he teach them truth when he was living a lie?

Hopelessness was not an emotion with which Marcus had any experience, but he was drowning in it now. He hated the sucking dark hole it created in his soul, but he didn't know what to do about it. The optimism and solutions that usually came with a good run down the oak-lined streets of their neighborhood evaded him this time. He increased his speed in desperation, but all it did was give him a stitch in his side.

He came to a stop, hands on his head to pull out the cramp, on the block where he'd found the little cottage house. He could see the For Sale sign in the yard six houses down. When he'd caught his breath, he turned to retrace his steps, not wanting to see yet another symbol of his shattered life. There would be no house buying now, not when he didn't know if he'd still have a job in a month. Or even still be in Wheatridge.

Feeling defeated, Marcus walked home, showered, then pulled the sale flyer for the cottage house from the fridge and stuffed it into the trash. He poured himself some lukewarm coffee and sat heavily in the dining room chair once more. He picked up a concordance and flipped to the index to look up *despair*, then copied down the verses listed. At least now he had a topic for his sermon.

Amelia woke after fitful sleep to another day when she should have been teaching at Blue Note. Instead she'd called in sick the night before, just like she had the night before that, and now instead of getting up, she pulled the sheets over her head and burrowed deeper down. Marcus was already up and, with any luck, already gone. Otherwise he might realize she was awake and try to make her eat something. Her appetite, however, had fled hand in hand with the buoyancy she'd felt the last couple weeks, and not even the knowledge that her baby needed sustenance drove her to the kitchen. She'd read somewhere that a mother's body would sacrifice itself for an unborn child, diverting energy and calories to the baby instead of the mother if there weren't enough for both. She was fine with that.

She'd said nothing to Marcus, but she knew he'd figured out she was depressed again. It explained why he was so quiet, why he wasn't talking to her anymore. Her very presence was an irritation to him; he went on more runs than usual and could barely focus enough to write his sermons. The last two weekends she'd heard him up working in the middle of the night, no doubt trying to catch up on the things he couldn't do when she was around. And his last two sermons, on despair and anger, had obviously been directed at her.

She didn't blame him anymore for not telling her directly how he felt. Marcus was a good man; he wouldn't want to hurt her feelings. That he would try to reach her at all, even if it was through sermons that she may or may not attend, was more kindness than she deserved. She couldn't bring herself to apologize, to talk about it at all—to acknowledge it in front of him felt like failure, and she had enough of that on her plate already. It was a blessing to operate under the guise of normality instead of having to face his disappointment head-on. His silence was painful, but not as painful as his spoken disillusionment with her would be.

The mid-May sunshine striped the bedroom walls through the blinds, but did nothing to make Amelia feel better. In fact, the glaring light served to illuminate how lacking in light she was. *You're pathetic,* the voice in her head told her. *A black hole of need. There's nothing good left in you.*

She'd felt desperation before, but it had never been accompanied by voices this judgmental. She felt twitches of panic in her chest. She was torn between wanting to succumb to the fear in the hopes that it would do her in completely, and wanting to resist it for the sake of her baby. Without thinking about whether or not he could even help, Amelia grabbed her cell off the nightstand and called Marcus at the church.

He answered just before his voice mail picked up. "Hey."

"Hi." Stupid girl. She hadn't even thought about what she'd say.

"Need something?" His voice was terse. Its tension triggered her guilt.

"I … um … I just wanted to …" *To what? Beg you to forgive me? To make this better? To put me out of my misery?*

"I can't really talk right now, Amelia. Can this wait until I get home?"

His tone was so abrupt her words caught in her throat. "I—yes, of course. That's—that's fine."

"All right. 'Bye."

"'Bye." But the line had already gone dead.

The panic kicked up a notch. She looked at the clock. Marcus wouldn't be home for another four hours. How was she going to last?

Something clicked. Marcus wouldn't be home for another four hours. She had four hours left with which to take care of all this herself.

At the thought, the panic died in her chest. The peace she felt almost made her weep. Of course. Why hadn't she done this earlier?

She rolled from the bed and headed for the medicine cabinet. She grabbed the first bottle she found, a rarely used container of Motrin, and took it to the kitchen where she poured herself a tall glass of water. Pausing only to write "I'm sorry. I love you," on a piece of paper and leave it on the kitchen table, she popped the top off the bottle and alternated swallows of pills and water until the bottle was empty.

She left both on the counter and returned to bed. Tears ran down her cheeks, mostly from relief, though she did feel bad about the baby. *Trust me,* she thought to the child in her womb, *it's much better this way. I would have been an awful mother. And you probably would have ended up with the same crazy brain that I have.*

Amelia curled herself around her pillow and closed her eyes. *I wonder how long this will take,* she thought as she felt the tension fleeing her body ahead of the inevitable and welcome end. With any luck she'd fall asleep and die before she woke. The thought was pure bliss.

Sleep had just about set in when her stomach gave a lurch. Her throat spasmed as her body attempted to vomit. *No!* She sat up and barely got her head over the edge of the bed in time to throw up onto the carpet instead of the mattress. She'd barely caught her breath when her throat caught again. She fumbled off the bed, threw up once more, and stumbled toward the bathroom. But that seemed to be the end. Her stomach rolled uneasily, but nothing actually happened.

That's it? she thought, staring at the mess she'd made on the bedroom floor. *That's the worst it can do?*

What a waste.

She rinsed out her mouth and walked on shaky legs into the kitchen, leaving the mess behind to clean up later. There was a host of possibilities there—knives, cleaning supplies, gas oven. Her eyes roamed the room, taking inventory of her options, but she couldn't bring herself to a decision. The last thing she wanted to do was screw it up again. She threw away the note and Motrin bottle, then sat down at the table to think of her next move.

I need to do some research. The thought brought an odd kind of relief as she went to the dining room where Marcus's laptop stood open. Her fingers hesitated over the keyboard for a moment before pecking out "how to kill yourself" in the search engine. An eclectic list appeared, and Amelia began clicking the links to see if any of them were achievable with what she had on hand.

It wasn't long before she was sidetracked by the bizarre and disturbing sites she discovered as she indiscriminately selected links to click. Some were text-based versions of a train wreck she couldn't tear her eyes from. Others were surprisingly well-written and thoughtful, but with an underlying darkness that both fascinated and repulsed. She gave up her goal of researching and let herself be pulled along on a virtual tour of messed-up psyches and desperate individuals as the clock ticked the minutes away. When she checked the time she realized she had less than two hours left before Marcus would be home.

That's all right, she thought as she clicked another link. *I'll get another chance eventually.* She didn't allow herself to examine the sense of comfort that came with the decision. She simply continued to read, tucking all the information away for another empty day.

CHAPTER 10

"I can't really talk right now, Amelia. Can this wait until I get home?" Marcus rubbed a hand over his eyes as Amelia stammered out some kind of affirmative answer. "All right. 'Bye." He snapped his phone shut and dropped it next to the pile of papers he'd amassed on his desk. The stack overwhelmed him, though he prayed they'd give him some insights into what he ought to do next.

He picked up the first set of papers on the pile. After stapling them together, he flipped through the pages, scanning the information for anything that might give him a quick fix. He did the same to the second and third stapled stacks, but uncovered nothing that would save him from the hard work he'd had a hunch he'd have to do. With a sigh, he returned to the first packet, titled "*The Finding Your Dream Job E-Book*" and began to read.

An hour later Marcus dropped the packet on the desk and groaned in frustration. What a waste of time that had been. It wasn't that the information was bad—it was just the wrong information. Despite the immediacy of needing a job, he couldn't expect to figure out what kind of job to take until he had untangled who he really was and what he really wanted. And so far he hadn't found a website or e-book to help with that.

His eye caught the photo of him and Amelia that sat in a frame on the bookshelf. Pangs of guilt shot through him whenever he thought of her. How was he ever going to tell her all of this? He couldn't hide things much longer; if he didn't start talking to someone about everything soon he was going to go crazy.

Enough. He'd done nothing but run circles in his mind—and through town—ever since he'd read that email from his father. Nothing was going to get better unless he confided in Amelia and Dane, maybe even Ed, and started seeking professional help. Amelia needed a therapist too—maybe they could therapist shop together.

Marcus stood, stacked all the stapled packets together and stuffed them into his file cabinet. He'd come back to those later, after he'd done a little more work on the real issues. He pocketed his cell, locked his office, and told his secretary he was leaving early.

The closer he got to home, the more nervous he became. What would Amelia say when she told him? She'd be sympathetic, at least at first—she could relate to having parents who messed with your head. But after her initial empathy played out, what would she think? And what about Ed? He had to tell him eventually. Surely the elder already suspected something was going on—Marcus knew his last few sermons had been sorely lacking in depth and quality. Would he be fired? They'd lose their insurance then. He groaned at the thought of having a baby without insurance. *I wonder how much a home birth is …*

He pulled into the apartment complex's parking lot and sat in the car for a moment, praying for Amelia's response. Then, gathering his courage, he went inside.

Amelia shrieked when he opened the front door. "Sorry, babe," he said, feeling sheepish when he saw the look of surprise on her face.

She slapped his laptop shut and stood. "Why are you home so early?"

"I felt bad for being so short with you earlier. And I wasn't getting much work done anyway."

Her eyes darted toward the bedroom and then back to the laptop as she slowly sat back down again. "I was in the middle of something," she said as she opened the machine and rotated it slightly toward the far wall.

"Um … okay." He shrugged and crossed the room to go change his clothes.

"Wait!"

He stopped and turned. "What?"

"Um … there's a … mess. In there. I was going to clean it but I got distracted."

He waved a hand. "I don't care."

"No, I mean—"

He opened the door and the smell hit him before the sight did. "What the heck? Amelia?"

He heard her muttering under her breath and then the click of his laptop shutting. "I, um … My stomach was a little upset …"

"A little?" He scratched his neck, looking from the small piles on the carpet to his wife who now stood beside him, her face red. "Are you sure you're all right?"

"Yeah, I'm fine."

Marcus moved past her to the kitchen and pulled out the cleaning supplies. "Go relax, I'll take care of this."

"No, I'll do it."

"No, really, it's all right." He kissed her cheek. "You should have told me you weren't feeling well when you called; I would have come home sooner."

She said nothing as she turned and went back to the dining room. Baffled, Marcus knelt to work on the carpet, hoping no permanent damage had been done. With rubber gloves on and a roll of paper towel in hand, he began to clean, noticing after a few minutes the small white lumps, smaller than peas, that littered the stains. *What the heck are those?*

Once finished, Marcus returned to Amelia's side. "So, what happened? Did you eat something … weird?"

She shrugged as she stood, having once more shut the laptop when he'd come out of the bedroom. "No, nothing weird." She nodded to the living room. "I'm going to go, um, sit."

He walked her to the couch and sat beside her, troubled by how guarded she was being. Aside from the minute he'd walked in the door, she hadn't looked him in the eyes yet, and she seemed off somehow. He got the sense she was hiding something. *Aren't we all?*

He decided not to push, trusting she'd open up when she was ready. For now, he'd just try to mend things between them as best he could without going into any details. He had a feeling this wouldn't be a good time to tell her his own secret. "Hey, I'm sorry about earlier—when you called. Now that I know you were getting sick, I feel really bad." He stopped, forced himself to tell the truth. "Honestly, I felt bad before I knew you were sick. I'm sorry I haven't been very … attentive … lately. I've just been really preoccupied."

She looked at him with surprise in her eyes. She opened her mouth, shut it, and then with trepidation in her voice, asked, "With what?"

"Well … long story. We'll talk about it later. I just wanted to apologize and tell you that I'm going to try to be better for you. Okay?"

"Is—is it me?"

He frowned. "Is what you?"

"Whatever it is you don't want to talk about right now. Is it about me?"

He shook his head, guilt flooding his heart. "No, babe. No, it's totally not you. And I'm so sorry if I've done anything to make you think it is."

She didn't look that relieved as she pulled invisible lint from her shirt hem. "I wouldn't have been surprised if it was. I know I've been awful lately."

"You? No you haven't."

She looked at him, bewildered. "I haven't?"

"No, babe, not at all." He kissed her forehead, trying not to let his nose wrinkle from the smell that still clung to her. "You've been great, like always. Trust me, it's not you."

The side of her mouth twitched in a half smile, but it didn't make him feel any better. What kind of a husband was he? How could he be so self-centered that he didn't even realize Amelia was blaming herself for his moodiness?

He stood. "I'm going to go make myself some dinner." He went to the kitchen and stood in front of the open fridge, looking for something easy to make. But in reality he didn't have an appetite anymore. He was too preoccupied with how bad he felt. The list of things he needed to fix in his life just kept getting longer.

He shut the fridge and went instead to his laptop on the dining room table. It was definitely time to find a therapist.

Amelia didn't think she'd ever feel like more of a failure than her mother was. But at least her mother had been able to off herself properly.

She'd waited all night for Marcus to put two and two together and figure out what she'd tried to do. The anticipation of it was maddening. Every time he spoke her whole body tensed, waiting for the accusation. But bedtime rolled around without him saying anything about it, and she breathed a sigh of relief as she pulled the sheets over her head and tried to fall asleep.

Of course, sleep was impossible. The voice of shame was louder than ever, and she was too busy trying to figure out what to try next. She'd always thought a bottle of any kind of medicine was enough to do someone in, but now she knew the truth. She didn't have it in her to research anymore, but she had to come up with a different plan, one that would work the first time. She couldn't afford to screw it up again.

Marcus came to bed after a while, and Amelia faked sleeping so she wouldn't have to talk. She evened her breathing and tried to send out sleeping vibes as Marcus got comfortable and turned on his lamp to read. But after a few minutes she heard him whispering. At first she thought he was talking to her, but then his words became clearer, and she realized he was praying.

"I don't know what to do, God. I'm so overwhelmed. Please show me what to do to fix all this."

Fix what? Why is he so overwhelmed? She couldn't help rolling her eyes. How bad could his life possibly be? He had the job he'd always wanted. He wasn't losing his mind. He didn't want to kill himself. He didn't have the crazymaking genes that she did.

After a few minutes of aimless thinking, she came to another question. When was the last time she'd prayed? When was the last time she'd given God any thought at all? She honestly couldn't remember. Even at church when Marcus spoke, as much as she tried to be a good wife and listen, she was too easily distracted. It was like listening to a lecture on some foreign culture's mythology. It had no meaning to her, no bearing on her situation. The more she thought about it, the more she realized that's how it had always been with her.

She wasn't bothered by the realization. God didn't seem to be doing much good for Marcus, and if a pastor couldn't get help from Him, what chance did she have? It was probably all phony anyway. Just another way for people to try to make sense of their world when it was spinning out of control. Amelia didn't care to find rhyme or reason for things anymore. She just wanted to get off the ride.

The next day Amelia called in sick again for her piano lessons and stayed in bed as long as she could without rousing Marcus's suspicion. The pregnancy was proving to be a handy excuse for such times. All she had to say was how tired she was when she didn't feel like getting out of bed, or how her stomach was feeling off when Marcus tried to get her to eat and she had no appetite. When she felt she'd reached her daily limit of justification, she'd relocate to the living room with a book and have some tea and a few crackers to keep Marcus happy.

That's what she'd just done, a few minutes before noon. Marcus had stayed home, concerned that she might relapse, and was working at the dining room table on that weekend's sermon. Supposedly, anyway. She could tell he wasn't getting anything done. He spent more time staring out the window, or at his laptop screen even though he wasn't typing or using the trackpad. The look on his face was more foul than she'd ever seen on him before. She wondered what it was that had him so tense.

He came out of what seemed like a trance and looked around at the books on the table. Out of nowhere he slammed one book shut after another, then his laptop, then made a growl that startled Amelia even though she'd been watching him the whole time. She twitched in her seat with surprise, and Marcus caught the movement and was instantly contrite. "I'm sorry. I'm just ... incredibly frustrated right now."

"That's okay."

He ground a fist into the palm of his other hand and muttered, "Sometimes I just want to kill myself."

Amelia let out a snort. "Whatever you do, don't try Motrin."

The words were out before she could stop them. She tried to play it cool but had no idea if her expression was one of disinterested boredom, as she was aiming for, or of the sheer terror she felt inside.

Marcus cocked his head and gave her a look that was more penetrating than usual. "Why do you say that?"

She could see the wheels turning. "I read it, in *Cosmo*. An article on, um, people who tried to kill themselves. That always stuck in my head because, you know, it seems like something that would work, right? People are always OD'ing on painkillers like that." Her mouth was moving without much input from her brain, and she didn't know what would be worse: to keep going, or to stop. *Change the subject!* "Anyway, you shouldn't be saying things like that, Marcus."

He rubbed his eyes with the heels of his hands. "You're right. I shouldn't have said that. I'm just … There's a lot on my mind."

"Like what?" Maybe now she'd get some answers.

He opened his mouth, then shut it with a shake of his head. "Long story. I don't want to burden you with it. Just some stuff I have to deal with." He paused, as though rethinking what he'd said, then gave a slight shake of his head and left for the kitchen. Amelia's shoulders slumped. She thought she'd finally get some answers. Though the longer he went without telling her, the less she wanted to know. If he'd waited this long, it must be pretty bad, and she had her fill of things to worry about.

The next day Marcus had a meeting with the elders. As soon as he'd left the house she went to the medicine cabinet to see what else she had to work with.

It was virtually empty.

Amelia frowned as she stared at the bottle of mouthwash and the tube of toothpaste, the only two ingestible items in the cabinet. There had been more in here the other day. Nail polish remover. Rubbing alcohol. Hydrogen peroxide. Where had they gone?

She went to the kitchen and opened the cabinet where they kept their cleaning supplies. She hadn't tried them first because they usually bought all-natural cleaners and Amelia figured they wouldn't do much harm. But now, with her other options gone, she was desperate. But the cleaning supplies were missing as well.

She went back to the bedroom, thinking Marcus had left them all in there after cleaning her mess. But they weren't there. A thorough and frantic search of the apartment revealed that anything remotely dangerous had been removed. Even the knives were missing.

Marcus was on to her.

She was embarrassed. And furious. How dare he treat her like some child who couldn't be trusted. It was her life, her body—she should be allowed to do whatever she wanted with both.

She went back to the bathroom and pulled out the mouthwash. It was a large bottle, but less than two-thirds full. She glanced at the ingredients, but they didn't tell her enough. She took the bottle to the dining room table, opened the Internet browser, and typed "can you overdose on mouthwash" into the search engine. It took longer than she'd expected to find an answer, but once she found a forum where people were trading stories of loved ones who had died using it, she knew she was at least on the right track.

She looked at the bottle again. Was it enough? She didn't have the energy—or the time, since Marcus was coming back after the meeting—to go downtown and buy something else. And with Marcus obviously on to her, her opportunities would be few and far between now. And it would take forever to wait for them to finish the mouthwash and buy a new bottle.

Amelia returned to the bedroom and uncapped the bottle. The minty smell made her eyes water as she brought the bottle closer to her face. She held her nose and began to drink. It took a few minutes to get the entire bottle down, but once she did, the calm she'd felt after downing the Motrin returned, even though her gut was churning. She felt it in her bones—this was going to work.

The elder meeting was over, and Marcus couldn't get out of the church fast enough. He'd felt like a fraud giving input to their discussions, but until he had a chance to talk to Ed, he had to keep up the illusion that he still belonged there. He'd almost called the elder a handful of times, but every time he picked up the phone he chickened out. He didn't know how to talk about his struggles without setting himself up to be fired, and he couldn't afford to lose his job, not with the baby coming. But it was going to be a long five months playing this game.

Marcus was almost to his car when he heard Ed call his name. He winced, stopped, and turned to see him crossing the parking lot. This was not good timing. He was anxious to get home, knowing now what Amelia was capable of. The lengths he'd gone to that morning while she slept were probably enough, though he hadn't had time to double-check his efforts, and he still wasn't about to leave her alone any longer than he had to. He waited until Ed had caught up with him, then said apologetically, "I can't really stay, Ed, I need to get home."

"I won't keep you long, Marcus. I just wanted to make sure you're okay."

"Um ... make sure I'm okay?"

Ed gave him a look. "I'm concerned about you."

Marcus glanced over his shoulder in the direction of the apartment, then back at Ed, arms crossed. "Oh?"

"Forgive my boldness, but ... you haven't quite been yourself these last couple weeks. I know I don't know you well, but I'm usually a pretty good judge of these things."

Marcus ran a hand through his hair, torn between spilling his guts before he lost his courage and glossing over things so he could get home. "You're right," he said, trying to walk a middle ground. "There's a lot going on with me right now, I admit that. Right now isn't the best time to talk about it, though—I need to get home to Amelia."

Ed frowned. "Is she all right?"

"Um … Yes, she's fine. Just … struggling still, with the adjustment."

Ed nodded. "I understand. But listen, Marcus, I hope you know you can talk to me about anything. I'm a good confidant. And just because you're the senior pastor doesn't mean you don't need a listening ear or some guidance now and then."

The words gave Marcus hope. He'd feared that admitting he needed help would immediately send the elders into doubt over their decision to hire him. "Thanks, Ed."

"You're welcome. Now, let me pray for you before you go."

Marcus hoped his impatience didn't show on his face. The elder placed a hand on Marcus's shoulder and began to pray, then stopped midsentence. "Marcus, you need to get home."

"What?"

Ed's face was troubled. He nodded toward Marcus's car. "Get home. I feel like God wants you to get home."

CHAPTER 11

Marcus's stomach leapt into his throat. Without a word he ran to his car. *Please don't take Amelia. Please, God, protect her.*

He sped down the residential streets, berating himself for his stupidity. He should have confronted her when he'd figured out what she'd done. He should have called … someone. Her doctor. Even Ed. But he'd been embarrassed for her, hadn't wanted to focus any attention on something so desperate as trying to kill herself. She hadn't seemed so bad off; he'd figured she was over it.

"Don't let her die," he prayed aloud as he rolled through a four-way stop. "Please, God. I'm sorry I didn't do anything. I can't believe I was that stupid—how could You let me be that stupid, God?"

He pulled into the parking lot and into the first spot he saw. He jabbed the elevator button until the doors opened, then did the same to the third-floor button, breathing hard with fear. As he ran down the hall to their door, he pulled his phone from his pocket in case he had to call 911, then let himself in as quickly as he could. "Amelia?"

There was no answer. He ran for the bedroom.

✳

An older woman, not wearing scrubs or a doctor's coat, walked over to Marcus, offered a hand to shake, and introduced herself as the hospital's social worker. "I've spoken with Amelia, and she gave me permission to discuss her situation with you." She sat beside him and folded her hands over the chart in her lap. "Amelia admitted to having attempted suicide."

Despite expecting this, the words were a knife in his heart. He rubbed a hand slowly over his face, not knowing what to say.

"Based on her personal history and the fact that she's still feeling suicidal, I'm recommending an inpatient program. We don't have one here, unfortunately; the nearest hospital I'd recommend is in Omaha."

"Omaha?" He groaned. "That's over an hour away. There isn't anything here in Wheatridge?"

"I'm afraid not. She needs to be given a full psychological examination and placed somewhere where she can be monitored 24/7."

"I can take off from work—"

"Mr. Sheffield, I understand how difficult this is. Unfortunately, by law she has to be committed. And given the severity of her depression, she'll likely require medication, and it will be helpful to have her monitored while that is being adjusted and we wait for her mood to stabilize."

"But—she's been on antidepressants. Are they just not working?"

The social worker gave him a sympathetic look. "Actually, she told me she'd never started them."

"Oh." He rubbed a hand over his eyes, overwhelmed. "Okay then."

"When she's been cleared for discharge, I'll come talk to you about transferring her to Omaha." With a sympathetic smile and another handshake, the social worker left. Marcus dropped his head into his hands and continued to pray.

The next morning Marcus arrived at the hospital to learn Amelia was ready to be discharged. As she had promised, the social worker returned to explain the details of the transfer, and after a ridiculous amount of paperwork, Amelia went on a gurney to an ambulance, which Marcus followed in his car.

The drive was agony. He wanted to be with Amelia, not driving alone. The social worker had assured him he'd get the chance to spend some time with her once they arrived, but he couldn't shake visions of her being torn away from him by thug-like orderlies and dragged down the hall through lockdown doors. He tried to convince himself such things only happened in movies, but the dubious side of his brain reminded him that the idea for those movie scenes had to come from somewhere.

When they reached the hospital, he parked in the visitors' lot and ran to the admissions desk. "My wife was brought in as a transfer from Wheatridge Medical," he said. "She's being admitted to the psych unit. Where would she be?"

The attendant pointed him down the hall, and again he ran at full tilt, afraid she'd be hidden away before he could say good-bye. But no, there she was with a nurse at her side, sitting in a small waiting room outside the psych ward entrance.

Marcus helped complete the admission papers, then the nurse stood aside so they could say their good-byes.

Marcus pulled her into his arms and kissed her hair. "I love you, Amelia. I'm so sorry for whatever I might have done that contributed to all of this."

"It's not your fault," Amelia said, her voice muffled against his shoulder. "It's me. I'm the one who's broken."

Marcus sighed. "You're not broken, babe."

"Of course I am." The words were empty of emotion, spoken as simple fact. Marcus wanted to counter them but knew nothing he said would make a difference.

"I'll come up for visiting hours tomorrow."

"You have to work."

"I know. I'll figure it out."

They stood, silent, until the nurse cleared her throat. "Amelia?" A note of sympathy underlined her tone. "We should get going."

"I love you." Marcus released his wife and watched her walk through the door. Stuffing his hands into his pockets, he walked back to the car to start the lonely drive home.

That afternoon Amelia met with a psychologist who made her detail again her family history and the events of the last few months. More questions followed, and by the end of the interview Amelia felt like her brain had been wrung out. The doctor completed his notes in her chart and then dropped the bombshell.

"Amelia, I think you may have bipolar disorder."

She frowned. "Wait—like, manic depression?"

"That's a common term for it, yes."

"But … I didn't have mania, did I? I mean, I thought people who were manic were all … I don't know … giddy and thought they were God or something?"

"That's one way a mania manifests. But it's not the only way. The period of time where your energy came back and you started meeting friends and getting involved at your church was the beginning of it."

"But that was a good time for me."

"Yes, but it devolved to a period of chronic irritation, binge shopping, and insomnia, among other things. It's what we'd call a hypomanic state. It wasn't as severe as a typical mania, but it was a mania nonetheless. The fact that you dropped into depression imme- diately after is another indicator."

Amelia's already foggy head was spinning. "But ... isn't that sort of thing genetic? My mom wasn't bipolar, or my dad."

The doctor's eyebrows raised slightly. "Given the description you provided of your mother, I am fairly confident she would have been diagnosed as such had she sought help."

Not lazy. Not "creatively jammed." Not just starved for atten- tion. None of the things Amelia, or even Amelia's father, might have guessed. Her view of her childhood took on a new cast. She'd come to terms with being the daughter of the town crazy. But having the label of "bipolar" applied to her mother's condition created a significant shift in her heart. There really wasn't anything she could have done, short of medication, to change herself. Her father's demands that she grow up, snap out of it, and stop being so self-centered hadn't stood a chance against the forces warring in her mother's head. How different could things have been if she'd been evaluated? Could she have made her way back to the stage? Would her parents have stayed together? Would she still be alive? The thought of her mother's lost years made Amelia want to cry.

"We're going to start you on a mood stabilizer and see how that works for you. Our options are limited, given the pregnancy, but we'll work with what we have and focus as much as we can on behav- ioral therapy."

"How long will I be here?"

"Well, that depends on a few things—how well the medication works, whether or not you do the work we prescribe in therapy, that sort of thing. Some of it you can control, some of it you can't. Typically, pregnancy hormones tend to even out the moods of bipolar women, but in the rare case—like yours—it seems to exacerbate the symptoms instead."

Amelia went cold. "I could be here until the end of the pregnancy?"

"No, no—unless you're resistant to therapy or medication, which I doubt you'll be, you should be out in a matter of days or weeks, not months."

She let out a sigh of relief. "All right then."

The doctor completed her chart and released Amelia back to the ward where dinner was just being served. Most of the other patients had congregated near each other to eat, but Amelia sat as far from everyone else as she could. The revelation about her mother was just starting to register, and she wanted to be alone while she tried to process it all.

Mom was bipolar. Mom had a known disorder that could have been treated. Amelia had always assumed her mother was just different—to an extreme. When she was old enough to know the stereotypes of artistic people, she chalked up her mother's unusual behavior and volatile personality to her artistic nature and to the fact that she was no longer pursuing her art as she once had. Her mother often spoke of her old life as an actress, and once Amelia began to follow in her performing footsteps, it made sense to her that someone who loved acting but couldn't work at it would be frustrated.

But the more she thought about it, the angrier Amelia became. Her father had tried to convince her mother to see a doctor, but she had refused. As Amelia had told Marcus, her mother believed medication would destroy her creativity. But what use had her creativity been anyway? She hadn't been doing anything with it—so what did she care? Did she enjoy being out of control, in bed for days, thought of as crazy by her family? Hadn't she known her behavior took a toll on the entire family, that her husband avoided her because she was so difficult to handle, that her children lived in fear of one of her outbursts? Memories long forgotten resurfaced as Amelia ate—of the perpetual knot in her stomach that only untied itself when she was immersed in her music, of the time she spent attempting to comfort her mother as she cried about how worthless she was to everyone, of the fights between her parents when her mother pulled another embarrassing stunt like driving to the market in nothing but her kimono or painting the living room red. She could have had a normal childhood—a normal mother. But her mother had been too ... selfish? Misguided? Fearful? What had *really* stopped her?

It didn't matter. She couldn't do anything about it now, other than deal with the aftermath—like the embarrassment and enormous self-loathing she felt from having failed to kill herself and how she was ever going to face Marcus again. And that was plenty to deal with.

CHAPTER 12

The silence in the apartment was like a fog that hemmed Marcus in and threatened to suffocate him with its weight. It was dusk now, and though he'd been home for hours, he still hadn't moved from the couch. The enormity of what the last twenty-four hours had revealed was too much for his already overloaded mind to handle; his brain was on tilt and his body shut down. But he couldn't stay like this. He had a sermon to prepare. He had to visit Amelia in the hospital tomorrow. He had to make meals, and eat them, and sleep, and …

Marcus's gaze went to his cell phone that sat on the coffee table. He had to talk to someone. That was the only way to get out from under this pressure. But who? Normally he'd call Dane, but even his best friend didn't seem fit for the task of helping Marcus haul his soul out of the pit in which it had settled. His wisdom was no greater than Marcus's, his life experience no more varied. This was the kind of situation in which he should be able to call his father. How supremely unfair that he should have a father so many people went to for help, but to whom he could never turn for anything without getting crushed.

A name came to mind. He owed the man a call, anyway, to let him know why he'd heard God telling Marcus to get home. He picked up his cell and dialed Ed's number. Nerves made his hands tremble. What would the elder think of him when he knew the truth?

"Marcus, hello! I'm glad you called. I've been wondering how things were."

Here goes nothing. "Things are actually pretty awful, Ed. I know it's last-minute, but I don't suppose you've got some time to get together this evening, do you?"

"Of course, Marcus, of course. Name the time and place and I'll be there."

"The diner on Main, at eight?"

"You've got it. I'll see you then."

The diner was virtually empty when Marcus arrived. The waitress sat him at a booth and brought him ice water while he waited for Ed to show up. His knee bounced beneath the table as he looked at the dessert menu, and when Ed clapped a hand on Marcus's shoulder his heart just about stopped from the shock.

"Sorry there, son," Ed chuckled as he slid into the seat opposite Marcus. "Didn't mean to startle you. You're not normally the jumpy type, though. Things really must be bad off."

The waitress arrived and took their order, then Ed folded his weathered hands on the Formica and said, "So, tell me what's wrong, and I'll do my best to help."

Marcus took a deep breath. "First of all—you were right to send me home so fast yesterday. Amelia tried to kill herself."

Ed's eyes went wide. "Oh no. Marcus, I'm so sorry. Is she all right?"

"She's at a hospital up in Omaha; the one here didn't have the kind of program she needed to be in. They took her up this afternoon."

"How is the baby?"

"Fine, apparently. And physically I think Amelia is all right, too. But … I just don't know what to expect now. Hopefully I'll get more information tomorrow, find out what her diagnosis actually is, all that stuff. But ..."

"It's a lot to take in."

"Yes. And if it were just that, it would be overwhelming enough. But there's something else, and ..." Marcus fought to keep eye contact. "I'm concerned it might lead to my termination."

Marcus waited for Ed's defenses to go up, but his face remained as kind and open as ever. "It would have to be pretty extreme for that to happen, Marcus, and somehow I don't think you're the extreme type. Tell me what it is."

Marcus took a deep breath to steady his nerves, then spilled the entire story about his father and their dysfunctional relationship. "And now," he said in conclusion, "I don't know what to think about myself anymore. I feel like I don't know who I am. Everything I've done has been to try to win this man's approval. I've never done anything, besides marrying Amelia, that wasn't driven by some attempt to prove myself to him. Heck—even marrying Amelia was done with that motive, now that I think about it. Not that I don't love her, but I knew my father valued family and—" He stopped, the irony of his words catching up with him. He let out a sardonic laugh. "He values family, but not *his* family. And you know what else is sick? I've been going down that same path. I've been working my tail off at the church and my side job, and I completely neglected Amelia and missed the signs that she was so depressed. I've put more time and energy into my jobs than into my marriage, and now my wife is in some mental-health ward ..." His voice broke and he covered his eyes with his hand as grief and embarrassment overcame him.

Ed was silent as Marcus's shoulders shook. When Marcus finally had his emotions under control, he trained his eyes on his plate of untouched pie and continued. "The bottom line is, Ed, I don't know if I'm even supposed to be a pastor. I've only pursued it because of him. And it makes me wonder if the reason I've struggled so much since taking this job is because it's not where I'm really supposed to be." He shrugged, unsure of what to say next, and took a chance with a quick glance at the elder to try to gauge his thoughts.

Ed slowly nodded, his brow furrowed in thought. "That's a lot of weight to carry. And a devastating discovery to make, I'm sure. I'm sorry you've been struggling with this, Marcus. I'm sorry I haven't been more attentive to you and how difficult things have been."

"That's not your responsibility, Ed. You're not—" He chuckled. "You're not my father."

Ed sat up tall. "Oh, on the contrary. As one of the elders, I'm a father figure to the whole church—including you. *Especially* you. A young husband, soon-to-be-father, first-time pastor—you shouldn't be expected to find your way in all those roles on your own. But I've let you fly under the radar, so to speak, because you seemed so mature and capable. I shouldn't have made such assumptions. *Not* that I don't think you're mature and capable." He smiled. "But even if you are, it doesn't mean you're Superman."

Marcus felt the weight of his fear melting in the face of Ed's understanding. "I … I don't think I've ever heard the role of an elder described like that. At our church growing up, the elders were there to run the place, for the most part—take care of the details so the pastors could preach and take care of the people."

Ed shrugged. "I think many churches do operate like that. And we do too, to an extent. But the longer I'm a Christian the more I come to believe that the church isn't just a place we're supposed to come to once or twice a week and give money to and make a building for. It's supposed to be a family. And not the kind of family you only talk to on holidays." Elbows on the table, he tented his fingers and leaned in, his eyes locked on Marcus's as he spoke. "You should have been able to come to me with all this when it first happened, because you should have known I was here to be a father in faith to you and Amelia." The thought of Ed as his father threatened to pull Marcus's concentration down a rabbit trail. He forced himself to focus on Ed as he continued. "But you didn't know that because we—New Hope—haven't embraced that paradigm yet. It's something I've been praying a lot about lately, and now I know why. What other hurts are people in our congregation struggling with because they don't have anyone to turn to? What kind of faith community are we if people don't feel they have that kind of support here?"

Marcus thought of all the meetings he'd had with parishioners the first few weeks he'd been on staff. He knew all sorts of hurts and struggles that the community was weathering. Who knew what others had gone unmentioned in those meetings, what circumstances were eating people up inside and making them miserable. It would explain why people weren't engaging at church—they didn't feel like they could be themselves, like they could open themselves up to the people sitting around them in the pews. Maybe the fix wasn't in events and ministries, but in facilitating deeper friendships so that their community could become a true community of encouragement and support instead of a shallow weekly gathering of religiously like-minded people.

Marcus rubbed a hand on his neck. "I think you may be on to something here, Ed." A spark lit inside him and brought with it a thin ray of hope. "The idea of a family … of this church being more than just a bunch of people who know each other but only see each other on Sunday … Obviously I studied stuff like this in seminary, but it was usually house churches that were described as functioning that way, and there was definitely a bias against that approach. I remember one professor talking about how the tight community the first-century church formed was a means of self-protection against the anti-Christian sentiment of the time, and how the idealized view some Christians have of that kind of community isn't really achievable in this day and age." He gave Ed a genuine smile. "But I can see how we could pull it off—or, at least, a twenty-first-century version of it. I don't know what else to say, other than it sounds amazing."

Ed returned the smile and clapped his hands together. "I knew you'd see it that way. When we interviewed you, I kept praying that God would bring us to agreement on this. I didn't know when it would happen, but I knew it would eventually."

Marcus gave him a sheepish, lopsided smile. "So I'm not fired?"

"Fired? Good heavens, son, not at all! We still need a teacher, and regardless of the doubts you may have about your ability, I can assure you you're a good one. You may have come out here for what you think are all the wrong reasons, but God was guiding you, every step of the way."

It was humbling to think of God directing his path even when he was so headstrong in his own desires and so misguided in his pursuits.

But when he thought about what New Hope could be if it gave itself wholeheartedly to the goal of being an intimate community—a family—the excitement he felt told him he was definitely in the right place. Even if he'd taken a crooked path to get there.

✳

The next morning Marcus stopped off at the church to pick up his mail and let the secretary know he wouldn't be in for the rest of the week. Atop his mail stack were a handful of phone messages from the other elders, offering everything from meals to housecleaning to rides up to Omaha and back. Ed had asked for Marcus's permission to share with the elder board the fact that Amelia was hospitalized, but Marcus hadn't expected this kind of outpouring in return. Apparently Ed wasn't alone in his views on the church as a family.

"Ed told me he'd be doing the message this week too," the secretary said. "And that, if you try to come in to work, I should tell you to leave or risk formal disciplinary action."

Marcus laughed. "He can be a little pushy when he wants to be, eh?"

She grinned. "I think I'd call it protective."

"Ah. You've got that exactly right." Marcus looked again at the messages. "Man, the phones must have been busy this morning."

"Most of them were on the machine when I got here, actually."

Marcus shook his head in wonder. "I have to say, it's humbling."

The secretary gave him an empathetic smile. "Well, we all go through something eventually that requires the help of others to deal with. There's no shame in that."

"You're right." Marcus slapped the stack of mail in his palm. "It's not at all how I was raised, but I'm going to have to just get over that."

"I know what that's like. There's all sorts of mess from my childhood that's made it hard to live right sometimes. But God gives me strength."

"Amen to that."

Marcus checked his email one last time, then left for Omaha. The drive felt far less depressing than it had yesterday. Even though he still hadn't decided whether or not to tell Amelia about his father and the things he'd been dealing with, Marcus was definitely going to tell her about his discussion with Ed and how supportive the elders were being. He felt light and unburdened for the first time in … Now that he thought about it, he couldn't remember the last time he'd felt this way. There had always been a shadow behind him, pushing and driving and goading. Ed's words had been revolutionary.

It's going to be different now, God. I'm going to be different. I don't want to neglect my family the way my dad did. I don't want to live behind some mask of strength and think I have to make everything okay on my own. Thank You for Ed. Thank You for this church. He thought a moment as the cornfields rolled past. *One of these days I may even be able to thank You for putting me through all this.*

He smiled, an unfamiliar but pleasant sense of peace enveloping him, and set his thoughts on the things he'd talk about with Amelia. Despite where she was and what she had done, he couldn't wait to see her.

Amelia's first twenty-four hours on the ward had been nothing like she'd expected. Her only frame of reference for mental hospitals was a movie she'd seen back in high school and a book she'd read in college. From those she had inferred that the staff would be abusive and her fellow patients either psychopathic or delirious. Neither, thank God, were true.

The staff, while not the most nurturing people in the world, were not sinister or cruel. They upheld the rules in no uncertain terms, but they had been helpful to Amelia as she'd been settling in and made sure she was doing all right. The other patients were on the ward for a variety of reasons, but only two of them shared Amelia's diagnosis. One of them, Kristine, was her roommate.

Kristine was currently experiencing what she told Amelia was called mixed states. She was suicidally depressed but revved with mania. "It's a heckuva thing to be so sad that you want to die but so powered up you also want to run a marathon," she'd told Amelia as they'd dressed for bed that first night. "I'm lucky because my manias are actually kinda fun, when I'm not experiencing them in mixed state, anyway. I play trombone and I'm a painter, too, so I just stay up all night and paint and write music and play and play and play. I have synesthesia, too—do you know what that is? It's where you see sound as color. So my paintings and my compositions are all coordinated. I play them and then I paint them." The whole time she talked she was twisting the end of her shirt until Amelia thought she'd rip the fabric. "So I'm guessing this is your first time being hospitalized, huh? You don't look like someone who's done this before."

"First time, yeah. I just got diagnosed."

"Aw man, that's a bummer. I mean, it's good that you know what it is, but it sucks that you've got it too. Medication is good, when it's working. Mine isn't working because I stopped taking it."

"Why'd you do that?"

"Because I didn't want to anymore." She raked her nails up her arms, leaving angry red tracks. "Did they give you something to help you sleep? They gave me something, but I don't think it's going to work. It usually doesn't when I'm like this. I apologize now if I keep you up. I don't mean to."

"It's all right. I probably won't sleep well anyway."

"Naw, you will, it's good stuff, the stuff they give us to help us sleep. When it works."

A nurse had come in and told Kristine to can it so Amelia could sleep. But when they woke the next morning, Kristine started in again and didn't stop until group therapy after breakfast. "So when you're not so depressed that you want to kill yourself, what do you do? Do you have a job? I haven't had a job in forever; I can't keep stable long enough to hold one. It sucks. Where do you work?"

"I'm a pianist. But right now I'm not working. I just moved here from California because my husband got a job here."

"You're a musician too! That's awesome! I wish I had my trombone here; we could jam. Although you don't hear a lot of piano-trombone duets, do you? We could write one. And then I could paint it. That would be awesome. So what does your husband do?"

Amelia fidgeted in her chair as she pushed greasy sausage links around her plate. "He's a pastor."

"A Christian one?"

"Yeah." She kept her eyes down, hoping Kristine would move on to something else. She didn't want to talk about Marcus. It made her miss him even more.

"Hey, I'm a Christian too! That's awesome!"

"Girl, leave Amelia alone and let her eat." This came from one of the other patients, a woman whose name Amelia couldn't remember but who reminded her of the black nurse on *Scrubs*.

"I *am* letting her eat. You'll notice I'm doing most of the talking."

"Yeah—isn't there something the nurses can give you for that?"

Kristine stuck her tongue out at the woman and turned back to Amelia. "So you're a Christian too, then, huh? I am too. I don't think I've ever met another Christian on the ward before."

Amelia gave up on the sausage and pushed her plate away. "Yeah. Well … sort of. I mean … actually … I'm not sure I am anymore."

Kristine's eyes grew big. "Oh. Why? Because of the bipolar?"

"No … maybe. I don't know. A lot of things, not just that. I'm not sure if I ever really and truly was in the first place. I did it more to protect myself."

"From what?"

Amelia gestured to the ward. "From this. From the crazy that my mom had. She disappeared when I was in college; everyone says she killed herself. She was always unstable, always messed up. She had an amazing career and lost it, and I didn't want to be like her. My roommate was a Christian, and I figured it was worth a shot if it kept me from turning into her."

"Did it?"

"Nope."

"That doesn't mean anything."

"Shouldn't it, though?"

Kristine shrugged. "I dunno. I'm not a theologian. But I'm not a Christian because of what it does for me."

Amelia frowned. "But if it doesn't work, then what good is it?"

One of the therapists came by the table. "Group therapy in five, folks." The others stood to take their trays to the cart, but Amelia remained in her seat.

"Aren't you coming?" Kristine asked.

"Is it mandatory?"

"Um … no."

"Then no."

"But you're not going to get out of here unless you're participating and getting better."

"I know."

"Don't you want to leave?"

"Yeah … eventually. But not until I'm ready. There are … things I need to figure out first."

Kristine gave her a puzzled look but said nothing as she stood with her tray and left the table.

Amelia propped her chin in her hand and stared, unseeing, at her breakfast. The silence in the room as the others disappeared into the therapy room gave her space to think. Everything she'd said to Kristine was true, and the more she thought about it, the more convinced she became that God didn't figure in to her future. She had no reason to trust Him—if He was even real—and she didn't want to waste her time trying to toe some religious line that just made life more difficult.

There was only one problem. She was married to a minister.

A phone rang at the front desk. A nurse answered, then called out, "Amelia, your husband is here to see you."

Oh no. Amelia bit her lip, thinking. "Tell him ..." She stared at the space where her wedding ring had been before the nurses had confiscated it for the duration of her stay. She wanted to see him, but she was so embarrassed over the behavior that had landed her here, and so confused about who she was. She also didn't have it in her to keep up a facade, and she wasn't ready to be honest with him about what she was thinking.

Amelia looked to the nurse. "Tell him I don't want to talk." She heard the nurse relay the message as she stood and brought her tray to the cart, then curled up on the couch and began to cry.

Marcus sat in his car and eyed the hospital building through the rain-covered windshield. He'd been resolute when he'd left the apartment, telling himself it didn't matter if she wanted to see him or not; the important thing was to show up. But two days in a row of being shot down were beginning to wear on his perseverance.

He pulled an umbrella from the floor of the backseat and left the car with a sigh. He knew the route by heart now, and followed it without thinking as his mind contemplated how he should respond today if Amelia still refused to see him. He didn't have a lot of options; it's not like he could storm the ward and demand she talk to him. But maybe he could talk to her therapist and ask her to convince Amelia to at least explain why she wouldn't meet him.

He shook out the umbrella at the lobby doors and followed the damp carpet path to the reception desk. The receptionist gave him a small smile. "Back again."

"A glutton for punishment."

She dialed the phone. "Marcus Sheffield is here to see his wife, Amelia."

A jumbling of nerves in his solar plexus was put to rest yet again when the receptionist hung up and said, "I'm sorry."

"Thanks." He gave her a terse smile and turned to leave, then stopped. "If I wanted to write her a letter, how would I get it to her?"

"Just leave it here with me. I'll make sure it's delivered."

He nodded. "All right then. Thanks." Inspired, he followed the signs to the gift shop and purchased a spiral bound journal and a cheap pen. *Where there's a will,* he thought, *there's a way.*

He was halfway to the cafeteria when he saw a sign for the chapel. *Even better.* He followed the arrow and came upon a wooden door propped open at the end of a hall. Inside were eight rows of short pews and a platform on which stood a simple wooden stand. A bank of tea lights stood against one wall on a table draped in wine-red velvet, and an upright piano sat in the opposite corner. The sight of the piano made his heart hurt.

He sat in one of the pews and opened the journal.

Dear Amelia,

He stopped, thinking about what exactly he should write. What he *wanted* to write was not likely to convince her to see him, though getting it out of his system would certainly make him feel better. *Any ideas, God?*

After a few minutes he began to write a rough draft, telling himself he'd just say whatever he wanted first and then rewrite a final letter later. He certainly had the time.

Dear Amelia,

Hey babe. How is it in there? I keep picturing it like the cafeteria, for some reason, but without the buffet. Have you had the red Jell-O yet? Good stuff.

So … I miss you. I'd like to think you miss me, but given how the last few days have gone, I'm guessing you probably don't. Is it something I said? Or didn't say? I know this is new territory for you, but it is for me, too, so if I've done something wrong I hope you'll give me a do-over. Or maybe you're embarrassed, or scared. You don't have to be, because I love you. That's what it all comes down to. I love you.

Marcus reread what he'd written and decided a straight-from-the-heart letter was better than something edited and polished as though destined for public consumption. He carefully ripped the page from the journal and folded it, then walked it back to reception. "Don't suppose you have an envelope, do you? I promise to bring my own next time."

The receptionist chuckled and pulled one from a drawer. "On the house."

"Thanks." He sealed the letter inside and wrote Amelia's name on the front before handing it back.

"You're welcome." She gave him a sincere smile. "I hope you get to see her soon."

Marcus nodded. "Thanks. Me, too."

Marcus had visions of Amelia calling in tears, begging forgiveness for refusing him and promising to see him whenever he wanted. But it didn't happen. The resolve he'd felt earlier dissipated in the face of her silence as the day wore on, and when Marcus went to bed that night he decided not to go back up the next morning. He wasn't going to keep going if she had no intention of seeing him.

He showed up at work the next morning and the secretary wagged a finger at him in mock disappointment. "Pastor Sheffield, don't make me call Ed."

He flashed a terse smile. "I don't really have a reason not to come in today. I'll be in my office." He took his mail from the corner of her desk and closed his office door behind him a tad too loudly. He didn't really want to be here, either. He just didn't know where else to go.

He'd just finished emptying his inbox when his phone rang. "I hear you're in to work today," said Ed's jovial voice.

Marcus glared at the door. "Yes, I am. I'm being paid to do a job, not to sit at the hospital and wait for my wife to decide to see me. And since I don't know when that's actually going to happen, I figured it made more sense to be here."

"Your wife needs you, Marcus."

"You know, I don't think she does. I've been up there the last three days, and every single time she's refused to see me. I'm over it. When she's ready to talk she can call me, and I'll be happy to go up then."

"I can tell you're frustrated, Marcus—"

He snorted. "Can you?"

"—but I think you need to go back up there anyway."

"What for? So I can waste more gas and another two hours in the car just to have the receptionist give me that look of pity again?"

"No. So Amelia sees just how committed to her you really are."

"She knows."

"Does she?"

Marcus was irked. "Of course she does."

"Remember that actions speak louder than words. It doesn't matter how much you say it, if what you do tells a different story."

Marcus was about to spout off a list of ways he'd shown Amelia his commitment, but couldn't come up with a list. A different one, however, queued up easily. He'd put his career ahead of hers, he'd been working the kinds of hours his father had always worked and that Marcus had always resented, and now he was essentially giving up on her until she'd proven herself to him.

Marcus shut down his computer with a sigh. "All right. I'll go."

"I think that's wise."

"Thanks."

"Anytime, son. Anytime."

The chapel was as good a place as any to spend his time while in Omaha, so after being rejected yet again, Marcus returned with his notebook and pen, an envelope folded in his back pocket, and sat in the same pew as before to write another note to Amelia.

So … you don't want to see me. Okay. Are you … I don't know … testing me or something? I wouldn't mind if you were, though I would appreciate knowing how long it was going to last and what I had to do to pass. You are okay in there, aren't you? I need to know you're all right.

Ed is doing all the preaching this month—isn't that kind of him? He's an amazing man. I know you haven't talked with him much, but I think you'd really like him. When things are back to normal, we'll have to have him and his wife Lucy over for dinner. We'll order takeout so we don't have to cook. I know it's not your favorite thing.

Not that we'll ever get back to our old normal, hm? So … once we figure out our new normal, then we'll have them over.

New is good, by the way. You don't have to be afraid of it.

Marcus slipped the note into the envelope and sealed it closed. But instead of leaving for reception like he had before, he waited, the letter sitting beside him on the pew, and stared at the candles on the table against the wall. He didn't try to focus on anything in particular, just let his mind wander, and after a few minutes he started praying.

So how much of my father have I projected onto You, God? Not only do I not know who I am…. I have a feeling I don't really know who You are, either. If my views of what it means to be a pastor were as skewed as they were, then I can only imagine how messed up my views of You are.

He sat up straighter in the pew, cutting off the train of thought. He wasn't ready to do that kind of detective work yet. He stood and left the chapel, heading for the sympathetic receptionist, and hoped this would be the day Amelia put him out of his misery.

When Amelia woke on her sixth morning in the hospital, her first thought was of the chocolate-chip pancakes her mother used to make on birthday mornings when she wasn't bedridden from depression. Where the memory came from she didn't know, but it made her mouth water with craving as she stretched beneath the sheets. Her second thought was of how much she missed the six-hundred-count sheets she and Marcus had on their bed—a wedding present from Dane and Jill and much more comfortable than these. Her third thought was of how tired she was of being in the hospital.

The fact that she was still depressed was not the fourth, or fifth, or even sixth thought she had that morning. Her eighth thought was one of surprise: She didn't feel nearly as desperate and despairing as she had when she'd first arrived. *I'm actually getting better.*

That small amount of improvement turned out to be just enough for her to see more clearly what her life had been like the last few months—what parts of it she could remember—and even though she was still depressed, she felt better able to think straight, and she had a lot to think about.

"You look … different." Kristine set her breakfast tray beside Amelia's and slid into the seat. Her mixed states had evened out and now she was just straight-up depressed. "Meds kicking in?"

"I guess so, yeah. I'm still depressed, but … not as bad, you know?"

"You'll probably get to go home soon then."

Amelia sat up from her slouch over the plate of lukewarm French toast. "What? But I don't want to yet. I'm not ready."

"Why not? Why would you want to stay here any longer than absolutely necessary?"

"Because I … I'm not sure I want to go back to my old life." She let the words come out without too much thinking, just to see what she'd say. They felt right.

"What life *do* you want to go back to?"

Amelia pulled her fork through a puddle of syrup and let herself daydream. "One where I'm back in California. One where I'm not married to a pastor." Though she did still want to be married to Marcus. With the heavy fog of the depression lifting, she missed him even more. "One where … one where I'm not a Christian anymore."

"Wow. A really, really different life."

"Yes."

"I don't think you can just do that. I mean, you can give yourself a makeover, or go back to school to learn to be something else besides a pianist, and I guess you can go back to California if you want. But I don't think you can just up and stop being married." She sliced her French toast in precise squares. "I'm not sure about the not-being-a-Christian-anymore thing, either. I mean, how do you just erase all that thinking from your head and start … not thinking that way?"

Amelia sighed. "I know. But that's why I don't want to leave yet. I need to figure out first how I can make that my new life. How I can get back to Cali, and shake off all the Christian thinking, and ..." She couldn't bring herself to vocalize what it would take to no longer be married, even though the thought of being single again was enticing.

And that was the moment the baby chose to make herself known.

"Oh my gosh." Amelia's hand dropped to her stomach, her eyes wide. She sat still, waiting to see if it happened again.

"What? What is it?" Kristine looked worried. "Want me to call the nurse?"

"No, no, it's all right, it's just ..." Amelia bit her lip as the sensation came again. "I think I just felt the baby move."

"Oh, wow. Cool."

"Yeah." Amelia tried to smile, but instead she felt tears welling in her eyes as her own version of mixed states began.

The baby's existence had been obvious ever since her stomach had begun to swell a month ago. The fact that she was pregnant had never exactly slipped her mind. But actually feeling the baby move solidified its presence in a way that no other indicator had. She couldn't make her plans without factoring in this new being. She couldn't just up and leave for LA without knowing what she'd do for childcare and how she'd juggle the demands of both a job and a baby. And as Marcus had pointed out, he had rights too—if she left, she'd be separating father from child, and she couldn't do that in good conscience.

Amelia scrubbed a paper napkin over her tearstained cheeks and stood. She had to get alone somewhere and think. "See you in group," she said to Kristine, then returned her half-eaten breakfast to the tray cart and headed for the sofa at the far end of the community room. There was an understanding between the patients that sitting on that sofa was the equivalent of sequestering yourself in your bedroom—something that was not allowed on the ward during the day. She curled up in the corner and faced the window. *I'm smart. I can figure this out.*

A religion she no longer believed, a town she wanted to leave, a baby she didn't want, and a husband she didn't want to be with anymore. *That's not true.* She frowned. What was it about Marcus, then, that made her want to leave? His workaholic tendencies? The pathetic way he chased after his father's approval like an addict chasing his next fix? The way he wouldn't take the hint and leave her alone?

No—it's not him. It's everything that comes with him. Marriage to Marcus meant living in Nebraska. It meant being a pastor's wife. It meant having religion shoved in her face all the time. And it meant placing his desires ahead of hers. It wasn't that she didn't love him— she just didn't love what it meant to be married to him now.

And honestly—she didn't want him to have to be married to her. Not when she was full of doubt about his beliefs and couldn't give him the support he deserved. Not when her mind could crack at any moment and send her back to the hospital. How much time had he lost at work already while he tried in spite of her to be a good husband? He deserved someone who could keep house and raise children and be a doting wife without stealing away to her piano to cope with her sadness or resenting the sacrifices she'd made for him. She didn't think she'd ever be that.

"Amelia, your husband is here. Again."

She heard the note of irritation in the nurse's voice and knew it was directed at her. She knew everyone thought she was an ingrate for not at least letting him say hello, but she needed to have her plan figured out before she saw him, or he might talk her out of it, even if he didn't know what she was planning. All it would take is for him to be himself—loving, sweet, gentle, smart, funny—and she'd be right back to where she'd been before: caving to his ideas and letting him set the agenda. She couldn't let that happen again.

Amelia looked to the nurse, who watched her with a critical expression, and shook her head. The nurse sighed, relayed the message and hung up, muttering to herself. She almost changed her mind, just to stop the nurse from thinking poorly of her, but she held fast to her decision by chanting "New life, new life, new life" to herself under her breath. That nurse didn't know what Amelia was up against.

Amelia joined the group-therapy session despite knowing it would reflect well on her recovery and count another point toward her being released sooner rather than later. The focus of the group was learning coping skills, and when she was out on her own again she was going to need those. No more running back to Marcus if she was depressed. She had to learn how to handle her illness on her own.

When therapy was over and she'd reentered the community room, the desk nurse called to her and waved a white envelope. Amelia rolled her eyes and accepted it, then retreated to the couch again to read Marcus's latest missive.

Dear Amelia,

You should see it outside today, it's absolutely beautiful.
Well, I'm sure you can see it, I'm sure they've got windows
there somewhere—I just wish you could come out in it.
Doesn't sunlight help with depression? I'm pretty sure I've
read that before; they really should bring you guys outside
more often.

So, guess what I came home to last night? A cleaned
apartment and dinner cooking. Remember how I told you
a couple days ago about the talk Ed and I had about the
church being a community that takes care of its members?
Well, I don't think I told you how many people offered to
bring me dinner and help out with stuff at the apartment if
I needed it. Pretty much the entire elder board. Ed knows
the details of why you're hospitalized, but I told him not to
tell anyone, so don't worry, you can tell people on your own
time. All they know is that you're in the hospital—I think
a lot of them assume it has something to do with the baby.
Anyway, point being, Ed asked me to drop off a spare key
at the church before coming up here yesterday, so I did, and
when I got back the place had been cleaned and a crockpot
of stew had been left on the counter.

I know you haven't been all that enamored with New
Hope, but I really think things are going to be changing
there in big ways. No necessarily on Sunday mornings, but
in the way people relate to each other, in the way the church
functions ... Who knows, maybe Sunday morning will

change. Point being, I think you'll feel more at home there in the coming months. I can see us both forming some really great friendships there. It'll definitely make things easier when the baby comes, too.

A lightbulb went on in her head. Amelia quickly scanned the rest of the letter, not letting herself dwell too much on the last paragraph of the note that was filled with all the "I love yous" that might make her doubt herself. She folded the letter and put it back in the envelope as the wheels turned.

Everything was falling into place. Marcus had a supportive community full of people who could take care of him *and* the baby. Better them than her—who knew what kind of damage she'd do as a parent, or as a mentally ill wife. She'd done enough damage already. She could wait until she'd recovered from the birth and then just … leave.

The flood of relief brought a smile to her face. She had a plan. She had a while to wait—almost five months, but with the end in sight she could do it. It would give her time to sort out the details, stash money away, and start looking for jobs and a place to live.

And Marcus … poor Marcus. She knew this would crush him. But he'd be crushed either way—might as well get it over with now rather than five years down the road when she snapped from regret and resentment, and they'd lived that many more years of their lives together. It was only going to get worse from here on out.

Really, she would just be putting him out of his misery.

CHAPTER 13

Marcus sealed yet another note in yet another envelope in the comforting stillness of the hospital chapel. He'd wrestled with God—and with Ed's voice in his head—on the way there this morning, nearly deciding to just make his customary call to the psych ward and then go home. Surely Amelia was sick of him trying to contact her when she obviously didn't want to talk. How far was he going to let this go before he finally gave up?

But then he'd think of Ed's words, and imagine from her perspective the day when he didn't call or write. Now that he'd taken it this far, to stop would send a completely different message than he would mean to, and the last thing Marcus wanted was for her to think he'd given up on her.

As had become part of the routine, Marcus remained in his seat with the note beside him on the pew, letting his thoughts toss like stones in a rock tumbler in the hope they'd polish into something that made sense. Truth was, this reprieve from real life had become a good hiding place, but he knew once Amelia was released he'd have to face it all again. He needed a plan.

First he had to decide whether or not he'd stay in Nebraska if it really made that big of a difference in Amelia's emotional state. He'd come to really like Wheatridge, but knowing how miserable it made Amelia, it would be cruel to stay. Yet the thought of going back to California—the cost of living, the pace of life, the politics—left a bad taste in his mouth, especially without a job lined up first.

But what kind of job do I even look for?

The door to the chapel groaned softly as it opened, and Marcus glanced back to see who was joining him in the normally empty room. A tall man, gray at the temples and holding a Bible, zeroed in on Marcus and approached him with an outstretched hand. "Pastor Ryan. I don't want to disturb you; just wanted to let you know I'm here if you need prayer or a listening ear."

Marcus smiled and shook his hand. "Pastor Marcus. Thanks for the offer."

Ryan's face lit. "What church, if I may ask?"

"New Hope, down in Wheatridge."

"Wheatridge, eh? Visiting a parishioner?"

"Ah, no. My wife is here."

Ryan's face softened with concern. "I'm sorry to hear that. Is there anything I can do?"

"She's not talking to me," he admitted without thinking. He gave a sheepish wave of his letter. "I show up here every day and write her a letter and then pray like crazy that she'll finally call me, but she doesn't. She … she tried to kill herself. And she's pregnant. And—" Marcus clenched his jaw, embarrassed to have shared so much with a stranger. "Suffice it to say, things are … difficult right now."

Ryan sat in the pew across the aisle from Marcus and rested his elbows on his knees. "I'm sorry to hear that, Marcus." His tone was sincere, and Marcus was surprised how comfortable he felt talking to a virtual stranger. "I'd be happy to pray for you both."

"Thanks. I'd really appreciate that." Ryan bowed his head and began to pray, and Marcus tried not to let his emotions get the better of him as he listened to this fellow pastor intercede with such conviction and passion for a total stranger and his wife. He was drawn to Ryan's kindness, and when the man uttered his "amen" and looked back to Marcus, Marcus took a chance. "Do you have a few minutes to talk?"

Ryan smiled. "It's why I'm here."

"It's not about my wife—well, who knows, maybe I'll talk about that, too. But, if you don't mind me asking … how did you know you were supposed to be a minister?"

Ryan settled back in the pew as a nostalgic expression came to his face. "I came to the Lord at an early age, and was the only believer in my family for a long time. As early as ten years old I remember thinking about being a pastor, but without the support from my family I didn't have the courage to pursue it. But the idea—or, God, more accurately—wouldn't leave me alone." He shrugged and spread his hands. "I went into business and should have loved it, but I didn't. Same with education. It wasn't until I was almost forty that I finally went to seminary. So I guess the answer to your question is that, in the back of my mind, I always knew it's what I was supposed to be."

Marcus nodded slowly, trying to mask his disappointment. He'd hoped for a more illuminating and relevant answer. "Thanks for sharing that."

"You're welcome. And how about you? How did you know?"

Marcus gave him a rueful grin. "That's the sixty-four-thousand dollar question I can't seem to answer."

Ryan chuckled knowingly. "So you're not sure why you became a pastor?"

"No, I know exactly why. I just know now it was the wrong reason, and I'm trying to figure out if I'm supposed to be one or not."

"Ah, I see." Ryan studied him as he idly spun his wedding band around his finger. "Is there something in particular, besides your original motivation, that is making you question things?"

Marcus nodded with a rueful grin. "Yeah—the fact that I hate the job."

"Oh, yes, that will do it!" Ryan settled in the pew, an arm thrown over the back. "I went through that, too, when I first went into ministry."

"Really?"

"Yes. I was a director of spiritual growth at a fairly large church. It was a new role, so the board only had ideas of what they wanted from me, no previously tested programs or anything. I'd had visions of working directly with the congregation, either one-on-one as a kind of spiritual counselor, or with small groups and Bible studies—but the reality was that I spent almost all my time in my office researching other churches and what they'd done and trying to get a program together that the board liked. They wanted things their way, I wanted them my way, and neither of us was getting what we wanted."

"So what happened?"

His warm smile crinkled the corners of his eyes. "Well, eventually I pretty much threw up my hands and said, 'Seriously, God? All those years of dogging me to go into ministry and this is the job You had waiting for me? What gives?'"

Marcus laughed. "Yes! That's exactly how I feel. I had all these dreams of what it would be like to be a pastor, and so far it's nothing like that at all. I spend all my time listening to people who want to gripe, trying to help heal people who were wounded by the old pastor, trying to get ministries off the ground that people seem to want—though once I do no one seems to care—and then somewhere in there I'm supposed to research and write sermons. And I keep thinking that, if I was really supposed to be doing this, it would be easier. I'd enjoy it more. I'd see some actual results, rather than seeing a bunch of blank faces staring up at me on Sunday morning."

Ryan was silent for a moment, then leaned in again, hands clasped, and spoke in careful tones. "Marcus—may I make an observation?"

"Yes, please, by all means."

He went silent again, then said quietly, "I think maybe you're going about things all wrong."

Marcus felt his defenses rise. He'd expected an observation about the church, not about him. "How so?"

"It sounds like you're taking an awful lot of responsibility for these people."

"Well … yeah. Of course I am. I'm their pastor; I *am* responsible for them."

Ryan shook his head. "No, that's not how I meant it. You're responsible for providing the things a pastor should provide, yes— but I meant you're taking a lot of responsibility for their reactions. It sounds as though you think you're failing because people aren't reacting the way you think they should. But you can't control their actions—that's *their* job. You can't change their hearts—that's *God's* job. Your job isn't to make these people better—it's to …" He paused, then shrugged with a sheepish smile. "Well, I don't know what your job is. That's between you and God. But I'm confident it's not what you think, because what you're striving for is impossible."

Ryan sat back. "The church board and I had to learn that lesson, too. We all wanted, in our own ways, to make our church the most spiritually mature church in the world. We had grand plans for everyone, and we cajoled and guilted and flat-out bribed people to participate—but in the end none of it mattered because God didn't move the people's hearts to respond to our plans."

Marcus frowned. "But … then what was the point of you taking that job?"

Ryan crossed ankle over knee. "To learn that only God can change hearts? To learn that, just because the desired outcome of a plan seems admirable, it doesn't always mean it's what God wants? To meet the people I met while I was there? Only God knows why He put me there, and I mean that literally. None of our programs worked, and I was let go two years after I was hired."

Marcus squeezed his eyes shut and pressed his fingertips to his temples. "So … what are you saying? That I shouldn't be doing anything for these people?"

"No, Marcus. I'm saying that you need to stop thinking of yourself as The Fixer who should be able to make everything better, and maybe start asking God what exactly He wants you to do there."

"But if people there are hurting, wouldn't He want them healed?"

Ryan gave a tight shake of his head. "I no longer make any assumptions about what God does and doesn't want. I'm seeing such a small, limited bit of the whole picture; there's no way I can begin to account for why He does what He does. All I can do—all any of us can do—is ask Him to guide our steps, and to be faithful to what He asks us to do. We can't force people to cooperate. We can't force people to want to be Christians, or to want to grow in their faith. All we can do is love them and offer them the things God leads us to offer them, and then sit back and let God do the rest."

"But what if they don't ever come around?"

Ryan shrugged, then gently pointed a finger in Marcus's direction. "It's not your responsibility. You'll be judged for *your* actions, not for the actions of others."

Marcus shook his head. "No—I mean, what if all the people who are threatening to leave really do leave, and the people who complain but do nothing to help make changes continue to refuse to pitch in? The church could split, or fall apart, or die out."

Ryan nodded. "I suppose it could."

"But how can that possibly be what God wants?"

Ryan leaned in, hitched up the sleeves of his blue button-down, and rested his elbows back on his knees as he fixed Marcus with a focused stare. "Who are you to say what God wants, Marcus? You don't know what phoenix could rise from those ashes. You don't know what rock bottom someone might have to reach before finally opening their eyes to their own spiritual depravity. You can't read minds and souls, Marcus. You can't know God's heart in all things. It's entirely possible that the collapse of your church could be the catalyst that changes the heart of a parishioner who goes on to be the next Billy Graham. It could be the catalyst that brings you to a new plane of spiritual maturity. *You don't know.* And you need to let go of those fears and just accept that God has you here for a reason that you don't yet know. Don't ask God to make these people respond to you. Ask Him what you're supposed to do, and then do it—no matter what you think the outcome might be. You're not in this position on accident. There are no accidents or coincidences in life. God orchestrates it all."

Marcus sat back in his seat, eyes trained on the floor as he pondered what Ryan had said. "It feels like a cop-out," he finally said.

Ryan laughed. "How so?"

"I feel like I should have more …"

"Power?"

Marcus looked up sharply. "I was thinking more like … well, responsibility."

Ryan raised one eyebrow as a small smile tugged at the side of his mouth. "Why is that?"

"Because I'm the pastor!"

"So?"

"So?!" But Marcus found he didn't know what else to say. Ryan had been right. He *did* want more power—because, yet again, his father's example had taught him that being a pastor meant being in control. The thought of being a pastor who couldn't make his congregation do what he knew they needed to do made him feel inadequate. He let out a moan of frustration.

Ryan leaned across the aisle and laid a hand on Marcus's shoulder. "From one pastor to another, Marcus, I think there's more going on here than just questioning whether or not you're in the right place. Instead of asking God where else you should be, try asking Him what you should do now that you're here." He stood and pulled a business card from his wallet. "I'm sensing you need some space to think. Please don't hesitate to call if there's anything I can do."

Marcus took the card and Ryan shook his hand, then turned and left the chapel. Feeling emotionally ragged and strangely weary,

Marcus slouched in the pew and laid his head back, eyes closed, and prayed God would make sense of the confusion the conversation had caused.

Morning number thirteen turned out to be Amelia's last on the ward. When she woke, she could tell something had shifted in the night. Her mind was calmer and less clouded. Her emotions, while still down, were more within the range of her typical emotional experience. And when she met with the therapist, he deemed her safe enough to leave.

Had she not been working on her life plan, the news would have been terrifying. But with a return to LA in mind and a plan for the baby in place—at least in her head—she felt better equipped to handle the thought of real life. The only thing she dreaded was seeing Marcus.

Amelia was allowed into her bedroom after therapy to pack. When Kristine had packed to leave three days ago, Amelia had sat outside the door to keep her company. "I can't believe you're leaving," she'd moped as Kristine had tucked her clothes into a small suitcase. "You're the only person here I feel like I can talk to."

"Wow." Kristine had stopped, her pajamas in her hands, and given Amelia her full attention. "I'm really flattered."

"I mean it. The therapists are fine, but they don't know what it's like to be in our heads. At least you get me."

"Yeah, I know what you mean." She'd smiled and adjusted her glasses on her face. "I seem to always click with one other patient when I'm admitted, and it's always someone else with bipolar. It's a unique and unfortunate sisterhood—or brotherhood I guess if it's a guy—and when you find someone who understands you, it can be a real relief."

Amelia's fingers had tapped out Bach on her pretzel-crossed legs as she'd watched Kristine finish her packing. Her quirky roommate had been a nuisance more than anything else when Amelia had first arrived, but now Amelia couldn't imagine life on the ward without her. "So, if you don't have a job, what do you do all day when you're not gracing the mental wing with your effervescence?"

Kristine had let out a good laugh at that. "Yeah, that's what it is." She'd zipped the bag and flopped onto the bed beside it. "Well, I paint. And play my trombone. And go over to my church and volunteer to help with whatever needs doing. There's a hint for you: Volunteering is a really good way to fight depression when you feel it coming on. It keeps your mind off yourself." She'd twitched her mouth back and forth as she thought, a habit Amelia ended up picking up from watching Kristine do it so often. "I'd like to go back to work someday. I try to keep up with what's going on in my field so I can find a job once I get my meds worked out right. But engineering is hard to just read about. I get it more when I'm actually doing it. So, who knows, maybe I'll never get to go back to work."

"That's depressing, don't say that."

Kristine had shrugged. "But it's reality. It bothers me sometimes, but I figure God's got a plan, so I shouldn't worry too much about it." She'd looked to Amelia then with a sympathetic face. "What about you? What are you going to do when you get out?"

Amelia hadn't been able to answer her. By then she'd had most of her plan worked out in her mind, but she hadn't wanted to admit it to Kristine because she knew she'd try to talk her out of it. But now, as she zipped her duffel closed and carried it to the community room to wait for Marcus to arrive, she wished she had. Not because she thought Kristine would approve, but because she knew Kristine would have shared some nugget of truth that would have helped make sense of the chaos she felt inside.

Amelia sat alone on the couch and stared at the doors that led off the ward. She hadn't thought to ask Kristine about the transition back into real life. She wished she had. What did Kristine tell the people in her life when she disappeared for inpatient treatment? How open was she about her disorder? What did the people at her church think about it? Amelia had no idea what she was going to say when people asked where she'd been and why.

She looked at the clock. Still at least half an hour before Marcus arrived. Not willing to engage with the other patients, she opened her bag and pulled out her notebook to try to journal as her therapist had suggested. She flipped open the cover, and an unfamiliar piece of paper fluttered to the floor. She picked it up and unfolded it, confused at the unfamiliar handwriting, then glanced down at the end and saw Kristine's name.

Dear Amelia,

I'm really glad I had the chance to meet you. I'm sorry you're stuck with this diagnosis, but trust me, it's not too bad once you figure out the right meds—and so long as you stay on them. I know I'm not one to talk, seeing as I was in because I stopped, but the thing is, you start feeling better and you can trick yourself into thinking you're okay now and don't need them anymore. Don't do that, okay?

I know you've been questioning your belief in God, but I wanted to put in one last word for Him in case it changed your mind. I think you were probably right about having believed in Him for the wrong reasons, but I think you may be giving up on Him for the wrong reasons too. Just because you didn't want to turn out like your mom, and you did anyway, doesn't mean there's not a God. It just means that there's a reason for you to be who you are. He needs you like this for some reason. You can either accept that and work with it, or you can deny it and run, but either way, it doesn't change who you are. You're bipolar, regardless.

I know you think a different life would be better, but just remember we can't always see what's coming up the road. Going back to California might sound better than living in Nebraska, but what if it's not? Being single again might sound better than being married to a pastor, but I have to say, your husband seems pretty amazing. A lot of people get ditched by their boyfriends and husbands when they develop BP. I did. It's a pretty special kind of love that is not only willing to stick with you, but is as tenacious as Marcus has been in the face of your rejection. Don't underestimate the kind of difference a love like that can make in your life.

And, because God's Word never comes back void, let me quote a quick verse. In John somewhere, a bunch of Jesus' followers stopped following, and Jesus asked His disciples if they wanted to leave too. And Peter said, "To whom shall we go? You have the words of eternal life." It's not about how God can make your life better. It's about reality. Whether you like it or not, God is real. And you can make this life as perfect as you want—but you're still going to die someday. And then what?

I'll be praying for you and your baby. Here's my contact info in case you want to keep in touch. I'll understand if you don't, though, so no pressure.

—Kristine

Amelia folded the note as tears blurred the words before her. She'd felt so confident in her plans, prepared to face the months ahead while she waited for the baby to be born so she could leave. And with a few scrawled paragraphs Kristine had undone it all.

"Amelia, your husband is here."

A surge of fear flooded her body. Amelia clutched the handles of her duffel and headed for the windowless double doors that led to the rest of the hospital. The desk nurse triggered the door release, and Amelia walked out to the hall where Marcus stood.

He looked nervous, like it was their first date. "Hey, Ames." He reached out a hand. "Let me take your bag."

She handed it to him and swallowed against the anxious dryness that invaded her mouth. "Thanks."

"Of course." A shy smile spread across his face, and her heart ached with the realization of how hurt he must have been by her silence. "I missed you, Ames."

"I—missed you, too."

"For real?"

She nodded.

Marcus let out a deep sigh. "Whew. I was really, really worried for a while there." He reached for her hand as they walked to the door, and she let him take it even though she'd planned to keep her emotional distance. She'd figured the cooler she could keep things between them in the coming months, the less painful her eventual departure would be. But now ...

The drive home was awkward. Marcus tried a few times to engage her in conversation, but she was too preoccupied—with Kristine's letter and the doubts it had cast on her intentions, with the weight of the real world she had to somehow fit back into, with sadness over how she had shunned Marcus while hospitalized. "I'm still not a hundred percent," she told him, hoping it would ease the blow. "I'm still depressed. They don't keep you there until you're completely better, just until you're not suicidal. They kept me a little longer because of the baby and trying to make sure the meds were kicking in."

"Ah, gotcha." Marcus squeezed her knee. "I'll shut up, then. Just tell me if there's anything I can do."

"I will."

The smile he beamed her way wrenched her heart even more. It had been easy to think about leaving Nebraska when she'd been isolated, but now, back in Marcus's gravity, her resolve was wavering even more.

When they got home she expected him to drop her off and go back to work. When he followed her inside and began to fix a snack, she asked when he was leaving.

"I'm sort of taking a sabbatical," he said.

She was surprised. "You told me Ed's teaching this month," she said, feeling her face flush at the indirect nod to the letters he'd written, "but I'm home now, so I figured you'd go back."

Marcus kept his eyes on the apple he was slicing. "Actually that's not the only reason."

"It's not?"

"No—but you've got your own stuff to deal with right now; I don't want to go into all my garbage on top of it. Don't worry, though; it's all good." He flashed her a smile and went back to his apple, leaving Amelia to wonder what he was talking about but too wrapped up in her own turmoil to want to press for details.

Not knowing what else to do with herself, Amelia curled up on the couch and shut her eyes. She cursed Kristine for leaving her that message. She'd had a good thing going before that, and it had given her hope that she wouldn't be stuck in this life she'd grown to despise. But all that talk about God being real whether she wanted Him to be or not, and that her bipolar might actually be a good thing … She still wasn't sure she bought any of it, but it made just enough sense to throw everything out of whack.

The baby fluttered in her abdomen. She put a hand to her stomach, patted it gently, then lay down to take a nap. Now that the edge was off the depression, sleep came more easily, and she might as well take advantage of it. Anything that gave her an excuse not to contemplate her life.

✳

Having Amelia home wasn't what Marcus thought it would be. She'd been in therapy, he'd been working through his problems with Ed, and he'd naively thought they'd be in a better place now. He hadn't expected her to still be struggling as much as she was, and to have to chart her moods for her therapist, and to still be trying to avoid him. He thought that's what she was doing with all those naps, anyway.

It felt similar to when they'd been living in different states. Marcus had this interior life full of chaos and questions about who he was, and God was slowly revealing more and more of who and what Marcus was supposed to be—and Amelia knew nothing about it. And he could tell Amelia was experiencing something like it too. She almost never stayed this quiet for this long, and whenever she did, it was because she was really wrapped up in something. What was going on in her head?

While they'd driven the long, awkward ride home from the hospital, he had vowed to himself that he'd be a better husband. No more escaping to work to avoid uncomfortable discussions and feelings. No more allowing their communication to stagnate. And no more tiptoeing around Amelia and letting her retreat into her head. He loved her too much to lose her to another depression.

"So ... how are you?" he asked her one night as they sat worlds away from each other on the couch and stared at a Hallmark movie.

She shrugged. "Fine."

"You're not ... you're not suicidal again, are you?"

She looked surprised. "What? No, not at all. I'm actually feeling almost normal. Why?"

He shifted on the couch so he was facing her, and slowly reached over to take her hand that was resting in her lap. "You've been so quiet. I miss talking with you. I don't know what you're thinking anymore. And ... I guess now I'm worried that, since I didn't see the signs of your depression the first time, I'm going to miss them the next time too."

He thought he saw a glimmer of the old Amelia in her expression as she nudged him gently with her foot. "I promise—I really promise—I'm not suicidal. I'm hardly even sad anymore. The medication they've got me on is definitely doing something good. I just have a ... a lot on my mind."

"I know how that goes." He swallowed hard, knowing she'd be mad that he'd waited so long to tell her about his father. "We're both hiding something."

Her guarded look returned. "Both of us, hm?"

"I'll trade you, my secret for yours."

Her mouth twitched. "I'm curious what yours is, but ... I'm not ready yet." She stood. "I'm going to go to bed."

The hope that had briefly flared in his chest died out as she gave his knee a pat and headed for the bedroom.

Marcus hadn't talked to anyone about his conversation with Pastor Ryan. But he'd ruminated on the man's words long enough. It was time to hash them out with another person. A week after Amelia had come home, Marcus met Ed at the diner once again. "So how's

Amelia?" Ed asked as he doctored his coffee with sugar and cream. "Was her time at the hospital helpful?"

Marcus filled him in with what few details he knew. "There's something she's not telling me, though. I'm not sure if I should be worried or not."

Ed frowned as he stirred. "Secrets in a marriage are no good."

Marcus's guilt kicked in. "You're right. But I can't force her to tell me what's going on, either."

"No, that's true. Best just to make sure you're nurturing your relationship as best you can so she feels safe telling you."

Marcus nodded, glad he had his pie to focus on. "On a different topic, I had an interesting conversation with the hospital chaplain." He told Ed what Ryan had said, noting especially the other pastor's admonition to stop thinking about whether he was in the wrong place and concentrate instead on what God wanted him to do at New Hope. "I've been going crazy trying to get things off the ground here—you've experienced that yourself. And I know neither of us wants to see the church collapse around us. But … I've been praying about what he said, and it makes more and more sense every day."

Ed's gaze was steady on his pie, but Marcus could tell he was thinking. "That's excellent advice," he finally said. "I'm disappointed that I didn't think of that myself." He glanced up at Marcus. "And has God revealed anything to you about what your purpose is here?"

"I think so, actually. I—I really think I am supposed to be a pastor."

Ed chuckled. "I could have told you that, son. Anyone who listens to you preach knows you're a born teacher. And your sermons are some of the best I've heard. Very impressive for a man so young."

The compliment was heady stuff. Marcus tried not to let his giddy appreciation show too much. "Thanks, Ed. That means a lot."

"You're welcome. I guess the next question is, what do we do now?"

"Well ..." Marcus tapped his fork on his pie, nervous about the suggestion he was about to make. "I think the board needs to draw a line in the sand, saying *this* is what we're about, and if you're in, great. If you're not ..." He shrugged.

"Show them the door?"

"Maybe not quite like that, but make it clear that we're not going to accommodate attitudes and behavior that are detrimental to the body."

"Set some boundaries."

"Precisely." Marcus pushed his pie away, his energy focused entirely now on the conversation. The passion he'd felt for the job when he'd first been hired was smoldering again. "When I think about the vision you had, of a community that really took care of its own, I get so fired up. I want to be a part of that. And I really think God wants me to be a part of it too. And I can see there's going to be a rocky road ahead as the members are called upon to either get serious or go home. There are going to be some hurt feelings, some big anger—because people have grown complacent and they like things the way they are, not because I foresee us being mean in our delivery. But what's going to come out of it ... I think it's going to be amazing."

Ed smiled. "A phoenix rising from the ashes."

Marcus's heart knocked in his chest. "Yes. Yes, exactly like that."

They spent the rest of their time together brainstorming, and when Marcus left for home, he felt like a new man. Everything was falling into place. His purpose was clear again, and without the weight of the congregation's health on his shoulders, he felt that he actually had the strength to handle whatever they might throw at him when changes started to happen.

There was only one thing left to do: Show Amelia that her secret was safe with him.

＊

A month out of the hospital, Amelia's depression had greatly improved, though she still felt emotionally wobbly on some days. Unfortunately, the stability didn't translate to her plans. She changed her mind about her future and her faith almost daily. Ruminations about motherhood would send her dreaming of running away to LA after the baby was born, but the next day she'd see a mom with a newborn at the store and find herself taken by the perfect little bundle in the stroller. She'd be comfortable with the idea of a godless world, only to have Marcus read her something he'd found interesting in one of his preaching magazines that made it more obvious than ever that God had to be real. Her soul was suffering from a bad case of whiplash.

Having Marcus around so much made it worse. She longed for the connection they'd had before New Hope had sent him that letter. It was killing her not to open up to him, especially after he'd admitted how much he missed talking with her. And when he'd said he had a secret too—it had taken all her willpower not to capitulate just so she could hear it. She didn't like the idea of him having a secret from her. But who was she to complain?

She still held to the belief that leaving was the right thing to do, but she still had so much to figure out, and she didn't have space to think with him always there. She was afraid her doubts and thoughts of leaving would show up somehow on her face. And it was harder to think about leaving when she was surrounded by the scent of his cologne and distracted by his very presence. They hadn't had sex the entire time she'd been depressed, but since coming home from the hospital the combination of a stabilized mood and the absence of intimacy for so long had her longing to make love to him, and he was more than willing to comply when she admitted her desire. But the act left her feeling tremendously guilty—how she could give him her body in bed, but not share her soul and deepest thoughts?

And as if it wasn't already difficult enough to commit herself to leaving, Marcus's blatant—and effective—attempts at expressing his support and love for her nearly did her in. He'd started going back to the church to work, but he would leave her little notes if she was still sleeping, or make her breakfast if she was awake and deliver it to her on the couch with a kiss. He catered to the silly cravings the pregnancy brought about, even anticipating them before they hit and coming home from work with a collection of random items that he predicted she'd want at two in the morning. Regardless of whether she did or not, she'd indulge him by eating them at one point or another, loath to hurt his feelings and secretly tickled that he put so much thought into something as weird as her changing tastes.

In an effort to contribute to their life again and to try to make up for her secrecy, she returned to teaching piano for Blue Note. Six students came to their apartment throughout the week for hour-long

sessions, and while the money wasn't much, it was better than nothing. The bigger payoff came in feeling like she was still able to be
productive even though her brain was so defective. Her self-esteem
had taken a major hit with the diagnosis, and even though teaching
was one of the last things she wanted to do with her life, she was glad
to know she could still do at least one thing to contribute to society
and make a living.

One Wednesday morning at the end of June, she went out to the
coffee shop on Main just to get out of the house for a while. Armed
with a book and a wide-open afternoon, she claimed a beat-up armchair in the corner and made a halfhearted attempt to read. But the
group of women gathered around a nearby table stole her attention
and unwittingly cured Amelia's indecision about her life.

"Guess who got eight solid hours of sleep last night?" said a
woman with bright lipstick.

"Don't rub it in," said one with her hair in a messy ponytail. "I'd
kill you out of jealousy, but I'm too tired." She drank deeply from her
coffee while the others laughed.

"Dave got eight hours," added a woman in a too-tight shirt.
"Maybe even nine. Slept right through Izzy's screaming fit at two
thirty. I don't know how he does it."

"Men have some weird ability to sleep through anything their
children do at night," said Ponytail. "They only respond to orders
barked from a mother on the edge of insanity."

"Well, of course—it's *our* job to take care of the kids, remember?" said another woman. "Because they have to, you know, go sit
at a desk for eight hours, and that's *really* tiring." More laughter as
she rolled her eyes.

"The minute Greg walks in the door I tell him he's on duty with the kids," said Lipstick. "I've had it with them by the time he gets home. The whining—seriously, I feel like my ears are bleeding half the time." The others were vocal in their commiseration.

Amelia had heard enough. This was the last thing she needed. Leaving her nearly finished drink on the window ledge near her chair, she fled from the coffee shop. Was *that* what it was like to be a mother? There was clear resentment and sarcasm in these women's tones. It was what she'd always heard from her own mom, but she'd always assumed other people thought differently, that her mother's venom had found its source in her craziness. But apparently it was a more common view than she'd thought.

Amelia didn't want her life to become one giant gripe session. It would be hard enough to resist with the stupid bipolar thing hanging over her.

She drove to the library and waited for one of the public terminals to open up, then sat down to do some research. She'd had enough waffling. She was getting out of here.

When Amelia arrived home, the apartment was empty. A note on the kitchen counter told her Marcus had gone out for a run. She took advantage of the solitude to start writing out notes on her plan at the dining room table. She started with a list of necessities— travel back to LA, a place to stay, a job—then began to brainstorm options. Her research at the library had been scattered and aimless, driven more by the need to take some kind of step in the direction of leaving than by an attempt to find useful information. When her initial burst of energy diminished and her frantic hunger for a way out abated, she'd come home in order to give her mind time to digest everything she'd taken in. Now she set about plugging that information into her list and fleshing out the details. She had less than four months to get it all laid out; once the baby was born she'd have to start implementing.

Amelia's thoughts were on Karis and whether she'd make a good wife for Marcus when her cell rang and startled her like a sudden crash of thunder. She jumped, the pen fumbling from her fingers, and grabbed it before another ring could jar her again. "Hello?"

"Hey, Ames, it's me."

Jill's voice came as a surprise that knocked Amelia off balance. They hadn't talked much since Amelia had moved, though Jill had certainly tried more than Amelia had to keep their friendship alive. "Oh—Jill, hey. How are you?"

"I'm pretty good now that it's official: I'm a mom."

Amelia gasped. "The baby? You had the baby?"

"This morning, yeah. Seven pounds, seven ounces, will one day answer to the name Bradley Michael."

Amelia didn't really want to hear about this—it made the impending birth of her own baby all too real. But she couldn't get out of it now. She did her best to fake her enthusiasm. "Oh my goodness, Jill. That's—that's wonderful. Congratulations. How are you feeling?"

"I'm all right. I'm still not sure what was worse: labor or the first six months of the pregnancy when I couldn't eat a blasted thing."

Amelia winced. "Well, it's all over now."

"Yes it is. Thank the Lord. How are you feeling?"

"I'm … doing all right."

"Good, I'm glad to hear it. I promise not to tell you any awful stories about giving birth. I know you're not psyched about it in the first place. But honestly, once it's over, you realize it wasn't *that* bad."

"Heh, thanks."

"So you and Marcus have to plan a trip out here soon, before you can't fly anymore. I want you to meet Brad. Plus, I miss you."

"Aw, you're sweet." And then, to avoid more baby talk or the possibility that Jill would try to get all sentimental with her, Amelia took a chance and changed the subject. "But I'm moving back, so eventually I'll be around all the time again."

"You are? Oh wow—I didn't think you ever actually would. Is Marcus coming back, too?"

"No—just me."

"What about the baby?"

"Well, actually … I'm leaving the baby with Marcus."

The pause before Jill answered made Amelia sweat. "Seriously?"

"Yes."

"Um, I feel like I'm missing something. How exactly are you going to work this?"

Amelia sat up straighter, gathering her courage to seal her new truth by speaking it aloud. "I'm leaving Marcus, Jill. I'm turning the baby over to him and coming back to LA."

The silence on Jill's end made panic start to percolate in her middle. She started talking to fill the space. "I've put a lot of thought into this," she said, standing to pace. "Ever since my time in the hospital, I've struggled with the idea of staying here and trying to be this homemaker-slash-pastor's wife. It's not what I thought it would be, and I'm not the right girl for the job. Remember when we went out for sushi, back before Christmas, and you said you weren't even sure I was a Christian?"

"Y-yeah—but remember, I—"

"No, Jill, you were right. I mean, I guess maybe I sort of was, but it was for all the wrong reasons, and lately I've realized I'm just not convinced about it all. Marcus can't be married to a woman who doesn't even share his beliefs. He's a pastor, for crying out loud." She wandered the apartment, afraid to stop talking, sensing Jill would read her the riot act when she got the chance. "When my mom disappeared, I was desperate for anything that would give me hope that I wouldn't turn out like her. You and your faith were right there in my face, so I grabbed it when you offered it. But I would have grabbed anything. I didn't think about it, I didn't study it—you looked like you had it all together, the stuff you told me about God made enough sense, so I went for it. And then I made that ridiculous decision to transfer out of Juilliard, and I met Marcus.… Honestly, if I hadn't met him I don't know if I would have lasted this long as a Christian. But I can't keep faking it. And it's not fair to him if I stick around."

"Amelia, you can't just leave him with the baby."

"Why not? He's going to be a great dad, he's got a ton of support here—"

"That's not what I mean. I mean, you seem to think it's going to be like handing over a—a box of books or something. 'I'm moving but I don't want to bring these; here, take all my paperback romances.' This is your *baby*, Amelia. A living, breathing piece of yourself. Trust me, you have no idea how you're going to feel about this child until you've given birth."

"Jill, listen, I didn't want this baby in the first place. I don't want to be a mom. I've never wanted that." She punched a pillow on the bed, frustrated that she had to justify herself and afraid that, when she laid it out like this, she'd find her reasoning too flimsy to follow through on. "I don't want to look back on my life in twenty years and hate myself for getting stuck with a kid I don't know how to raise, a husband who believes something I don't, and for missing my chance to actually do something with my life and prove myself. But by then I'll be so entrenched, I won't be able to leave. I still have a chance if I do it now. Marcus will have a chance to find a wife he can depend on to be the Christian woman he thought I was when he married me, someone who knows what to do with a baby."

She ran out of words and let herself sink to the bed. The line was quiet for a moment, then Jill said, "I can't believe I'm hearing this. I can't believe you're actually talking about walking out on your family."

Amelia rubbed a hand over her forehead and squeezed her eyes shut. She really wanted this conversation to end. "What's better, Jill—to deny who I am and make all three of us suffer for it? Or to let them move on with their lives and find someone who makes sense in the life they want, and move on with mine and be who I really am?"

"You're out of your mind, Amelia. Is your medication balanced?"

"Oh please—I'm bipolar, not delusional."

"I'm not so sure about that."

Amelia rubbed a hand over her eyes. "Look, pretend I never said anything, okay? Obviously I shouldn't have brought it up. I shouldn't have expected you to be supportive. I'm just excited about getting my life back on track, and I wanted to share it with someone, so I figured I'd tell my best friend. My mistake. Congrats on the baby; I'll talk to you later." She shut her phone and sucked in a deep breath, then let it out in a huff as she stood to return to her list in the dining room. Why did she go and complicate things like that? Now she'd have to worry about Jill telling Dane, and Dane telling—

"Marcus."

He stood outside the bedroom, arms folded across his chest that heaved with measured breaths. She tried to think of something to say, but her mind was blank with horror. They stared at each other for what felt like hours, until Marcus finally broke the standoff.

"You're leaving me?"

CHAPTER 14

Marcus's heart was pounding, and not just from his run. Amelia wrung her hands, started and stopped sentences before they made any sense, and finally pushed past him and said, "It's for the best."

He felt like he was in *The Twilight Zone*. Who was this woman? "It's for the best? It's for the *best?* How can there be a single iota of 'best' in walking out on your husband and child? My gosh, Amelia, who have you been talking to?"

"No one! You think someone talked me into this?"

"I don't know what else to think—why else would my wife be talking like this?"

"Because your wife isn't who you think she is!"

"Yeah, so I heard." He hadn't believed it when he'd heard it, and he still didn't believe it now. "Not a Christian anymore, either?"

"I never was, Marcus. Not really. I thought I was, but come on—you must have seen it, too."

He shook his head. "No. I saw someone who was young in her faith and still working her way through it. Why didn't you tell me you'd begun to have doubts?"

Her laughter was hollow. "Tell you? Tell my pastor-husband that I thought God was a hoax? Yeah, that would have gone over real well."

"I can promise it would have gone over a lot better than this."

She buried her face in her hands, then slid them down to her neck. "Look, Marcus. This place suits you. You fit right in with the Main Street, USA, community and the quaint little church. Me—not so much."

"You were settling in—"

"Settling in isn't the same. And this is about so much more than just not liking Wheatridge. This is about a—a baby I'm terrified of, a husband whose job I can't support—what would the elders say when they found out I wasn't a believer anymore? You're having a hard enough time there without people talking behind your back about your crazy wife."

Marcus cut her off with a slice of his hand through the space between them. He thought he'd been scared and angry when he'd realized she'd tried to kill herself, but what he was feeling now trumped all that, and then some. "Stop. Look, do you love me or not?"

"Of course I love you, Marcus. What isn't there to love? You've been absolutely amazing, aside from the whole moving-to-Nebraska thing. And it's because I love you that I need to leave. I want you to have someone who wants the same life you do."

"Baloney. You don't love me and you don't have the guts to just come out and say it."

"That's not true!" She shouted it, fists balled at her sides. "I do love you!" Her face crumpled as tears slid down her cheeks. "Do you know how frightening it is to think I'll never meet someone who loves me as much as you do? Or that you really were the right one and I was too broken to make it work? Of course I love you, Marcus!"

Praying with all the strength he had, Marcus stepped forward and pulled Amelia into his arms. "Then please, Amelia, don't leave me."

Amelia began to bawl, clinging to Marcus as though in danger of being sucked away into quicksand. He wrapped his arms around her as tightly as he could with the bump of their baby between them and held her until she'd exhausted her tears. He led her to the bed and pulled her down beside him, never letting go of her hand for fear he'd never get it back. "There's something I want to tell you."

She sniffed and looked at him, frowning. "What?"

"Before you went into the hospital, I got an email from my dad." He took a deep breath, then told her the whole story—not only his revelation about his father, but about his doubts about himself and his calling, about his fear that he'd dragged Amelia to Wheatridge for no good reason, and his conversations with Ed and Pastor Ryan. "I understand, way better than you realize, what it's like to fear your future and to think your life isn't what it's supposed to be. I know what it's like to learn something about a parent that completely upends your world and makes you question who you are. The difference between you and me, though, is that eventually I let out those fears and questions and sought input from people who were wiser than me. You've just—trusted your own mind. There's nothing wrong with being independent, but you can't expect to always come up with the right answers on your own."

Marcus squeezed her hand. *Please speak to her, God.* Handing her another tissue from the box on the nightstand, he said, "If you'd said you didn't love me anymore, then I might have let you walk away. But I can't when I know you're just running scared. Give me a chance to help you sort things out, Amelia. Let me lay out some arguments for God. Let me brainstorm with you on how we can make this work. And if we can't, and you want to leave … I won't force you to stay."

She crumpled the used tissue in her hands, her expression dubious. "Seriously?"

"Yes."

She was quiet a moment, looking lost in thought. "This sounds like another agreement we came to once upon a time."

He nodded soberly. "I mean it."

She stared at her hands, then nodded. "Okay."

"Thank you, God." He kissed her, relief overwhelming him. He leaned his forehead against hers and willed the adrenaline pumping through his system to abate. "I love you so much, Amelia. I can't even begin to tell you how much."

"Even though I nearly …"

"Even though." He kissed her again, then stood and held out a hand. "Come on. I'm taking you out for dinner."

She let him pull her from the sofa and wrap his arm around her. With few words, but more peace in the air than he'd felt since December, they changed clothes and drove to the only Italian eatery in town after Amelia shyly admitted to a craving for lasagna. With the dam of secrecy broken, Amelia asked gentle questions regarding Marcus's revelations about his calling and his father, and Marcus carefully broached the subject of the baby and what decisions they still needed to make so Amelia felt prepared for the birth. By the time they were pulling into the parking lot at the apartment complex, their argument felt like it had happened days ago, instead of hours. And finally, despite the agreement they'd reached that left the door open for Amelia to leave, Marcus felt some hope for their future.

Marcus hung his keys on their hook and kicked off his shoes. "Can I get you anything? Ice cream? Water?"

Amelia gave him a sheepish grin. "Both?"

"You've got it."

He kissed her and walked to the kitchen, trying to remember if she'd finished the hot fudge he'd gotten her the week before. He was about to start looking when Amelia made a noise that made his heart skip a beat. He ran back to the living room. She was grasping the back of the armchair, her other arm hugging her belly. Her face was pinched and white.

Marcus's blood went cold. "What? What is it?"

She shook her head, breathing hard, and grabbed his hand when he tried to wrap his arm around her. "I ... I think it's ... a contraction."

His mouth went dry. He swallowed hard as his thoughts raced to queue up a plan of attack. "Wait—it can't be, you're only six months along."

"I know. Oh God. Marcus—"

"Don't worry, here, sit down." He led her to the sofa, then ran to the kitchen for water. "Here, drink this, maybe you're just dehydrated."

She drank down the entire glass as Marcus looked on and prayed. When she gasped again five minutes later, Marcus grabbed her phone from the table and scrolled through the numbers to find her OB. *Please, God, protect the baby. Protect Amelia.* He left a message with the answering service, then knelt in front of Amelia and took her hands. "I'm going to pack up some stuff for you in case we have to go to the hospital, okay? Just hang tight."

He kissed her and went into the bedroom, praying under his breath as he pulled clothes from the closet and stuffed them into the same duffel Amelia had taken to the hospital in Omaha. When the doctor called back and heard what was going on, she directed them to go straight to the ER, promising to meet them there. He grabbed clothes for himself, added them to the bag, and went back to the living room. "Okay, babe," he said, helping her up from the couch. "Let's get to the hospital and *not* have a baby."

It took over twenty-four hours for the OB to be sure, but after an array of medical interventions Amelia was declared to no longer be in labor and sent home on strict bed rest. She spent the first week scoping out daytime television and reading books, and the second week playing games on the Internet. Once she'd wrung the life out of every pastime, she had nothing left to do but think.

The day spent in the hospital had brought into sharp clarity how uncertain life could be. Despite her reticence about the baby, Amelia had been terrified at the thought of something being wrong with her—or him—and feared it was her inability to accept the pregnancy that might be causing the baby to attempt a breakout. After she'd been cleared and sent home, she'd tried not to think about any of it—the impending birth, what had almost happened, the baby—but without anything else to do, it was hard to keep her mind off it all.

She'd done some reading last week about how in-utero babies could be affected by their mothers' emotions, and how a mother could turn a breech baby just by talking to it. If that were really true, then who knew what kind of damage she'd done to her child already with all her negativity, not to mention the depression. Guilt prompted her to apologize. "I didn't know all this stuff before," she said to her stomach as she visualized the baby politely listening. "If I had, I would have been more careful with how I thought about you. Don't take any of this personally, okay? It's really not about you. Heh—it's not you, it's me. I'm just … I'm not cut out to be a mom. And you're going to have it hard enough, being a pastor's kid and having my genes. I'm really sorry if you end up with bipolar too. Believe me, if there was anything I could do to make sure you didn't get it, I would." The thought came without her planning it, and she was glad to see she harbored enough goodwill toward the baby to wish she could prevent it from inheriting her faulty mind. "You know, if it were true that it's the thought that counts, then I might feel a little better about all this, because it's not like I have anything against kids in general. I'd love to be a great mom. I'd love to think I could handle this and that I'd figure it all out eventually. But wanting to be good enough won't make up for the damage I do."

This wasn't helping at all. Dwelling on her shortcomings just made her feel worse. Amelia shifted on the couch, her backside aching from being there all morning, and tried to think of something else she could say to the baby that wasn't so depressing.

"Your dad is awesome, by the way. He's superhandsome, and really smart, and you would not believe how excited he is about you. The two of you are going to have a lot of fun, I think."

She considered Marcus's relationship with his parents and wondered how he would do things differently as a dad. There were some obvious things, like not resenting your children and actually telling them he loved them. But what little things did she not know about from his childhood that would figure in to how he parented?

Amelia's eyes went wide as she had a revelation.

Marcus was in the same boat she was—having grown up with a parent who did everything wrong and whose lousy example left him unprepared for his new role. He'd never want to follow in his father's shoes. And yet, he wasn't afraid of messing up their baby. He wasn't terrified of falling into the same patterns. Why?

Amelia picked up her cell from the table and dialed. "Why aren't you freaking out about being a dad?" she asked without preamble when Marcus answered.

"Um … why would I be?"

"Because your dad sucked. Why aren't you afraid of turning into him?"

"I—I don't know, I haven't really thought about it. I just feel like this is different—that this is an opportunity for me to take a wrong and make it right, in a way. Like, I can use his example as an anti-example, as in, 'If you want to be a good dad, don't do this.'" He chuckled. "Does that make sense?"

Amelia let out a frustrated sigh. "Sort of. Why can't I think like that? I just realized we're both coming at this whole parenting thing with major role-model deficiencies, but we're responding in totally different ways."

"Maybe it's because our expectations were different from the get-go. I wanted kids; I always imagined us having them. You saw them as something that might happen someday, but they weren't a goal for you, they weren't something you were actually looking forward to the way I was."

"Hm. Maybe."

"Don't stress about it, babe. Just keep telling yourself, 'I am not my mom.'"

"But I am."

"No you're not! You're not at all your mom, given what you've told me about her. You've done way more to better your situation than your mom ever did. She didn't get help. She didn't go to therapy. She didn't let her husband take care of her the way you let me take care of you. And your devotion to pursuing music is so admirable, so much more passionate than your mom ever was about her art … Believe me, babe, you are nothing like her."

Tears stood in Amelia's eyes at Marcus's affirmation. "Really?"

"Really. Just do what I'm doing: Picture everything she did as an example of how not to be an awesome mom—and then just do the opposite. I know you don't believe it, but babe, you've got the makings of being a truly fantastic mother. Remember when we worked with the inner-city kids during college? You were a natural, and they all loved you. You always seemed to know what they needed to hear. You made them feel important, and cared for, and respected. You're fun, you're funny, you're passionate, you love like crazy.… What kid wouldn't want a mom like that?"

Amelia wanted to hug him through the phone. "Thank you, Marcus."

"Anytime, babe. I love you."

"I love you, too."

They hung up and Amelia let her hands rest on her growing stomach. She took a deep breath, blew it out through pursed lips, then said, "Okay, kiddo. We're going to give this a shot, okay?" She closed her eyes and imagined holding the baby and enjoying it. She pictured herself pushing the stroller down Main Street, doing dinner dishes with the baby in the wrap she'd seen on a mom at church, sitting on the couch with Marcus and staring at him/her on the cushion between them. She pictured diaper changes, late-night feedings, baths in the kitchen sink. After a few minutes she opened her eyes and let out her breath as though she'd been holding it.

"That wasn't too bad. I guess at the beginning it's pretty easy to be a decent mom, right? Feed you, clothe you, change your diaper, put you to sleep … I think I can do that." The baby gave a kick and Amelia chuckled. "Glad you agree."

A contraction seized her around the middle, driving her breath from her lungs. When the tension released she grabbed her water bottle and downed it all, then picked up her phone and squeezed it as she stared at the clock on the DVD player. A minute passed, then another, and after the third Amelia began to relax. "Are you just playing with me? Because I don't actually find that amusing."

Six minutes passed before another one struck, and this time Amelia was dialing Marcus before it even finished. "Contractions again," she said through clenched teeth when he answered. "Six minutes apart."

"I'm on my way."

At the hospital, Amelia was dosed with terbutaline and a steroid to mature the baby's lungs. After twenty-four hours, the contractions still hadn't stopped, and her OB prepared them for the possibility that the baby would be born in the next day or two. "But I'm only twenty-seven weeks along," Amelia said, trying not to panic. "The poor thing will barely be …"

The OB put a hand on Ameila's shoulder. "Odds for survival at this stage are good, though—80 to 85 percent. And the facility here is excellent; this is the hospital you want to be at if you can't be in Omaha or Lincoln. We'll do everything we can to put this off, but you need to stay positive and prepare yourself for the possibility of labor soon."

When she'd left Marcus and Amelia alone, Amelia groaned and buried her face in her hands. "What am I doing wrong? Why does this keep happening?"

"I don't know, Ames, but listen, it's not your fault, all right? There's nothing you did to start it and nothing you can do to stop it. You just have to go with it and try to stay positive. Whatever happens, God's in control. I know you're having a hard time believing that these days, but I believe it and I'm confident that no matter what happens, God will use it for good." He kissed her hair. "Now, is there anything I can do for you? Anything you can think of that we didn't bring from home that you might want?"

Amelia shook her head, her arm over her eyes. "No. Nothing."

"Would you mind if I prayed? I'll do it in my head if you want— I just want to be with you when I do."

She shrugged. "Okay."

They used to pray together all the time, but Marcus's prayer now was nothing like the ones he used to pray. He'd always sounded so confident, so eloquent, so *pastorly* when he prayed. But this time, the first time she'd heard him pray for her since before he'd moved to Nebraska, the posturing was gone. Instead, his words were humble, simple, and straight to the point. "God, we're scared for our baby, but I know You know what's going to happen and that, whatever it is, it's what has to happen for Your plan to be fulfilled. But even so, God, I'm asking You to please protect him or her, and protect Amelia, too. Prepare us for what's coming next, and help us to cling to You for our peace and comfort. Amen."

"Thank you," Amelia whispered.

"You're welcome."

She peeked out at him. "Would you feel awful if I wanted to be alone for a bit?"

He smiled. "Not at all. If you need me, just tell the nurse I went down to the lobby. I'm going to call Ed and let him know what's going on. Okay?"

She nodded and they kissed once more before Marcus disappeared down the hall. Amelia brushed tears from her cheeks and whispered, "What are you up to in there?" Another contraction was the baby's reply, and when it was over Amelia squeezed her eyes shut and took a chance.

All right, God. I'm desperate here. I don't know what else to do. I'm scared about labor, I'm scared the baby is going to have all sorts of problems ... I can barely imagine parenting a normal child, God; I can't even begin to fathom parenting one that has special needs from being born too soon. If You're real, then please don't shut me out here. Give me some hope or something. Reassure me that whatever happens, I can actually handle it. Because honestly, all this is making me want to flee the state even more than the thought of being a mom to a regular baby did. I know I told Marcus I'd give it a shot, but that was when I thought things would be normal. I don't know if I can agree to that if things go south here.

Amelia opened her eyes and shook her head at her prayer and muttered to herself, "That was so lame."

I want your honesty.

Amelia twitched, startled by the strong impression that had flashed into her mind. Had that been real, or just her imagination? She took a deep breath to calm her racing heart before the nurses thought she was going into distress. "God?" she whispered. "Was that You?"

Nothing happened, and Amelia tried to rub away the goosebumps that had risen on her arms. She didn't know who else it would be, but if it *was* God, then she had to appreciate the sentiment.

All right then. In case it was You … I'm mad at You, about the whole bipolar thing, and the baby thing. Really, You thought the timing of all this was good? I don't see how You could. It sucks, all of it. I do not get Your way of thinking.

A verse came to mind. ***My thoughts are not your thoughts, neither are your ways my ways.***

Okay, so maybe I can't see the big picture like You can, she prayed further. Was there a big picture? Or just random crap that had no meaning and would never get redeemed somehow? *And I don't just mean the bipolar and the baby,* she prayed. *I mean all of it—not being the pianist I always wanted to be, not living the life I thought I'd live.*

She looked up at the ceiling, wishing she could see past the roof and the atmosphere and the stars and look God in the eyes. *Tell me I'll be able to look back on all this at the end of my life and see how it all came together for good like Marcus thinks it will.*

The impression that came next was so strong she thought it must have been a memory of something that had already happened. In a millisecond flash Amelia saw herself and Marcus and a young woman she knew was the baby she was carrying now. She was beautiful, with Amelia's red hair and Marcus's eyes, and she was playing Mozart on a baby grand in a living room somewhere. It came and went so quickly she had no time to study it, but she was overwhelmed with confidence, with no explanation as to why, that everything really was going to be all right.

A contraction gripped her, followed quickly by a second and a third. Two nurses ran in, and Amelia sent one after Marcus, knowing in her heart that this was it. The other nurse performed an internal check and said to Amelia, "You're nearly ten centimeters. Dang, that was fast."

"Is the baby all right?"

"Baby's at station one—you're in active labor, Amelia."

Marcus came on the heels of the second nurse, who began to convert the room for delivery at the instructions of the first, who was paging the OB. Marcus grabbed her hand. "Are you all right?"

With the picture of their daughter burned into her memory, Amelia couldn't help but smile. "I am. You were right. Everything is going to be okay."

CHAPTER 15

Within an hour of Amelia's vision, Hope Aisling Sheffield was born and taken straight to the NICU. Amelia sent Marcus to be with her and to observe what they did so he could give her a play-by-play later on, but he wished she hadn't. Seeing his daughter surrounded by wires and hooked up to a ventilator just about killed him.

"When can we hold her?" he asked Marcela, the NICU nurse who was on shift when Marcus followed Hope down to the ward.

"Not until she's off the vent," she said with a sympathetic smile. "But once we're sure she's stable, we'll start some touch therapy. That'll be you just stroking her with a finger. Some babies can't handle much of it, but it's all just trial and error. We'll do as much as we can without overstimulating her."

Marcus stared through the incubator at Hope's thin chest rising and falling with the rhythm of the vent. He could see her veins just below the surface of her jaundiced skin. He didn't want to stare, but he couldn't help it—she was a miracle.

When he'd asked every question Amelia had given him, Marcus returned to her room to give her an update. "One pound, twelve ounces; fourteen inches long exactly. She's on a vent for breathing right now; they said it'll take a while before they know if there are any complications. So far, though, everything looks good."

Amelia reached out to hug him and then burst into tears. He sat beside her on the bed and wrapped his arms around her. "Hey, babe, it's gonna be okay, remember? God's got this, He's totally in control." He smiled a little. "I guess this means you're more attached to her than you thought you'd be, hm?"

She hiccuped a chuckle and nodded against his shoulder. "I didn't expect this," she said when she was able to talk. "I didn't expect to feel so … protective."

"Well, you're a mom now. That's what happens when you have a kid of your own, I guess." He grinned. "Hey—we're parents."

"I know." She sniffed and gave him a quavery smile. "For better or worse, huh?"

"Definitely better. Better than we both had." He kissed her, relieved that she was doing as well as she was. He'd been encouraged by her sudden change in mind-set but had worried it would dissipate when they learned of the obstacles Hope would face. For all they knew, worse things were down the road, but for Hope to be this healthy was a true miracle, and the longer Amelia could rest in the belief that all would be well, the better she'd be if things started going downhill.

He also wondered if that belief was going to translate to their marriage. His heart was already filled to capacity with love for Hope, but he didn't see how he'd ever be able to raise her and work at the same time. And the thought of not having Amelia there, not just as a mom but as his partner through it all, made that almost-bursting heart want to break.

He knew it might not be the best time, but he had to know what she was thinking about her life. If he was going to be raising Hope alone, he wanted to know that now, so he could start figuring out exactly how he'd make it work. "Amelia. I need to ask you something."

Her face clouded. "Okay."

"Listen. I know we had an arrangement all worked out. But …
You seem more at peace with things now than you were when we last
talked about it. And that's raising my hopes, but if there really isn't
any hope I don't want to—"

"Marcus, you're not making sense."

He took a deep breath and said in a rush, "Are you still thinking
you might leave us?"

She blinked. "Ah." She licked her lips, her eyes trained on something beyond his shoulder. He tried not to read anything into how
long it was taking her to respond. "Um—"

Marcus waved a hand and mentally cursed his impatience. "I
shouldn't have brought this up now. I'm sorry. I just—when you said
everything was going to be okay I thought maybe—"

"No, it's all right, I understand." She held his hand and smiled,
though her eyes looked weary. "I … I want to say that I'll stay."

"You *want* to?"

"Yes."

"But you can't."

She bit her lip, then said, "I think I need to figure out first how
I can make sure I can follow through with it."

His hopes went up another notch. "Okay, okay. We can figure
that out. Like—therapy, together? God knows—literally—that I
would benefit from it."

She nodded slowly. "Yes … That might help."

"And time alone to keep up with your music? Although …" He
stopped, not sure if he should say what had just become clear to him.

"Although what?"

"Well … Hear me out here, and don't read anything in to what I'm saying, okay? Take my words at face value."

She rolled her eyes. "All right, what is it already?"

Marcus mulled a few more seconds, then began slowly as he tried to figure out the best way to say it. "Since you've been here—and I know a lot of that time was spent depressed, so maybe that skews things—piano has gone to the back burner for you. And the more I think about it, it seems like maybe your dreams about piano and touring and your career weren't so much because you're so in love with music and performing, but because of what you were trying to prove." His pace picked up as his idea found sure footing in his mind. "Like me and pastoring—I didn't start down that road because I had some revelation from God when I was a kid that I was born to preach, or even because I had a passion for sharing Christ. I did it because I wanted my dad to love me. Everything I did was because of him and what I was trying to get from him. Maybe—maybe piano has been the same for you. You needed to prove to yourself that you weren't your mom, that you weren't going to waste your life and squander your talents and make your family miserable. You thought music could save you from becoming her. But now that you've been diagnosed, and you're getting healthy, you don't have to worry about that anymore. You don't need piano to justify or save you anymore." He stopped, afraid he'd already gone too far. "Does that make sense?"

Amelia looked dumbstruck. Her gaze slid away from him and she said nothing for a long time, and Marcus fought the compulsion to fill the silence with more blathering and armchair psychology. When she spoke it was so quiet he couldn't understand her. "What, babe?"

"By George, I think he's got it."

He smiled. "Really?"

She sniffed, brushing away the tears that had come to her eyes. "I—I'm afraid to admit it, but I think so." Her eyes went wide. "But if I'm not a career pianist, I don't know *what* I am."

He chuckled and pulled her into his arms. "I know the feeling." He leaned back, looked her full in the face. "But I can tell you this much. You're still a pianist—an incredibly talented one. And you're a wife—a really, really wonderful wife. And you're a mom. And even though I haven't had a chance to see you in action, I think you're going to be a fine one."

She smiled through her tears. "Well, when you put it that way." She leaned into him again, her head on his chest, then said the words that made him cry with her. "All right then. I'll stay."

❉

Amelia reached a hand into the incubator and let a single finger rest on Hope's belly. Nurse Marcela stood beside her, monitoring Hope's vitals. "Holding steady," she said. "That's a great sign."

Amelia stared at her daughter, taking in the complication of wires and hoses and tape that had turned her into some human-machine hybrid. Her pink knit cap was baggy on her head, and the diaper looked like it was intended for a toddler. She was only a week old, but she'd already endured a litany of tests to determine the extent of her challenges from being born a trimester early. And to the doctors' amazement, every single one had come back clear. "Truly a miracle," they'd said. Amelia was beginning to believe them.

Which begged the question: A miracle worked by whom?

They continued the touch therapy until Hope's vitals began to waver, then Amelia withdrew her hand and stood. "I'm going to get some tea," she told the nurse once she'd ensured Hope was stable. "Can I get you something?"

"You're a doll. No thanks, though."

Amelia headed for the cafeteria on autopilot, having walked this route dozens of times over the last week. She'd been released two days after the birth, but showed up every morning after breakfast to sit beside Hope until dinner. The first couple of days she'd brought things to keep herself busy—a few books to read, stationery to write letters—but she soon stopped, unable to concentrate on them. Her prior feelings of resentment and ambivalence toward the baby had been erased in those minutes after Hope's birth and then replaced by fierce mama-bear instincts that left her tormented at seeing her daughter laid out like a science experiment in the isolette. She had no patience for things that might steal her attention from her baby. Instead, she sat and stared. And when the stress of seeing Hope that way became too much, she walked. And thought.

Today's musings had gravitated toward New Hope. The name made her smile now. So did the lengths the congregation was going to for the Sheffields. They'd provided dinner every day since Marcus and Amelia had been home. Cards and flowers arrived daily to their home or the hospital, making Hope's corner of the NICU the most decorated on the ward and their apartment smell like a flower shop. And offers of help in every imaginable form came from people Amelia had no memory of even meeting on the few Sundays she'd attended.

She hadn't expected to receive so much support from people she hardly knew, especially given how absent she'd been from the church in the months since she'd arrived. She'd assumed she'd have to prove to them that she was worthy of so much encouragement. And while she knew Marcus was their pastor, she was surprised they were as caring as they were, given the hassle so many of them had given him when he'd started. She had no choice now but to own up to the fact that she'd misjudged them, that she'd never really given them a fair chance in her heart or mind.

Granted, none of them, besides Ed, knew why she'd been hospitalized. Would they be so caring now if they did? Or if they knew she wasn't even sure God was real?

You're jumping to conclusions again, she thought to herself. Why was she so sure the congregation would eventually turn on her? Why couldn't she give them the benefit of the doubt? *Besides, you're becoming a lot more sure about God now than you were before.*

She sat by a window in the cafeteria, sipping her tea and mulling over this thought. It was true. Had she not had Hope early and seen for herself the way God—or Someone—was taking care of her, she wouldn't have had any reason to question her doubt. But hearing one doctor after another use the word *miracle* had forced her to rethink her incredulity.

So had her promise to Marcus to stay with him and Hope and not return to LA. If she was going to make good on it, she had to figure out how to be a pastor's wife. And she didn't think she could be a decent one without at least believing in God.

She was jumpy to get back to the NICU, but forced herself to remain still for a few more minutes, reminding herself that they'd page her if anything happened. And when she was there, she couldn't concentrate on anything but Hope. If she was going to figure any of this God stuff out, she had to take some time alone to do it.

Amelia stared out at the world beyond the windows, taking in the colors and the complexity of the natural landscape: green fields polka-dotted with dandelions and clover, strands of trees that lined the bank of a small creek that ran past the hospital, a sky the same blue as Hope's eyes. That thought brought her back to her daughter, to the miracle of birth, no matter how early or late a baby was, and the intricacy of the human body and all its inner workings. She'd been raised with the theory of evolution, but it had never sat well with her. To think there was a Creator behind it all made more sense.

But the belief in a Creator was a jumping-off point for lots of religions—could she just hop onto the Christianity train without considering the others? She didn't know much about any other faiths; she'd been raised without any religious leanings and the tidbits she'd learned over the years were picked up from the media and comments by friends, none of whom had been very religious themselves. But did any of those religions get it right?

I suppose I could ask that Creator for a little guidance.

She smiled faintly at the thought, but then considered it seriously. Why not? Why not ask for a little help in figuring it all out? If there really was a God, then chances were He wanted people to know Him, and if someone flat-out asked, what reason would He have to not respond?

Amelia wrapped her hands around her tea and stared into the dark liquid. She stole a glance at her watch and took a deep breath, trying to keep her thoughts focused and promising herself she'd head back to the NICU in two minutes. *All right then,* she prayed. *God—or whoever You are—I want to know You're there. I want to know which religion to fall in with. I guess I'm kind of hoping it's Christianity, because that's going to make my marriage a lot easier. But if it's not, I want to know that, too. I don't want to live a lie, that's all. I don't want to call myself anything—a Christian, a Buddhist, whatever—without knowing as well as I can that it's true. So ... have at it. I'm ready and willing. Lay it on me.*

She sat back and braced herself, not really expecting to be zapped in the head with a giant body of knowledge, but hopeful that she'd feel at least a little something or once again hear the voice that had asked for her honesty in the moments before Hope's birth—the voice that might have been a fluke of her own imagination. The allotted two minutes passed without any glimpses of truth or dazzling epiphanies, and as soon as her time was up, she took her tea back to the NICU.

When she got there, the pulmonologist from Hope's medical team was standing at her incubator. Amelia's heart dropped to her feet, seeing him there when rounds were already over. "Oh God— what's wrong?"

He turned, and when she saw his face, her heart beat again. He was smiling.

"Nurse Marcela called me down," he said. "Hope was breathing over her vent."

"What does that mean?"

His smile got wider. "It means she's breathing on her own. It means she may not need the vent." He chuckled, scratching his chin. "For a micropreemie to be off the vent this quickly—well, most of them born at this age spend at least a few weeks, sometimes months. It's pretty miraculous for them to come off after just seven days."

Amelia clapped a hand to her mouth, afraid she'd let out either a scream or a sob. The doctor detailed the process of weaning Hope off the respirator, then left, leaving her to stare once more at her miracle baby. She sank into the rocking chair beside the incubator and gazed at the tiny body sleeping inside, blinking away tears so she could see her better. "Marcus!" she gasped, then pulled out her cell and texted him, knowing he wouldn't want to wait until he came after lunch to hear the news. *H coming off vent soon!!! Dr says total miracle.*

Within a few minutes her phone chirped with his response. *Thank U Jesus!!!*

She read it and felt something click inside. She sat still, as though moving might dislodge the feelings of warmth and peace that were spreading from her center to the farthest boundaries of her body. After a moment, through more tears, she texted him back.

Amen.

EPILOGUE

THREE MONTHS LATER

"Well done, Christy," Amelia said to her pupil. "I can tell you really practiced this week. Keep that up, and you'll have this piece ready in time for the recital in December." She smiled at the girl as she wrote the next assignment in a notebook. "Here you go. Pay attention to measures thirty through forty-two, where it gets a little trickier. Try to practice that part ten times a day. Cool?"

"Okay, thanks, Mrs. Sheffield." Christy hopped off the piano bench and took her notebook from Amelia, then left for the parking lot where her mother awaited her. Amelia turned off the keyboard and headed for the kitchen to start dinner. The timing was just right; she had half an hour left before Hope woke from her nap. She'd have time to get the casserole warmed through and go over her notes for the evening.

Once dinner was in the oven, Amelia sat with a cup of tea at the kitchen table with her notes spread before her. At the top of the first page was the title: *Community Band Info Meeting*. Ideas without organization covered the rest of the page and two more besides; with a pen she added details here and there and then started an agenda for the meeting. Since she didn't know how many people to expect, her main goal for the evening was just to see what kind of interest there might be in her plan. She hoped she'd get a decent turnout. Surely there had to be some other musicians hanging around Wheatridge looking for an outlet for performance.

When Hope awoke, Amelia put her notes away and brought her into the living room. "Good afternoon, my love," she said to the swaddled baby. Hope smacked her lips in anticipation of her post-nap feed, and Amelia settled with her on the sofa and propped her feet on the coffee table. "That was a good nap. Thank you for letting Mommy work." She stroked Hope's silken strawberry-tinted hair and smiled as the baby locked eyes with her. The instant when Hope looked at her that way always felt like the engaging of a magnet on Amelia's heart. It pulled her from her own thoughts and self and connected her in an otherworldly way with the miracle child whose existence still astounded her daily. Only days old according to her estimated birthday, but just over three months in the world, Hope's tiny frame was beginning to look more like Amelia had expected it to, back before the premature delivery. Her newborn clothes didn't hang quite so roomily anymore. She didn't look nearly as alien as she had just a week or two ago. But it was her eyes Amelia couldn't get enough of. Giant blue eyes, just like her daddy's, which would focus on Amelia as though she were the only thing in the room and seemed to have the wisdom of the world locked behind them.

Marcus came home just as Hope was finishing her snack. "There's Daddy," Amelia cooed, unlatching Hope from her breast and handing her over to Marcus. "Just in time for burping."

"Ah, my favorite job," he said with a grin. "Gotta teach my girl how to represent. Come on now, Hopesy, don't be shy, let it rip for Daddy."

Amelia laughed as she put her shirt back to rights. "Nice, Marcus."

"I do what I can." He gave her a kiss and sniffed the air. "Smells good. Lucy's chicken and rice?"

"No, Holly's chicken and rice."

He chuckled. "Knew it was someone's." He rubbed Hope's back and kissed her temple. "Ready for tonight?"

Amelia wrinkled her nose. "I'm nervous. What if no one shows up?"

"People will show up, I promise."

She smirked. "Why, you paying people to come to protect my pride?"

"Yes—bribing them with our overabundance of casseroles." He winkled. "Seriously though, you have nothing to worry about. Don't forget there *was* a band at one point. And I doubt those people have all moved. They've just been waiting for the right person to come along and lead them. And here you are."

She sighed, then stood as the kitchen timer beeped. "I know, I know. Can't help worrying, though."

"The elders prayed their hearts out this morning over it, so I don't think you have anything to fear."

She grinned as she pulled the casserole from the oven and sat it on the range while she set the table. "That was sweet of them."

"Well, you know them."

She did. And she was glad of it.

Marcus adjusted Hope in the Mei Tai carrier Amelia had shown him how to use and started working on the dinner dishes while Amelia showered before the meeting. "I talked to Grandpa Ed today about you. He thinks you're pretty great, did you know that? We all do."

He kissed the top of her head. "I asked him if he would christen you this weekend when Auntie Jill and Uncle Dane come into town. You don't mind if he does it instead of me, do you? It would be nice to just be dad for that, and not the pastor, too." He dropped the knives and forks into the dishwasher's silverware caddy. "Grandpa Ed is a good guy. You're really going to like him. I think you'll like Grandpa Sheffield and Grandpa Rimes, too, but unfortunately they're not very close by." Marcus made a mental note to extend another invitation to his parents to visit. His mother had come out just after Hope was released from the hospital in September, but his father hadn't been willing to take the time off from work. Marcus had worked hard not to let it bother him. He'd been mostly successful.

Marcus brought his thoughts back to the suds-filled sink. "Mommy bought you a beautiful dress that I think is actually going to fit you. How nice will that be, clothes that fit?" He kissed her head again. "You're getting there, sugarplum. Auntie Jill and Uncle Dane can't wait to meet you. And you're gonna love Bradley. He's a cutie. Mommy and Auntie Jill are already plotting your wedding. Though if Bradley turns out anything like his parents, then you'd be wise to grab him when you can. They're good people. Mommy and Daddy introduced them, did you know that?" He shut the dishwasher and turned it on, then rinsed out the sink. "Mommy and Auntie Jill went to school together, and so did Daddy and Uncle Dane. We had a double wedding on the beach after graduation." Marcus stopped swaying as his mind automatically did the math. "Man. That was only a year and a half ago. Do you have any idea how much has happened in the last, what, seventeen months?" Marcus shook his head as he dried his hands. "It was the best of times, it was the worst of times. Seriously. But in retrospect, it was all worth it." He patted Hope's diapered bottom through the Mei Tai and went to the bedroom with swaying steps. "Especially since we got you in the end."

※

Amelia followed Marcus into the library's meeting room, where ten rows of chairs were set up for her meeting. "Oh man, too many seats. Even with a good turnout it's going to feel empty in here."

Marcus chuckled and began to stack the last row against the wall. "Stop stressing, babe."

"I know, I know." Amelia took a deep breath and set her notes on the rickety podium at the front, then freed Hope from her carrier. "Remember, if she starts crying, just bring her in and I'll feed her."

"She just ate, Ames, she'll be fine."

"Well, you never know if she's in a growth spurt or something. It's not like you can predict that sort of thing." She straightened the hat and socks that always seemed to spin on Hope's tiny head and feet, then picked her up and cradled her against her chest. "And if you think anyone near you is sick, go somewhere else. I don't want anyone sneezing or coughing around her."

"I *know*, Amelia. I was in the discharge meeting too, remember?"

She gave Marcus a sheepish look. "I'm sorry."

He chuckled. "Relax."

"Okay. I'll try."

She topped off Hope as she reviewed her notes, then at seven o'clock, Marcus put the baby in the wrap again and gave Amelia a kiss. "Knock 'em dead, babe."

"Thanks."

Marcus and Hope left, and Amelia chewed her lip as she anxiously watched the clock and the door. The weather had turned in the last two hours, and now a cold rain fell outside the large windows that made up one wall of the room. *Just watch—now no one will come.*

At five after seven, a tall woman with long dark hair entered the room looking as unsure as Amelia felt. "Are you Amelia Sheffield?"

Amelia sprang up from her chair. "Yes, that's me. Hi." She walked over to shake hands, then motioned to the chairs. "Better grab a seat before they're all taken." They shared a smile as they sat down. "I'm sorry, your name is …"

"Oh, forgive me—Gloria Stedman."

"Nice to meet you, Gloria. What instrument do you play?"

"Oboe and clarinet."

"Very cool. As a hobby? Or professionally?"

"Mostly as a hobby, though I was in the orchestra that played for that Nebraska tourism commercial they came out with last year, so I've had one paying gig."

Amelia nodded and smiled. "Nice. How long—" Two more people walked into the room, and Amelia stood to welcome them. Three more trickled in, and by quarter after seven, there were twelve people in the chairs and Amelia started the meeting. The turnout was heavy on brass and light on strings, but she could tell from the questions people asked and by how engaged they seemed to be that the group that had assembled that night would be an excellent way to start.

By eight o'clock, Amelia had exhausted her agenda and the group had decided on a rehearsal schedule. "I don't have anything else to add," she said when she saw Marcus appear in the doorway. "Feel free to stay and socialize, otherwise I'll see you all at New Hope Church next Wednesday at seven."

Most people left, but a few sat to talk with people they apparently already knew, and just as Amelia was sitting down to nurse, Gloria came by and touched her shoulder. "I just wanted to thank you for organizing this," she said. "I hope we get a chance to talk some more later."

Amelia nodded to the chair beside her. "If you're not uncomfortable with me nursing, I'd love to chat more now."

Gloria sat down with a chuckle. "I have two of my own—it definitely doesn't bother me."

"How old are your kids?"

"My daughter is three and my son is eighteen months." She hesitated, then said, "I hope you don't mind me asking, but ... do you go to New Hope?"

"My husband is the pastor there, yes."

Gloria nodded. "I'd heard Pastor Carmichael had left—or been removed, or whatever."

Amelia raised a brow. "Did you know him?"

"We used to go there, about six years ago. My husband and I left when Pastor Carmichael started going off the rails. My husband's family had been there for decades. We all left together, and it was painful for us, but ten times more so for them. I take it things have changed a lot?"

Amelia chuckled. "I think so, yes." She told Gloria about how the congregation had rallied around her and Marcus when Hope had been born, and how even now, three months later, they still got at least one dinner a week from someone. "The church we were at in California was a lot bigger, but I only knew a handful of people intimately. Now I feel like I've got a huge extended family here in Wheatridge. I went through a … a difficult time with my faith, back before Hope came, and I never thought I'd be able to tell anyone at New Hope about that." She smiled. "But I have. And people have been wonderful. Not just by letting me vent and ask questions, or by saying they'll pray for me. But by *really* talking with me, and listening, and asking questions and actively helping me find answers. It's incredible."

Gloria shook her head. "That's nothing like what it was like before. I'm really glad to hear things are so much better."

"What church are you at now?"

Gloria shrugged. "You know, we never really found another one we liked. We'd attend a place for a month or two, but nothing clicked."

"Maybe you guys should try New Hope again."

Gloria smiled. "Maybe we will."

By eight thirty, Hope had fallen asleep in Amelia's arms, and Gloria and Amelia had become friends. When Gloria's husband texted that the kids were restless for bed and wanted their mom, they said good-bye with a promise to meet for coffee the next day. Alone in the meeting room, Amelia prayed as she transferred Hope to the car seat, thanking God for the meeting going well and for having the chance to talk to Gloria. *I feel like we clicked. I haven't felt that kind of connection with anyone in a long time. I'm really looking forward to seeing her again tomorrow.*

Marcus walked in, a stack of books in his hands. "So who was that?

"Gloria Stedman. Oboe and clarinet player and ex-New Hope parishioner."

"Really now?"

"*And* we're getting together tomorrow to hang out."

Marcus's face lit up. "Hey, Ames, that's fantastic."

"I know, isn't it?" Amelia checked the straps on the car seat and then stood to put on her coat.

"And the meeting? You had a good turnout, looked like. "

"Awesome. Everyone is in for Wednesday-night rehearsals, and apparently there are at least three people who wanted to come tonight but couldn't. Incredible."

Marcus kissed her cheek and nodded to the books. "Want to trade and I'll take the baby?"

"No, that's all right, I've got her." Amelia adjusted her hood to shield herself from the rain and draped a blanket over the carrier. They walked out to the parking lot, and Amelia let out a sigh. "The air smells delicious, doesn't it? I love the smell of rain."

"You used to hate the rain in California."

"I know. Funny, huh? I love it here."

Marcus froze. "What did you just say?"

Amelia snorted and punched his arm. "I meant I love the rain here."

"Ah."

"But …" She shrugged. "I guess I wouldn't be lying if I said that I maybe, sorta, kinda liked it here now." She set the car seat into its base in the backseat and winked playfully at Marcus. Then she shut the door and let herself into the passenger's seat.

Marcus leaned over and kissed her. "I'm so glad."

Amelia smiled, relishing the unexpected feeling of contentment her little family gave her as Marcus drove them home. She was far from completely healed, far from confident that she wouldn't still mess up this new role of mom and ministry wife.

But she had hope.

... a little more ...

When a delightful concert comes to an end,

the orchestra might offer an encore.

When a fine meal comes to an end,

it's always nice to savor a bit of dessert.

When a great story comes to an end,

we think you may want to linger.

And so, we offer ...

AfterWords—just a little something more after you

have finished a David C Cook novel.

We invite you to stay awhile in the story.

Thanks for reading!

Turn the page for ...

- **Reader's Guide**
- **Author Interview**

READER'S GUIDE

Spoiler Alert!

1. At the beginning of the story, Amelia and Marcus both are "stuck" in dead-end jobs. Have you been in a similar place? How did you respond?

2. Do you think Amelia holds too tightly to her career dreams? Why or why not?

3. How do you handle decisions in important relationships? Do you agree with the "inaction until unity" concept?

4. Do you think Marcus was justified in accepting the job in Nebraska, breaking his promise to Amelia? How would you have reacted?

5. Was Dane's suggestion that Amelia stay in LA when Marcus moved to Wheatridge a wise one? Why or why not?

6. Why didn't Marcus confront Amelia right away about her suicide attempt? What would you have done in his place?

7. Kristine tells Amelia she's not a Christian because of what it "does" for her. What do you think of this idea?

8. Marcus learns that it is not his responsibility as a pastor to "make" the congregation participate. Do you agree with this? What is the proper role for a pastor?

9. Both Marcus and Amelia struggle with wounds from their parents. How does this impact their sense of identity? How can they help each other in the healing process?

10. What is the big difference between how Amelia and Marcus view their roles as parents?

11. After Hope is born, Amelia still wonders what the "right" religion is. How do you deal with similar doubts?

12. Do Marcus and Amelia strike you as being truly compatible as a couple? What is it that keeps them together?

AUTHOR INTERVIEW

1. Where did the inspiration for *Composing Amelia* come from? Do you remember when you first had the idea?

My best friend/roommate in college developed bipolar disorder our junior year. She became a Christian at the end of our freshman year, so her faith was really young—but those two years had been filled with trials that had strengthened it, which I think really helped when she was deep in her depressions. The way other Christians handled it, though, when she told them what was wrong, really made both of us angry. There was a lot of, "You're just not praying hard enough for healing" and "This is punishment for something; you need to confess your hidden sins." The experience made me want to write a book about Christians and mental illness, and I still have an outline for a nonfiction book for the loved ones of people with BP that I started back when we were in the thick of her disease. When I started writing *Composing Amelia*, I envisioned it dealing a lot more with those kinds of issues, but it turned out God's vision was a little different. Maybe someday I'll write that other book, though!

2. Were there some alternate endings of the story? How did you settle on this one?

There was an entire alternate *book*, actually! My first draft of the story was very different from this one—Amelia went to Wheatridge at the same time Marcus did, the parishioners of the church played a much bigger role and were very unaccepting of Amelia and her artistic ways, and the whole baby Hope subplot was entirely different. But I was really pushing my agenda, wanting the book to focus more on how misinformed the people at the church were about BP, and it was clear I was forcing the story to be something other than what God wanted it to be. My developmental editor, Nicci Hubert, walked me through a total rewrite that got the story to about 90 percent of what the final version is. It was a tough job, letting go of what *I* wanted the book to be about, but in the end it's not my book to write, it's God's to dictate, so I had to step back and allow Him to guide the story.

3. Tell us about the writing process. Did you have a favorite spot to go to or certain music you listened to as you wrote?

In an ideal world I'd spend my writing time in a café or the library. But my reality is that I'm a work-at-home mom, and because of my girls' ages—my youngest one, especially—it's difficult for me to be away from home for the four to five hours I work every afternoon. So my writing spot is my home office, which I can't complain about too much, since the view of the Rockies is downright gorgeous. (I have to situate my computer away from the window or else I spend way too much time daydreaming as I stare at the view!)

Because I was writing a character with a classical-music background, I spent some time listening to piano-driven classical "hits" to give me some ideas for songs Amelia could play in certain situations. I can't write and listen to music (or anything, really) at the same time, so I'd set aside blocks of time to just sit and listen to the CDs I found with piano compositions. It was so nice to have an excuse to just chill and listen to this beautiful music! I thought readers might enjoy hearing those pieces too, so I've posted a playlist on my website of all the songs mentioned in the book. Check out http://www.alisonstrobel.com/coam for this and other "backstage" content.

4. Amelia and Marcus travel to some pretty dark places emotionally. How did it feel to enter into that?

God has blessed me with a weird ability to shield myself from getting too involved in my characters' emotional tumult. I don't have the luxury of hiding away to process difficult emotions because I go straight from writing to taking care of my family. If I got wrapped up in the darkness of my characters' lives, I wouldn't be able to function! And it probably helps that I'm not a person who is prone to dark thoughts—which is odd, in a way, because I write them all the time!

5. What do you hope readers learn from Amelia and Marcus's relationship?

Marriage isn't easy, and society's cavalier attitude toward marriage and divorce has eroded the expectation that spouses fulfill the "for better or for worse" part of their vows. Obviously there are times when divorce is necessary—in matters of abuse or abandonment, for example—but too often people think a marriage can't be saved when, in fact, God is fully capable of restoring even the most broken of relationships.* Amelia assumed there was no way she'd ever be happy in her marriage again, given the resentment she felt toward Marcus for moving them to Wheatridge and how uneven their faiths were. But God grew both her and Marcus, and was able to bring healing to a marriage that could easily have dissolved. If both parties of a struggling relationship are willing to turn to the Lord for help, I do believe He will answer those prayers.

*However, just because He *can* doesn't mean He *will*, and I am not advocating that anyone remain in a marriage with a toxic person who is unwilling to change.

6. Amelia obviously loves her piano. Are you a musician?

My two favorite things to do have always been writing and singing. I was a choir geek through high school and helped lead worship in all the various churches I was involved with through college and after graduation. I took piano for a few years but it never seemed to stick—but I'm going to give it a shot again soon so I can at least play Christmas carols and hymns for family worship and teach my girls the basics.

7. What role do you think art—music, writing, or something else—should have in a Christian's life, especially as a wife and mom? How do you find that balance?

I think interacting with art is a vital part of a Christian's walk. God is the ultimate artist, the source of all creativity, and we're missing out on a major facet of who He is when we neglect it. But, that being said, it doesn't have to be some formal, complicated, or time-consuming thing. Just taking time to really look at the flowers in your garden or switching over to the classical station in the car for a while can give you a new connection to God. And, as a mom, those little moments are a great way to teach my girls about how God is involved in our world on that level—how the sunsets, the harmonies, the tints and shades of a Renaissance master's painting all find their start in Him.

EVER WANTED TO REINVENT YOURSELF?

A true-to-life story that will draw you in and keep you on the edge of your seat until the very end.

www.alisonstrobel.com

800.323.7543 • DavidCCook.com

David C Cook
transforming lives together

Childhood Wonder, Powerful Truth

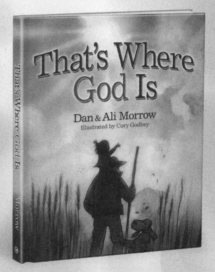

When a little boy wonders where God is, his grandfather sends him on an adventure of discovery. While exploring his everyday world, the boy uncovers God's presence everywhere.

Available anywhere books are sold.

800.323.7543 • DavidCCook.com

David C Cook
transforming lives together

Even Little Prayer Lives Can Grow Deep

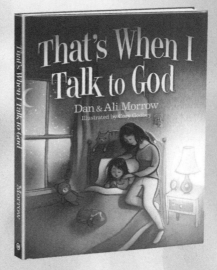

A child discovers she can pray anywhere, at any time, and about anything. When prayer becomes more than a bedtime ritual, nothing seems the same, especially her relationship with God.

Available anywhere books are sold.

800.323.7543 • DavidCCook.com

David C Cook
transforming lives together